Praise for *Once Again a Bride*

"A near-perfect example of everything that makes this genre an escapist joy to read: unsought love triumphs despite difficult circumstances, unpleasantness is resolved and mysteries cleared, and good people get the happy lives they deserve."

—*Publishers Weekly*

"A bit of gothic suspense, a double love story, and the right touches of humor and sensuality add up to this delightfully fast-paced read about second chances and love's redeeming power."

—*RT Book Reviews*, 4 Stars

"Well-rendered, relatable characters, superb writing, an excellent sense of time and place, and gentle wit make this a romance that shouldn't be missed... Ashford returns with a Regency winner that will please her longtime fans and garner new ones."

—*Library Journal*

"It's so nice to have one of the premier Regency writers return to the published world. Ms. Ashford has written a superbly crafted story with elements of political unrest, some gothic suspense, and an interesting romance."

—*Fresh Fiction*

"Jane Ashford's characters are true to their times, yet they radiate the freshness of tod

The *Bride* Insists

JANE ASHFORD

sourcebooks
casablanca

Published by Sourcebooks Casablanca, an imprint of Sourcebooks,
Inc.
P. O. Box 4410, Naperville, Illinois 60567-4410
(630) 961-3900
Fax: (630) 961-2168
www.sourcebooks.com

Printed and bound in the United States of America.
WOZ 10 9 8 7 6 5 4 3 2 1

One

THE SCHOOLROOM OF THE BENSON HOUSEHOLD WAS agreeably cozy on this bitter winter afternoon. A good fire kept the London cold at bay, so that one hardly noticed the sleet scratching at the windows. In one corner, there were comfortable armchairs for reading any one of the many books on the shelves. A costly globe rested in another corner, nearly as tall as the room's youngest occupant. Scattered across a large oak table, perfect for lessons, were a well-worn abacus, pens and pencils, and all the other tools necessary for learning.

"I am utterly bored," declared seventeen-year-old Bella Benson, sprawled on the sofa under the dormer window. "I hate winter. Will the season never start?"

"You could finish that piece of embroidery for…"

"You are not my governess any longer," the girl interrupted with a toss of her head. "I don't have to do what you say. I've left the schoolroom."

And yet here you are, thought Clare Greenough. But she kept the sentiment to herself, as she did almost all of her personal opinions. Clare's employer set the tone of this household, and it was peevish.

All three children had picked up Mrs. Benson's whiny, complaining manner, and Clare was not encouraged to reprimand them when they used it. "It's true that you needn't be in the schoolroom," she replied mildly. She sorted through a pile of paper labels marked with the names of world capitals. The child who could correctly attach the largest number of these to their proper places on the huge globe would get a cream cake for tea. Clare had an arrangement with Cook to provide the treats. It was always easier to make a game of lessons than to play the stern disciplinarian, particularly in this house.

"I won't do what you say either," chimed in twelve-year-old Susan Benson, as usual following her older sister's lead.

"Me neither," agreed ten-year-old Charles.

Clare suppressed a sigh, not bothering to correct his grammar. Charles would leave for school in the spring. Only a lingering cough had kept him home this term. He was hardly her responsibility any longer. Bella would be presented to society in a few weeks, effectively disappearing from the world of this room. And Clare would be left with Susan, a singularly unappealing child. Clare felt guilty at the adjective, but the evidence of a year's teaching was overwhelming. Susan had no curiosity or imagination and, of the three children, was most like her never-satisfied, irritable mother. She treated Clare as a possession designed to entertain her, and then consistently refused to *be* entertained. The thought of being her main companion for another four years was exceedingly dreary. Surely Clare could find a better position?

But leaving a post without a clear good reason was always a risk. There would be questions that Clare couldn't answer with the simple truth: *My charge is dull and intractable. I couldn't bear another moment of her company.* Inconvenienced, Mrs. Benson might well refuse to give her a reference, which would make finding a new position nearly impossible. Clare wondered if she could… nudge Susan into asking for a new governess? Possibly—if she was very clever and devious, never giving the slightest hint that it was something *she* wanted. Or, perhaps with the others gone, Susan would improve. Wasn't it her duty to see that she did? Clare examined the girl's pinched expression and habitual pout. Mrs. Benson had undermined every effort Clare had made in that direction so far. It appeared to be a hopeless task.

Clare turned to survey Bella's changed appearance instead—her brown hair newly cut and styled in the latest fashion, her pretty sprigged muslin gown. At Bella's age, Clare had been about to make her entry into society. She had put her hair up and ordered new gowns, full of bright anticipation. And then had come Waterloo, and her beloved brother's death in battle, and the disintegration of her former life. Instead of stepping into the swirl and glitter of society, Clare was relegated to the background, doomed to watch a succession of younger women bloom and go off to take their places in a larger world.

Stop this, Clare ordered silently. She despised self-pity. It only made things worse, and she couldn't afford to indulge in it. Her job now was to regain control of the schoolroom. She shuffled her pile of paper labels. "I suppose I shall have to eat all the cream cakes myself then."

Susan and Charles voiced loud objections. Clare was about to maneuver them back into the geography game when the door opened and Edwina Benson swept in. This was so rare an occurrence that all four of them stared.

Bella jumped up at once and shook out the folds of her new gown. "Were you looking for me, Mama?"

"Not at present. Though why you are here in the schoolroom, Bella, I cannot imagine. I thought you were practicing on the pianoforte. Have you learned the new piece so quickly?"

"Uh…" Eyes gone evasive, Bella sidled out of the room. She left the door open, however, and Clare was sure she was listening from the corridor.

Mrs. Benson pursed narrow lips. "You have a visitor, Miss Greenough."

This was an even rarer event than her employer's appearance in the schoolroom. In fact, it was unprecedented.

"I do not recall anything in our arrangement that would suggest you might have callers arriving at my front door," the older woman added huffily.

Only humility worked with Mrs. Benson. She was impervious to reason. "No, ma'am. I cannot imagine who…"

"So I am at a loss as to why you have invited one."

"I didn't. I assure you I have no idea who it is."

Her employer eyed her suspiciously. Mrs. Benson's constant dissatisfaction and querulous complaints were beginning to etch themselves on her features, Clare thought. In a few years, the lines would be permanent, and her face would proclaim her character for all to see. "He was most insistent," Mrs. Benson added. "I would almost say impertinent."

You did say it, Clare responded silently. "He...?"

Mrs. Benson gave her a sour smile, designed to crush hope. "Some sort of business person, I gather." Her gaze sharpened again. "You haven't gotten into debt, have you?"

It was just like the woman to ask this in front of the children, who were listening with all their might. She was prying as well as peevish, and... pompous and proprietary. "Of course not." When would she have had the time to overspend? Even if she had the money.

Mrs. Benson's lips tightened further. "I suppose you must see him. But this is not to happen again. Is that quite clear? If you have... appointments, I expect you to fulfill them on your free day."

Her once-monthly free day? When she was invariably asked to do some errand for her employer or give the children an "outing"? But Clare had learned worlds about holding her tongue in six long years as a governess. "Thank you, Mrs. Benson." Empty expressions of gratitude no longer stuck in Clare's throat. Mrs. Benson liked and expected to be thanked. That there was no basis for gratitude was irrelevant. Thanks smoothed Clare's way in this household, as they had in others before this.

Clare followed her employer downstairs to the front parlor. The formal room was chilly. No fire had been lit there, as no one had been expected to call, and obviously no refreshment would be offered to the man who stood before the cold hearth. Below medium height and slender, he wore the sober dress of a man of business. From his graying hair and well-worn face, Clare judged he was past fifty. He took a step forward when they entered, waited a moment, then said, "I need to speak to Miss Greenough alone."

Edwina Benson bridled, her pale blue eyes bulging. "I beg your pardon? Do you presume to order me out of my own parlor?"

"It is a confidential legal matter," the man added, his tone the same quiet, informative baritone. He showed no reaction to Mrs. Benson's outrage. And something about the way he simply waited for her to go seemed to impel her. She sputtered and glared, but she moved toward the door. She did leave it ajar, no doubt to listen from the entry. But the man followed her and closed it with a definitive click. Clare was impressed; her visitor had a calm solidity that inspired confidence. Of course she would endure days of stinging reproaches and small humiliations because of this visit. But it was almost worth it to have watched him outmaneuver Edwina Benson. "My name is Everett Billingsley," he said then. "Do you think we dare sit down?"

Clare nearly smiled. He *had* noticed her employer's attitude. She took the armchair. He sat on the sofa. Clare waited to hear what this was about.

For his part, Billingsley took a moment to examine the young woman seated so silently across from him. Her hands were folded, her head slightly bowed so that he couldn't see the color of her eyes. She asked no questions about his unexpected visit. She didn't move. It was as if she were trying to disappear into the brocade of the chair.

Despite her youth, she actually wore a lace cap, which concealed all but a few strands of hair the color of a fine dry champagne. Her buff gown was loosely cut, designed, seemingly, to conceal rather than flatter a slender frame. A shade too slender, perhaps, just as her oval face and pleasantly regular features were a shade too pale. Here was a female doing everything she could to remain unnoticed, he concluded. She even seemed to breathe carefully. Everett Billingsley certainly understood the precarious position of genteel young women required to work for their bread. He could imagine why she might wish to appear unattractive and uninteresting, to remain unobtrusive. Her attempt to impersonate an ivory figurine made his mission even more gratifying. "I have some good news for you," he began. "I represent the estate of Sebastian Greenough, your great-uncle." This won him a tiny frown, but no other reaction.

Clare sorted through her memories. Sebastian Greenough was her grandfather's brother, the one who had gone out to India years before she was born. She had never met him.

"Mr. Greenough died in September. It has taken some time to receive all the documents, but they are now in place. He left everything he had to you."

Clare couldn't suppress a start of surprise. "To me?"

Billingsley nodded. "His last will was made in the year of your brother's death. In it, he expressed a wish to 'even things out.'"

Clare sat very still. Mention of her brother still hurt,

even after seven years. It evoked a cascade of loss—from the pain of his death, to the callous eviction from the home where she'd lived all her life, to the speedy decline in her mother's health in their new, straitened circumstances. How did one "even out" a catastrophe?

A bit puzzled by her continuing silence, Billingsley added, "Because the entail gave everything to your cousin. He wished to make up for that."

After he was dead and could not be inconvenienced in any way, Clare thought but did not say. Sebastian Greenough hadn't expressed the least interest in her while she was struggling to survive her losses.

"It is quite a substantial estate," Billingsley went on. "There is some property in India still to be liquidated. But the funds already transferred, and conservatively invested, will yield an income of more than five thousand pounds a year." At last the girl looked up. Her eyes were a striking pale green. She looked stunned. As well she might; it was a fortune.

"Five thousand a year," Clare murmured. It was more than fifty times her current salary. It was unbelievable. "Is this some kind of... confidence trick?"

Everett Billingsley smiled. "Indeed not. I have not brought all the documents here. I would ask that you call at my office to look them over. But I did bring this as a token of the change in your circumstances."

He took an envelope from the inner pocket of his coat and held it out. Clare accepted it and looked inside. The heavy cream paper bulged with banknotes.

"Five hundred pounds. For expenses until all is in place," Billingsley added. She could leave this oppressive household, purchase some pretty gowns, he thought. He was glad to see more animation in her face when she looked up again. "I should explain the arrangement. The legacy has flowed into a trust. It is to be overseen by me and your cousin Simon Greenough, as trustees, until..." He paused as all the dawning light in her face died.

"Simon." Her cousin would never let her touch any money he controlled.

Billingsley cleared his throat. "It seems that Mr. Simon Greenough wrote your great-uncle to say that he was watching over you. Making sure you had what you needed in the wake of his inheriting."

"He has never given me a penny," Clare responded through gritted teeth. He'd even refused to lend them money to purchase medicine and other necessities for her mother when she was ill. As far as Clare was concerned, he had killed her.

"So I have learned," responded Billingsley dryly. "I believe he also argued, quite forcefully, in their correspondence that your great-uncle's money should be left to him."

"I'm sure he did." Her cousin—the son of her father's younger brother, who had married early and unwisely—had been reared to resent Clare and her brother, to want revenge for their very existence. His greed was fathomless.

"But it was not," finished Everett Billingsley. "And you can be sure that he won't get his hands on it. I will see to that."

Clare believed him. Something about this man inspired trust. "But Simon will be in charge of what I can do with the money?"

"Partially. Along with me."

Clare's fingers closed around the envelope Billingsley had given her. Simon would move heaven and earth to ensure that she saw no more of the legacy than this.

"Until you are married, of course," her visitor added.

"What?"

"On the occasion of your marriage, the trust is naturally dissolved. Your cousin will have no further say in any matters pertaining to the estate."

"Because the control will pass to my husband." Clare knew that was the law. Married women couldn't own property; anything they had automatically went to their husbands as soon as the wedding vows were spoken.

"Correct," replied Billingsley. For the first time, the young woman met and held his gaze. A startling fire blazed in those pale green eyes. Her face seemed altered, too. The visage he had marked down as merely pleasant now shone with a spirited beauty, a patent intelligence. Miss Greenough had arranged to be thoroughly underestimated, he realized, like an actor inhabiting a role wholly unlike himself. There was far more to her than he had been allowed to see at first.

Clare felt as if parts of her were springing back to life after years of dormancy, like unused rooms when the draperies are pushed back and the sun streams in. Her mind raced. Cousin Simon would do anything to thwart her. Everett Billingsley didn't begin to understand the depth of that man's enmity. She would have no real control of this amazing windfall, or of her life, until her cousin was removed from the picture. Fleetingly, Clare wondered if one could hire murderers with a great deal of money. Not that she would, of course. The idea was morally repugnant. And unlikely to succeed, for any number of reasons. She would have to explore more conventional paths. But one thing was certain—Simon would not best her this time. He would not beggar her again.

Two

JAMES BOLEIGH, SEVENTH BARON TREHEARTH, LOUNGED in a gilt chair and watched his friends play whist. He sipped from his fourth glass of champagne. Or was it the fifth? He'd lost track, as he often did, in the humiliation of knowing that he couldn't even afford to spring for the next bottle, let alone match the high stakes passing across the gaming table. Andrew and Harry wouldn't mention this lapse. They wouldn't even think of it, really; that was the amazing thing about them. They were staunch friends, better than he deserved. Since their first year together at Eton, and through all the disaster that followed, they'd stuck by him. Not like the supposed friends who offered false sympathy while they angled for juicy details. Or, even worse, the ones who approached him with real pity. Intolerable! Andrew and Harry weren't oblivious to what had happened to him. Far from it. They were just… true friends. He didn't know how to describe it any better. He did understand, though he would never say it aloud, that he would have been lost without them. Then. Now… now he was as good as lost in any case. What was he going to do?

He was getting maudlin—none of that. Jamie drank more deeply. At least he'd made no wagers tonight. He wasn't stupid enough—any longer—to imagine that he could save himself at the gaming tables.

The noise of the crowded club swirled around him, a cacophony of men making bids, setting stakes, calling for wine. Smoke from a hundred candles, and not a few cigars, fogged the air. The place reeked of wax and tobacco and the sour sweat of those who desperately needed to win. All too easily he could recall the feeling—the trembling hands that must be hidden, the burning eyes, the choking sensation when your heart was in your throat at each toss of the dice. The black despair when you lost; the hardly lesser blow when you won, because a small gain was never enough. And then, inevitably, the odds turned against you, and it all came crashing down. There were men in that state here; he recognized the signs.

Jamie's roving gaze caught in the mirror on the nearby wall. There were his friends, reflected. Harry Simpson, the big, bluff guardsman with his close-cropped red hair; people often expected Harry to be slow-witted, but a sharp mind lay behind those blue eyes. Across the table, Andrew Tate was smaller, a wiry blond whose gray eyes glinted with irony. Many a fool feared his quick tongue. Few knew what boundless kindness lay behind his quips.

And there, just a little separated from them, was his own reflection, like the ghost at the feast. Hair, black; eyes, nearly so; skin tanned because he preferred the outdoors. Like his late lamented mother, he was dark as a gypsy. Like his dead father, he was tall and rangy, with angled cheekbones and a mouth that naturally turned down. Spirits only too prone to darkness as well; his father had certainly demonstrated that. Lolling back in the chair, watching his friends lay down their cards, the fellow in the mirror looked as if he hadn't a care in the world. He raised his glass to him, congratulating himself on a successful deception. Drink muted the pressure of a multitude of ills.

"Jamie?" Andrew's half smile acknowledged the raised goblet. Jamie lowered it.

The hand of cards had ended. "More champagne," called one of the other players, gesturing for a waiter. "Trehearth here is sponging it all off us."

Rage surged through Jamie at the taunt. He sprang up and had to catch his balance. It must have been five glasses after all. "I'll get it."

"He was jok—" began Harry.

"I'm getting it!" Jamie turned his back and stalked away. He would order two bottles; no, three, and be damned to it. What did it matter? All too soon, this life would be over, everything lost. He'd staved off ruin for as long as he could. His creditors were out of patience. The home that he loved so much that he could no longer bear to be there would be taken from him. The cost of a few bottles of wine would make no difference, except to silence the jibes of that bloody fool at the table. He could still manage that, at least. By God, he'd order a round dozen!

The evening played out as they so often did. Andrew and Harry, longtime partners at whist, won modestly.

Jamie kept drinking. It was nearly two by the time the trio made its way back to Andrew's rooms on Duke Street, and no one showed much inclination to go to bed. Harry had no duty the next day and no requirement to return to barracks. Andrew was naturally a night owl, and Jamie, his houseguest, was plagued by dark thoughts. He could hardly down enough wine to sleep well these days. They cracked a bottle of brandy, dropped into chairs in Andrew's comfortable sitting room, and let the crackling fire warm them.

"Why the glower, Jamie?" asked Andrew. "Taking up Byron's posturing now he's off in Greece?"

Jamie frowned into his liquor. With these old friends, he needed to finally tell the truth. "It's all over for me. I'm rolled up."

Andrew and Harry exchanged glances. Jamie was prone to black moods, but this seemed darker than usual. Harry tried a jovial tone. "You know what I always say, get yourself leg shackled to an heiress. When the season starts up—"

"It'll be too late by then," Jamie interrupted. He drank deeply. "And even if it weren't, you know I can't get near an heiress. Their mothers have me marked down as a damned bad bargain. Remember last season? The Laramys' ball? I tried to ask Annie Fitzgerald to dance, and her mother marched up and ordered me off."

"You were half sprung," Harry pointed out. "Doubt you could have kept your feet on the dance floor."

"I was not!" Jamie drank again.

"And you called her mother a hatchet-faced crone,"

remembered Andrew. "For everyone to hear. That wasn't exactly helpful."

"I wouldn't have done if she hadn't insulted me." Jamie emptied his glass at the burning memory of that walk across the ballroom after he'd been dismissed. The sniggering and whispers. "She is hatchet-faced, and mean as a snake," he added as he refilled his glass. With brandy on top of the champagne, he'd feel like hell eventually. But devil take it; he felt like hell now. When would the liquor drown the thoughts circling in his brain?

"I've heard it's easier to meet heiresses in Bath—" began Harry.

"I'm telling you, I'm out of time," Jamie interrupted. "I don't have another season. I don't have another month. The banks are taking Trehearth." His home, the wellspring of his name, would go to some well-heeled stranger. Money would purchase his heritage. He'd become one of those threadbare hangers-on, clinging to the edges of society, reminding people he was titled, if no longer landed. No, he wouldn't. He would never sink so low as that.

"Could you really claim to love a woman when all you wanted was her money?" wondered Andrew.

Harry slouched lower in the armchair, his long legs propped on a Turkish ottoman. "Well, it wouldn't be as stark as that, would it?" Brandy generally made Harry philosophical. He held up one finger. "We all mean to marry, yes? Duty to the line and all." He didn't wait for his friends' nods, but raised a second finger. "And we'd rather not disappoint our moth... families by getting riveted to some unacceptable female." Harry provided his own nod this time. "So…" His third finger joined the other two digits. "We have a certain…" A belch broke this sentence. "…field of operations. Why not set our sights on… er, targets with plenty of juice? Nothing says we can't discover one we like well enough."

"Only make up to women with money?" said Andrew. "Ridiculous. Taking that line, I would never have become acquainted with Alice."

"Eh, that would have been a tragedy," murmured Harry. Jamie threw him a look. They'd both suffered through Andrew's infatuation with Alice Whitsett last season. It had been appalling to see their intelligent, witty friend reduced to one single topic of conversation—his perfect love. A smile from the chit threw him into truly embarrassing transports; an imagined slight turned him so morose he snapped your head off. He'd even written a ghastly poem to his "heart's princess." "Hair like raven silk," or some such drivel, Jamie remembered with a grimace. And then Alice had gone and married another. That had been an excruciating month or two.

The groom's subsequent complaints about Alice's foul temper and extravagance had taken some of the wind out of Andrew's melancholy sails. The tide had turned when the fellow declared at the club that Alice was exactly like her mother. Jamie and Harry had seen Andrew's eyes bulge, and a shudder go through him, and known they were nearly home free. The mystery of the whole affair was—Alice had always seemed to them just an ordinary girl. Pretty enough, Jamie supposed, but by no means a beauty, and certainly not interesting to talk to. Thinking she might actually become his friend's wife, he'd tried. He could never see why she'd reduced his clever friend to maundering idiocy. What Andrew insisted was love seemed to Jamie sheer lunacy.

"There's got to be a way," said Harry. "You could marry Lily."

"No more brandy for you, my friend," said Andrew.

"You sh… saying I'm foxed? What's wrong with my sister?"

"She's still in the schoolroom?"

"She's making her debut this year," Harry pointed out.

But, thought Jamie, though she would bring a substantial portion to her marriage, it wouldn't be nearly enough, even if he would consider such a thing. Harry had no idea of the sums needed to restore Trehearth. And why should he? It wasn't his burden to bear. Of course Jamie would never make such use of Lily even if she had a larger dowry. Would he? "Thank you, Harry, but Lily deserves better. I have to face reality now. I have people to provide for. I can't postpone the inevitable any longer."

"What are you going to do?" asked Andrew.

"Finish the legalities. Cut the strings." Regret lanced through Jamie. "And look for some kind of employment."

"Employment?" Harry gazed owlishly at him. "What sort of employment could you…?" He closed his lips on the end of this potentially insulting sentence.

"I thought I could manage some large estate."

"Manage?"

"There are people buying properties these days who

have no experience caring for them." Successful trades-
men, grasping nabobs. The brandy curdled in Jamie's
stomach at the thought of submitting to such men.

"You'd be some city mushroom's steward?" said
Harry.

"It's the only thing I know how to do."

Jamie's bleak tone silenced the others. But it
couldn't mask the mixture of disbelief and sympathy
on their faces. Reaching for the bottle, Jamie poured
another brandy.

Clare Greenough sat in the neat offices of the agency
that had provided her last two posts as governess, in
a small chamber set aside for interviews. Farnham and
Hicks was considered the best source for the more
superior sort of governesses, companions, and high-
nosed dressers, those who were several steps up from
lady's maid. They had certainly treated her well over
the years. Clare trusted Mrs. Hicks as she did few other
people in the world.

She'd made her requirements very clear, and the
first two women she'd spoken with had been distinct
possibilities. But somehow not quite right. Clare
couldn't say precisely why, but she wanted to make
the perfect choice. And so, she waited for a third
candidate, forcing herself to be patient when all she
wanted was to rush into action.

During the last two weeks, she had called at Everett
Billingsley's chambers and signed the documents final-
izing her legacy. It was only then, reading through
the pages of legal jargon and seeing the ornate seals of

officials in far-off India, that she had truly believed it was real. She'd given her notice and left her position at the Bensons, a step that had been as rancorous as she'd expected. Edwina Benson had seemed to take Clare's new financial status as a personal affront, expressly designed to belittle and inconvenience her. Should Clare ever need a reference… But she wouldn't. Never again. Clare took a deep breath. She'd engaged rooms at Mivart's Hotel on Brook Street, and now she was here at the agency, ready to make the next move in her plan.

Mrs. Hicks opened the door and looked in. At a nod from Clare, she ushered another woman into the room. "This is Mrs. Selina Newton," she said. "Mrs. Newton, Miss Clare Greenough."

"Good morning." Clare remembered to smile as she indicated a chair opposite. The room was set up as a parlor to make these sorts of meetings more comfortable. The newcomer sat down, and Mrs. Hicks retreated, leaving them together.

Clare examined the other woman. She knew from the list of particulars Mrs. Hicks had provided that Selina Newton was forty-seven years old. She didn't look it. Her dark brown hair showed no hint of gray, and her round face only a few lines. These seemed to have been engraved by smiles rather than scowls, which was a good sign. Her hazel eyes held a promising warmth. She was neatly dressed, more fashionably than Clare actually, and comfortably attractive. "Could you tell me a bit about yourself?" She wanted to get the woman's story in her own voice, not from a piece of paper.

Selina surveyed the very badly dressed young

woman before her. Her fingers itched to unpick the seams of that drab, baggy gown and turn it into something more flattering to Miss Greenough's slender figure. Mrs. Hicks had been vague about the nature of this post, only saying that she thought it might suit Selina. So the interview was more difficult than usual. Selina settled for the customary combination of openness and omission. One shared enough history to establish trust and secure the position, while withholding the more personal details that no one else needed to know.

"Certainly," Selina began. "I married quite young, a Navy man, and was widowed after eight years." There was no need to add what she'd realized within a month of the wedding—that Ronald had married her only to gain a caretaker for his invalid mother. Or that he had been away at sea for the greater part of their marriage and might as well have been away when he was at home. Selina had nursed his mother through her final illness the year after Ronald was lost off the Australian coast, and found herself penniless when old Mrs. Newton died.

"Neither of our families had much money," was the way she put it to Miss Greenough. Certainly her own clergyman father had been in no position to assist her. "So I was obliged to seek employment. An aunt found me a position as companion to an aged relative. I remained with her until she died, and then moved to another similar post, and another after that. The woman I was working for most recently, Lady Harriet Vernley, was carried off by a lung complaint a few weeks ago. She was eighty-one and had been ill for some time."

Selina emphasized that last bit. There must be no suggestion of laxness in her care for her employer.

Clare liked her voice. It was low and pleasant, her manner straightforward and self-assured without a trace of... of peevishness. That was important. "So, you have always been employed by older ladies?"

Selina Newton nodded. She had, in fact, spent the greater part of her life catering to the whims and crochets of elderly females with enough money to afford such service. She assumed Miss Greenough had a relative in that position, though she didn't see why no one had yet said so. But Mrs. Hicks had suggested that the post was an interesting possibility for her, and Mrs. Hicks had never let her down. "I have a number of positive references," Selina replied with a polite smile.

Clare looked into the older woman's eyes and asked one of the list of questions she'd prepared that would determine her choice. "Do you have a plan for your future?"

"My...?"

"For the time when you can no longer serve as a companion?" Clare added. "Due to age or... other factors."

Selina stared at her. This was the dread hanging over every woman who came through the doors of this agency seeking work—the never-spoken terror of one's final years eked out in some dingy rooming house, tolerating whatever companions luck foisted upon you, pinching every penny and praying that they would last... long enough. No one talked about it. Or if they did, it was in whispers, as if speaking the words aloud might bring penury crashing down. Miss

Greenough looked thin and pale and diffident, but there was nothing waiflike about her clear green gaze. Now she was waiting for an answer as if she'd posed a perfectly conventional question.

It was a good test, Clare thought—how a person dealt with her fears. She knew only too well what it felt like to wake in the night and lie rigid, anxiety devouring all hope of rest.

Under those steady, serious eyes, Selina told the truth: "Each of my employers has included a small bequest to me in her will. It is the usual thing in my sort of post. I have set these sums aside and intend to continue the practice, building up a nest egg for my own old age." The amount she'd been able to accumulate was laughable, but there was no need to reveal that.

Clare nodded. It was an intelligent, realistic reply. She was beginning to think she had found the person she was seeking. "I'm looking for a companion," she said.

Why else was she here, Selina thought? "For your grandmother or—?"

"For myself."

Selina blinked in surprise.

"I am about to... enter society, and I have no family or acquaintances to call upon."

"So you require a chaperone?" Why had Mrs. Hicks contacted her about this post? It was not the sort of thing she did. Young women wishing to make their way in London society wanted—needed—sponsors who could introduce them into fashionable circles. Selina had observed high society from the far periphery—part of its invisible background—but she had no influence or connections. She couldn't help Miss Greenough.

Clare hadn't thought of it in that light. "More of a... counselor, I would say. Someone to consult and advise as I... proceed. A companion, as you have been." Clare had admitted to herself that the thought of living all alone was daunting.

"I see." Despite Mrs. Hicks's recommendation, the position was unattractive. Firstly, Selina feared she wouldn't be able to fulfill its requirements. Beyond that, an attractive young woman—which Miss Greenough was—possessing the funds to hire a superior companion would soon marry. Selina didn't wish to be looking for work again in such a short time. "I don't think I am suited..."

Seeing her reluctance made Clare more certain of her choice. She decided to go a step further than she had with the other candidates, tell more of her story. "I have been employed as a governess for six years, almost since I left the schoolroom myself." Clare smiled a little at the surprise in the other woman's face. How often did a governess hire a companion? "And now I have suddenly come into a large amount of money. I want someone to help me as I settle the circumstances of my life as I wish them to be."

A mixture of envy and wistfulness ran through Selina. It was the dream of any dependent—to gain the power to control one's own life. How very seldom it happened. "How... splendid for you." She hadn't meant the words to come out with that tinge of bitterness. She gathered her wits and set aside her emotions, as she knew so well how to do. "I must tell you that I am not well connected in society. And I know nothing about financial… arrangements. Surely you need a solicitor or…" She didn't even know who was appropriate.

Clare made up her mind. Selina Newton hadn't changed her tone when she heard there was a fortune involved. There'd been no gleam of greed in her hazel eyes or bend of sycophancy in her straight back. Clare thought this woman could be a resource and support as she carried out her plans. She decided to tell her the rest. "The terms of the legacy make it imperative that I marry as soon as possible." Imperative to her, at any rate. She would not remain under Simon's thumb for a moment longer than necessary. Clare took a breath and said it out loud for the first time. "So I intend to purchase a husband."

"I beg your pardon?" She couldn't have heard her correctly, Selina thought.

"People call the London season a Marriage Mart. I shall make use of it. I have the money." Or the promise of money. Clare twisted her hands together. Spoken so starkly, it did sound outrageous.

Selina stared at her. With her pale hair and dowdy gown, the young woman didn't look unbalanced. She'd sounded perfectly reasonable until now. "My dear Miss Greenough, that is only an expression people use—"

"And expressions commonly arise from some real basis."

"But—" Selina couldn't find any polite phrase to voice her true opinion.

"I want someone to aid me in this, I admit rather

odd, endeavor. Obviously, I will have to make very careful judgments. From what I have seen of you, I believe you would give me good advice. So I hope you will consent to be that aid."

Selina felt pinned by the young woman's striking green eyes. Why had she not noticed till now how they practically coruscated with energy? Used to doddering old women, Selina found the intensity of Miss Greenough's wrongheaded determination unsettling. She shook her head.

Clare spoke again before she could refuse. "I will undertake, in writing, to buy you an annuity of two hundred pounds a year, to begin as soon as I am married as I wish to be."

Selina's mouth dropped open. A guaranteed, lifetime income of two hundred a year! It was more than twice what she'd made at any post, and she knew very well how to stretch such an amount to cover a secure and comfortable life. It was a dream come true. It was a fantasy. "Is this some sort of joke? Did Mrs. Hicks…?" But the staid head of her own highly respected agency was the last person on earth to participate in a hoax.

"Absolutely not. I will sign a contract, drawn up by anyone you like, to assure you of the funds." Clare knew what a blessing she was extending. It was a pleasure to be able to do so.

The offer was astonishing. Selina could scarcely comprehend it—independence, the end of constant, nagging financial worries, of catering to old women's whims. It was irresistible. Selina felt herself being swayed. Even if it didn't work out, she would merely be back where she was now, searching for a position. And there was something else, she realized. She feared for this young woman, going out into the world with such a reckless plan. She wanted to help her. "All right."

Like a man sealing a business deal, Clare reached across the space between them and offered her hand. A bit dazed, Selina shook it.

Three

DESPITE A HEAD THAT FELT AS IF SOMEONE HAD STUFFED it with cotton wool and then set the material on fire, Jamie left Andrew's rooms at ten to find a hackney cab. His eyes ached, and his stomach roiled after another night of drowning his sorrows in whatever form of drink passed near his hands—which were shaking as he climbed into the carriage. He might have used these pains as an excuse to put off his morning appointment, but he wasn't going to bother. It was time for him to face up to things and give in, for others' sake if not his own. He'd delayed the inevitable as long as he could. It was ridiculous to pretend that something might change.

With clenched teeth, Jamie endured the bounce and rattle of the wheels over cobblestones, the swerves as the driver wove through a press of vehicles. He paid the fare and climbed the steps to his man of business's office like a condemned man mounting the gallows. The fellow would have called on him, of course, but Jamie had no desire to seal the ruin of his house with Andrew in the next room. His friends knew his situation; that was not the same as having them overhear every sordid detail.

The young clerk in the outer office tried to take his greatcoat, making Jamie realize he'd forgotten his hat. When Jamie refused to relinquish the garment, he was ushered directly in. "I'm ready to make the final arrangements," Jamie said as soon as the door shut behind the lad. "It's no use dragging it on any longer. I can't bear it."

Everett Billingsley looked up from the thick document before him and into a pair of agonized dark eyes. Young Lord Trehearth looked haggard. Billingsley had heard rumors of his drinking, and he could see the signs of sleepless nights. It was such a pity. "Sit down, my lord."

"There's nothing left to discuss." But Jamie dropped into a chair across the desk and faced the man who had been his adviser for nearly ten years. Some part of the pain of losing his estate was the sense that he had failed this stalwart ally.

"Would you care for tea?" Billingsley watched his visitor slap his gloves against his knee. He was wound tight as a watch spring.

"I just want to get it over with." *Would he feel any relief?* Jamie wondered. When it was all gone, when he'd acknowledged that he would never see Trehearth again, would the burden of grief lighten?

Billingsley sighed. He'd known the younger man all his life, and his parents before him. Billingsley's father had represented the interests of his grandfather. He genuinely liked young Lord Trehearth and had learned to respect him as they worked together to try to stave off the wreck of all his prospects. He hated seeing it end this way. The boy had tried so hard. "If only your father—"

"My father was a weakling and a coward!"

Billingsley hadn't meant to speak aloud. They had touched on this painful topic before, and it never went well. "I will never believe he meant to take his—"

"He killed himself," interrupted Jamie harshly. "And left an unholy mess in my hands. Obviously, he *meant* to escape it."

"He cared about you. He often said to me—"

"Cared? I was sixteen years old! My mother was barely three months dead."

"Well, I think that was the reason he wasn't paying proper attention—"

"It doesn't matter." Jamie cut off the conversation with a slashing gesture. Dredging up the past did no good. It simply hurt all over again, and the tremor in his voice when he spoke of it was downright humiliating. Had it been anyone other than Billingsley, who had gone through those dreadful years with him, he would have walked out of the room. "Let's just get on with it."

"I've negotiated with the holders of the mortgages, and they've given us three more weeks—"

"And what do you suppose will happen in a few weeks to make any difference?"

The words were clipped and harsh, but the older man took no offense. He understood the anguish behind them. "Very well, my lord. I'll have the papers drawn up."

"I would have thought you'd done that long ago.

Can't I sign and be finished with this?" Now that he'd made the decision, Jamie didn't want to wait.

Billingsley could have produced the documents in short order. But somehow, he felt they should wait those final few weeks. It made no sense, yet he couldn't resist the impulse to play the thing out to the bitter end. Miracles did occasionally happen. "We'll prepare everything and notify you, my lord."

"Oh, all right." Jamie rose, remembering that there was a tavern not too far from here where he could get a decent ale. That would ease his headache, at least. He didn't wait for Billingsley to see him out. He strode through the door, threw open the one in the outer office, and walked smack into a woman on the other side. He threw her off balance and into a second female just coming up the steps behind her. They teetered, and he had to grab them both and pull them away from the stairwell.

A flash of pale green eyes impaled him. They made Jamie think of a creature he'd seen once in a menagerie, a rare white tiger brought back from India, fierce and beautiful.

"You can let go of me now," said the owner of those amazing eyes.

Jamie dropped his hands and took a step back. "I beg your pardon." The woman was pale, with regular features and hair gleaming pale gold in the dimness. Her frame had felt light as a bird's in his grasp. The one behind her was older, a mature and attractive brunette. Jamie scarcely noticed her as his gaze strayed back to those tiger eyes. They held a cold, appraising stare.

Clare had to look up at the gentleman in Billingsley's doorway. He was tall, and from her cramped position, his broad shoulders nearly obscured the room beyond. He'd caught the two of them as if they were nothing, his arm around her like an iron bar. The set of his mouth was grim, which was unreasonable, since he'd careened into them. His eyes were so dark they seemed black in the dim light of the stairwell; they gazed at her with a spark that looked both intelligent and bitter. What ailed the man? She'd done nothing to him, and still he glared. Though he didn't move, he gave the impression of scarcely controlled energy, pouring off him in waves. Clare pressed back against the wall; here was a dark and brooding presence. "May we go past?"

"I beg your pardon," Jamie said again. Why had he been standing here like a looby? Awkwardly, they maneuvered around each other on the small landing, shoulders repeatedly brushing. For some reason, the touch made him think of the spark that sometimes crackled off the fur of a cat. Then he was free. He hurried down the steps, mind turning from the odd encounter to the foaming pitcher of ale that awaited. He didn't look back.

Clare Greenough and Selina Newton proceeded into Billingsley's outer office. They were early for their appointment. Clare hadn't been certain how long the cab journey would take. But the clerk showed them right in nonetheless.

Everett Billingsley stood to greet his next visitors and fought not to stare at the younger of them. This was a different person from the mousy governess who'd last called here to sign a pile of documents. Miss Greenough's cloak might be dull and shapeless, but her manner and expression were completely transformed. She stood straighter; her face glowed with purpose and intelligence.

"This is Mrs. Newton," Clare said. "She has been kind enough to... join my household and bear me company." Clare was still getting used to the idea that she might have a household of her own.

Billingsley met sparkling hazel eyes. The woman looked levelheaded and genteel, of an age to serve as chaperone. He approved.

"I've come to talk to you about a plan for my future," said Clare as they sat in the chairs before the desk. "Selina and I have discussed this matter at great length."

Now there was an understatement, Selina Newton thought. They had chewed over Clare's harebrained idea until they were both weary and annoyed. Though the debates had speeded the establishment of a friendship between them, Selina still thought the plan ridiculous. Why shouldn't Clare take her time, establish herself in town, make some acquaintances, enjoy herself a bit after years of servitude? But Clare wouldn't hear it. She remained convinced that this cousin of hers—Simon—would make any such scheme impossible. And despite everything Selina could say, Clare seemed to have some picture in her head of a marketplace where she could browse for a mate as one might buy vegetables.

"I cannot bear being under my cousin's control through this trust," Clare continued. She kept her voice even. Some emotional exchanges had made

Selina ask her why she was so unreasonably prejudiced against her cousin. "He will make it his business to forbid anything I want."

Billingsley folded his hands on his desk. It was true that his dealings with the young woman's cousin so far had been difficult. The man did seem bent on thwarting her.

"So, I wish to marry right away."

"Ah, there is some young man with whom you have formed...?"

"No. At first I thought I would advertise, but Selina has convinced me that would not be wise." Her horrified reaction had done as much as her arguments to quash this plan.

"Advertise?" Billingsley frowned in confusion.

"For a husband," Clare explained. "Selina thought we would get too many... unacceptable responses. And draw the wrong sort of attention." Clare had seen the truth of this argument right away. It had been a silly idea.

Everett Billingsley had to hide a shudder. Meeting Mrs. Newton's penetrating gaze, he saw the same consternation there.

Clare sat straighter. "But I do wish to come to some... immediate arrangement with a gentleman who is looking for a rich wife." It sounded rather bleak when she said it aloud. But that didn't matter. "Selina suggested that you might know how to proceed."

Selina had suggested it because she hoped he would talk her out of it, the older woman thought. She tried to convey this with her expression.

"But, my dear Miss Greenough." Billingsley searched

for words. "You should take your time, meet people, enjoy your new independence."

Clare sighed. She *had* thought things through. Why did people not see that? Why did they assume she was naive and witless? She steeled herself to go over it all once again. "You think I should rent a house in London? Perhaps try to secure invitations to some of the events of the season?"

"Yes, exactly. That would be most—"

"Can you advance me the funds to lease a suitable house?" Clare inquired. "And to purchase a proper wardrobe, of course, and... oh, rent a carriage, hire servants? I imagine this would be a significant sum."

"Ah." Billingsley had already received a searing letter from Simon Greenough about the five hundred pounds he'd withdrawn from the trust for Clare. The man had made it clear that he intended to monitor and approve every penny spent, and that he expected such a large initial amount to last a solitary young woman a year at least. He'd threatened to take Billingsley to law if he acted again without consultation.

"Mr. Billingsley?" Clare prompted.

"I do not have the sole authority to approve such a sum," he admitted.

"And is it your impression that my cousin would agree to do so?"

He'd intended to write the man and lay out a case for further expenditure. He thought his arguments quite powerful. But the intemperate tone of the man's letter did not make him optimistic. In truth, he didn't know how he was going to deal with the rift in the Greenough family. Rancorous complications loomed.

"No. Not immediately. I'm sure he could be brought around…"

"I imagine he thinks that the money you've already given me is sufficient for… oh, years."

Clearly, Miss Greenough knew her cousin better than he did.

"If I were still a governess, of course, it would be. And as long as Simon has charge of my finances, I may as well be a governess." Clare was trembling with anger and defiance, but she tried not to weaken her position by letting the others see it. They hadn't been present when Simon rejoiced at her brother's untimely death or sneered at her grief-stricken mother. They couldn't comprehend the depth of his malice. Or how desperate it made her feel to be under his control. His absence from her life had been one of the few good things about being an employee.

"I may be able to help convince him…"

"Mr. Billingsley, I beg you to believe me when I say that he will be immovable. There are many examples I could give you. My cousin allowed my grieving mother one week to vacate her home of thirty years, and he refused to let her take even one stick of furniture."

There was a moment of shocked silence. Selina saw the pain in Clare's face and how she tried to hide it. She'd learned a good deal about this young woman's character in a short time. And she'd found it admirable. She would do whatever she could to aid her.

Clare cleared her throat, clogged with old griefs, and strove to set the past aside. "So rather than wasting time remonstrating with Simon, I hope you will help me in another fashion, Mr. Billingsley," she continued.

Billingsley saw his own pity reflected in Mrs. Newton's gaze. "How?"

"When I inquired at the bank, I was told you represent some of the oldest and most distinguished families in England." Clare smiled at his surprised expression. "I wished to know something about my other trustee. They gave you the highest possible recommendation."

"I'm pleased," he said dryly. He *was* glad that she showed some business sense. But it had been years since he required anyone's recommendation.

"So, I thought you might be able to find me a husband."

"Find you a…?" Billingsley turned to Mrs. Newton, who nodded as if to say, *You see?*

"Through your work, you must be acquainted with many gentlemen, and privy to their financial circumstances. Of course you cannot reveal confidential information. But there couldn't be any harm in making a simple introduction. Or more than one," Clare conceded.

Billingsley felt dazed. "Are you asking me to be a matchmaker?"

"Precisely. And I have some very specific requirements." Pleased that they were at last getting to the heart of the matter, Clare took a folded piece of paper from her reticule.

Selina Newton had to smile at the stunned expression on Mr. Billingsley's face. She imagined that she'd looked just the same when Clare had first produced her list. It was comforting to have her sense of propriety reflected back to her.

"The first, and indeed the crucial, item is that this

man be willing to sign a document guaranteeing that I have control over my own money," Clare said. "This is the one nonnegotiable point. I'm sure you can draft such an instrument?" She looked at Billingsley.

"Well, yes, but…" That direct green gaze made the most outrageous things seem plausible.

"Other than that, I can be somewhat flexible. I would prefer that he be not more than forty years old, and of good family. I require some level of intelligence and good temper. And I don't see why he should not be… pleasant-looking." Clare felt a tremor of uncertainty. Was she really going to pledge her life to a complete stranger? She could take the funds she had and find inexpensive lodging, exercise economies… Then she thought of Cousin Simon and how he would enjoy reducing her good luck to that meager outcome.

"Miss Greenough, I don't really feel that…"

"Marriages are sometimes arranged." Clare didn't know whether she was telling him or herself.

Everett Billingsley suddenly remembered meeting his own wife, more than thirty years ago. He'd been an articled clerk, most of his hours devoted to drudgery, determined to make something of himself. He'd been drawn to Emily because she was attractive and kind—and because she was the daughter of a very successful solicitor with many useful connections. Would he have pursued her otherwise? He admitted to himself that he would not. Yet after all these years of marriage, children, and grandchildren, he loved her deeply and couldn't imagine any other choice. Perhaps Miss Greenough's scheme was not entirely insane. It was only when he acknowledged this possibility that the idea occurred to him. A fact that was to be a great comfort to him on many future occasions.

Clare saw the change in his expression. "You've thought of someone."

Billingsley was not accustomed to being read so easily. This young woman had managed what many ruthless negotiators had not: she'd thrown him off balance. "I don't say so," he replied. "I must consider your scheme." It was, he supposed, a kind of business transaction. Yet if that were so, he would be representing both sides, which was unacceptable. But if the action benefited both equally... His head spun. "You must give me a few days," he added.

Clare heard the finality in his tone. He would not be pushed. Accepting this, she smiled at him, then rose and held out her hand. "I am so grateful for all your help," she said.

Billingsley realized that it was the first time he'd seen her really smile. The effect was dazzling. Any young man would be putty in her hands, he thought. He felt in some danger of malleability himself.

The smile stayed on Clare's lips as they said their good-byes and as she and Selina walked down the stairs together. "He definitely knows of someone suitable," she said as they reached the street.

Perhaps he did, Selina thought. But was that good news?

Four

OVER THE NEXT FEW DAYS, SELINA HELPED CURB Clare's impatience by insisting on a thorough rehabilitation of the young woman's wardrobe. Though she understood the reasons behind Clare's choice of dull colors and unflattering cuts, the results continually pained Selina's keen fashion sense. And, she pointed out, those reasons no longer applied. Clare didn't need to fade into the background for fear of unwanted attentions or an employer's disapproval. She could dress just as she pleased.

Clare, however, refused to spend any of the money Billingsley had advanced on new clothing. "If things don't turn out well, we may need it for far more important purposes," she declared. And so Selina set about altering the gowns Clare already possessed.

A combination of exquisite taste and continual lack of funds had forced Selina Newton to become a skilled seamstress. And as she learned, over the years, to sketch a pattern, set a dart, gather ruffles, and sew invisible seams, she came to love everything about the process. From the inspiration for a new gown—from examples she admired or her own ever-expanding imagination—to finding just the right fabric, to constructing the garment, she found pleasure in it all. Clare's wardrobe became a challenge rather than an eyesore as she plunged into the task.

For her part, Clare was amazed at the magic her new friend was able to work on her dowdy old dresses. Her apprehension at seeing her limited store of clothing reduced to a pile of scraps, the seams all unpicked, soon turned to admiration. A line recut here, a tuck there, and Clare had gowns that made her look svelte and graceful—no longer a thin young woman bundled into a bag. Selina also convinced Clare to put away all the caps she had used to hide her hair and to try some new ways of dressing it. By the time the older woman had lured Clare out to the Pantheon Bazaar, she was primed to spend a little money on the amazing bargains they found there. She bought a shimmering scarf that echoed the green of her eyes, a bright paisley shawl, a spray of colorful flowers for retrimming a dull hat, and several pairs of silk stockings. After that, it was no great step to procuring tickets for a play and going out to show off her new look.

Clare enjoyed the performance. She enjoyed the cold supper they ordered afterward. Indeed, she was finding pure pleasure in many small things. For the first time in years, Clare could spend her days doing whatever she wanted, and with that freedom came an ability to savor the choices she made. She remembered how much she loved raspberry jam; on a walk in the park she watched people riding and recalled the wind in her hair as she galloped down a country lane. Each trivial action was transformed by the fact that no one had told her to do it or forbidden her to think of it. Though she'd lived in London for years, she now began to savor some of what the metropolis had to offer. It was like being released from a subdued, colorless limbo into a landscape flooded with brightness and life.

❦

Down in the city, Everett Billingsley frowned over a letter that had arrived in the morning post. Simon Greenough's reply to his missive suggesting that Miss Greenough needed to rent a house in town was couched in a positively insulting tone, as if he were addressing a servant. He declared that they would not be wasting his great-uncle's hard-earned fortune on "fripperies." The "girl," as he referred to his twenty-four-year-old cousin, would be better off in a room or two. She could hardly need more than a maid. Billingsley got the impression that he would have liked to suggest a nunnery. It seemed that Miss Greenough was right; it would be a continual battle to get a penny from this man. She would not be establishing herself in society on her own.

Billingsley put down the pages and wondered what to do. This difficulty did not mean that he should do as she'd asked. If he made an introduction, he was, in essence, benefiting another client at her expense. Literally, in fact, at her expense. Her fortune was the counter in this game. It was not a deception, of course. She'd urged him to do it, and she would also gain something she wanted. And yet... Billingsley's scrupulous soul revolted at the prospect, even as his kind heart ached at the thought of leaving two young people caught in familial traps when he might aid them. And then it came to him. It was quite simple. Should the matter go forward, and should Miss Greenough still refuse to engage her own advocate, he would ask an unbiased colleague to review all the documents he prepared and give an opinion. That should ensure all was fair and aboveboard. His conscience salved, Billingsley pulled out a piece of parchment and wrote a note.

❧

Jamie returned to Andrew's rooms in the late afternoon to find Harry already there. His two friends lounged on either side of the fireplace, absorbing its warmth on this icy February Tuesday. "That took you an age," said Andrew. "What was so urgent that you had to rush off to the city on such a filthy day? Not bad news, I hope."

Jamie threw his greatcoat onto the sofa and sank into the remaining armchair, still feeling a bit dazed. "My man of business has found me an heiress," he said.

The other two sat up straight and stared at him.

"She is prepared to marry a penniless man…"

"You're saved!" cried Harry. "Break out the champagne, Andrew."

"Under certain conditions."

"What sort of conditions?" Andrew wondered.

"What does it matter?" said Harry before Jamie could reply. "Take the heiress and run, my lad. Good God, isn't this what you've been praying for?"

"Harry, why aren't you off somewhere hunting with your aristocratic relations?" Andrew asked.

"Because I have duty here in town. Don't change the subject."

"What's the catch?" asked Andrew. "Is she a hunchback, or a shrew, or a madwoman?"

"Well, of course she's mad if she'll have Jamie," said Harry.

Jamie gave him a look. "She wants…" He hesitated. Somehow, he was reluctant to tell his friends that the young woman in question insisted on being in control of her money, and that he'd be required to sign documents guaranteeing this. It was… a bit humiliating. Billingsley had assured him that he wouldn't have to go to her for every penny he wished to spend. Still… A man should have control over his own household. "There would be a written agreement between… us," he temporized.

"A marriage contract." Harry nodded as if this were only natural.

Billingsley had told Jamie to think of what he would ask, what resources he needed to redeem Trehearth. But it was difficult to get his mind around the idea that his wife would control his finances.

"Which would ensure the funds to save Trehearth?" Andrew asked.

That was the crux of it. If he could get that, did the rest really matter? It didn't, Jamie thought. Trehearth was the important thing.

"*Is* she an antidote?" asked Harry.

"Billingsley promises that she is not."

"Well then? What's the problem?"

"There is none, I suppose." Jamie found that he couldn't confide any further. The agreement would be a private matter, after all. His friends would never know that he had relinquished the financial reins. "It's just... I know we've joked about it. But when it really comes down to taking a wife as a... business matter..."

Harry and Andrew looked at Jamie, and then at each other. Their friend seemed quite forlorn. He'd drifted into deeper waters than they were used to navigating.

"If you were in love with someone else, of course you couldn't consider it," Andrew acknowledged. "I know. After I met Alice, it was impossible even to look at another."

Harry opened his mouth to mock this sickly sentiment, then closed it again. Jamie's expression was so serious.

Jamie got up and went to the sideboard, where the brandy waited. He'd uncorked it, ready to pour, when he hesitated. If he really had a chance of saving his estate, then he didn't need to stick his head in a bottle any longer. "I still have to meet her," he said, to himself as much as his friends. "Perhaps she'll dislike me, and this will all be for naught." Jamie didn't dare really hope. He'd fallen into that trap before, hatching a host of schemes over the years to save his heritage. The blow when they failed was almost unendurable. It hurt so much more when you hoped. He poured himself a large glass of brandy.

"You must exert yourself to be charming," said Harry. "I can give you a few pointers, if you like."

"You?" hooted Andrew. "If you want to know how to woo a woman properly..."

"And send her right off into a rival's arms," Harry finished.

The conversation veered into comradely taunting. Jamie sipped his brandy and wondered precisely how one charmed a female who was perfectly aware that it was her money rather than her person that most attracted you.

⁕

Nothing could change the unenticing buff color of her best gown, Clare acknowledged. The hue did not flatter her. But with the new cut Selina had contrived and the green scarf draped over her arms, it had a fashionable look. And her hair was quite transformed, pulled up into a high knot, with curls clustering around her face. She could wish that she had more color in her cheeks, but the overall result in the mirror went a good way toward calming her nerves. "What time is it?" she asked Selina.

"It's just ten. You've half an hour to spare." Though she still had doubts, Selina didn't voice them. They'd heard from Billingsley about Simon Greenough's intransigence. It seemed that Clare was right about her cousin. And if Clare was forced back onto a governess's budget, the beautiful zest for life that Selina had seen emerging would be dimmed. That would be heartbreaking to see. Mr. Billingsley seemed a trustworthy man. Selina knew he wouldn't recommend a blackguard. But if she had any reservations at all about this Baron Trehearth after meeting him, she was not going to hold her tongue.

Less than half a mile away, Jamie stood before the

cheval glass in Andrew's bedchamber and regarded his reflection. His dark blue coat had been made by Weston; the quality was evident, but so was the age. New clothes had not been in his budget since he reached his full growth. He had no fashionable pantaloons, only breeches of the same vintage as the coat, and he was overly conscious of a tiny fray in the cuff of his fine linen shirt. Harry had insisted on lending him a new neckcloth. The kindness had not taken all the sting out of the necessity. Andrew had wanted to give him detailed advice on how to tie it, as if he didn't know perfectly well. He was glad they were both occupied this morning. He was in no state to take their teasing, or their genuine concern.

His face looked back at him from the mirror, dark and unsmiling. Was this the sort of engaging fellow likely to win an heiress? He tried a smile; it looked insincere to his hypercritical eyes. He told himself that he ought to feel grateful for the chance of salvation. But that was it, wasn't it? This was only a chance. He was about to present himself for approval. Some chit he'd never seen before was going to look him over like prize livestock and decide his fate. His brows came together at the thought. He hated the prospect. He'd almost rather chuck the whole thing than take the chance of rejection—and yet another painful collapse of all his hopes. Almost. "Smile," he told the fellow in the mirror. "And try to look like you mean it, for God's sake."

The bell rang. Everett Billingsley was fetching him for this delicate appointment. Jamie wasn't sure whether the man wanted to help or just be certain his candidate came up to scratch. When he went down the stairs and opened the door, however, Jamie found he was glad to see the older man. Over the years, Billingsley had always had his best interests at heart, and he seemed to think this eccentric plan could succeed. Through the short carriage journey, Jamie told himself to rally round and do his part.

∽

The employee of Mivart's Hotel who ushered the visitors upstairs to a spacious private parlor wondered what dire matter they were calling to discuss. Both the ladies within and the gentlemen arrivals looked serious as a funeral. But he was destined never to know the answer, for as soon as he had opened the door and announced their names, he was dismissed.

Clare and Jamie gazed at each other in surprise, each remembering the moment when they'd passed outside Billingsley's office. Unconscious of their previous encounter, the man himself stepped forward to make the introductions. He wasn't accustomed to feeling so awkward and would have been glad to be elsewhere. But he'd set this affair in motion. He had to be present to give what help he could.

As the couple greeted one another, Selina tried to get a sense of the young man. She also remembered him from the corridor outside Billingsley's office, where he'd seemed to simmer with angry energy. Observing him, she realized how much she cared for the happiness of a young woman she'd met only a few weeks ago. Clare was spirited, intelligent, kind. Selina would not stand by and see her throw her life away.

As she and Billingsley withdrew to a sofa on the far side of the room, giving Clare and Jamie space to get acquainted, Selina resolved to pump the man for every detail of Lord Trehearth's history and character.

It was the girl with the tiger eyes, Jamie thought as they sat down in a pair of armchairs before the fire. Without a shapeless cloak muffling her form, she looked spare and elegant. With that pale hair and skin, he might have said cold, if it weren't for the spark in those penetrating eyes. The feel of her slender frame in the curve of his arm came back to him. Light as a bird, he remembered. It made him wonder if the spark could catch fire.

A tension she'd hardly been conscious of relaxed as Clare gazed at him. She had to admit that she was glad he was handsome. She'd been braced to accept a plain man in order to achieve her goals; she would have, of course. But Lord Trehearth's dark good looks did no harm. He held himself with the poise of an athlete, and he still gave off that impression of barely contained energy she remembered from their first encounter. "It's rather hard to know how to begin," she said. It was, in fact, impossible. What could she say to a man she planned to purchase as a husband? The thought made her flush and smile.

Jamie blinked as the young woman before him seemed to spring to life. Color tinged her cheeks; emotion warmed her gaze. Far from cold, he thought. He smiled back.

The dazzle of white teeth against tanned skin made Clare's pulse jump. His answering smile felt like a hand reaching out to draw her close. Which was nonsense.

Lord Trehearth simply… He must see the humor in their situation, as did she. It was an immensely comforting idea. Clare took a breath. There was no point in trivial chitchat. She should simply plunge in.

"So you vouch for Lord Trehearth's good character?" Selina demanded quietly across the room. She had made what inquiries she could as soon as Billingsley had given Clare the young man's name. But Selina's close acquaintances did not stretch into the upper reaches of society, and the elderly ladies she felt able to consult had said merely that the Trehearth family was "all to pieces," which she already knew. Why else were they here?

"He's a fine lad," Billingsley assured her. "He has a bit of a wild streak, but I've heard that females find that attractive."

"Wild? In what sense? Is he a libertine? A gamester?" Selina's worst fears rose to haunt her.

"No, no. Of course not." Billingsley tore his attention from the young people. Distracted, he'd let his tongue run away with him. "I should never have brought him here if he had such grievous faults. He simply enjoys a bit of fun."

"What sort of fun?"

Billingsley shifted nervously on the sofa cushion. What was he doing? His information was all rumors, after all. "The sort any wellborn young gentleman enjoys. Convivial evenings with his friends…"

"He is a drunkard?"

"My dear Mrs. Newton…!" Billingsley found he was sweating under her interrogation. "Nothing of the kind."

Selina frowned suspiciously at the darkly handsome young man on the other side of the parlor.

Clare cleared her throat and once again urged herself onward. "I… ah… I imagine Mr. Billingsley told you that I worked as a governess for several years, due to… family circumstances." Billingsley had given her some basic information about the man she was to meet, and she supposed he had done the same for Lord Trehearth. But facts told one only so much. "I don't know if you realize what that means. I went from a luxurious, carefree childhood to being a sort of upper servant." This was coming out with more emotion than she'd planned. Clare's flush deepened. It was unsettling to reveal private matters to a stranger, and a man, but she felt the situation must be laid out between them. "Now, I have come into this money, but it is tied up in a trust partly controlled by a cousin who…" She wasn't going into that. Tales of her sadly broken family could await a closer acquaintance, if that developed. Clare leaned forward. "The point is, after six years of humbly taking orders, I cannot bear to lose control of this inheritance that has unexpectedly come my way!"

Her story, and her vehemence, struck a chord in Jamie. The painful decline in his prospects, year after year, had been beyond his control, no matter how hard he tried to mend things.

Embarrassed by the strength of her outburst, Clare started to speak.

"It's maddening," said Jamie. "To feel your whole life is at the mercy of those who care very little about you, who scarcely see you as an individual, in fact."

Clare's lips parted in wonderment at his ready understanding. "Yes, that is it, precisely."

"I tried very hard to initiate improvements on my estates. I've proposed various plans, at one time or another, to increase yields and allow me to gradually pay off the mortgages. But the bankers only pretended to listen, and then dismissed every idea I suggested, because they each required some fresh investment."

Just as Simon treated her wishes, Clare thought. Except he didn't even pretend to listen. "Tell me about your land."

Jamie sat back. His far-off acres rose in his mind—the towering sea cliffs and the pastures and fields that rolled away inland. He knew and loved every inch of it. He hardly knew where to begin a description.

"Is he a kind man?" Selina asked Everett Billingsley. "Does he treat members of his family well?"

There was a small quibble here, though a young man could hardly be blamed... "Lord Trehearth's parents are both deceased," Billingsley hedged.

"Has he no other family?"

"No aunts and uncles. Some distant cousins, perhaps. Sadly, the Trehearths have dwindled in this century. They have a long, proud heritage, you know. Lord Trehearth can trace his line back to the Normans."

Sensing something unspoken, Selina frowned again.

Jamie let out a sigh and said, "Trehearth is in Cornwall, about a half day's journey south of Penzance. The land has been in my family for centuries. It's beautiful country and full of promise if properly tended. Wild as a stormy ocean and soft as a spring mist."

A lilt came into his voice as he spoke of it, and the sense of barely restrained impatience that hung about him eased. Clare liked this side of him. "It sounds lovely. I grew up in the country."

She was thinking of the gentle countryside of the home counties, Jamie knew. He wondered if she really understood how far from London Trehearth lay. It was almost like another country; that was one of the things he loved about it. He had a momentary impulse to explain, but he hesitated. With a twinge of discomfort, he held back. He was not here to discourage her from funneling some of her fortune into his lands.

Clare decided she liked him enough to take this discussion a step further, into delicate territory. "You've come here today. I assume this means that you... feel you could allow a... a wife to take charge of the family's money?"

What was he to say to this? That he found the idea unnatural and humiliating, but would accept almost any conditions to save his heritage? Obviously not. When he'd thought about the condition in the days leading up to this encounter, it had seemed to him that a woman would soon tire of the details of business, become immersed in her household and children, and gratefully relinquish the reins. But this was clearly not the thing to say now either. Though Jamie was certain that carrying out such a scheme was not going to be as simple as she seemed to believe, in the end, he settled for a clipped, "Yes. With certain conditions."

Clare nodded. Naturally there were specifics to be discussed in this unconventional arrangement. She would not have trusted a man who grabbed too readily at her offer. But she found she was ready to move forward. The admirable Billingsley had found her a sensible man, amenable to reason, able to set aside common masculine sensitivities. She smiled again and felt that inner flutter when he responded. The fact that he was very attractive was a bonus, though irrelevant, of course. It would not affect the settlement between them. "Then I am willing to sit down together and set out our terms." It was such an arid way to describe a marriage. Was she making a mistake? "If you need some time to think about whether…"

"I also am prepared to do that," he put in. She was lovely, really, with that sense of a banked fire beneath her cool exterior. Once he'd ignited those fires—and there was a task to be anticipated—she'd want nothing more than for him to take charge. It was the way of things, after all. "We can pass along our thoughts to Billingsley and let him draft the papers. He has suggested that a neutral solicitor review the final…"

"No, we should talk face to face about each point. In order to be very clear. I have a list." She would show him just how practical and organized a woman could be. He need have no fears that she would be a poor manager.

Jamie suppressed a spurt of annoyance. This scheme of hers was going to tax his patience, of which he knew he had no great store. But she would soon abandon it, he assured himself. He need do no more than what came naturally. "I, of course, require an heir," he said, meeting those amazing green eyes with desire simmering in his own. Clare's pale skin went scarlet. Yes, Jamie thought, it was all going to work out, in time.

Seeing her young friend's flush, Selina rose to intervene. "You have absolutely no doubts about the wisdom of your recommendation?" she asked Billingsley, her voice full of challenge.

Was there any transaction that engendered no doubts at all? he wondered. Certainty was a rare commodity in this world. "Lord Trehearth is an honorable man," he answered. And with this Selina had to be satisfied.

Five

MISS CLARE GREENOUGH AND JAMES BOLEIGH, BARON Trehearth, were married two weeks later by special license, on a chill February morning in the parish church nearest the hotel. Neither had any family members present. Jamie was supported by his two best friends, and Clare by Selina Newton. Everett Billingsley was also invited, to see the fruition of the match he had set in motion. The notice in the *Morning Post* informed interested readers that the couple was leaving for Cornwall directly after the wedding. Since most prominent members of society resided in the country at this time of year, the news was not much marked.

The notice did not mention that the bride's companion was accompanying the newly wed couple on their western journey. The desire for Selina's company had washed over Clare as she sat in Billingsley's office, across the table from her proposed husband, discussing their future in terms of contractual guarantees and schedules of payment. She'd met his terms, signing documents to redeem mortgages and designate funds to restore the Trehearth estate, as he had accepted hers. And from time to time, she'd felt as if she were facing an adversary rather than a prospective partner. The language of legal documents seemed to foster that attitude. So even as Clare told herself that she was satisfied, delighted even, to have placed her inheritance safely under her own control, she found she didn't want to set off on a long journey alone, to a strange place, with a husband she barely knew.

Selina, sitting next to Clare in the luxurious post chaise, stretching stiff muscles and feeling her age a bit, knew that she could never have resisted Clare's request to stay on. Even though Clare had bought the promised annuity, granting Selina her independence, the bonds of friendship still held sway. But at times Selina wondered if she was a help or a hindrance on the journey. With Selina in the coach, Lord Trehearth was free to ride much of the way, rather than attend his bride. The two were not becoming better acquainted on this journey, as they should have been. They would arrive as they had set out— strangers. And the young man had made no objection to this arrangement. Selina fidgeted in her seat and wished that the roads were better. The bouncing of the chaise made handwork impossible and reading a queasy proposition. There was little to do but worry about the exact nature of her responsibilities. Years of fetching misplaced lornettes, coddling irritable pugs, and patiently listening to the querulous complaints of elderly women had not prepared Selina to counsel newlyweds. Particularly those who had entered into such a very odd match.

Selina gripped the leather strap above the window as they jounced over an especially deep set of ruts. A busy coaching inn was a poor spot for a wedding night, she told herself. A jolting carriage and broken sleep in lumpy beds promoted short tempers and potential regrets. The pair would grow closer as they made a home together. Clare would need her less and less. When her young friend was well settled in her new house, with her new husband, Selina could depart to establish a peaceful and ordered life for herself.

Pulling the coach blankets closer around her chilled feet, Selina leaned back and allowed herself the luxury of imagining a secure future. She was thinking of Bath as a place to settle. Society there was more welcoming for a mature single woman, and yet not so stuffy as Harrowgate or Wells. She would be able to afford comfortable rooms, with books and perhaps even a pianoforte, and a servant or two. She would make friends with other women in a similar position, inter-est herself in a local church and charities. She knew that her new income, though small by the world's standards, would allow her the satisfaction of helping others while she enjoyed herself. A calm and sooth-ing daily routine unfolded before her mind's eye and made her smile as the carriage swayed through a turn onto an even poorer road. It would not be long, really, before she was snugly installed in the placid life of her imaginings.

Despite the icy winds and stretches of half-frozen mud that dragged at the coach wheels and slowed them down, Jamie was conscious only of a rising ela-tion as they traveled farther away from London. This journey home was different from all others; this time he was returning to renew his land rather than mourn its decline. The fatigue of hours in the saddle scarcely touched him. Noting landmarks he'd passed countless times before, he thought of the tenants and dependents who would share his joy at this unanticipated redemption, and he was borne up by a heady mixture of pride and relief and eagerness. He could let go of the nagging guilt over those he'd neglected. He truly could, he thought, dismissing the familiar twinges.

This ferment left little room for thoughts of his new wife, for now simply a means to a much desired end. When he could spare any attention for Clare, he was merely glad she had a companion to keep her occupied. And on the final stage of their journey, with home tantalizingly close, he couldn't resist leaving the laboring post chaise behind and riding on to Trehearth.

❧

A full hour later, Clare climbed stiffly down from the carriage and gazed up at the massive gray pile that was now her home. The long stone facade, with two wings thrusting forward on either side to form a courtyard, looked like something out of a fairy tale. There were steep slate gables and arched windows and crenellations. The scudding clouds on this chilly afternoon added to the impression. She knew that Lord…

Jamie. He'd said that his friends called him Jamie, and that she should do so. It still felt awkward, which brought up uncomfortable thoughts such as—was she his friend? She was undoubtedly his wife. The ring on her finger was a constant reminder. But that did not necessarily equate with friendship.

Clare rotated her tight shoulders and looked up the sprawling house. There seemed to be no one about to welcome her. She knew that Jamie's grandfather had built this place on the site of a ruined castle, using the fallen stones, so it dated only from 1770. It stood on a sheer cliff above a cove formed by a small Cornish river. There was a fishing village below, she remembered. Jamie had said that his grandfather designed the house, too. With only limited success, Clare had to say, surveying the mishmash of styles that ran into one another along the frontage. His obsession with construction had nearly bankrupted the estate. That was why the place looked unkempt and shabby. It was, in a way, the reason she was here. Standing in the gravel courtyard, in the cold, alone. Where was Jamie?

"Well," said Selina, who had stepped down beside her. "Where is Lord Trehearth? Where are the servants? This is outrageous. To ride off like that with scarcely a word, and now no sign of a..."

The great wooden front door opened, and two small figures scurried out—boys of ten or so in white shirts and buckskin breeches above thick woolen hose. Or... Clare took in the long tangled black hair, big dark eyes, and delicate features. They weren't boys; they were girls, twins obviously. Why were they so oddly dressed? She took a step forward to greet them. Something moved in the dim doorway, and then shot out between the children and hurtled toward her.

In the next instant, Clare was flattened by a gigantic dog. It stood over her, feet planted on either side of her torso, and began to lick her face with a slavering red tongue. She pushed at its chest; it was immovable.

For a moment, Selina stood frozen, terrified by the largest canine she'd ever seen. Then she recovered and rushed over; she spied a collar around the creature's neck and grasped it. But her tugging had no effect. She might have been trying to shift a horse. The two scandalously dressed children had come closer. "Is this your dog?" Selina panted. "Remove him immediately."

"He likes you," said one, gazing down at Clare as she continued to try to fend off the beast's attentions. Her hands were now dripping with saliva.

"His name is Randolph," added the other.

"He's half wolfhound and half mastiff."

"The vicar's dog got into Mr. Fox's kennel."

"He was hopping mad," said the other twin, with sparkling eyes.

"Randolph was the only puppy in the litter. Mr. Fox was going to drown him!" Their dialogue was sending Selina's head back and forth like a pendulum.

"But we came to the rescue."

"We don't care if he's a mongol."

"Mongrel," corrected the other twin.

"Call him off!" Selina commanded.

The doorway erupted. Jamie ran out, followed by an older couple, the woman's hands flapping in dismay. Pushing Selina aside, Jamie grabbed the dog's collar and yanked him off. "Take him away," he told the twins as he helped Clare to her feet.

Her face was dripping stickily. Her clothes were marked with muddy paw prints. She had no doubt that her bonnet was ruined. *May I present the new mistress of your household*, she said silently, wondering whether to laugh or break down in hysterics.

The twins made no move to control the dog, who frisked about the group as if he'd done just as he ought. They were observing the scene like a scientific experiment.

"These are my sisters," Jamie said.

Startled, Clare met his dark eyes. "Sisters?"

Except for the capering dog, the scene froze as it became obvious to all present that this piece of information was wholly new to her. Faces exhibited a range of reactions, from Selina's astonished disapproval to the older couple's quickly stifled worry to the twins' resigned grimaces. Jamie had the grace to look shame-faced.

"I'm Tamsyn," said one twin then.

"I'm Tegan," chimed in the other. "It means 'pretty little thing' in Cornish." The girl smirked up at the adults.

Jamie put his hands firmly on the second girl's shoulders. "*Tamsyn* has a small mole on her neck," he said, his jaw tight.

Clare saw the tiny mark that identified the child. They'd been trying a trick that their brother clearly recognized.

Jamie moved to his other maddening sister and set warning hands on her shoulders. "*Tegan* is just a hair shorter."

Clare could see it if she looked carefully.

"It is quite *easy* to tell them apart," Jamie finished. *Except that they are both imps of Satan*, he added to himself. He'd written them with news of the wedding. He'd commanded them to be on their best behavior when they welcomed a new sister-in-law to Trehearth. He'd hoped to present them in a proper state. Of course it had been a forlorn hope that they would put on suitable gowns, which they certainly possessed, and pretend, at least, to be civilized. Allow Clare to believe, however briefly, that they were not going to be a plague on her existence. But as always, they'd ignored him. Or, no. Devil take it—this *was* their best behavior. They had no more manners than a pair of feral cats.

A familiar guilt mingled with his anger. Was it any wonder that he hadn't found an... opportunity to talk to Clare about them? They made it so difficult. But their lapses weren't his fault. What did he know of rearing young ladies? How could he have been expected to do any sort of job of it with not a penny to spare? Now, though, he would have to endure another lecture about his failures. His sisters should be at school; they should have a governess. Did people really think he was so stupid as not to have tried these things? Could they even imagine the disasters that had ensued?

The dog came over to fawn at Selina's feet. She backed away. The animal was buff colored, with floppy, darker brown ears and diamond-shaped black patches around his eyes that gave him the look of a mournful harlequin. He panted winsomely. She glared at him to indicate that she was not charmed, then shifted her icy gaze to Lord Trehearth. His conduct was also beyond the pale. "Perhaps we go should inside?" Selina suggested acidly.

Galvanized, Jamie offered Clare his arm and

escorted her across the gravel courtyard, up the two stone steps, and through the heavy wooden door into the great hall. The others trailed after them and reassembled in the large space. "May I present Mr. and Mrs. Pendennis," Jamie said, indicating the older couple. "John and Anna. They are the mainstays of the household. They've been here since I was a child, and they take care of the place and... my sisters."

"As well as we can," said the old woman darkly.

Clare realized that the twins had not come in with them. Nor had the dog, she was glad to see. She liked dogs, but those she'd lived with had been well-trained animals.

"They've stayed on through thick and thin," Jamie added. He tried to convey in his tone that the Pendennises were more than servants to him. "John, Anna, this is Lady Trehearth, and her friend Mrs. Selina Newton."

Rallying all her faculties, Clare smiled at the old couple. They looked rather alike, both short and broad, with round faces, the gnarled hands of hard workers, white hair, and bright blue eyes. "I'm very pleased to meet you," she said.

"I tied up that fool dog in the stables," said John Pendennis. Like his wife, he spoke in the accent of the West Country.

"I've no doubt of it," replied Jamie. He wondered how his sisters had arranged for Randolph to focus his uncouth attentions on Clare. They hadn't, he concluded. The lumbering creature was oblivious to commands. It had been sheer bad luck.

Further gathering her composure, Clare looked

around the large room that formed the entry of the house. It was not a comfortable sort of chamber. Two stories of dark wood paneling soared up to a row of high windows overlooking the courtyard. Dusty banners hung from the great beams that crossed the white plaster ceiling. The planked floor, stretching out to a huge stone fireplace on the inner side, was nearly empty. The lone table looked tiny and out of place. The space was clearly a nod to the castle that had once stood here, and not a chamber to really live in. Without meaning to, she sighed.

"It's been a tiring journey," responded Jamie. "Anna will show you to your room." And let him escape the complaints he imagined were waiting to burst out of Clare.

"While you are doing exactly what?" began Selina, her irritation breaking through in her tone.

"Thank you," Clare interrupted. She was too tired to argue. And she longed to clean up before discussing why he hadn't mentioned sisters—and anything else he might have left out. She remembered that she was the hostess here. "And Selina's bedchamber as well, please."

"I'll bring the luggage, milady," said Mr. Pendennis, turning back to the door.

The two women followed Anna Pendennis up a carved wooden staircase and into a long corridor that looked far more modern than the entry. It was lined with closed doors. A threadbare carpet ran down its length, and there was dust visible on the empty candle sconces. "We've not enough hands to keep up such a big place," said Mrs. Pendennis defensively.

"Of course not," said Clare.

"Mrs. Newton is in here, milady." The old woman went across to open a door to the left of the stair. "And you're along this way." She moved in the opposite direction. At a wave from Selina indicating she was well, Clare went into a spacious bedroom at the back of the house. Here, too, the figured carpet and blue hangings were old and worn. A massive four-poster bed and wardrobe in dark wood contrasted with a newer dressing table and mirror. A bright fire warmed the space. Clare walked over to one of the two wide windows. The cliff fell away beneath her, yielding a vertiginous view of the tossing sea.

"Master's room is through there." Mrs. Pendennis pointed to a connecting door in the right-hand wall. "John'll have your things up in a trice."

"Thank you. Would it be possible to have a bath?" Clare thought longingly of hot water and scented soap and warm towels.

Anna Pendennis's wrinkled face creased further. "We have a tin tub the girls use in front of the kitchen fire. We could carry it up, perhaps." Obviously trying to hide reluctance, she turned away. "I'll set the water on to heat."

"No, that's all right," replied Clare quickly. "Just a can of hot water will be fine." Clearly relieved, the old woman nodded and went out. Nothing in this house had been updated since its construction, Clare reminded herself. But she could not stifle a sinking feeling when she confirmed her suspicion that a screen in the corner hid a chamber pot. The state of the place was daunting.

Still, it was pleasant to be alone for the first time in days. She took off her battered bonnet and stained cloak and went to hold chilled hands out to the fire. And in that moment of relaxation, without warning, the enormity of what she'd done hit her. She was hundreds of miles from anything familiar. She'd pledged her life to a man she hardly knew. She'd taken on a household that seemed in complete disarray, including two unexpected, and clearly eccentric, children. How could Jamie not have told her about them! Clare watched her extended hands begin to tremble in the warm firelight.

Heralded by a knock, her trunk and satchel arrived, and then a can of steaming water to be poured into the washbasin that also waited behind the screen. Declining Anna Pendennis's diffident offers of help, Clare undressed and had a thorough wash. She was worn out, she told herself. She hadn't slept well during the nights on the road. Things would look better after a real rest. Digging out a fresh nightgown, she climbed into the huge bed. It was surprisingly comfortable. The sheets were soft and clean and smelled of lavender. Clare crawled between them and was almost instantly asleep.

When Selina tapped on the door and looked in a bit later, she smiled to see Clare lying so peacefully. Gently closing the door, she went downstairs to warn the Pendennises not to disturb their mistress until she woke on her own. Clare needed rest. Selina knew from her own state how tired she must be. And any situation looked better after a good night's sleep. At least, so she hoped.

Some time later, Jamie knocked on the door between their bedchambers and, after waiting a moment, came in. He was braced to apologize for not mentioning his sisters, for their poor behavior and that of their wretched pet. He was ready to assure his irate wife that he had reprimanded the twins, and to escort her downstairs to a dinner he knew would be only tolerable. Anna Pendennis was admirable in so many ways, but she was not a good cook.

Jamie found Clare sound asleep, her face sweetly peaceful against the white of the pillow. The dancing firelight picked out stray gleams in her pale hair and washed her cheeks with color. But there were dark smudges under her eyes, and exhaustion showed in the depth of her slumber. The journey had been hard on her; he knew that. He'd pushed because he was so eager to be home and get to work; his heart thrilled every time he thought of what he could now do for his tenants and acres. Still, he shouldn't have left her to arrive alone. It had been rude at best and thoughtless at worse. He'd been ready for reproaches about that lapse, knowing he deserved them.

Standing there, watching the soft rise and fall of her breath, Jamie saw that his lapse went further. Clare was not a guest, come for a passing visit; she was his wife. She would be here, sleeping in this bed, walking the corridors of his house, for the rest of their lives. He was *obliged* to treat her with respect, even though he knew so little of her. Jamie was conscious of a twinge of resentment. The bond felt artificial, the woman in the bed a stranger. Was he to be forced… At once, he stiffened. It was thanks to her that he had his chance.

He wouldn't shirk his duty, not like his father had. Quietly, he walked over and added wood to the dying fire. He drew the ancient curtains over the windows and stepped softly from the room.

Entering the dining room, Jamie received the reproaches he'd been expecting when Selina Newton waylaid him.

"Clare is asleep," the older woman said. "I've ordered that she not be disturbed for dinner." She waited a moment, then added, "I hope you know that her reception here was shameful."

Jamie bristled at the word. He knew he was in the wrong, but her judgment seemed harsh. And he didn't see why she should be handing out reproaches in his household. "I realize I should not have ridden ahead," he answered stiffly.

"Indeed." Selina eyed the man who had pledged to honor and keep her young friend. Handsome, yes. Spirited and capable of charm, no doubt. A dangerous spark in his dark eyes at being chided. None of that mattered to her. He needed to learn that this was no way to treat his wife.

"You have my apologies for the poor greeting," Jamie managed.

"You need to apologize to *Clare*."

"I *shall*."

"Splendid."

After that exchange, dinner was an uncomfortable meal. Selina was surprised to find that Lord Trehearth's sisters joined them at table, despite their tender age. They had, at least, exchanged their unacceptable attire for dresses, though they squirmed in them and plucked at tight sleeves and bodices. Clearly, the garments had been made when the girls were smaller. Selina made a few attempts at polite conversation, but the master of the house offered only minimal replies, and the twins looked sullen and said nothing. The roast was underdone and the potatoes cooked to sludge. The host continually refilled his wineglass. Selina was very glad to escape the family board and retire to her bedchamber for an early night.

Clare slept soundly right through the evening and the night, not stirring until early morning light filtered through the threadbare curtains. She woke much refreshed and very hungry. Throwing back the covers, she was struck by the chill of the room. The fire had nearly died. Hurrying over the cold floorboards, she shifted the fire screen and stirred the coals, then added logs from the bin beside the fireplace. As the flames sprang back, she splashed her face and hands with cold water remaining in the can from last night. It would have been so pleasant to have a cup of early tea, but she didn't blame Mrs. Pendennis for the lack. At her age, and with the size of place, it was no wonder the house was without amenities. One of Clare's first tasks was obviously hiring staff to help her.

Dressed, she went downstairs in search of breakfast. She was wondering which way to turn to find the kitchen when her new husband's twin sisters stepped out of a doorway and into her path, spreading out in an obvious ambush. They were still dressed as boys, and their long black hair fell in tangles down their backs. Did they never brush it? Not quite recovered from the surprise of discovering their existence, Clare began a greeting.

"We are *not* going to be made to wear dresses," said one of them.

Clare noticed the tiny mole. It was Tamsyn.

"Or make boring 'polite conversation,'" said Tegan.

"Or waste our time in a schoolroom."

"Or learn 'genteel accomplishments.'" Tegan almost spit the final word.

"Or take orders from a stupid city 'lady' who knows nothing about us." It was back to Tamsyn for the grim finish.

Clare heard hurt in that last sentence. These little girls had noticed her startlement at their very existence, and she was sorry for that, though it was not her fault. She met two pairs of intense dark eyes. The twins were trembling with determination and anxiety. Pity rose in her. Their world had changed, and they'd had no say in the revolution, not even a mention. She understood only too well what that felt like. It was tempting to open her arms, to offer them kindness and reassurance. But Clare knew that the softer emotions would be suspiciously rejected right now. Jamie's sisters were declaring war. They had no reason to trust her, and they would despise conciliation as much as rebukes.

For the first time, Clare was thankful that she'd been a governess for six years. She'd dealt with children so spoiled by indulgence that they'd scarcely heard the word "no," and with some whose heedless parents had allowed them to hatch schemes of amazing guile and complexity. She'd once had to quell a full-on tantrum in the middle of a crowded ballroom, while peers of the realm stood back in helpless consternation. The twins had no idea what they were up against. "I see. Is that all?" she said cordially.

The girls gaped at her.

"Can you tell me the way to the kitchen?" Clare added. "I'm looking for some breakfast."

After a further bewildered pause, Tamsyn pointed. Clare smiled at her and set off in the indicated direction. It would be amusing to hear what the sisters said to each other when she was gone. But she thought she could predict most of it.

The large old-fashioned kitchen, with its associated storerooms and a space for servants' meals, occupied the lower level of the north wing. Clare found Anna Pendennis stirring a pot of porridge that hung over a bed of coals in the big kitchen hearth. "Good morning," she said.

The old woman dropped a small curtsy. "Milady."

"I slept so long that I'm quite hungry," Clare added with a friendly smile.

The old woman nodded. "You look like you could use some feeding up, and no mistake. I've got this porridge here, and there's bread and good butter and jam. I'll tell you straight out, though, milady, I'm no great shakes as a cook. When the old master was alive, we had Mrs. Fitch to manage the kitchen. Gone up to Penzance years ago to work in some merchant's house."

"Ah." Clare could see from where she stood that the porridge was rather lumpy. "Is there tea?"

"Aye. That I can do." Mrs. Pendennis hooked a steaming iron kettle from over the fire and grasped it with a cloth. She poured the hot water over leaves already waiting in a china pot.

Clare sat down at the well-scrubbed kitchen table and began her meal. Mrs. Pendennis's lack of surprise at this informality told her more about the state of the household. "I'd like to get you some help as soon as possible. I wondered if you could recommend anyone?"

"There's a couple of girls in the village might do. They'd like the wages, I know." The old woman gave Clare a sharp glance, and Clare nodded carefully in response. Anna Pendennis pursed her wrinkled lips, satisfied. They understood each other. There would be regular wages from now on. "I'll put out the word, like."

"Good. I'll just tell his lordship—"

"Mr. Jamie's already out on the land," said Mrs. Pendennis. "Like to be gone all day, he said. Home for dinner."

"Oh." Clare was briefly taken aback. She hadn't even seen him since the dog debacle and the revelation that he had a pair of obstreperous sisters. She'd expected that they would talk this morning. She certainly had a few things to say to him. Clare sipped her tea and considered the likely course of that conversation. No doubt that was one reason he was gone—for the entire day.

She didn't know whether to smile or scowl. Was he going to require as much managing as Tamsyn and Tegan? Of course, there was also a great deal to be done on the land. He *had* mentioned that, repeatedly. "Well, I shall ask Selina when she comes down—"

"She was up betimes. Going out for a walk, she said."

"Oh," repeated Clare. Fleetingly, she felt abandoned. But that was ridiculous. She should turn her mind to the long list of tasks that lay ahead.

৵

At the foot of the path that led from Trehearth manor down to the village nestled in a cove, Selina turned right, toward the church. The steepled edifice was built of the same gray stone as the house above but looked much older. As she'd hoped, Selina found the doors unlatched. It was often so with village churches, and she'd taken advantage of that freedom from locks many times.

Slipping through the solid wooden door, she sat in a pew in one of the back rows and let the serenity of the space settle around her. Shafts of early sunlight shone through the stained-glass windows down either side of the church, lending color to the flagstone floor. The quiet that always seemed to come with the whoof of a church door closing embraced her. A bank of flowers before the altar scented the air. The stone pulpit at the front looked medieval.

Selina felt her internal balance returning in this peaceful place, home of reverence and familiar ritual. The building was different, but the feeling was the same as that she'd first found in her father's church as a child. She took a deep breath and let it out, grateful. In the past few weeks, her life had begun to seem like a tumult of unpredictable events. And now, on top of the deep fatigue of the journey, she faced dust and spiderwebs in corners, tattered hangings, and

barren gardens. Huge dogs and hoydenish children.
A truculent young man and a weight of unaccus-
tomed responsibility.

Selina breathed again, pushing away anxiety. She'd
felt like this when she had no post, she realized, and
her future was all uncertainty as she waited to find a
new one. To have no idea what was coming next! But
her situation was different now. She had her independence; she could leave whenever she liked. Yet leave
for what? Her new life was equally unknown, even
though the security Clare had provided was a blessing.
It had to be created from whole cloth.

Selina understood then how much she was comforted by routine—to rise knowing how the day
would unfold, to anticipate the smooth workings of a
well-regulated household, to rest in a bastion of good
manners and propriety. Had she always been that way?
Or was it because that had been her life, nearly all of it,
in the homes of her elderly charges? Despite the disad-
vantages of her situation, she'd enjoyed the—peace of
it. Her next breath came out in a sigh. There was no
prospect of such an ordered existence at the moment.
Feeling tugged in different directions, she bent her
head over clasped hands and asked for guidance.

Some twenty minutes later, the church door behind
her opened and closed; firm footsteps trod up the aisle.
Selina turned to see a tall, thin man in a clerical collar
passing by her. He had sandy hair going gray above a
pleasant bony face, scored by lines clearly etched by
good humor. He smiled and nodded.

He looked so cordial, and at the same time so careful not to interrupt a parishioner's meditations, that Selina said, "Hello."

He stopped beside her. "Good morning. Welcome. I'm Edward Carew, the vicar here." His smile was full of warmth.

"It's a lovely church," Selina said.

"Isn't it? A very peaceful feel, I find."

Startled at this precise echo of her own thoughts, Selina nodded. "Yes, exactly. I was so glad to be able come in."

"The doors are always open. Are you visiting the village?"

"No, I've come to stay at Trehearth manor."

"Oh… ah. Are you the new Lady Trehearth? I beg your pardon…"

Of course the village would have heard of Clare's marriage. No doubt it was the subject of great speculation. "No, I'm a… friend of hers. Selina Newton. We've just arrived." But he probably would know that. The chaise would have been spotted on the road.

"Well, welcome to the village," he responded. "I hope I will see you all on Sunday."

"Of course," said Selina, and then wondered if she should have been so quick to answer for the whole household. She couldn't imagine the twins, for example, in these hallowed environs. With their wild hair and pugnacious expressions, they'd be like feral cats in a duchess's drawing room.

Edward Carew simply nodded and moved on up the aisle. Selina rose and departed, to return to her duty.

Six

CLARE WAS WANDERING THE HALLS OF HER NEW domain when she encountered Selina taking her hat and cloak to her bedchamber. "Did you have a pleasant walk?" she asked the older woman.

"I did indeed."

"I hope you will find enough to amuse you in this—"

"I'm not here to be entertained," was the prompt reply. "How can I help you?"

"Well, I'm going to look over the house this morning and consider the most pressing needs. Obviously, I must hire staff. I've already spoken to Anna about that."

"Shall I come along?" Selina wondered. It would be a discouraging, dirty task.

"No need. I have a scheme in mind for the expedition."

Selina raised her dark eyebrows at her friend's odd expression, but didn't inquire further. "I could look over your linens and see what needs to be mended or discarded. Although I must say, I find no fault with the sheets on my bed."

"That would be splendid," Clare agreed. "Mind, I shall hire someone to do the mending. You should just make a list." The two women exchanged a smile. They had found they shared a reliance on lists—indeed a real pleasure in making them and ticking off the tasks when accomplished.

As Selina went to inquire about the location of the linen press, the twins skulked into the hallway. Clare had asked Anna to find them and request that they join her there. From the set of their identical jaws, the summons had not been welcome. *Were they sought out only for scoldings?* Clare wondered. Or to be forced to do things they did not wish to do? "I was hoping you'd show me around the house," she said. She made no reference, in word or expression, to their earlier encounter. "It's your home. I'm sure no one knows it better."

Tamsyn and Tegan looked at each other, then back at Clare. She thought she saw a spark of gratification in their dark eyes, along with the speculative mischief she had naturally expected. "We can do that," Tamsyn said.

"We should start in the cellars," Tegan added. Her sister's sly smile told Clare all she needed to know about the foundations of her new home.

Thus began an odyssey covering every inch of Trehearth House. The twins dragged Clare down through numberless dim basement chambers and up through furlongs of dusty attics. They showed her chaotic storerooms and vacant guest chambers. They obviously reveled in making her crawl under filthy beams and squeeze past piles of moldering boxes. With increasingly puzzled looks as the morning passed, they waited for her to break down and flee. Clare had come prepared, however. She'd put on her oldest, dowdiest gown; she didn't care if it became crusted with dirt. She'd tied a bit of cloth over her hair. And perhaps most importantly, she'd steeled herself in advance against the worst excesses of a neglected dwelling. When she didn't flinch at the nest of squirming baby mice between attic rafters or the scurry of black beetles across a damp brick cellar floor, the sisters softened a bit and began to talk.

The huge entry hall had been their grandfather's pride, they informed Clare. He'd had an actual suit of armor standing at the foot of the carved staircase. "We don't know what happened to it," Tegan complained.

"We've looked everywhere," agreed her sister.

"But we can't find it."

They must have heard stories about the house from the Pendennises, Clare thought. And perhaps others as well. She had no doubt that the girls were masters of information gathering, by whatever means available.

When they'd exhausted all the truly grimy choices, the twins walked her through the dining room on the north rear corner of the building, conveniently next to the kitchen wing. They showed her a large library, with ranks of dark shelves rising to a high ceiling. Moth-eaten armchairs dotted the room, flanking a large table for spreading out oversized volumes and maps. The room's fireplace backed up to the cavernous hearth in the great hall, and its windows looked cozily over the courtyard. "You've certainly had plenty to read," she dared to comment, running her eyes over the serried ranks of books. She wondered what sort of schooling the girls had had. Some, surely? They spoke well and appeared intelligent. But she knew it would be a mistake to inquire.

"There's lots of books on Cornish history," Tegan offered.

"And plants," said Tamsyn.

"And fauna," her sister added. "They call animals 'fauna' because—"

"It's Latin."

"And scientists name things in Latin."

Clare merely nodded, tucking away this indication of their interests and education. Someone, at some time, had taught them. She would find out who. But not now. She felt that a delicate balance was being established, and with any push from her, it would disintegrate.

"Come see the best room," Tegan urged.

Clare followed them to a space that spanned most of the back of the house. "You can divide it into three," said Tamsyn, pulling on a recessed panel that slid across to close off a third of the area.

"Or leave it open to make a ballroom," supplied Tegan, pushing the panel back.

It would make a fine one, Clare thought. French doors lined the far wall, opening onto a stone terrace that extended almost to the edge of the sea cliffs. Two fireplaces punctuated the inner side of the room, each surmounted by a portrait. "That's Grandfather," Tamsyn said of one.

"And Grandmother." Tegan stood before the other. "She was a witch."

"She was not," snapped Tamsyn.

The builder of this house looked a bit like Jamie, Clare thought, examining the paintings. He had the same dark hair and eyes. His frame was burlier, though; he faced the viewer with the solidity of a boulder.

"She was too," Tegan insisted. "I heard John say that the whole county was under her spell."

"Because she was 'bewitching,'" her sister retorted. "That's not the same as a witch."

The subject of their debate was slender, with tumbling raven hair and hazel eyes that seemed to jump from the portrait to skewer the observer. Based on the painting, she wasn't beautiful; her features were too dominant, her face too pointed for that. But her appearance was compelling. The image managed to convey some of the crackling energy that also animated Jamie. And his sisters. The portrait rather reminded Clare of them.

"Sounds the same," muttered the other twin.

"It isn't, Tegan! You can't just ignore what a word *means*."

The girls seemed to have forgotten Clare momentarily, and the passion in Tamsyn's tone caught her interest. Clare filed it away with the other characteristics she'd noted in the girls as she walked down the long room. There were several islands of faded sofas and chairs arranged along it, anchored by dusty rugs, but she couldn't imagine sitting here of an evening— even with the fires lit and burning candles in all the holders. Like the great hall, the room was cavernous. It swallowed the sound of voices; it made one feel small. It seemed that the builder of this house had provided no cozy public rooms. She might be forced to adopt one of the empty bedchambers upstairs for her own retreat.

But their final stop on the main floor changed her mind. The twins led her into a parlor on the south corner of the house, with banks of long windows opening onto the terrace on one side and a neglected garden on the other. The space was empty, but it had a pretty parquet floor and a handsome marble mantelpiece. And it was not so large that one felt like a mouse in a barrel.

"Grandpapa called this the solar," Tamsyn informed her.

"The vicar says that's a medieval de-designation," added her sister.

"It means 'sun.' In Latin."

"Because this is the sunniest room," Tegan finished.

And it would be her sanctuary, Clare decided. She would have the walls painted in a blue that mirrored the sea, and bring in beautiful, comfortable furniture, a rich rug. These windows would indeed catch any sun available, and she would hang draperies—something sumptuous—to draw across them when the light was gone. Some inner tension relaxed as the picture rose in her mind. She could be contented in such a room.

Reluctantly, she allowed the twins to urge her onward. The south wing contained the estate offices and more storerooms below, and rooms for male servants above, next to box rooms for storing luggage and unused furnishings. The upper floor of the main block boasted nine bedchambers. The twins shared one of the largest on the north corner, as far as possible, Clare noticed, from Jamie's room at the south. The Pendennises had quarters above the kitchen in the north wing, next to rooms for female servants, a spacious sewing room, and linen storage, where they encountered Selina. "Great heavens," the older woman cried when they appeared in the doorway. "What happened to you? Are you all right?"

Clare looked down at her filthy gown. Her hands were black with dirt, and she suspected her face was smudged as well. She put a hand to the cloth over her hair and came away with a bit of spiderweb.

Selina had rounded on the twins, who exhibited their own share of dirt. "What have you—?"

"We've just been exploring the house," interrupted Clare. The girls' expressions had hardened. "We're nearly done." She turned away before a dispute could erupt. "Is there more than one staircase?"

There was. Besides the grand sweep of steps in the great hall, each wing contained a small stair for the staff's use. Had there been any staff. *How many would it take to put this dilapidated place to rights?* Clare wondered.

Her list now filled both sides of the page she'd carried with her; her pencil was worn down to a nub. Everywhere were dust-laden threadbare carpets and tattered draperies, moth-eaten upholstery and cracked windowpanes. It was a setting straight out of a gothic novel. Except that such stories airily glossed over accessories like mildew and black beetles, rat droppings and woodworm, which Trehearth offered in plenty. Not to mention enough dirt to choke a whole herd of horses. A good portion of which currently covered her from head to foot, made her skin itch, and roused desperate yearnings for a real bath. But the home Jamie had described with such love had nothing resembling a bathroom. Clare thought wistfully of some of the gleaming modern versions she'd seen in fine London houses. One of the smallest bedchambers was ripe for conversion—if she could find workmen here in the country to do it. She shook her head. No, she *would* find them. What was the point of inheriting a fortune if you couldn't indulge in a bit of practical luxury?

Clare scribbled more notes as they made their way downstairs again. Her pencil lead gave out completely. She would have to find a penknife to sharpen it.

"That's all the rooms," said Tamsyn.

"We're going outside now," added Tegan.

"We need to let Randolph out of the stables."

"He gets very lonely there." The tone was reproachful, the look accusing.

"He howls."

Clare thought that they were actually rather bored, which was better than rebellious or sullen. It was a small step. The girls didn't seem to mind the dust that streaked their shirts and breeches. "I'm sure he would enjoy a run," she said. "Thank you for showing me—"

The front door opened and Jamie strode in, greatcoat flapping, bringing a rush of cold, fresh air into the great hall. His circuit of the land had brought him near the house, and guilt had brought him inside. That, and the thought that he could snatch some bread and cheese from the kitchen and save himself time.

Pushing the door closed, he was confronted by a trio of filthy, disheveled figures; it took him a moment to identify them as his wife and sisters. They all looked as if someone had dragged them through a chimney backward.

He was inured to seeing the twins dirty. They so often were. But the sight of the elegant, fastidious Clare with smudges of dust on her cheeks and forehead, dirt and mold streaking her arms and gown, pale hair wrapped in a blackened rag, was appalling. "What have you done?" he exploded. He had told the twins, repeatedly, in writing, that they were to treat his new wife with consideration and respect. But as usual, they'd ignored him. Of course they'd played some prank that had reduced her to a shambling wreck. Jamie remembered the time his sisters had lured a prospective governess into the midden heap. They'd barely escaped legal proceedings that time. At least Clare wasn't crying. Yet. He strode closer and loomed over his sisters. "I gave you very clear instructions, and you chose to pay me no heed. You are confined to your room except at meal…"

The twins began a storm of protests: "We didn't do anything." "We were helping." "She asked us."

Jamie raised his voice to be heard over them. "…times. At which you will appear properly dressed and *clean*. You will cease roaming the countryside like tinkers. And I'm getting rid of that blasted dog!"

"Noo," Tegan wailed.

"That isn't fair!" Tamsyn cried.

Once again, their voices overlapped in a maddening cacophony. "Randolph didn't…" "We were help-ing." "She wanted to see…"

Under her coating of dust, Clare burned with humiliation. Was she destined to look a fright whenever she saw Jamie in this house? But he was undoing the modicum of progress she'd made with the twins. She couldn't run for cover. She had to intervene. "It's all right."

Her remark was lost in the chorus of shouting.

"It's all right," she yelled as loudly as she could.

The other three fell silent in surprise.

"We've been exploring the house," Clare said. "I asked Tamsyn and Tegan to take me around. It's… badly in need of cleaning." She shook her skirts and only managed to raise a cloud of dust motes around her head. She suppressed a cough.

Jamie hesitated. His sisters stared up at him with the wide, hurt eyes of the unjustly accused. Clare avoided his gaze as if he were indeed the villain of the piece. "I must go and tidy up," she added in a choked voice. She turned and fled up the stairs.

Should he go after her? Jamie wondered. He'd only been trying to protect her. Apparently he'd been hasty, but… Perhaps his sisters hadn't been making mischief this time. But their history promised that they inevitably would be. Soon.

"We're going outside," declared Tamsyn, her chin stuck out rebelliously.

"To get our blasted dog," said Tegan.

"And roam the countryside like tinkers."

"And if you take Randolph away from us, we will *never* come back!"

Before he could point out the illogic of that last comment, they slipped by him and out of the house. Jamie yanked the door back open and shouted after them, "Fetch your coats and hats!" Then he shut the door again, heroically resisting the impulse to slam it, and stalked off to the kitchen. There, at least, was a female he could trust not to rail at him. Anna Pendennis would be only too happy to feed him, no questions asked.

His pique sent Jamie south to the farthest edge of the Trehearth estate. There, he found that one of the tenant cottages had collapsed completely. There was no sign of its former inhabitants. Since he had not been able to employ an estate agent for some time, he had not been informed of this loss. But the family living in a neighboring cottage, also in very poor repair, was only too happy to tell the tale of an autumn storm, a constantly leaking roof that had at last given way, drenched children and possessions, and a flight to better prospects in the north. By the time he had heard them out, and assured them that repairs would be made immediately to their own dwelling, the sun was setting. He would never reach home in time for dinner, he realized. He'd tried to do too much too quickly. On top of the long journey from London, another day in the saddle had worn him out.

As he slumped over his horse's neck while the beast picked its way along the lane in the growing dimness, Jamie faced the fact that he didn't have a good reputation on his own land. He had heard friends speak of cordial dealings with their tenants and dependents— years and even generations of working together. But he'd maintained a distance from those living here at Trehearth, ashamed and angry, because he couldn't offer them needed assistance. And now they received him with skepticism and a litany of complaints. It would take time, no doubt, to change that.

The moon rose, fat and yellow, on the horizon. Jamie patted his mount's neck, thankful for the added light to guide him along. Lulled by the slow clop of hooves, he sank deeper into melancholy. He'd neglected his sisters for some of the same reasons, he admitted. They loved Trehearth so much. He'd known its loss would fall on them like a thunderbolt. How did you warn children of impending catastrophe? How to explain mortgages and creditors and your inability to do anything to save their home? He'd never been able to face that conversation. In their earliest years, he'd hoped; then he'd despaired, and the hovering doom had colored every visit home. And so he'd withdrawn, let the twins run wild. He knew he should have done more, though he couldn't conceive just what. His sisters, however, had taken that license and run with it. Those small heads could hatch more mischief than a gang of London apprentices. Their… eccentricity wasn't all his fault.

Or perhaps it was. He'd made mistakes. God knew he'd made mistakes. Jamie drew his coat collar closer against the night chill. He ought to feel triumphant right now. He *had* found a way to save Trehearth. Against the odds, he would be able to redeem it. But in this moment, he was simply overwhelmed by the extent of the disorder. It was too bad he hadn't put a flask in his pocket. He could really use a fortifying draught or two right now.

No one was about when he reached home, damp and cold from a mist that had risen from the wet earth. The Pendennises had gone to bed, for which he couldn't blame them. They rose early and worked hard, had for many more years than he'd been alive. And so, despite his fatigue, Jamie had to tend his horse himself. He found a covered dish of cold meat in the kitchen, and picked at it without much appetite. The knowledge that he must speak to Clare oppressed him. She'd fled in a huff this afternoon. She was probably still fuming, goaded by his lateness, primed to point out his shortcomings as a brother and host... no, husband. Husband. Jamie remembered a play he'd seen a few years ago in London, with a ranting wife whose voice cut like a razor. His bones ached. He longed to leave the confrontation till tomorrow. But he wouldn't. There would be no more evasions of responsibility.

Quietly he entered his bedchamber—the room that had been his since his father's death. The huge four-poster loomed in the light of his single taper, flanked by the massive wardrobe. He lit more candles, then went to the cabinet in the corner near his shaving stand. Pouring a drink from a bottle of brandy he kept there, he took a generous swallow, and then another. The liquor hit his nearly empty stomach and spread welcome warmth through his veins. The tension in his neck and shoulders relaxed somewhat.

Jamie shed his mud-spattered boots and coat, and washed with cold water left from the morning. He started to build up the fire, then admitted he was only delaying the inevitable. In shirtsleeves and breeches, he went to the connecting door and listened. There was no sound from the other side. Perhaps Clare was already asleep, and he was reprieved. He tapped lightly, heard nothing, and gently opened the door.

On the far side of the room, Clare sat at the dressing table, brushing her hair with long, smooth strokes. In the dancing light of the fire and a pair of candles, the pale strands glowed like summer sunshine. A creamy nightgown foamed around her, nearly slipping off one white shoulder. Her illuminated figure, so bright against the darkness of the rest of the bedchamber, was delicate and lovely as a renaissance masterpiece. Jamie was struck speechless for a moment. He stood in the dim doorway and gazed at her as if she were a celestial vision that had materialized in his rundown house.

Clare enjoyed the feel of the brush running through her clean hair. Together, she and Selina and Anna Pendennis had set up the tin tub before the big kitchen hearth and filled it with steaming water. She had had as luxurious a bath as the household could currently provide, and she felt vastly better for it.

He was here to speak to his wife, not gawk like a schoolboy, Jamie told himself. He stepped forward. "Clare?" She jumped and turned, causing the gown to slip farther down her satiny shoulder. Jamie swallowed. "I'm sorry I was not at dinner. I rode farther than I meant to and got caught up with some tenant problems." He congratulated himself on how reasonable that had sounded—only a little stilted.

It was startling to discover a man in her bedroom at such a late hour. No, not a "man," Clare amended, her husband. A spark of excitement followed the thought. She'd been concerned, and yes, annoyed, when he didn't return for the evening meal. Beyond mere courtesy, she was full of plans for the house that she'd wanted to share with him. But just now, he looked very tired, and nervous for some reason. "It's all right."

"It isn't. I shall do better in future." Now that sounded pompous, he thought. The beautiful sight of her was scrambling his senses. "Also, I jumped to the wrong conclusion earlier today because my sisters have a habit of making mischief. I beg your pardon for shouting."

"It's not…"

He hurried on, years of defensive arguments rising to his lips, weary of apologies. "It was wrong of me not to tell you about them. I do know that. It's just… I didn't know how to explain. I've never known what to do about them. You will say that they should have had better supervision. A governess or other teachers. Of course I have tried employing these." His voice had gone accusing; he throttled it back. "The twins drove every one of them away with their pranks and intransigence. Even those who might have managed to tolerate their devilment found the condition of the house and the isolation intolerable. I looked for others, but…"

The spate of words touched Clare. Jamie looked so harried and guilty. Yes, he should have told her about his sisters. But what had she told him about her family? Next to nothing. They'd had no time for confidences. "I can handle the twins," she said. Indeed, she was certain she could.

Jamie fell silent and stared at her. No one who had actually met them, in all their years, had ever said that, let alone with such confidence.

"I have all the experience of a hired governess and a number of advantages over an employee," she added. She was prepared to explain further, but he was looking at her so oddly. Meeting his dark eyes, she nearly lost herself in them. A wave of heat passed over her skin.

Jamie had to move closer. He couldn't help himself. His universe had narrowed to that one smooth white shoulder, exposed by the slipping nightgown; he had to just touch it. He reached out. Her skin was as he'd anticipated, like warm silk.

A memory flashed through Clare's mind—that moment when he'd looked straight at her and declared that he required an heir. The same flush suffused her now: self-consciousness, curiosity, a hint of desire. The brush of his fingers was like a spark to tinder.

The scents of rosewater and lavender rose in warm, intoxicating waves around him. Jamie shifted his hand to her bright hair, lightly touching the soft strands and then letting his fingers drift down to rest on her bare shoulder again. When Clare shivered slightly, he could do nothing but bend and kiss her parted lips. They were as luscious as they looked. Grasping her upper arms, Jamie pulled his wife upright against him and guided her into a kiss that went much deeper.

It raced through Clare like wildfire. She felt his hands on her, his exploring lips, but more than that—a shock of sensation arced down her body. It spoke for her, arching up to meet him.

Enflamed by this encouragement, Jamie cupped a breast under the creamy silk of her nightgown, teased her with his thumb.

It felt astonishing. Following the cues of her own desires, Clare ran her hands up his shirtfront to enlace around his neck, pressing tighter, wanting more.

Jamie danced her back toward the great four-poster, kissing her neck, her bare shoulder, her responsive lips once again. He lifted her onto the bed, pulling at his shirt to be rid of it.

Firelight gleamed on his skin as he loomed over her; his eyes were black as the night. Clare felt an instant's nervousness, and then he was kissing her again, and it fell away. When he slipped his hand under the lacy hem of her nightdress and let his fingertips slide lightly up her leg, she forgot everything but the aching fire that had blazed to life at her core.

She was lithe curves wrapped in softness, the taste of peppermint, the scent of flowers. Through a haze of desire, Jamie reminded himself to consider her inexperience, to go slowly. But when his fingers reached their goal, he found her ready. She moaned at his touch.

Roused to a fever pitch, every inch of Clare opened to him, silently urging him to continue his delicious attentions. Her husband obliged, drawing her further and further into a torrent of sensation, until there was nothing left in her world but the two of them, in the firelight, together. The feeling became almost unbearably intense, and then it burst into waves of delight that shook her to the depths.

Feeling her response, Jamie plunged into the mysteries of marriage like a madman diving off the sea cliff behind Trehearth. A flash of vertigo, and then he was immersed, riding a tide of pleasure that carried him far beyond the realms of rational thought.

Clare felt a flash of pain, a mere nothing compared with what she had just experienced. She held Jamie as he moved within her, and felt an odd sort of pride when he cried out in an ecstasy of release. She'd made him lose control, just as he had done to her. There was a sort of reciprocal power in it, as well as delight.

He held her in his arms, their hearts pounding together, breath gradually slowing. Then Jamie slipped away to lie beside her on the white pillows. He didn't speak, and after a while Clare grew self-conscious. "I suppose we are truly married now," she said. When he didn't reply, she risked a glance. Jamie was asleep in a tangle of limbs next to her. The long days of riding had caught up with him.

Freed now to look as much as she liked, Clare turned on her side and watched him. The planes of his face were smoothed in repose, and he looked younger and more vulnerable. She wanted to brush his black hair back off his forehead, but she didn't dare disturb him. *What would it be like to trace the outline of those skillful lips with a fingertip?* she wondered. Or to explore all the contours of his male body with her hands, as he had hers? A thrill went through her as she realized that she could soon find the answers to those questions. There would be a thousand other nights like this. More than a thousand. She'd feared that her unorthodox marriage would make this part of life difficult. She was very glad to have been proved quite, quite wrong.

Seven

WAKING JUST PAST DAWN, JAMIE WAS AT FIRST DISORI-
ented by the angle of light filtering through the
ancient curtains. The bed was on the wrong wall.
Then his perceptions realigned, and he remembered
he was in Clare's room. She lay beside him, gleaming
hair scattered across the pillow, breath soft and even.
Her face, which could sometimes seem remote in the
waking world, was an image of peaceful beauty. He
hadn't woken once in the night, he realized. It was
years since he'd slept that well, a seemingly endless
period of bolting upright in the small hours, sweating
with fear about the future. He had Clare to thank for
that in a number of ways.

She was so lovely, lying there, unconscious of his
gaze. His hand reached out to touch that silken skin.
If last night was any measure, she would welcome him
with open arms. He imagined those pale eyelids lifting,
her tiger eyes meeting his, and his hand pulled back.
Jamie Boleigh had never been in a relationship with
an adult woman that he could not easily break off. His
liaisons had been pleasurable and fleeting—with no

occasion to wonder what a lover might think of him. Night and morning were such different creatures. He didn't want to put a foot wrong. His stomach growled, protesting yesterday's near fast. His head throbbed with an echo of its usual morning ache. He had so much to do.

Jamie slipped out of bed, quietly added wood to the coals of the fire, and gathered his scattered clothing. He eased through the connecting door to his own room, fruitlessly wishing that he would find a can of hot water there. And a cup of strong tea. He would have done much for a simple cup of tea.

Clare felt precisely the same longings when she woke a while later. In the households where she'd lived, even a governess received those small luxuries. Today, she would absolutely find Mrs. Pendennis some help. And tomorrow, perhaps, the cup of tea would be forthcoming. She threw back the covers and rose. She felt full of energy, and as she dressed, she realized that she was humming. Meeting her own eyes in the dressing table mirror, Clare saw that she wore a secret smile. Last night lingered in her memory like a gentle caress. When she was ready to go down, she tapped on Jamie's door and then looked in. He wasn't there.

In the dining room, Clare found a young girl bent over two somewhat tarnished chafing dishes. "Good morning."

The girl started and turned, revealing a lighted taper in her hand. She dropped a brief curtsy. "Ma'am. Er, milady?"

"I'm Lady Trehearth. And you…?"

"Gwen, milady. Mrs. Pendennis spoke to my mum about a position here at the house?"

"Indeed. Welcome."

"Thank you, milady. She got out these warming dishes. I'll have them lit in a tick."

"Splendid. Is there tea?"

"Yes, milady." With another bobbed curtsy, she went out.

By the time Gwen returned with a pot, Selina had come down. They enjoyed a steaming cup together as the girl got the chafing dishes warming. She was filling them with eggs and sausages when the twins arrived, stopping in the doorway to stare.

"Tamsyn, Tegan, this is Gwen. She's come to help out in the house."

"You live in the village," said Tegan. She made it sound like an accusation.

"Yes… er, miss."

Gwen couldn't be blamed for the hesitation, Clare thought. The twins were again dressed as boys, though they did look fairly clean. Jamie walked in as they took their seats, and although Clare felt self-conscious, she was also proud to be able to offer him a proper breakfast. As he dug in with a gratifying appetite, she looked around the table, for the first time feeling like the mistress of her own household. At last, things were going well. "I've been making plans for some changes to the house," she said to Jamie. "Is there anything you don't want touched or altered?"

"Changes?" asked Tegan.

"What sort of changes?" said Tamsyn. Both twins frowned at her.

It was enough to make Jamie say, "No, it is entirely up to you." He couldn't bring to mind any sentimental attachment to bits of furniture in any case.

Clare answered the girls' scowls. "Well, first off, a thorough cleaning. We'll begin as soon as Anna and I can assemble enough hands."

"There will be a lot of new people in our house?" asked Tegan.

"Yes." Clare spoke firmly. This was not negotiable.

"Absolutely." Jamie backed her up.

The twins exchanged a frown, as if suspecting a new governess might be included in this influx. "They won't have anything to do with us!" declared Tamsyn.

"Or our room," confirmed Tegan.

Clare spoke before Jamie could utter the reprimand she saw in his expression. "And then I want to install a bathroom, so that we don't have to bathe before the kitchen hearth. I thought the smallest bedchamber on the courtyard side would do very well for the purpose."

Jamie nodded his consent as his sisters considered this fresh intrusion.

"New curtains, rugs, furniture, of course."

"Not in our room!" repeated Tegan.

Clare had not yet been granted sight of this sanctum. The twins' tour had not included it, and she was not stupid enough to enter on her own. She tried to imagine what the room might look like, and failed. "You can choose what you would like to have done in your room."

"I'm not sure that is a good—" began Jamie.

"Whatever we want?" said Tegan.

Clare looked her right in the eye, aware of the risks, and said, "Yes."

Jamie decided this must be part of the handling she'd promised. Did she really understand what his sisters were capable of? Though full of doubts, he left her to it.

Selina, who more than shared his uneasiness, decided to add, "Within reason."

The girls' heads swiveled to Selina, then back to Clare. Clare decided that a hint of restraint wasn't a bad notion. "A dash of reason never did anyone any harm." She continued before they could speak. "I thought I would take the solar as my own sitting room. The light is so pleasant there."

"There's nothing to sit on," Tegan pointed out.

Clare smiled at her, relieved that the twins had not voiced any particular attachment to the solar. "Which is why we need new furniture."

"It will make a comfortable parlor," said Selina.

Jamie rose. "I must go. I'm meeting with a local builder this morning."

"Could you ask him about installing a bathtub?" Clare said.

He wondered what old Jenkins would say about such a project. Or he didn't have to wonder; he could easily imagine the man's derision. "Repairing the tenant cottages has to be the first priority." Around the table, Jamie saw disappointment on Clare's face, smirks from his sisters, disapproval in Mrs. Newton's expression. How had he ended up in a household of females? Wife, sisters, an older woman who might as well be a mother-in-law from the way she regarded him. He edged toward the door.

"Can Randolph come back in the house today?" Tegan called after him.

"He's *used to* living in the house," said Tamsyn.

"And he's very lonely in the stables."

"He howls."

"Didn't you hear him last night?"

Fortunately, the stables were a good distance from the house. Jamie paused. He hadn't heard anything when he put his horse in the stall last night. That should have roused the dog. No, it definitely would have. "*Was* he in the stables last night?" His sisters evaded his gaze. "And where is he right now?"

"Everything's spoiled since you brought *her* here," replied Tegan.

"Randolph's atrocious manners have nothing to do with Clare," Jamie replied. "Take him out to the stables and leave him there." He hurried away before they could argue. But he hadn't counted on Clare following him.

"Have they always kept their dog indoors?" she asked when she caught up with him in the hall.

He had no choice but to pause. "I suppose so. But Randolph clearly belongs outside. He's no lapdog, for God's sake."

"You think he's dangerous?"

"No, no. He's docile enough, in his overbearing fashion. I wouldn't have allowed them to keep him if he hadn't had a good temper. And to make sure, I had the farrier treat him as we do the surplus bull calves."

"As...? Oh."

"He won't be repeating his sire's indiscretions and making trouble with the neighbors. Er, I didn't mention this to my sisters."

Clare nodded.

"That wretched dog is up in their room right now, you know. I told you they were incorrigible."

"We'll come to some accommodation on Randolph. But about the builder?"

"Many of my tenants are living with leaky roofs and backed-up drains. Several cottages are uninhabitable. One at least has completely collapsed. I can't put work on my own house ahead of those repairs, Clare."

"But it is such a simple…"

"This estate had been neglected for forty years. Everyone in the neighborhood knows it. For most of my life I've been bombarded with complaints and criticisms that I could do nothing about. Now I can. This comes before any other work."

The reminder that he had married her for her money felt like a slap in the face. Of course, she knew it. She had arranged the matter. But this morning it was harder to hear.

"Fripperies will have to wait," Jamie added. Could she imagine how it rankled, to see neighboring landowners eye him with pity and, from some, contempt?

"A bath is not a frippery," she murmured, though of course she understood that its lack didn't compare with rain on your head or noisome drains.

"Buy whatever you like. Those decisions are up to you." Jamie felt he was being eminently reasonable. He couldn't hear the trace of bitterness in his tone. "But I can't ask Jenkins to work on a 'bathroom' just now."

He said the word as if it were indeed just a piece of foolishness. Clare swallowed the sense that he was throwing their agreement back in her face. She'd wanted control of her money. She had it. She *could* buy whatever she wished. And if she wanted to search for another builder, she could do that, too. It needn't have anything to do with him. She'd imagined that he would have some interest in the refurbishment of his—their—home, but if he did not…

The stiffening of her face made Jamie uneasy. She didn't seem to understand his point. "I must go. Jenkins will be waiting." With guilty relief, he made his escape.

❧

Selina Newton sat in the sewing room simply holding a piece of mending in her hands. Needlework had always soothed her nerves, comforted her even, perhaps because she'd learned the skills at her mother's knee. Whether it was repairing a tear, neatly finishing a long seam, or embroidering a garland of flowers onto a cushion cover, there was something deeply satisfying about the process. Occasionally, she felt it even rose to the level of art, as she created a new gown from a raw length of cloth.

This room was just the sort of place she loved, too. The wide table, now pushed against the side wall, was ideal for laying out and cutting fabric. The shelves against the whitewashed walls held spools of thread in all manner of colors, boxes of pins and papers of needles, several sizes of scissors, measuring tapes, and tailor's chalk. Early morning sunlight poured through two windows, giving plenty of light to work by. There were sconces for candles as well. And the place was wonderfully quiet, well separated from the bustle of the household. No sullen children glowered across a dining table at her. No arrogant young men gave her dark looks.

Selina sat there, relaxing, and asked herself if she really could not endure any life but the careful routine of aged women whose days were mostly past? Had her long years as a companion, often anxious and precarious, made her unfit for anything else? When she set up her own frugal household, was that to be the extent of it? Days designed to be all the same, acquaintances who were guaranteed to be predictable? If so, she was not going to be any help to Clare, and she might as well leave this house right now.

Selina gazed out at the undulating cliff and the surging sea below it. So much had happened to her in the last few weeks. It was only just sinking in. For perhaps the first time in her life, she had the luxury of doing as she pleased. What was that to be? She looked around the silent room. She thought of years that ran together in sameness. She considered the excitements as well as the upsets of the past month. Her jaw firmed, and her spine straightened. She would not run back toward narrowness and routine. She would try to expand her horizons.

Selina Newton put aside the torn sheet, rose, and shook out her skirts. In any case, she couldn't abandon Clare. Those clever and devious children were obviously up to no good, and Lord Trehearth clearly had a temper.

Eight

CLARE RETURNED TO THE DINING ROOM. GWEN WAS clearing the dishes away; the room was otherwise empty. She suspected that the twins had gone to move Randolph to another location, but she wondered what had become of Selina. She checked her friend's bedchamber and found it empty. An intuition took her onward to the sewing room, and she met Selina coming out. "Well, we should get to work!" the older woman said. "What shall we tackle first?"

She looked remarkably determined, and her voice had a ringing, hearty quality Clare hadn't noticed in it before. "I came to see if you would go for a walk with me."

"A walk?"

"I have an errand in the village."

"Oh, an errand! Of course."

The two women fetched hats and cloaks and set out. Clare took the path down to the village in the cove. "I asked Anna what education the twins have received," she explained. The old woman had grown positively chatty after they listed the servants to be hired. She'd been lonely, Clare thought, and was delighted to have female company, as well as assistance. "We're going to talk with their most recent teacher."

"It's difficult to believe they have had one," Selina replied. "A French anarchist perhaps?"

Clare couldn't help but laugh. "They're not so bad."

"My dear, you can see nefarious plots continually running behind their eyes. Perhaps this teacher set them lessons from Machiavelli?"

Smiling, Clare shook her head. "We will channel that intelligence into more positive pursuits." She drew in deep lungfuls of the sharp sea air and admired the sparkle of the waves below. The sunshine and exercise cheered her. Trehearth was a lovely spot on a fresh March day like this one. She could learn to love it here, Clare thought, her mood lifting once again.

In ten minutes they had descended to the village and found their way to the pleasant stone vicarage beside the church. For reasons she could not quite define, Selina said nothing as they rang and were admitted by a pleasant housekeeper. The vicar was in, she told them, and they were conducted to a book-lined study that overlooked the churchyard.

Edward Carew rose from behind the desk. "Good morning," he said. Against the light from the window, the tall thin man looked like one of the effigies from his church.

"Good morning, vicar," said Clare. "I am Lady Trehearth, and this is my friend Mrs. Selina Newton. We had hoped to speak with you, if it is not inconvenient."

"Not at all. Please sit down. Edward Carew, at your service. Good day, Mrs. Newton." His warm smile acknowledged their previous meeting without making a point of it.

"I was talking with Anna Pendennis about Tamsyn and Tegan," Clare continued. "I understand that you have been instructing them…"

"You?" burst from Selina. "They've been taught by a man of the cloth? But they're little better than savages."

Carew stiffened in his chair. "I beg your pardon, but I cannot agree with you."

"They wear boys' clothing," Selina said. "They keep a huge intractable dog and apparently wander the countryside wholly unsupervised. They have the manners of street urchins. They—"

"Selina," began Clare, startled by her friend's vehemence.

"They are two little girls who have been left alone far too much of the time," snapped Reverend Carew before Clare could continue.

"From all I could see, they prefer it that way."

"Selina!" said Clare more forcefully. "Reverend Carew."

Selina sat back in her chair and looked down, flushed. The vicar pressed his lips together as if shocked at himself. "Pray excuse me," he said. "I spoke hastily."

"I hoped we might discuss how best to deal with Tamsyn and Tegan in the future," Clare said in a calming tone. "I understand they have had a governess—or two."

"Indeed," the man answered, still a bit stiff. "They attended an infants' school here in the village when they were very small and learned basic reading and writing and sums. Over the last four years, they have had three governesses. All of them left after a very short time, so I don't imagine they taught much. The question of school was… broached. They flatly refused to leave home. Their reluctance and the matter of… fees ended that discussion."

"So Jamie… Lord Trehearth has tried to make provision for their education?" began Clare. The word "alone" rang in her ears.

"Of course. Repeatedly. I know it has been quite difficult for him."

Hearing a lingering tinge of reproof, Clare added, "Anna told me that their mother died at their birth?" She'd said that the twins had come after several miscarriages, when their mother was a bit old for childbearing.

Carew nodded. "I was not here then."

"And then their father was killed very soon after, in a fall from the cliffs. Was that at the house?"

"No, he was walking along the shore a mile or so away, I believe."

That was a relief. She wouldn't have wanted to think of a death from her very doorstep.

Selina wondered at their host's altered tone. Mrs. Pendennis was the same when the subject of the former baron arose. People didn't seem to want to talk about him.

"Lord Trehearth was only sixteen," Clare pointed out. "A boy of that age is hardly equipped to care for babies." Clare thought of two infants abruptly orphaned, and of Jamie, so young himself, suddenly in charge of them. Called home from school and presented with an estate in shambles and two tiny sisters, it must have been very frightening. Clare's own childhood seemed idyllic in contrast. For fifteen years, she'd had two loving parents and a big brother with no more cares than passing his examinations and winning a coveted military commission. Her home had been nurturing. Her three years of school had been interesting and full of friendships. Tamsyn and Tegan had had none of these things. For the first time, her heart went out to them. Clare realized that her companions were looking at her. Had one asked a question?

"Since the departure of their last governess, the twins' education has come mainly from me," Reverend Carew said.

Selina pressed her lips together.

"We first met tramping about the countryside," explained the vicar. "I discovered that we shared an interest in local history and botany. Knowing something of their... situation, I... Well, I suppose I lured them into a few lessons." His blue eyes glinted. "Baited with my housekeeper's excellent scones."

"So you probably know the girls better than anyone except the Pendennises?" Clare said. "Anna said it's been three years or more since she could keep up with them."

Carew nodded. "Tamsyn and Tegan are very intelligent and curious children. They will work hard at subjects that interest them."

"And not at all at those that don't," suggested Clare.

"True, I'm afraid. They're not much used to discipline."

"Discipline?" echoed Selina. "As far as I can see, they don't know the meaning of the word."

"Oh, they're quite good with words, particularly

Tamsyn," responded the vicar, his blue eyes meeting Selina's hazel ones. Clare almost felt she could hear a sound, like swords clashing.

"Lord Trehearth might have made more use of one particular word—'no.'"

"If he had been here," was the vicar's acid response.

Clare felt she should defend her husband. But it was true that Jamie had not seemed overly concerned with his sisters. His failure to mention them was only the most obvious sign of it. His attention was focused on restoring his acres and how he was viewed by his neighbors.

"He *has* tried," interjected the vicar. His thin cheeks had reddened. "Pardon me if I spoke too rashly once again. Lord Trehearth has had more than his full share of problems to overcome. But I can tell you one thing. At this point, it's very little use scolding the twins."

Clare was glad to hear her own conclusions echoed. "They are inured to it."

The vicar nodded.

"Well, I don't intend to scold." When the others turned to look at her, she added, "I have quite another plan."

Selina looked dubious. Edward Carew was impressed with her ladyship's insight and the compassion he saw in her face. Many people dismissed Tamsyn and Tegan Boleigh as hooligans. He thought that it took a rather special person to see through their belligerent manner so quickly.

"I hope you will keep up your lessons with the twins," Clare went on. "They've had so many changes. If that's all right with you, of course."

Perhaps the vicar had been looking forward to relinquishing this responsibility.

"Quite all right," he said. "Although…"

"They must also attend to those subjects that do *not* interest them," Clare replied. "I know, I will see to that."

"Really?" Edward Carew wondered if the new lady of Trehearth really understood what she was up against. And then he thought that perhaps she did.

"We must go back," Clare added, rising. "There's so much to do at the house."

"And great speculation in the neighborhood about what is going to be done," said the vicar, also standing.

She liked him, Clare thought. Despite his sharp remarks, the twinkle in his blue eyes was thoroughly good-humored. From the tone of her farewells, however, it seemed that Selina might not share her good opinion.

When they reached Trehearth House once more, Clare found that Anna Pendennis had solved one of her dilemmas by recruiting a team of cleaners. "There's lots who aren't looking for regular positions, but'd like to earn a bit extra for a one-time job," she told her. "They can come up whenever you like."

"Send for them," Clare replied. "The sooner we tackle all this dirt, the better."

❧

Thus, Jamie returned from his consultation about cottage repairs to a whirlwind of activity. There seemed to be village women, and a few boys, everywhere—scrubbing floors and walls, polishing windows, beating carpets in the courtyard. For a while, he couldn't even find Clare, and when he did, she seemed too busy to speak to him, moving through the chaos like a general marshaling her troops. He retreated to the estate office, which had not yet been touched, and tried to look over some accounts. He was tired from another day riding the land and oppressed by the size of the task ahead of him.

He was also beginning to be concerned that he hadn't asked for sufficient funds in the marriage agreement. Restoring Trehearth was going to cost even more than had been designated for the task. But the idea of going to Clare with this discovery and requesting more money grated on his sensibilities. A man who married an heiress got a fortune; that was understood. It was the way of the world. He didn't have to beg, hat in hand, for the advance of another thousand pounds. He took charge of his own destiny. Otherwise, what was the point? It was certainly what Jenkins the builder, and no doubt the rest of the neighborhood, expected to be the case. Jamie went to a cabinet in the corner and poured himself a small brandy. He needed to give it time, he told himself. Clare was already fully occupied with the house, not to mention the twins. Before long, she would be delighted to hand over the financial reins to him. Patience was all that was required. The trouble was, his mind was filled with projects that could not wait.

∽≈

The five of them sat down to dinner that evening in a sparkling dining room, with a snowy, if much mended, cloth on the table. Mrs. Pendennis's meal might have been only passable, but the candlesticks shone and the chafing dishes on the sideboard no longer had a spot of tarnish. Clare found the change immensely satisfying. "I understand that the service is at ten tomorrow in the village church," she said. "Is it your custom to walk down?" *Was there even a carriage here?* she wondered. She hadn't had time to examine the stables. Jamie had his mount. Were there other horses?

Jamie had forgotten that the next day was Sunday. His heart sank. He reached for his wineglass and drank.

"We don't go to church," said Tamsyn.

"You have to wear dresses," agreed Tegan.

"And sit still for ages," added her sister.

"And be quiet."

"Everyone stares so," said Tegan.

"And says 'you poor little things.'"

"As if we were infants."

Both twins glared at Clare as if this were somehow her fault.

"We will all attend church," Clare stated. She had always done so, and she was shocked to find that the girls had not, especially after learning they had lessons with the vicar.

The twins' heads swiveled to their brother, clearly expecting him to object.

Jamie nodded heavily. As a landowner and the head of his family, he must take his place in their traditional pew. But he would have liked a little more time before he faced all the neighbors. It suddenly occurred to him that one usually received a round of calls on the occasion of marriage. The neighborhood must know of the wedding. But no one had called at Trehearth; no one had acknowledged him or his new wife.

He'd never made himself part of local society. He was barely acquainted with his neighbors. It had always been too humiliating to mingle with them as his estate fell in ruin. Wary of their pity and disapproval, he'd turned to his London friends for society and solace. That must change now, but he dreaded it. The twins were right; people would stare. In fact, they would gape—surreptitiously. The whole service would be like being onstage. He poured a third glass of wine. At least his grandfather's cellar had survived the wreck of their fortunes. It still contained ranked bottles of quite decent vintages.

"We won't go," said Tegan.

"You can't make us," said Tamsyn.

Was this where Clare "handled" his sisters? Jamie wondered. Or was it just another occasion when he shouted himself hoarse with absolutely no effect?

Clare looked at Selina; she had discussed this with her beforehand, and Selina had agreed to help. "Well…" said Selina, drawing out the word.

"If you don't mind people whispering about you behind their hands," added Clare in the same dubious tone.

"What?" Tamsyn frowned at her.

"If they don't appear with the family at church, everyone will assume there's something to hide." Selina spoke directly to Clare, leaving the twins out of it.

"I would find it uncomfortable myself," Clare allowed.

"Everybody knows us," said Tegan.

Clare nodded. "They see you walking in the countryside."

"In your unsuitable clothing," remarked Selina. Clare gave her a cautionary glance.

"Wandering like tinkers," said Tamsyn, defiance and a hint of uncertainty in her tone.

"Appearances are so capable of misinterpretation," Selina said, speaking only to Clare again.

"Yes, when you're not really acquainted with a person…" Clare let her voice trail off.

What were they up to? Jamie wondered.

"We don't want to be acquainted," declared Tegan.

Clare nodded again, as if her defiant stance was quite reasonable. "Social obligations can be wearisome, but if you are never met or spoken to…"

Selina looked grave. "People will make up reasons for their absence," she said to Clare.

"They tend to do so, and very odd ones seem to be preferred."

Tamsyn scowled. "We don't care what they…"

"If they can't be seen in public, now that the family is officially in residence…" began Selina.

Clare pursed her lips. "Then perhaps they are… unfit for society."

"Uncouth," said Selina.

"What is un…?"

"Or even mad," the older woman continued.

"We are not!"

Clare shook her head at the vagaries of society. "Or… malformed somehow."

"Mal…?"

"And that their brother is ashamed to be seen with them," Selina finished.

Jamie sat up straighter at this one. "I am not," he

responded. And then wondered if he had been supposed to say something different, to follow what was
obviously a prepared script. But he wouldn't pretend
to be ashamed of his sisters. Driven distracted, yes,
absolutely; but not ashamed.

"Of course not," Clare agreed. "But once one
becomes the subject of gossip, it spreads like wildfire."

"The most idiotic tales are believed," said Selina.
"I've seen it so often. I think, as you said, Clare, that
people *prefer* the more outlandish stories."

"And then it's nearly impossible to be rid of them,"
agreed Clare. "They'll be told and re-told for years,
even when they've been proven false and—"

"All right, we'll go!" cried Tamsyn. She and her
twin exchanged a heated glance. Clare was certain
the girls could communicate a wealth of information
without a word.

"Just to stop you from talking and talking," conceded Tegan.

"But we really don't care what *anyone* thinks!"
Tamsyn's hard stare made it clear that this sentiment
was aimed at Clare.

The girls rose from the table and stood side by side
in solidarity. Clare merely smiled at them and turned
away. "Shall we all walk to church then? Do we have
a carriage?"

"An ancient one," Jamie replied. He avoided his
sisters' smoldering gazes. "And no proper team to pull
it just now."

"A lovely brisk walk then. We can meet in the hall."

"Nine thirty perhaps?" said Selina.

"I think that would be ample time." Clare rose as

well. "I had a sofa and some chairs moved into the solar. Shall we retire there this evening?"

Selina stood. "That sounds pleasant."

The two women went out, leaving Jamie alone with the glowering twins. He shifted uneasily in his chair. So much of the time they'd spent together had involved wrangling. Should he congratulate them on their cooperation? No, definitely a mistake.

"We're not stupid," said Tegan.

"We know we're doing what she wanted," affirmed her sister.

"It's just that Anna's niece told Alys Mason that we're daft." Tegan's lower lip trembled very slightly. Or, no, he'd imagined it, Jamie thought. That wasn't possible. Not Tegan.

"So we will go to church this *once*."

"And show them that we are *not*!"

"But that is *all*!"

Turning in unison, they marched out of the dining room—shoulders square, their small forms almost birdlike in their ridiculous shirts and breeches. A tremor of unease went through Jamie. It made his throat tighten, though he couldn't pinpoint the cause. He refilled his wineglass, emptying the bottle, although no one else had drunk any. Sipping, he sat alone in his newly scrubbed dining room, savoring the taste of the vintage.

His wife and her companion sat in the solar. His sisters were closed in their room, undoubtedly accompanied by Randolph. He'd seen no sign of the dog in the stables. Jamie didn't feel as if he belonged in either place. He sipped again, and was reminded of other nights in this room, when he'd slumped over a second, or a third, bottle and tried to blot out the certainty of a bleak future. He'd averted disaster. And he did feel triumphant. Truly, he did. Old Jenkins had been full of praise for his renovation plans.

He was just tired this evening, his mind overwhelmed by myriad tasks, his body by days in the saddle. Jamie's eyelids drooped, and he nodded over his glass. His head bowed, then jerked up. Once, and again. He finished his wine, stood unsteadily, and made his way out into the great hall. He should go and speak to Clare about… what was it? He couldn't remember.

His toe caught on an uneven floorboard, and Jamie tripped, barely avoiding a fall. He wasn't in the best condition to converse, he realized. As Harry and Andrew always said, when you're three sheets to the wind better head for a safe harbor. He'd lie down for a little while, recover his wits. Jamie turned toward the stairs and stumbled up them. In his room, he pulled off his boots and lay on the mattress fully clothed, falling headlong into sleep.

Later that evening, as Clare brushed her hair, her mind drifted irresistibly to last night. The memories were so vivid and enticing. She listened for sounds from the adjoining chamber and heard nothing. Their encounter seemed almost like a dream, or something from a different epoch, as if there were two layers to reality. She and Jamie hurried from task to task, and had disagreed a bit sharply, in a busy sunlit world. They'd caressed and exulted in a dim, sensuous realm. Tonight, the latter lay quiescent, apparently out of reach. She climbed into bed alone.

Nine

THE TREHEARTH PARTY SET OFF FOR CHURCH NOT TOO much after nine thirty. Randolph had been the cause of a short delay, when it was discovered that he had chewed up Tegan's best dress—most likely because she'd spilled gravy down the bodice, and then crumpled it into a ball so that no one would notice and stuffed it into the bottom of her wardrobe. Another was found, even more ill-fitting than the ones Clare had already seen, and she briefly wondered whether to leave the girls behind after all. At their age, she would have been mortified to be seen in such dowdy dresses. They seemed oblivious to fashion, however, and she let it go. Their cloaks covered the worst of it. But she would have to provide the twins with a new wardrobe, which would undoubtedly be a process fraught with difficulties.

The Pendennises walked with the other household members down the path that branched from the drive and wound down the cliffs to the village in the cove. The March day was chilly but not bitter. Clare had noticed that the winter temperatures in this westerly part of the country varied little between day and night. The climate was milder than London.

Jamie had an aching head and a severe shortage of patience. He should have left some wine in that bottle, he thought, or skipped the brandy beforehand. He'd nearly downed a dose of the latter as he dressed. He'd resisted the impulse, though, substituting liberal applications of cold water to snap himself awake. His mirror told him that he was pale, with some red in his eyes that wouldn't be missed by sharp-eyed village gossips. He wasn't in the best state to be put on display to the entire neighborhood.

He ran his gaze over the rest of his party, trying to see them as strangers would. The Pendennises were as forthright and solid as ever; he knew they were respected in the village—and deservedly so. Clare looked slim and elegant, her pale hair stirred by the morning breeze. Her bonnet and cloak might be drab, but the beauty of her face and grace of her carriage more than made up for it. He'd be proud to have her on his arm. Mrs. Newton was equally respectable, if not as lovely and alluring as his wife. As for his sisters... Jamie sighed. Somehow, when dressed as young ladies, Tamsyn and Tegan always managed to look like wild creatures, captured and stuffed into alien garments that chafed at them and hampered their natural grace. He supposed that they'd brushed their hair. They must have. Yet the strands had reverted to wild black tangles; they always did, as if they possessed a life of their own. And their set expressions—martyrs being marched to the stake—didn't improve the picture.

"It's a fine church," said Clare. She and Selina

hadn't ventured inside the previous day. "It looks quite old."

Jamie gathered his wits to respond and to smile, suddenly conscious that they were undoubtedly under observation now that they'd entered the village. "The tower was built in the fifteenth century. It's been used for beacon fires since Tudor times. The rest of the building is a bit later. Made of local stone." They passed under the archway, through the vestibule, and into the church proper. Jamie was aware of heads turning and eyes following as they walked to the pew at the front, set aside for the Trehearth family. He'd never liked sitting there. Everyone could watch them, and they could see no one but the vicar.

Clare enjoyed the service. Reverend Carew's sermon was both thoughtful and accessible. The choir boasted some exceptional voices, which rang through the old stone arches under the domed ceiling and seemed to rise on shafts of jeweled light from the stained glass. She would like worshiping here, she decided. Meeting Selina's eyes across the smaller frames of the twins, she saw less approval in the older woman's gaze.

The Trehearth party was among the last parishioners to file out after the service. The vicar stood just outside the door, offering everyone a word. "Edward Carew," he said to Jamie when they emerged. "I don't believe we've met, Lord Trehearth."

Jamie shook his hand. "May I present my wife, and her friend Mrs. Newton?"

"I've had that pleasure already," he replied, to Jamie's surprise. "Hello, Tamsyn, Tegan," he added.

The twins turned from their observation of the lingering crowd, dropped small curtsies, and smiled up at the older man. Jamie had to clench his jaw to keep it from dropping. "I finished that book about the hinges," said Tegan.

"Henges," Tamsyn corrected.

Her sister shrugged. "It was very good."

The pastor smiled down at them. His blue eyes were full of kindness for his pupils, Clare thought. The twins could not have happened upon a better mentor for pursuing their local interests. "I've just received another volume from London," he said. "I'll show it to you when you have the time."

"We could look now," Tegan began.

The bright curiosity in her face was a very good sign, Clare noted. Whatever these girls' rebellious antics, they clearly loved to learn. And she firmly believed that a child who loved to learn—loved rather than saw it an advantage or curried favor by it—was sound at heart.

"Unfortunately, I am occupied at the moment," said the vicar with twinkling eyes. He indicated the still busy churchyard and watched his sometime pupils subside into self-consciousness. Reverend Carew fervently hoped that the arrival of ladies at Trehearth would be the social salvation of Tamsyn and Tegan Boleigh. He was fond of the prickly children and, in fact, rather admired them. They'd faced a difficult lot in life with resolution and zest. If they occasionally misbehaved, he found it understandable. He also thought that their waywardness could be mended. Not easily, perhaps. But he'd seen what a bit of kindness and interest could accomplish. Turning, the vicar encountered Lady Trehearth's quite extraordinary green eyes, and he had the odd feeling that she'd followed his thoughts and agreed with them.

Feeling another gaze on him, he shifted his attention to the hazel eyes of her friend. There he found challenge and reserve, yet also some other element that drew him in a way he hadn't experienced in years. It was unsettling and quite an effort to pull his attention back to his duties. But he'd formed a plan for this post-service interlude. "Would you allow me to present some of your neighbors?" he asked Lord Trehearth. "I know you've been in London a great deal and may not have met them all."

The village would know practically everything about them, Clare realized. Country neighborhoods were rife with gossip. They needed to find their place within this one.

As the vicar shepherded them gently toward a knot of people near the churchyard gate, Jamie felt both stiff and grateful. The man must have heard his whole history. No doubt his neighbors had been all too eager to retail it—at least as they saw it. So Reverend Carew must be well aware that Jamie was a near stranger here, despite his family's long residence. Some of his neighbors he hadn't seen since before his father's death. He hadn't had the temerity to call when he was in his teens, and no heart for it after that, while the estate teetered on the verge of bankruptcy.

"Of course you know Sir Harold and Lady Halcombe," continued Reverend Carew smoothly.

Jamie vaguely remembered the older couple. Their land was a few miles west. His parents had visited them, and vice versa. He thought he'd met their sons—several years older than he and not much interested in a "squirt" of his vintage. But he bowed and agreed. "Of course."

"Mr. and Mrs. Palgrove recently moved into the manor at Vanyl," the vicar continued.

"Teddy," said a blond young man. "My wife, Marianne."

The pretty young woman beside him smiled and started to speak. Then her blue eyes shifted. "Arthur! Leave those flowers alone. Come here." A small blond boy snatched his hand away from the spray of blooms decorating the church door and ran over to join them. Only then did Jamie notice a little girl hiding behind Marianne Palgrove's skirts.

"And Mr. and Mrs. Fox from Damson House," the vicar finished.

"Graham," supplied the middle-aged gentleman who was the last in the group. "My wife, Elizabeth."

Jamie introduced Clare, Selina Newton, and his sisters. The twins curtsied again, to his renewed astonishment. "Knew your parents well," said Sir Harold. Stocky and square-jawed, he was the picture of a ruddy English landowner.

"Indeed, your mother was a dear friend of mine," added his wife.

Jamie didn't know whether this was meant as an assurance of regard or a reproach for dropping the connection.

Clare looked down as the small Palgroves gazed up. "Hello."

"This is Margaret and Arthur," said their mother. "We left baby Sidney at home because he *will* cry during the sermon."

"Might have a budding dissenter on your hands, vicar," joked her husband.

Reverend Carew merely smiled. The group chatted for a few minutes, exchanging news of the neighborhood and promises to call. "How's that dratted dog?" Mr. Fox asked the twins as the conversation was breaking up.

"Very well, thank you," replied Tamsyn.

"Happy not to be drowned," Tegan muttered.

Jamie couldn't tell if the man heard. They'd all been turning away toward home. He was half chagrined, half oddly relieved, to see that his sisters had not suddenly transformed into models of propriety. That would have been downright uncanny.

"I need better clothes," Clare said to Selina as they walked back up the path side by side. She'd been conscious of the contrast between her aged, dowdy cloak and the more fashionable attire of the neighbors.

"I would be delighted to help with that," Selina replied.

"So do the twins," Clare said, more quietly.

"What they need and what they can be made to accept may not quite agree."

"Indeed. How we will manage it I do not know." Clare was cheered, however, by the evidence that the twins could behave, if they wished to. Somewhere along the line, they had been taught proper manners.

After a cold luncheon, Clare and Selina went upstairs and arrayed Clare's current wardrobe over the big four-poster bed. Indulging their mutual love of list making, they decided what might be worth further alteration and what other sorts of attire she most needed. With her drab gowns lying across the mattress and then draped over the armchair, and Selina full of ideas about what colors would most become her, Clare rediscovered her love of fashion. Like so many of her enthusiasms, it had been suppressed while she lived in an employer's household. Now it could reemerge, another of those inner chambers opening to the light. She could go riding again, she realized. She needed only a proper mount, and one could surely be found. Her heart beat a little faster at the thought of galloping along the sea cliff and feeling the wind on her face.

When they'd finished, Clare sought out John Pendennis and asked him about the state of their stables. He told her that the building itself was sound, but the only inhabitant was Jamie's horse. The coach dated from Jamie's grandfather's time and had a cracked axle. "We borrow a wagon and team from the home farm for hauling," the old man informed her. But she had something more sprightly in mind. As they walked back through the gardens, Clare consulted Pendennis about hiring help to restore overgrown beds and cut back a rampant shrubbery. By this time her mind was racing with things to be done and how the result would appear.

Jamie, wrestling with columns of figures in the estate office, heard them when they passed under the window and felt a spurt of resentment. He knew he'd told her to do whatever she liked with the house. He ought to be grateful for her energy, as well as her money, he supposed. But hearing Clare issuing orders to his old retainer, he felt suddenly constricted. Signing the marriage agreement, he hadn't imagined this sort of scene, and it felt as if he'd given up a larger measure of control than he'd bargained for. Oh, Clare would consult him. He could contradict her, and she would listen. They might not even disagree, in many instances. But, except out on the land, he couldn't form schemes of his own and simply order them done. He had to ask his wife. Call it what you will, it came down to that. He had to go, hat in hand, and beg for permission. It rankled far more than he'd realized it would when he'd been desperate to save his heritage.

The conversation at dinner that evening was carried on mainly between Clare and Selina, discussing a shopping expedition to Penzance. Jamie found they'd already sent down to the village and hired a carriage to take them. And why shouldn't they? He had no objections to proffer. He had no right to expect that he would have been consulted. And so he kept his own counsel, sipping from another bottle of his grandfather's wine. When asked, he advised them on where to go to make various sorts of purchases, but he did not otherwise join the discussion.

Clare purposefully did not include Tamsyn and Tegan in the talk, though she observed their reactions sidelong. The way the twins listened to their plans gave her hope for a scheme she was hatching. By the end of the meal, she was confident it would work.

She was taking hold, she thought. She was ticking items off her lists, getting things done. Sitting in the solar that evening, joining Selina in some mending, Clare felt a satisfying sense of accomplishment. It buoyed her up until she climbed the stairs to bed and sat alone before her dressing table.

There was no sound from the room next door. Jamie had said that he was going to work in the estate office after dinner, and she didn't know if he was still there or just a wall away. Their one night together seemed to have receded in time, until it felt like far more than two days ago. It had become almost like a dream. Softly, Clare rose and walked over to the connecting door. She listened more closely and still heard nothing. She could turn the knob and go through. He was her husband. He had stepped over this threshold without hesitation. Clare flushed at the memory of that night. A part of her yearned for his touch, the fire of his lips on hers. But their exchanges since then had been so mundane, so terse. Tonight, Jamie had seemed as distant as a stranger. So, although her hand remained on the doorknob for several minutes, Clare couldn't quite bring herself to turn it.

After breakfast the following morning, Clare went up to the twins' bedchamber and knocked on the door. She was dressed for the outdoors. After a silent pause, it was opened a crack, exposing one dark eye. "Shouldn't you let Randolph out for a run?" Clare asked. "I'm sure he'd like that."

"Randolph?" answered one of the twins. Clare couldn't tell which with so little of the girl visible. "He's out in the st—" A sharp series of barks from within cut her off.

"I wondered if I might come along?" Clare added,

showing no sign of disapproval. "I should like to learn some good walks nearby. I'm sure you know them all."

The door closed on a whispered consultation, then opened wider to reveal both girls in their boyish attire, barring entry with their bodies. Clare heard the click of canine claws on the floorboards and braced herself. But Randolph merely thrust his massive head between the twins and gazed up at her, pink tongue lolling. "Hello, Randolph," she said. The diamond-shaped brown patches around his eyes gave him a mournful air, but Clare would have sworn the dog's brown gaze held a twinkle. He wiggled and jostled and pushed free of his guardians, bounding into the smaller corridor that ran down the north wing. Clearly he was accustomed to using the back steps there rather than the main staircase.

Clare took the opportunity to look over the twins' heads into their room. It was as individual as she'd expected. They had another of the huge four-posters against the inner wall, with a large wardrobe on the other side. Two armchairs were drawn up to the hearth, a table between them pleasantly cluttered with books, shiny stones, bird nests, and other bits collected from the surrounding country. Windows in the two outer walls showed the sea. The far corner held a pile of blankets for Randolph. The girls had also amassed objects from around the house to brighten their haven—a jewel-toned carpet, colorful silk cushions, a pair of silver candlesticks. Somewhat to Clare's surprise, it all appeared to be clean. Perhaps she wouldn't have to persuade them to admit the scouring team, which was a relief. She gathered all this in a quick glance, then said, "Shall we go?"

The twins looked at each other, then grabbed their jackets and came, closing the door definitively behind them.

Randolph was already down the stairs and gone. Anna Pendennis cast Clare a surprised look as they followed him out through the scullery door and into the sunny air. The great dog capered and barked when he saw them, overjoyed to be out. "Where is your favorite walk?" Clare asked, speaking to the dog rather than the girls. Randolph turned and trotted off toward the cliffs. The twins gaped at Clare as she went after him.

For a while, she said nothing. The big dog moved fast, and she used her breath to keep up with him and two active children. It was a blustery day, the great rushes of wind invigorating, the crash of the waves on the rocks below like the sea's heartbeat. They took a path that wound its way above the surf, far enough from the cliff edge to feel safe. There were few trees, and those small, but the ground was covered with bushy plants and green spears that Clare thought were nascent wildflowers. At last, when Randolph was sniffing at some fascinating bit of greenery, she dared, "He is so happy outdoors, isn't he? He can't like being shut up in one room." She ignored the issue of the stables.

"He used to live in the whole house," replied Tegan with a jutting jaw.

"*Before*," agreed her sister, putting a wealth of emotion into the word.

"I suppose he could again, if he were trained," Clare replied. "We had dogs about the house when I was a child."

"You won't beat him!" declared Tamsyn.

"Why would I do that?"

"John said he needed some sense beat into him," said Tegan.

"But we won't allow it."

"We will throw ourselves in the way and—"

"What was Randolph doing when John said that?" Clare wondered, suspecting that the old man had been at the end of his rope.

The twins looked away. "Eating some roast beef," Tamsyn murmured.

"Off the kitchen table," Tegan admitted.

"We know he mustn't climb on the furniture."

"But Anna left the joint just sitting there."

"She knows he…" Tamsyn didn't seem to have an ending for this sentence that she wished to share. Randolph anointed the branch he'd been sniffing with his own interesting odor and moved on. As they followed, Clare said, "If you teach him better behavior, he can have the freedom of the house again. Mind, he cannot jump up on visitors. I will not have that."

The girls looked at their giant pet, bounding through the bushes as if his legs had springs. "He doesn't always listen," allowed Tamsyn regretfully.

"He never listens," Tegan corrected. "Except to Jamie."

Tamsyn looked at her sister. They communed silently for a moment, then looked away from each other again.

"Well, there is the solution, then. He can help you train Randolph." It seemed an obvious idea to Clare. She couldn't understand why they hadn't done this already. But as she watched identical expressions pass across the girls' faces—hope, regret, then a careful stoicism—she realized it might be more complicated than she knew.

Tamsyn shook her head. Tegan bent hers in a resigned gesture that seemed all too habitual. "I don't think he would have time to do that," Tamsyn said.

Clare read a whole history in the simple sentence—of promises made and broken. "I will ask him to do so," said Clare. A tremor of uneasiness went through her as the twins raised startled dark eyes to hers. Would Jamie agree? Had he ever glimpsed that fearful longing in his sisters' faces? Was he the sort of man who could ignore it? She didn't want to think so, yet the twins had clearly been disappointed before.

Ahead of them, Randolph leapt into the air, barking at a diving gull. The bird teased him closer to the cliff edge, and the twins ran forward, calling the dog's name. With a final defiant snap of his great jaws at the bird, he turned and loped toward them, ears flapping, eyes bright within their dark diamonds of fur. The meeting of children and dog on the path was the very picture of joy. He bounced between them, licking hands and faces, egged on by their laughter. It was the first time Clare had seen Tamsyn and Tegan romping like carefree children, and the sight made her laugh as well. It was settled; Randolph was part of the household. He would not be ejected.

They walked on a little farther and then turned back toward the house. When Clare judged that the girls' suspicions were at their lowest ebb, she sprang the trap she'd been preparing. "I wondered if you would care to come along on the expedition to Penzance?"

The twins stopped moving and stared at her.

"Have you been there before?"

In unison, they shook their heads.

"We will have to stay overnight, of course."

"At an inn?" asked Tamsyn.

"Yes, your brother says there is a very pleasant one, The Admiral Benbow."

"Why?" demanded Tegan.

Clare raised her eyebrows, waiting for more.

"Why would you take us?" the girl added. "No one…"

"We've never…" began her sister at the same moment.

Clare saw them withdrawing, retreating from the risk of disappointment. "You need some new clothes, just as I do," she said. "We're going to see about dressmakers in Penzance. Or, more likely, purchase cloth. Selina… Mrs. Newton is an accomplished seamstress."

"Dressmakers," repeated Tamsyn.

"Yes." Clare met their dark eyes, her own steady and uncompromising, making it clear that new clothes were in their future, however it was accomplished. She dared another nudge. "Did you notice the charming gown Margaret Palgrove was wearing?" She'd wondered if the twins had marked the contrast between their shabby attire and the other little girl's lovely outfit. From the flicker in their gazes, they had.

"So, we can go to Penzance to get dresses," Tamsyn said slowly.

"But if we don't *want* dresses?" Tegan ventured.

"Then there wouldn't be any need for you to make a tiring journey," Clare said.

The girls looked at each other, then back at Clare.

"You're going to be buying furniture, too." It wasn't a question. Clearly, they'd been paying attention to the dinner conversations.

"Yes, I am."

"We might like some things for our room."

Clare smiled down at them. They gazed up. The gauntlet she'd thrown down had been taken. The bargaining had begun.

Ten

THE FEMALES OF THE TREHEARTH HOUSEHOLD LEFT FOR Penzance early the next morning, on a brisk, sunny March day that was ideal for travel. Their hired carriage was a bit crowded, but fortunately the twins were small and did not object to sitting forward. They had even donned gowns and cloaks without protest. The distance was not great, but the roads were winding and narrow, so the journey took some hours. The girls stared avidly out the windows all the way.

Their eyes grew large when the carriage entered the bustling market town with its broad harbor. Penzance was nothing compared to London, but it was far larger than any village the twins had seen before. With its docks full of ships, it had an active trade with the capital, and Clare knew that she could easily communicate with her bank and any sort of merchant she required.

They left their valises at The Admiral Benbow and, armed with directions from the innkeeper, set off into the streets. Visits to two local dressmakers quickly convinced Selina that she could do far better herself, and as soon as they were outside once again, she said so. "Are you sure?" Clare asked her. "You are a guest at Trehearth, not a seamstress. I don't wish to take advantage of you."

"I shall enjoy it," Selina assured her. "It will be such a pleasure to choose whatever cloth we like best, without worrying about the cost." She raised her brows to show she was half joking. "And trimmings? I shall indulge myself shamefully with trimmings." She rubbed her hands together like a stage villain, making Clare laugh. "You know I am far more familiar with London fashions than the people here."

"You are." Clare glanced at the twins, who were peering through the window of a tea shop a little way ahead. Fitting them was unlikely to be a pleasure.

Seeing the direction of her gaze, Selina shrugged. "I shall count on you to deal with them," she added.

This decided, they set off for the dry goods emporium that Jamie had recommended and spent a happy two hours examining bolts of cloth. To Clare's surprise, Tamsyn and Tegan did not appear to be bored. Though they pretended disinterest at first, after only a little while they began to listen to Selina's astute judgments on colors and quality and expressed decided opinions on the patterns they preferred. Catching Tamsyn fingering a length of bright silk, Clare and Selina exchanged a secret glance. The girls were not so indifferent to fashion after all.

The delighted proprietor cut and folded their selections, for draperies and cushion covers as well as gowns, and filled out an order for fabric Selina wanted that he did not have. He assured them that he could procure these, and whatever else they might wish, from London in a matter of two weeks. When they had completed their transactions, he sent his assistant along to carry their large bundles back to the inn. There, they ate a late luncheon and then proceeded to the premises of another merchant, down near the quay. This enterprising gentleman had come up with the idea of stocking samples of goods from London in his warehouse. Local residents could view them and place orders, which he then had shipped down from town. The innovation had made him one of the richest men in Penzance.

Hearing of Lady Trehearth's visit, and aware of her hefty bank balance from discreet hints at the local businessman's club, he guided them around the large building himself. Clare chose sofas, chairs, and tables from the models he displayed, specifying upholstery fabrics from a selection of pattern cards he kept, and was promised that her orders would be sent off by the very next ship. Tamsyn and Tegan discovered several pieces they admired and were allowed to choose one each. Clare had never felt more in charity with them.

The day was waning by the time they'd finished, and they walked back to the inn in the slanting light of sunset. "A productive expedition," Selina commented. Clare agreed and then realized that Tamsyn and Tegan were no longer trailing behind them. Perhaps they had finally gotten bored. She feared some prank or outburst as she turned to look for them.

The girls were only a little way back, however, their noses pressed against the windows of a harness maker. The shop was closed, but a fine saddle was prominently displayed, the leather finely worked and

highly polished. Tegan was pointing out a feature
to her sister. Clare started to call to them and then
walked quietly back along the street instead. "Do you
remember when old Samkins let us ride his pony?"
Tegan was saying.

Tamsyn nodded fervently. "It was glorious."

"He was just a fat old plodder," Tegan scoffed.
"But do you think *she* would…?" Noticing Clare's
approach, she broke off. Clare simply smiled, congratulated herself on her sharp hearing, and made a
silent note for the future.

Sitting down to dinner that evening, Jamie found that
the dining room seemed much larger and very empty.
Though he'd often wished for peace and quiet here, after
some wrangle with his incorrigible sisters, tonight he
missed the sound of chatter, even Tamsyn's and Tegan's
pert replies. In a surprisingly short time he'd become
accustomed to conversation around the table at the end
of a busy day, and the lilt of one voice in particular.

The whirlwind of cleaning and scouring that had
seemed an irritation when it was all happening around
him had opened the place up. Trehearth had gone
from dusty and forlorn to bustling with life, and now
back to echoing silence, even though the new maid
Gwen and the Pendennises were in the kitchen. Clare
had wrought the change, Jamie thought. She'd given
his home new energy. But with her gone, the rooms
threatened to fall back into neglected stupor. He
sipped his wine and knew he was very glad that she
was returning tomorrow.

❦

The next morning Clare and Selina took care of a few other commissions, ordering smaller items for the house and visiting a local hiring agency. The carriage had been summoned for the journey back to Trehearth when the twins came to them with an urgent request. They wanted to visit Lescudjack Castle. "We haven't seen anything but shops," argued Tegan, stretching the truth a bit.

"It isn't far," said Tamsyn.

"It would be very educational," her sister added, using the magic word that nearly always swayed adults.

"I didn't know there was a castle here," Selina commented. She had a weakness for ramparts. "Shall we, Clare?"

"Why not?" Clare was elated at the success of her shopping and the twins' good behavior. She was happy to reward them by adding this viewing to their travels.

After getting advice from the innkeeper, they drove up the coast for several miles, in the opposite direction from Trehearth, finally pulling up before a great turfed hill. The twins were out of the carriage in a flash and running up it. Clare and Selina followed as quickly as they could manage. "But where is the castle?" Selina wondered. "Are you sure we're in the right place?"

"The driver says so," Clare replied.

Near the top of the rise they traversed a deep ditch, struggling up a sharp incline on the other side. The twins stood atop it, looking down. "Breeches are much better for exploring," Tamsyn said when they joined the girls, puffing a bit from the exertion.

"Skirts are stupid," Tegan agreed.

Saving her breath, Clare looked out at the scene before them. The hilltop was ringed by a great oval wall of stones and earth and grass, part of which they stood upon. A steep valley fell away to the east, and the slope went down to the sea on the south and west. Inside the oval were circles of old stones and mounds that might have been ruins. "Why do they call it a castle?" she wondered. The word evoked stone towers and crenellations in her mind. This was more an earthwork.

"Because people are stupid," Tegan replied. "It's a hill fort."

"No one even says it right," Tamsyn added. "*Lys Scosek* means shielded stronghold in the old people's language."

"That's what John calls them—the old people."

"Reverend Carew says they were the ancient Britons."

"There are ruins of their houses and circles of stones all over the countryside."

"They lived here?" Clare hadn't seen the twins so animated before.

The twins shook their heads in unison. "They came up here when there was danger," Tamsyn answered.

"They could fight off their enemies from the walls."

"There's room for a whole tribe, and their animals and all."

"There'll be a spring somewhere," Tegan continued. "For water."

"Let's look for it," Clare suggested.

Tegan, who had clearly been about to argue for permission to do just that, blinked. Then the girls were off, running down the inner slope into the center of the oval.

The women followed more slowly. "They obviously have a passion for this subject," Selina observed. Her tone was somewhat grudging, but her face showed that she was impressed by the girls' knowledge.

One of the twins suddenly disappeared from view. Clare hurried forward, only to find that she had stepped down into a shallow pit surrounded by a rough stone wall. "This was one of their houses," Tamsyn said.

Watching her footing, Clare joined her. She examined the rocks, the hint of a hearth in the center. "A family lived here—long ago?"

"When there were battles," Tamsyn replied.

Clare imagined women and children crouched in this little structure, listening to the clash of arms from the surrounding walls, overhearing the blows that would decide their fate. Or perhaps they weren't here, but nearer the defenses, aiding the fighters, playing their own part. Why not? She met Tamsyn's dark eyes and saw her curiosity and awe mirrored there. "You can almost feel echoes of them still here."

The girl held her gaze. After a moment, she nodded, acknowledging an instant of fellow feeling. Clare wanted to smile, but she didn't; the rapprochement felt too fragile. Any expression might be misinterpreted. But privately she thought that the twins' unusual lives, though plagued by difficulties, had produced a pair of very interesting children.

"I found the spring," called Tegan from across the grassy expanse. They all hurried over to look at a seep of water at the base of the wall. It was nearly silted up, but signs of a stone pool could still be seen.

"It must flow through the earth down to the sea," said Selina.

"They would have lined the pool with clay," Tegan informed them. "To hold the water."

"And pulled it out with buckets," Tamsyn said. The girls bent over the spring like consulting scholars, then ran off to circle the entire oval, searching for more discoveries.

Reluctant to curb the twins' excitement, and actually glad for them to work off some energy before the carriage journey, Clare allowed their visit to extend through the morning. They ate the picnic lunch the inn had provided next to the swell of the forted hill and set off far later than she'd planned. It was growing dark by the time they reached Trehearth, and all of them were very ready to be home.

Jamie rushed out to meet the carriage as soon as it pulled up. "Where have you been? I expected you hours ago." The anxiety that had been building in him as the afternoon passed flashed into irritation when he saw them all safe.

"We stopped to see an ancient site," Clare answered. "It was very…"

Jamie turned on the twins. "Your idea, no doubt." He'd been sitting in Clare's solar with a bottle of claret, imagining shattered axles and broken bodies tossed bloodily into the road with increasing vividness as the level of wine went down. His worries seemed foolish now, but it was not the first time in his life that he'd felt vulnerable to the vagaries of fate. Far from it. And this one had cut with a particular edge. His irritation spiked unreasonably. "You must always have your way, no matter how much it inconveniences…"

"Jamie."

The quiet way that Clare spoke his name stopped him cold. Jamie saw his small sisters standing beside the coach, their shoulders hunched, their identical faces gone stony. He turned away to hide his shame. "Dinner is waiting."

The group dispersed to doff their cloaks and wash their faces. John Pendennis appeared to help the driver unload the mound of parcels they'd brought with them. Much more would arrive by wagon tomorrow. Over dinner, Clare and Selina reviewed their successful purchases for the master of the house, but the meal was not convivial. Tamsyn and Tegan had gone silent and withdrawn. Jamie brooded. Everyone seemed relieved when Clare suggested an early bedtime after their journey.

She herself welcomed the solitude of her bedchamber, the bright fire, the quiet after the rattle and bounce of the carriage. Yet when she sat down to read, she could not keep her eyes on the page. She was a little tired, but not actually sleepy; physically worn, but restless. The details of the evening nagged at her, lowering her mood.

It was the character of her new family, she realized. Jamie and his sisters seemed scarcely able to speak to each other without clashing. In Penzance, she'd felt she was learning more about the twins, perhaps gaining their confidence in a small way. As soon as they reached home, however, that budding rapport was shattered by Jamie's harsh remarks. And the resulting tension had made the whole household unhappy. He was so quick to blame them.

Clare had no doubt that the twins had played a host of pranks, amply earning his distrust. But perhaps they'd had reason. They seemed to have been left to their own devices far too much. One thing she knew for certain: expecting them to rebel was not the way to change their behavior. Clare rose and paced from her chair to the long window overlooking the sea. She hadn't properly explained her ideas on how to handle them. She should speak to Jamie now, when there was no possibility of the twins overhearing.

Clare went to the door that divided their bed-chambers. She hesitated a moment, still a bit shy, then knocked. When she heard a response, she opened the door and found Jamie sprawled in a chair by the fire, bootless, a glass of brandy in his hand. He looked up, and Clare felt as if his gaze brushed her with heat. *How could his dark eyes seem at once hot and fathomless?* she wondered. "I wanted to speak to you about your sisters," she said before they could distract her completely. She sat in the chair on the opposite side of the hearth.

"It's no use complaining to me about their manners," he replied quickly. "I have done every—"

"I have no complaints." Clare almost smiled at his startled expression. He and the twins had more in common than they realized. They'd grown accustomed to a certain pattern of behavior, and they fell into it automatically. It was a kind of trap. Changing that was the key to her schemes for improvement. "Tamsyn and Tegan are intelligent girls."

"Too intelligent sometimes," he muttered.

"I believe that if we show them the advantages of behaving differently, they will do so."

Jamie sat straighter. The candlelight made an aureole of Clare's pale hair. It brushed her face with warmth.

"They have spent too much time alone." Clare raised a hand before he could speak. "We needn't apportion blame for that."

She was charitable, but he was to blame, Jamie thought. In his despair, he'd had no attention to spare for his sisters.

"But I think they're very happy to see an end to that." Clare was sure of it, actually. She'd glimpsed the yearning in their eyes. They wanted to trust. They longed for certainties. It was just a matter of convincing them that things had truly changed. She started to tell Jamie this, but his expression stopped her. The grim line of his mouth suggested that he would take it as a reproach. "They were interested in the idea of new gowns," she said instead.

"Gowns? Are you sure? That doesn't sound like my sisters."

Clare smiled. "I think there is more to them than you know. They simply need encouragement to act as members of polite society."

Jamie frowned, full of doubt. "Encouragement? I've told them a thousand times..."

It was not the moment to explore the difference between encouragement and harangues. "Perhaps bargain is a better word to use," Clare went on. "For example, I have told them that Randolph can live in the house if they allow you to help them train him."

Jamie's jaw dropped. "You what?"

"I know it must be possible. We had dogs about all the time when I was a child. They were quite well behaved. And you said he was good-tempered."

"But Randolph... Randolph is a..." Various words occurred to him—"rogue," "lunatic," "misbegotten mongrel."

"My brother used to insist that all dogs were trainable." Clare thought of him with a bittersweet sadness. How he would have laughed at the way the huge dog greeted her.

"Proper dogs, not mismated offspring of—"

"The twins said that Randolph listens to you."

Seeing the serene confidence in her face, Jamie couldn't protest again. He thought of the way his home had changed, gained new life. Was it possible his sisters could be reformed by the same hand? In that moment, he almost believed it. He'd try to make some time for the wretched dog, though he didn't see where it was to come from.

"Also, I suspect from things they said that Tamsyn and Tegan would love to have ponies," Clare continued, happily unaware of his skepticism.

"So they can ride off into the countryside like gypsies and play least in sight for hours," Jamie retorted.

"Gypsies, or tinkers?"

At her roguish look, Jamie had to laugh. But he wasn't convinced. "I shudder to think of the mischief they'd get up to on horseback."

"For the promise of their own mounts, they would make promises in return," Clare said confidently.

"Promises!"

"Have they ever broken their word to you?" She was genuinely curious about this.

Jamie started to assure her that of course they had, repeatedly. Then he paused. His sisters had played a host of tricks, exhibited maddening stubbornness, driven him and others to distraction. But had they ever gone back on an actual promise? Running through the years of their history, he couldn't recall an instance. They'd never promised to be good or obedient, he realized. On the contrary, they'd been careful never to promise much of anything. Had he asked them to? Perhaps not. Their conversations tended to be short and acrimonious.

"I believe that if we keep our bargains with them, they will do the same," Clare finished.

Jamie contemplated the possibility. "We can but try, I suppose."

Clare smiled at him, satisfied with this beginning of what would undoubtedly be a long process.

Jamie gazed at her, seated across the hearth in his bedchamber. The times when he'd told his sisters that he would be down to see them, and then not come, fled from his mind. He could think of nothing but the moment when Clare had turned from her dressing table and looked at him, and he had touched her silken shoulder.

"I'm glad you agree," she said. She shifted in the chair. His expression had changed. The heat was back in his gaze.

Jamie nodded with no thought for what he was agreeing to. He stood and took a step toward her. When he saw a spark in her pale green tiger eyes, he took another.

His stare seemed to draw her to her feet, like a hand pulling her up. Clare swallowed. The warmth from the fire suddenly seemed as nothing to the flash of heat that went through her.

Two more steps brought her into his arms. Jamie drew her close and bent his head. With the first brush of the kiss, all other concerns fell away. Her body was lithe and thrilling under his hands. Her arms came around his neck and pressed her nearer.

His lips moving on hers woke a surge of desire in Clare. Memories of the last time he'd held her blurred into the vivid sensations of the moment, setting her skin afire.

Jamie's fingers found the row of small buttons at the front of her gown and undid them one by one. He pushed the cloth down her shoulder and set his lips to that white slope, then slid them up the curve of her neck to find her mouth again. The gown slipped lower, and he caressed her breast, enticingly soft and round. Her breath caught, and he reveled in the sound.

Suddenly impatient, Clare pulled his shirt loose from his breeches and ran her hands up the muscles of his back. He felt like sprung steel sheathed in velvet. Their kiss deepened, and her hands flexed, nails scraping lightly across his torso.

And then both of them were shoving at folds of cloth, slipping out of constricting garments, throwing aside bits of raiment, desperate to be rid of all impediments on their way to his bed. Clare left her gown in a heap on the floor. Jamie tossed his shirt into a corner. She pulled up her shift and yanked it over her head to drop behind her as he shed his stockings and breeches.

Unveiled, they stood for a moment, gazing at mutual nakedness revealed, then they reached for each other. Jamie pressed her back against the edge of the bed, every inch of him blazing. As he kissed her again, he ran his hands up and down the length of her, urging her closer still.

Clare arched to his touch. She was burning up. They fell together onto the bed, and she copied him, running her own lips along his shoulder and back up to his demanding mouth. Her hands roamed the softer skin of his ribs, rousing a thrilling shiver of yearning.

Jamie rose over her. She was so beautiful against the dark coverlet, her green eyes drowning in desire. He eased one leg between hers and exulted as she opened to him. He followed it with trailing fingers, slow up the silken inside of her thigh. When she murmured his name to urge him onward, triumph throbbed in him. He let his hand wander farther, and Clare cried out as he reached his goal. He wanted to drive her as mad with longing as he was; he took her mouth again.

Clare melted into the kiss. She gripped her husband's broad shoulders and soared on a wave of pleasure that went on and on, until it broke into a thousand bright shards of delight. Heart pounding, she pulled him closer. She wanted more.

Every fiber of him concentrated into pulsing desire, Jamie at last let himself go. They moved together in a dance that made everything else in the world disappear, leading and following each other up step after step to a peak of shared ecstasy. It lasted a breathtaking moment, and forever. And then they held on while their hearts pounded in tandem at the end of the race. The world swirled and shimmered and slowly settled.

And then they were once again aware of the crackling of the fire, the whisper of a night breeze outside the windows, the scent of lavender rising from the bed linens. In a delicious languor, Clare didn't want to talk. What could there be to say that would rival what had just happened? She lay there, limbs tangled with his, and drifted toward sleep.

Seeing her eyelids droop, Jamie moved and lifted her so that he could push back the coverlet and slip beside her between the soft sheets. Clare nestled into his bed and up against him, her head trustingly on his shoulder. With every sense satiated, it seemed to Jamie that all his worries had been swept away. He couldn't remember what problem he might have been chewing over before she knocked on his door. Resting his head beside hers on the pillow, he relaxed and let sleep pull him down. And all through all the dark hours of the night, they slumbered peacefully side by side.

Eleven

CLARE WOKE TO THE SHOCKING CONSCIOUSNESS THAT she was in bed naked. Where was her nightdress? Why were there hairpins sticking into her scalp, as if she hadn't even brushed her hair before sleep? And most perplexing of all, what was that touch lightly trailing over her breast, circling and circling inward, sending bolts of delicious sensation through her unclothed body?

Clare turned her head and met her husband's dark eyes on the other pillow. They gleamed with satisfaction when she gasped as his fingers finished their circling and began to tease. Sunlight poured between the crevices of the draperies. The fire had died to coals. It was morning, and not so very early from the slant of the light. The household would be up.

Jamie rose on one elbow and looked down at her, reveling in the combination of surprise and arousal in Clare's face. He bent and substituted lips for fingertips. She moaned softly. His hand slid down her ribs to find another spot to tantalize. Her back arched. "Jamie, it's morning," she managed to gasp.

He raised his head. "So?" He loved watching her amazing eyes begin to soften with need.

"We have to get up. Everyone will be wondering—"

"Let them wonder."

"But they will know that we are—" Another gasp cut off this sentence.

Jamie smiled. "We *are* married, Clare. I imagine they already suspect." He bent his head and resumed his previous activity. Shivering with longing, Clare abandoned her concerns and surrendered to the rising tide of desire.

A full hour passed before she gathered up her scattered clothing and slipped through the connecting door to her own bedchamber. There was a can of hot water on the washstand, and the fire had been rekindled. She was thankful for it, but it also meant that Gwen the maid had seen her untouched bed and drawn the obvious conclusion as to her whereabouts. Selina would also know what to think about her late appearance at the breakfast table. It was nothing wrong, of course, but it did make her feel a bit self-conscious.

Moving across the room toward the washstand, Clare caught a glimpse of herself in the dressing table mirror. Her hair was a wild, pale tangle around her face. Her lips were rosy from many kisses, her eyes wide and soft. Bits of pale skin peeked out from behind the bundle of crumpled clothing she clutched. She hardly recognized herself.

Some impulse made her let the garments go. They slid to the floor, revealing all of her to the staring reflection. Sunlight through the closed curtains threw stripes of gold across her body. Every place she looked,

Jamie had touched. He'd drawn the most amazing sensations from this slender body gazing back at her. She raised her head and stood straighter, watching her breasts rise naked and proud. This was a completely different person from the reluctant governess who'd worked so hard to escape any sort of notice. There was no longer a need to hide. She could step fully into her life, all facets revealed. The knowledge sent a thrill of joy through her. She'd done it; she'd changed her fate.

Clare shivered. Even with the fire, the room was too cold for bare skin. She needed to wash and dress and begin the work of the day. Her lips curved in a secret smile, she stepped over to the washstand to do just that.

Selina and the twins were finishing breakfast by the time Clare came down, and Jamie was well into a piled plate. He gave her a broad smile, but no one else seemed to notice her late rising. At least, no one remarked on it. By the time she'd eaten, he'd gone out to see to the endless list of tasks on the land. Clare found Anna Pendennis and was pleased to hear that she and her husband had found a number of other local people interested in positions at Trehearth. She offered three more maids and several boys for the stables and gardens. The latter had no experience, but Anna thought they would do for a start. Clare, meeting the bevy of young people filling the kitchen, approved her choices. She was able to add that she'd done her part at the small agency in Penzance and engaged a highly recommended cook. By the time these matters were settled, the wagon had arrived with their purchases, and most of her new staff joined in the excitement of carrying the various parcels to their proper places.

Selina established herself in the sewing room, opening brown paper wrappings and spreading out the fabrics they'd bought. She couldn't restrain occasional murmurs of delight; it was such a luxury not to have to scrimp and make do to create the new gowns that filled her imagination. The feel and the clean scent of new cloth buoyed her up and somehow comforted her at the same time.

"I'll have Anna line up the best of the village seamstresses as your helpers," Clare told her. "You can lay out the designs and cut, but you mustn't be burdened with all the sewing." She found she was quite eager for a new gown in the pale green muslin they'd chosen. It was to be trimmed with bunches of darker green ribbon. And Selina had urged her to purchase a length of deep blue satin for an evening dress as well. Clare couldn't wait for Jamie to see her in it. She wanted to see his dark eyes go smoky and…

Clare blushed, glad that her thoughts were open only to herself. She turned and pretended to be engrossed by one of the fashion periodicals they'd brought back from Penzance.

❧

The Reverend Edward Carew rode slowly along the track that skirted the sea cliff above the village. The morning was crystalline—the deep blue ocean edged with lacy white in the surf, the air crisp and melodic with birdsong. On a spring day like this one, he positively reveled in the beautiful spot where he'd landed. He'd pulled some strings to remove to this place six years ago, unable to remain in his old parish after the death of his wife. Back there, every turn of landscape, every service and meeting, reminded him of her, and it had been unbearable. Here, all was new and diverting, even the lashing winter storms. Over time, his grief had eased, if not disappeared, but his life was still very different without her. Lonely.

His position as village priest made him the confidant of many, a reliable listener who would hold their secrets sacrosanct. He was expected to be a bulwark in illness and despair, and he was glad to fill that role. Part of what had drawn him to the church was a wish to help people, to ease their pain as much as he could and offer hope. But with the loss of his wife, he had no such resource himself. The vicar did not bring his troubles to his parishioners. It was best if he did not appear to have any. A sigh punctuated the thought.

Beyond the strains of his position, there was the simple emptiness of the chair opposite as he ate his meals, the vacancy of the parsonage in the evenings, when his admirable housekeeper had returned to her own family dwelling. He missed the warm presence of another human being, reading on the opposite side of the hearth, sharing a hot drink before bed, breathing beside him through the long hours of the night. Silent companionship could be as comforting as talk.

A gull cried directly overhead, startling his horse. Carew shook himself and sat straighter in the saddle. He'd enjoyed many happy years with Katharine. Their children were grown and well settled. He had much to be grateful for. Indeed, all around his parish people experienced far greater hardships than he'd had to endure. They didn't need a melancholy vicar showing them a mournful face. A bit of cheer and compassion could heal the spirit as much as tangible aid eased the body. It was his profession and his pleasure to offer both, and his bent to be optimistic. At the age of fifty-four, he hoped he had many years of service ahead of him.

Carew's mind turned back to the young farming family he'd just visited. They had two sick children and hardly enough blankets to keep them warm. He could do something about that. More, he was eager to enlist the new Lady Trehearth into his regiment of local helpers, and this seemed a perfect opportunity. Having met her, he was confident she would want to take up the chatelaine's traditional position and offer aid to tenants on the estate. Carew turned his horse onto a path that led to Trehearth.

At midmorning, Gwen came into the sewing room and announced that the vicar had called. Clare and Selina, their heads together over a sketch, turned at once. "Thank you, Gwen," said Clare. "Show him into the solar. We'll be right down. And bring some refreshment."

"Yes, my lady. What shall I...?"

"Ask Mrs. Pendennis."

They found Reverend Carew standing before the glass doors at the end of the solar, looking out over the terrace at the sea, hands clasped behind him.

"Good morning," Clare said.

He turned at once. "Good morning, Lady Trehearth, Mrs. Newton. I hope I'm not disturbing you. I was passing this way, and I thought I would stop in."

"You're most welcome," Clare responded. "Please sit down."

Clare and Selina took the sofa, the vicar an armchair. The furniture looked worn and shabby in the bright light of day, but their visitor showed no sign of noticing or caring. Clare's favorable impression of the man increased further when he said, "This is a very pleasant room."

"I've taken it for my own," Clare agreed. "Once we've refurbished it a bit, it will be a lovely place to sit, I think."

Gwen came in, carefully balancing a tray holding a teapot and cups. "Would you care for tea, vicar?" Clare asked.

"Thank you."

Clare nodded to Gwen, and the new maid poured with great concentration, then handed round the cups as if they were likely to shatter at a touch. She'd barely finished and gone out when Tamsyn and Tegan came running into the room.

They were back in their breeches, as they had been at breakfast. *Where did they get them?* Clare wondered. And how could she prevent them from getting more? Edward Carew showed no surprise at this garb. Did they go to the parsonage for their lessons dressed this way? Clare was fairly certain she knew the answer. Perhaps the village was inured to it.

"We heard you were here," said Tamsyn to their visitor.

"We went to Lescudjack Castle!" her sister chimed in. "Tegan found the spring."

"And we walked all around."

"We saw where the huts were, and the big fire pit."

Carew merely smiled at this onslaught. "Did you indeed?" Clare stifled her urge to tell the twins to sit down and speak more temperately.

"Tamsyn drew up a plan."

"It shows the spring," Tamsyn informed him.

Tegan tugged at his sleeve. "Come and see it!"

This was too much. Clare started to object.

"I should very much like to see it," replied the vicar. "Another time. I'm talking with Lady Trehearth and Mrs. Newton right now."

"Oh." Tamsyn looked around as if she was just noticing the whole group.

"You could bring it along when you come for a lesson," Carew added.

"Yes. I will." To Clare's surprise, Tamsyn put a hand on Tegan's arm and pulled her toward the door. Tegan turned to frown at Clare, who hoped her expression was quite neutral, then shrugged and followed her sister out.

"As I told you, the twins and I share a keen interest in the ancient inhabitants of this region," Carew explained when the girls were gone. "We've had many a good delve through the nearby ruins."

"They shouldn't be out wandering alone," Selina said.

"It's perfectly safe," the vicar assured her. "They're well-known in the neighborhood. No one would harm them."

"But a fall, or if they should lose their way…"

"Tamsyn and Tegan know the countryside as well as they know this house." He smiled at her. "Far better than I do."

He had a truly engaging smile, Selina thought. She couldn't help returning it, though she did not agree with his opinions about the twins. For his part, Carew found that he did not want to look away from Mrs. Newton's sparkling hazel eyes.

"They can't go on as they have," Clare said. "In just a few years, they will be young ladies." Wearing breeches at age ten was one thing; at fifteen, or eighteen, it was quite another.

The vicar recalled himself and acknowledged this with a nod.

"So their… reform is left to me?" *Did he have any idea what a daunting task that was?* Clare wondered.

From the twinkle in his eye, he did. "I suspect you're up to it."

"Can I count on your help?" Clare thought she could, after their previous meeting, but she found she needed some reassurance.

"Of course you can," he answered. There was a pause as he sipped his tea. "Actually, I came today with a hope of enlisting *your* help for some of the tenant families hereabouts."

Immediately diverted, Clare asked for details. The vicar explained some of the most pressing needs, and she at once agreed to provide for them. "Please tell me when anything of this nature arises," she said. "It will take me some time to get to know the people on the estate."

This satisfactorily settled, Edward Carew asked, "Did you all enjoy your expedition to Penzance?"

Selina eyed the man. "How did you know that we…?"

"This is a country neighborhood, Mrs. Newton," he replied. "Novelty is scarce. Discussing the other inhabitants' doings is a common amusement."

"Gossip," Selina snorted. She was more than familiar with this drive to dissect the activities and character of one's acquaintances. It was the chief interest of most of the elderly ladies who had employed her. She'd encountered men of the cloth who indulged them, too. And deplored it.

"Oh, I never gossip," replied Carew with a twinkle in his sharp blue eyes. "I may pass along a few interesting items of news, as I go on my pastoral rounds."

"How can you joke…?" Selina began.

"What are the neighbors saying about us?" Clare wondered at the same moment.

Carew addressed Selina first. "I would never break a confidence, or repeat a malicious rumor, or feed a feud. But the free flow of information can knit up bonds in a community." He waited until Selina gave a grudging nod, then turned to Clare. "Everyone has concluded that Lord Trehearth indeed married an heiress. The hiring of staff, the purchases, you see."

Clare said nothing, knowing her silence would be taken for confirmation.

"The village is delighted to have the house… open again. And the tenants about the repairs being put in train, of course. The prominent families are reserving judgment."

"Judgment of what?" Selina at once felt protective of her friend.

The vicar paused to find the right phrases. "I have

lived here only a few years. As I understand it, Lord Trehearth has never made any effort to know his neighbors. He was either in London or here but not... available. He paid no calls, extended no invitations." Carew gave an apologetic shrug. "He did not even attend church and make himself visible there. Some of the high sticklers disapprove of his manners. A few of the landowners grumble that he let the estate go to rack and ruin."

"That was not his fault!" Clare exclaimed. What had they expected he could do with every cent tied up in mortgages?

"Indeed. His predicament was... known. Yet it did not prevent him from observing the social niceties with men like Sir Harold Halcombe."

Clare could not argue with this, but neither would she acknowledge criticisms of her husband. Resolutely, she shifted the subject. "I thought I might invite the Palgrove children to visit," Clare tried. "And their mother, of course."

"Lord Trehearth must call on Sir Harold, Mr. Palgrove, and Mr. Fox before anything else. There's no way around that," Carew replied. "And I'm not sure the twins would make good playmates for Margaret Palgrove. Arthur, now..." He smiled. "That lad could be led into six kinds of mischief with no effort at all."

As if to underline this danger, a clatter erupted in the hall outside the solar, followed by a thud. Clare rose at once and went to find the source. In the corridor, Randolph stood over the youngest housemaid, a tiny girl who had barely learned her way about the big house. Clearly, he had just greeted her as he did Clare when she first arrived. The girl lay on the floor fending off slurps of the huge dog's tongue with both hands. Soapy water from a dropped bucket spread around them in a widening puddle. Clare turned back to the solar. "It's all right," she called. "A small mishap." Sympathetic as the vicar was, she didn't want him to see the still-chaotic state of her household. Moving closer to the scene of the melee, she grabbed Randolph's collar and yanked. "Off," she commanded.

He'd gotten to know her well enough by this time to obey. As Clare half dragged him toward the front door, she told the maid to fetch more rags and mop up the water. When the girl apologized, Clare shook her head. "It wasn't your fault, Maggie. His lordship has to do something about this dog."

In the solar, Selina took the hint in the tone of Clare's voice and sat on to keep Reverend Carew occupied. She also had a scheme in mind. "As you make your 'pastoral rounds,' you might pass along some items of news about *this* household."

Carew nodded as if to ask, What would you like me to say?

With that, Selina understood that Reverend Carew was offering to help the new residents of Trehearth get established in the neighborhood. He could do much to prepare the ground for cordial relations. Selina began to feel more in charity with the man. What should she tell him?

There was no harm in mentioning the near ruin of the estate, Selina thought. That was clear to everyone in the area already. The story of Clare's marriage, however, required careful editing. The gossips would require some plausible story; they would not get the full tale. In the end, she simply said that the two had met in London and been taken with each other. It was the truth. She'd seen it happen. Clare's significant inheritance from a great-uncle required no further explanation. And the details were no one's business.

Watching Mrs. Newton think and speak so carefully, Edward Carew admired the depth of her concern for her friends. He also couldn't help noticing how very attractive that care made her.

The talk might have been awkward, yet somehow it wasn't. In fact, Selina felt a fleeting sense of déjà vu, as if she'd sat with this man on many other occasions, relaxed and companionable. The feeling was so odd that she had to question. "You're being very kind about…" What was the word she wanted? "Cushioning the Trehearths' arrival in the area. Why?"

"Christian charity," Reverend Carew replied immediately.

When Selina raised her eyebrows, he smiled. It lit his blue eyes and gave his narrow face an exceedingly pleasant look.

"You do not believe in Christian charity?" he wondered, in response to her expression.

"Most assuredly I do. I try to practice it at every opportunity."

"There, you see. And I am a vicar." His tone was lightly teasing.

"So you are." Selina had to smile back. "One who likes harmony in his parish, I suspect. And does his best to discourage bad feelings and… casual malice."

Carew laughed. "You've caught me. I admit I'd rather preside over a wedding than settle a quarrel. I prefer celebration to mediation."

"Most understandable." Their gazes held in a moment of perfect amity.

"Are you a relation of Lady Trehearth's?"

Selina appreciated the delicate way of asking why she was here with a pair of young newlyweds. "No. Just a friend. She was moving a long way from home and wished for—"

"An anchor and a support," said Carew, before she could find the end of her sentence. "And I believe she chose well."

To her own surprise, Selina flushed. It had been many years since she received a compliment.

"But you have no family obligations of your own to call you away?" Carew wondered, finding he was very interested in the answer.

"No, I am a widow with no… obligations."

"Ah. I have lost a spouse. I know how very difficult it is."

Seeing a shadow of grief in his eyes, Selina did not say that in her case the difficulties had been almost entirely financial.

Carew rose to depart, and Selina stood. "Thank you for coming," she said.

"It was my pleasure," he answered. "I'm always grateful when my duty is so enjoyable."

His tone was level and sincere, not at all as if he were flirting. Of course he wasn't, Selina told herself. The idea was ridiculous. Where on earth had it come from? The vicar offered a small bow and went out.

Several minutes passed before Selina shook herself out of a brown study and returned to her work in the sewing room.

Twelve

RANDOLPH AND THE TWINS WERE OUT IN THE COURT-
yard when Jamie returned to the house around four
o'clock. The dog raced and leapt like a creature let
out of confinement, his buff fur pale against the gray
stone of the walls. Jamie nearly walked by them with
a simple nod. Then he remembered what Clare had
said about training the dog. It was ridiculous, of
course. The huge mutt was intractable. But she'd
made such a point of it. If it could be done… With
a sigh he changed direction and headed toward the
group. He saw his sisters brace for a scolding. Did
he never speak to them except to complain? That
couldn't be.

"We always play here," said Tamsyn before he
uttered a word.

"Randolph doesn't dig," Tegan added.

Jamie looked at the overgrown flowerbeds, the
weed-infested gravel of the drive. What harm could the
dog do in this wasteland? He needed to find a real gar-
dener, not just some village lads. "Nice spot," he lied.

The siblings eyed each other warily. Jamie searched

for words and finally settled on the stark truth: "Clare said you wanted to train the dog."

"He is trained," Tegan objected.

"He does what we want," Tamsyn agreed.

"Like knock people to the ground?"

For some reason, his sisters gaped at him. "How did you...?" Tamsyn poked Tegan with an elbow to cut her off, then they both quickly looked away. Long experience told Jamie that some new outrage had occurred, but he decided not to ask.

"That was a..." Tegan began, eyes fixed on the ground.

"A lapse, an accident? I hope you're not going to tell me that Randolph was doing what you wanted when he jumped on Clare?" Accusation had crept into his tone. He was so often called upon to correct them, Jamie told himself. He couldn't be blamed for the habits they'd created by their pranks.

"No!"

"He was just excited," Tegan supplied. "No one ever comes here."

"Came," corrected Tamsyn.

"Well, they do now. So Randolph will have to learn to behave." At this moment, the dog was rolling ecstatically in a drift of dead leaves. His wriggles scattered them onto the drive. Jamie hoped they weren't imbued with some enticing, disgusting smell.

"What if he doesn't?" Tegan glared up at him. "If you send him away, we'll go with him!"

An irritated reply rose to Jamie's lips. Just before it escaped, he felt a tugging at his coat and looked down into Tamsyn's dark eyes, so like his own. They pleaded with him. "How do you train a dog?" she asked.

Randolph rolled to his feet and shook himself, dry leaves flying. Spotting Jamie, he loped over, pink tongue lolling, and gathered himself for a flying leap. "No!" Jamie said. The sharp sound checked the dog momentarily. Jamie took the further precaution of stepping forward and grasping the loose fur at the back of his neck. Randolph gazed happily up at him. With his black nose and the dark diamond-shaped patches of fur around his eyes, the animal looked deceptively mournful. In fact, he was perhaps the least mournful creature Jamie had ever encountered. "You must let a dog know that you are his master," he said.

"We will *never* beat him," said Tegan fiercely.

She'd said that before, Jamie remembered. Did his sisters actually imagine that he would hit a dog? Randolph made a whuffing sound. Jamie risked releasing his grip. Randolph sat and looked up at him. That made three pairs of young eyes, fixed and waiting for him to make things right. "Of course not," said Jamie uneasily. "There is no question of that."

"So what do we *do*?" asked Tamsyn.

He marshaled his thoughts. It was only a dog after all. "Dogs want to please you. It is in their nature."

The twins glanced at each other. They seemed torn between liking the idea of being pleased and mistrusting the thought of such a pliant creature.

"You need a way to communicate clearly what you require of him," Jamie continued.

"We already communicate," said Tegan.

"He understands us when we speak to him, don't you, Randolph?" Tamsyn rubbed the dog's brown ears. His pink tongue slurped her face from chin to forehead, and she laughed.

"Then you are telling him the wrong things," responded Jamie automatically, even as he was wondering when he'd last heard one of his sisters laugh so freely. "If he is to join in polite society—"

"He doesn't want to be a member of polite society!" Tegan interrupted passionately. "He despises it! He hates all the stupid rules and the—"

"He wants to live in the house," Tamsyn interrupted, eyes on her twin. "With the new maids... and all."

Jamie watched as Tegan grappled with her temper. The battle was obvious in her snapping dark eyes, tight mouth, and clenched fists. He had to admire the way she pushed down her anger. He'd had no notion that the twins were capable of such self-control.

Randolph danced between them. Jamie set a hand on his back to still his capering. "Let's see what we can do. Randolph, sit!" He pushed the huge dog's hindquarters down to the earth, not an easy task. He had to squat to manage it. "Good dog! Well done," he said when Randolph was sitting. The dog sprang up, tail whipping, ready to lick any part of Jamie he could reach. Jamie gripped his jaws and held him still for a long moment. Then he repeated the whole process. "You must show him what you want him to do as you utter a command," Jamie explained. "Then he will associate the word with the action. Afterward, you praise him, so that he sees you are pleased by what he has done."

When he'd demonstrated the exercise several more

times, he had his sisters try. Surprisingly, they were able to push the huge dog down to sit. Randolph was actually beginning to get the point. After a few more repetitions, feeling that he'd done enough for now, and urging them to keep practicing, Jamie went indoors.

Clare greeted him in the hall, her smile enough to warm a man right through. "I saw you out the window," she said. "It... seemed to go well." Moved that he had done as she asked, and still full of last night, she had to move closer, to touch his arm. He at once pulled her close. The kiss they shared sizzled along their nerves like heat lightning.

Clare drew back first. "Someone may come in."

"And so?" But he let her go. In just a few hours, they'd be alone, upstairs. "I spoke to Jem Varryl. He knows all the livestock for miles around here. He thought he could put his hand on a pair of ponies for the twins." Jamie had also asked about a mount for Clare, but he was saving that as a surprise.

He hadn't forgotten! "That's wonderful," Clare said. "We won't mention it..."

"Until you make your bargains with them," Jamie finished. "I got the message."

"Will they be very costly?"

The question soured Jamie's mood slightly. The purchase of mounts was his realm, his decision. Clare had exhibited no particular knowledge of horseflesh. How would she even judge the wisdom of his choices if he presented the bills? Yes, he'd agreed on her right to ask, but it rankled. He said only, "Jem and I will get a good price."

"Of course you will." Clare smiled up at him again,

seeing only his agreement with her ideas on how to influence the twins. She was so very grateful for their perfect accord.

When Jamie knocked at her bedroom door that night and came in to her, it seemed more than natural. It was as if they'd always been together. As they touched and kissed and the passion rose between them, Jamie felt sure that his wife would soon see that she wanted nothing more than to rely on him. He wanted to take care of her; it was the way it should be. He was designed by nature to make the decisions, control their joint resources. She would realize it, feel it, just as she responded so eagerly to his caresses, rose to the peak of desire under his hands.

Falling toward glorious release, Clare reveled in the knowledge that she had a lover who was also a partner. She'd been so very fortunate in her choice. How many husbands could allow their wives the scope she'd required? But then, how many husbands were like hers? Few. None. He was... Clare lost all coherent thought in a blaze of delicious sensation.

The new cook arrived three days later, taking that responsibility from the shoulders of a very grateful Anna Pendennis. The rest of the household was soon equally thankful, because Branwyn Telmore was an artist in the kitchen. It changed from a utilitarian room where tasks were doggedly performed into a creative and bustling place full of luscious smells. They added a young kitchen maid to help her and receive training that would take her far.

The sewing room housed a similar center of happy industry. Several village women, eager for the extra earnings, trekked up each day to work under Selina's supervision on new draperies, cushion covers, and clothing for the female part of the household. Within two weeks, Trehearth had become a different place altogether, Jamie marveled. Windows sparkled; color gradually bloomed in the furnishings. He returned from busy days on the land to a place rapidly becoming a haven of beauty and serenity and comfort. Even the incorrigible Randolph had started to make progress. Once the twins understood the training method, they took it up with great enthusiasm and surprising patience. Jamie was astonished by their focused determination. But all of that was as nothing to his nights! His nights with Clare were all that he'd ever imagined passion could offer. In a miraculously short time, his life had completely changed.

She'd changed, Clare thought, as she gazed at her reflection in the cheval glass set up in the sewing room. At first she couldn't decide just what it was. Then she realized that she looked happy. It had been years since she saw anything but resignation and endurance in the mirror.

Selina, moving around her with a pincushion fastened over her wrist, making small adjustments to the gown Clare was modeling, thought how much better her friend appeared now that she had filled out a bit, lost that overthin, pinched reticence. It seemed her doubts about this marriage had been misplaced. "There," she said, pushing in a last pin. "What do you think?"

"It's wonderful." Clare gazed at the sweep of emerald silk, one of the indulgences she'd allowed herself at the drapers. Selina had fashioned it into a glorious gown, with a scooped neck, small puffed sleeves, and a long, sleek fall of skirt. The vivid color made her eyes seem both deeper and brighter. It was an evening dress to rival any she'd seen on fashionable guests at her former employers'. Clare turned, and the silk belled out with a soft whisper. "Oh, Selina, it's gorgeous. You're a marvel!"

"It did come out very well," the older woman acknowledged with satisfaction.

Clare had spied a small head peeking around the sewing room door. "Come in and tell me what you think... ah... Tamsyn." She'd spotted the identifying mole just in time. Clare had noticed that despite the games they might play with newcomers, the twins did not actually like being confused with one another.

Slowly, the girl came into the room. She reached out—Selina had to restrain herself from asking if the child's hands were clean—and brushed the silk with her fingertips. "It's beautiful," she said. The twins still insisted on breeches for daily wear, but Clare was confident that she could entice them, or wear them down, with the new garments Selina would produce. Tamsyn in particular had revealed a fondness for rich fabric.

Her confidence rose even higher that night when Jamie told her that his man had found two suitable ponies. "Sure-footed and gentle but not plodders," he said.

"Shall I come and see them?" Clare asked. "What sort of price shall we offer?"

Jamie stiffened. It hadn't occurred to him to take her to see the animals. The presence of a lady would have made all concerned in the transaction uncomfortable. "I bought them," he answered. "I thought you were eager to have mounts for my sisters."

His clipped tone startled Clare. He looked annoyed. Why? She started to ask him, but then an inner voice suggested that she knew very little about horses. She wouldn't have been able to judge their quality. "Of course. I am. Where are they now?"

"Still at their original stables. I understood that you did not wish them to be brought here until you had spoken to Tamsyn and Tegan." Jamie couldn't quite shake off the resentment her queries had roused.

"Exactly right."

Clare smiled up at him, and Jamie's irritation dissolved. She was so very beautiful. There were moments, such as this one, when he couldn't believe his luck in having made her his wife.

❧

The following afternoon the twins had fittings for some of their new dresses. Selina stood first one, then the other, on a small stool and walked around pinning in small alterations to the cut and fit. And first Tamsyn, then Tegan, wriggled and fidgeted through the session, the latter clearly teetering on the edge of rebellion. "You look so pretty in this primrose shade," Selina tried. The child glared at her as if this was an insult, as if fine new gowns were a burden to be borne. It was on the tip of Selina's tongue to tell them how much she would have loved to have such a dress at their age, but she wasn't entirely a fool.

"You do indeed," agreed Clare, who sat by the window, lending support for this ordeal.

"Who wants to be pretty?" Tegan retorted.

"What's the harm in it?" Clare said.

"Pretty girls are stupid ninnyhammers," was the quick reply. Tegan stared at her sister, demanding support for her position.

"They are bird-witted," agreed Tamsyn. But she didn't sound entirely convinced.

"And whining tattlers as well," said her sister. "Oww!"

"You must stand still until I finish pinning." She'd been rushing, Selina acknowledged silently. She was eager to complete this chore and get back to more pleasant sewing.

"Do you think I am a stupid ninnyhammer?" Clare asked, wondering just how the twins had formed their opinion of pretty girls.

Two pairs of dark, childish eyes narrowed and fixed on her, clearly wondering if there was some trick hidden in this question.

"Because I have been told I am pretty. Now and then." Jamie had said "beautiful." Clare's blood warmed at the memory.

The twins looked at each other, then back at Clare. She'd begun to think that she had at last brought them to a stand when Tegan intoned, "There are exceptions to every rule."

Clare bit back a laugh. *Should she feel complimented or thwarted?* she wondered.

"All right, that's done," said Selina. She had one

other gown pieced together for Tegan, but she wasn't going to fit it now. "Wait! Let me take it off," she added before the girl could pull out all the pins in her eagerness to shed the unwanted garment.

When Tegan had changed back into her boyish costume, and both twins were poised to bolt, Clare said, "I wanted to speak to you." They marched behind her to the solar with jutting jaws and burning eyes, clearly primed for a reprimand. Clare felt that she could read them rather well by this time, and she thought they were anticipating injustice. They had kept their part of the bargain, their expressions said, enduring the purgatory of dress fittings. Now they were going to be berated for the *way* they had done so. Had they ever promised to *like* it? Once again, Clare had to repress a smile. She could almost hear their indignant protests, and she so enjoyed upending their expectations.

In her sitting room, she settled herself on the old sofa. "Your brother has been making some purchases for the stables," she began. This got their attention. "We wondered if you would care to have a pair of ponies for your own use?"

The girls froze. They seemed to hold their breath. "Ponies?" whispered Tegan. Her face showed that she had longed for this so much, for so long, that she didn't dare believe.

"Of course, if you are not interested..." Clare couldn't resist teasing just a little.

"Yes!" exclaimed Tegan.

"We are," cried Tamsyn at the same instant.

"Splendid. We will get some mounts then for the two young ladies of Trehearth."

Tegan's dark eyes narrowed. "Ladies," Tamsyn repeated.

Clare smiled. The twins looked at each other, then went and sat down opposite her like canny traders in the market square. "I expect we will have many more visitors from now on," Clare continued. "Your brother has been calling at our neighbors' houses. We'll no doubt receive calls in return."

"*You* will," responded Tegan. Her sister kicked her ankle. "Ow!"

"The family will. And I think it would show a... commendable respect for others' sensibilities if you wore your lovely new dresses rather than your... old clothes."

"When there are callers," said Tamsyn.

"Well, yes, but we cannot always predict when people may call, can we?" Clare pointed out. "So it would be best to be prepared..."

"You want us to wear dresses *all day*?" burst from Tegan.

"I would like that to be your habitual clothing," Clare replied, voice firm. "When you are out on your ponies, of course..."

"I will *never* ride sidesaddle," Tegan declared, eyes flashing as if she would go to the stake over this issue.

"You may wear your breeches when you are riding in the countryside." It was Clare's big concession, though she doubted the twins would see it so. She hoped to gradually wean them into proper riding habits.

The girls looked into each other's eyes, communing in silent debate. The phrase "riding in the countryside" had obviously exerted an extraordinary pull. "All right," said Tamsyn finally.

"I have your word?" Clare waited until Tegan nodded as well. "And when you do go riding, you must always tell someone where you're going. And return at an agreed-upon time."

"What if something happens and we're late?" Tegan said. "Or if I... we forget about the dresses, make a mistake? Will you take the ponies away from us?"

In their faces Clare read a whole history of disappointments, of solitude, perhaps of mockery, of hopes continually dashed. She also thought she glimpsed a heartbreaking desire to trust, though she wasn't certain the twins were aware of it. Why was she bargaining with children? "No, I won't do that," she said.

The girls' dark eyes said they wanted to believe her. Obviously, they didn't quite dare.

"We might restrict your riding time, depending on the circumstances. You won't be blamed for things that are not your fault. But you will be expected to be responsible." Surely parents did it that way, Clare thought? And then she went stock-still on the sofa. Parents. She hadn't borne the twins, but she would be in the position of their mother for the next eight years, at least. It hadn't really hit her till now. She'd been thinking of them as a challenging task, a puzzle to be worked out—not as her children. But these weren't her charges as governess, to be cajoled and taught for a few years and then left behind—ultimately the responsibility of someone else. They were, for all intents and purposes, hers. The idea was frightening and oddly exciting at the same time.

The twins were looking at her strangely. "We would very much like to have ponies," said Tamsyn carefully.

Clare watched her make an effort to speak properly and sit very straight, as one of their late unlamented governesses must have nagged them to do.

"Yes, please," said Tegan. Aware of her sister, as always, she mimicked her posture.

"We will wear the dresses," said Tamsyn. "And we will be careful—"

"And take really good care of them!" Tegan broke in.

Clare smiled. "That's settled then. I believe the ponies will arrive tomorrow."

"You bought them already?"

Was this an admission of weakness? Clare wondered. She found she didn't care. "I thought I could count on you."

Tamsyn blinked as if startled.

"What…?" Tegan had to swallow before continuing. "What time will they come?"

"I'm not sure about that. I will have to ask your brother. It might not be till quite late in the day," Clare warned. Then and there, she vowed she would send John Pendennis to fetch the ponies if no one else was available.

Tegan nodded and stood up. Tamsyn rose beside her, then pulled at her sister's sleeve as Tegan turned to go. Tegan met her eyes. Together, they turned to Clare. "Thank you," they said in perfect unison.

"You're most welcome." She smiled again when she heard the girls' footsteps speed up into a run once they had passed through the doorway.

❧

Despite Clare's warning, the twins were up at six and haunting the stables by eight. They were wearing dresses, however—some of their old ones that wouldn't be harmed by a bit of dirt. They moved rather awkwardly in them and occasionally shook out their skirts as if they were irritants. But they didn't complain.

The ponies arrived at eleven, led by a countryman on a horse not much larger. They were handsome dark brown animals, Clare saw when she came out to look them over, equipped with their own tack. Even better, they didn't take exception to Randolph, a complication that had only occurred to Clare the previous evening, *after* she had promised them the mounts. In fact, they seemed to find the huge dog a source of cordial interest, though he nearly matched their height at the shoulder. They didn't shy as Randolph bounded around the stableyard with his pink tongue hanging out, even when he attempted to lick them.

The twins hovered over their new mounts, touched them as if they might be illusions. Each girl talked quietly to her pony as they bent their necks. They'd come prepared with some bits of apple in their pockets. Clare watched them as they fell in love. "Do they know how to ride?" she asked John Pendennis quietly.

The old man nodded. "I've seen 'em on horseback a time or two. They're naturals, they are. But Albert and I will see that they can keep their seats before they ride off anywhere." Albert, the new stableman, handled horses with genial expertise. Clare was content to leave matters in their hands.

When Jamie returned from inspecting the foundations for a new tenant cottage a bit later, he discovered his sisters back in their breeches, astride their new ponies, and in a state of mixed impatience and bliss. He could see that they were desperate to ride off immediately into the countryside. Before he put his foot in it by forbidding any premature expeditions, however, he became aware of the subtle cunning with which they were being manipulated. As the girls rode round and round one of the paddocks, getting accustomed to the new saddles and the ponies' gaits, Albert and John Pendennis talked, seemingly to each other, in clearly audible voices.

"A pony's got to trust you know what you're doing," John said.

"Aye," Albert agreed. Small and wiry, he was much younger than John, but he seemed to delight in taking on the manner of a codger. "They count on their riders and no mistake."

"Jerk on the reins and you can tear up their mouths right bad."

"Very delicate," Albert affirmed. Jamie watched his sisters ease their grip on the leathers.

"Take 'em too fast over a bad spot of ground, and they can step in a rabbit hole and break a leg," John Pendennis added.

His companion blew out a breath and shook his head. "Not much you can do when that happens."

"It's a sad, sad thing to have to put a horse down."

"Aye. It is that."

The horror on his sisters' faces told Jamie that there was nothing he need do here. His sisters were in capable hands. He went inside to find Clare. "I've finished my round of calls," he reported. "I stopped to see Graham Fox on my way south this morning." The visits to his neighbors, which he'd resisted as long as possible, had turned out to be less difficult than he'd feared. He'd found the nearby landowners open and ready to welcome him, if he intended now to become an active part of the neighborhood.

"Oh good. I had a card from Marianne Palgrove inviting Tamsyn and Tegan to a children's party next week. It's Margaret's birthday."

"Mar…?"

"The Palgroves' daughter."

"That pretty little girl at church?" Jamie winced. "Are you joking? The twins will make mincemeat of her."

"I don't think so. The arrival of their ponies has made a big difference. Thank you for finding them."

Her smile warmed his heart but didn't still his doubts. "Clare, my sisters will see a children's party as an irresistible invitation to pull a prank. Everyone will end up covered in mud from the mill pond or… worse." His mind boggled at the possibilities.

"I have some thoughts on that," replied Clare serenely. Or perhaps insanely, Jamie thought. "And I will be there," she added.

"Better you than me." Jamie shuddered. "On your head be it then."

"They have to learn to go about in society, Jamie."

He knew that was true; he just didn't believe it could happen, despite recent improvements. "You haven't had to explain to the mistress of an infant school that your little sisters do *not* have permission to keep a pet snake. Or retrieve their brand-new bonnets from the manure pile."

Clare couldn't help but laugh. "Surely *you* didn't…?"

"Who was I to ask to wade into the muck? John? Anna? Ruined my old buckskin breeches. The smell never came out. Yes, I can see how amusing that is."

"I'm sorry. I'm sure it was quite horrid."

"You have no notion."

"I think they will try harder now that they have their ponies to... deserve."

"I hope you're right." Jamie didn't want to think further about his sisters' low standard of behavior and how much of it might be his fault.

"I promise I will keep an eye on them."

She would, Jamie thought. And she had made great inroads already. It was a minor miracle. He wished he had something to give her in return, but he had not yet discovered a horse that matched his vision of a proper mount for his wife.

❧

"It went well, generally," Clare was able to report the following week. She and Jamie lay together in the tumbled sheets of her bed, bare skin painted by the firelight, senses sated by tumultuous lovemaking. Her whole body sang with the aftermath. Almost as pleasurable was the habit they'd begun to form of talking over the day as they drowsed toward sleep. "There was some difficulty when they were not allowed to ride their ponies to the party."

"Mutiny, you mean," murmured Jamie. He ran a fingertip along the curve of her shoulder and enjoyed seeing her shiver at his touch.

"Nearly," Clare admitted. "And I thought they were going to take even further against their new dresses because they cannot ride in them. But we found a compromise."

"They held you up for some concession," Jamie translated.

"I am not so easily outsmarted."

"Of course you are not." He let his fingers wander down her silken arm and back up. Perhaps he wasn't particularly sleepy after all.

Clare's breath caught. His touch never failed to enflame her. "We agreed that they could make an expedition to an old stone circle on their ponies and take a picnic lunch, if they did well at the party."

"Which stones?"

"The Merry Maidens."

Not too far then, a matter of two miles, perhaps. Still, he couldn't quite imagine loosing the mounted twins on the countryside on their own. "I'm not sure…"

"Ah," said Clare.

"Ah?" Jamie allowed his hand to rove over the curve of her breast, wanting to hear that syllable in a quite different tone.

He got his wish. "I'm… I'm going to arrange with the vicar to 'encounter' them there. To… umm… ohh… to see that they're all right. I chose a day when I know he often rambles." Clare knew this because Reverend Carew seemed very often to include Trehearth on his walks and end up talking to Selina in the solar.

"Devious." Jamie bent to let his lips follow the course of his fingertips.

"Indeed," Clare breathed.

He raised his head and gazed into her tiger eyes.

They were a bit blurred with arousal already. "I had no idea you could plot so twistily. I believe I must look... deeper into your... character."

"My... character is well worth explor—oh! Oh, Jamie!"

Thirteen

APRIL ARRIVED; FLOWERS BLOOMED IN THE CLEARED-
out garden beds, new plantings lending color to the
grounds around Trehearth. The furniture Clare had
ordered in Penzance arrived by ship, directly to the
cove in the village below, and new furnishings further
improved the feel of the house. Their neighbors
became more than just names as they were included
in the social life of the area. Comfortable in her transformed sitting room on a soft misty day, pouring tea
for a trio of callers, Clare marveled at the change in the
place. The combination of hard work and loving care
had made Trehearth a real home.

Selina and the vicar had their heads together across
the room. By now Clare was certain that her friend
was Reverend Carew's main object in his calls here.
The sight of them talking so easily together amused
and delighted her.

Elizabeth Fox, sitting next to Clare on the sofa,
accepted her cup with a smile. "How did you and
Jamie meet?" she asked. "Was it at a ball?" The older
woman sighed. "Graham and I first met at a ball. I

think dancing must be the most romantic way to begin a connection."

"We were... introduced by a mutual acquaintance," Clare replied. She met her husband's eyes across the room; they both smiled. Everett Billingsley was a mutual acquaintance, if not the sort their caller was no doubt visualizing.

"Astonishing," Graham Fox said to the twins. On the far side of the room, Randolph had sat on command beside the man's chair. And then he had held out a giant paw to be shaken. The dog looked from one guest to another, eyes bright, looking for applause. "You've done wonders with him. I'd have sworn it wasn't possible."

Jamie would have said the same about his sisters, but there they were, dressed in proper gowns, speaking quite civilly to the guests. The most amazing thing about it was their cheerfulness. They almost looked as if they were enjoying themselves. There were no scowls or attempts to slip out once they'd said the barest of hellos. There were no furtive glances to presage a disruptive prank. They looked... they looked like well-brought-up girls at ease in the midst of their family. Jamie turned to gaze at Clare. By some inexplicable magic, she'd made them a family in this short time. He'd married her to get the money to save his estate. And she'd shown him that Trehearth was far more than a stretch of acres and buildings.

Solemnly, Randolph offered a huge paw to Graham Fox for the third time. Amiably, the man shook it again, and Jamie joined in the group's appreciative laughter. What a clever choice he'd made, he thought.

Later, Jamie escorted the Foxes out to their carriage.

When he turned back to the front door, he found his sisters coming out of it.

"We're taking Randolph for a run," Tamsyn said.

"He gets tired of being on his best behavior," Tegan added.

Jamie imagined that the twins did, too. He was tired of chitchat and teacups himself. He felt a wave of kinship and affection for his sisters. "Shall I come along? We could go down the cliff path." They weren't supposed to go that way by themselves, though of course he knew they did. He shared their delight in the steep twists of it.

Tamsyn and Tegan smiled—identical, brilliant smiles that lit their dark eyes. "Yes!" they said at the same moment. Smiling back, Jamie set off with girls and dog for a good ramble.

❦

"I had a particular reason for coming today," said the vicar back in the solar. "I believe I have found someone who could do the work on your bathing room."

"Really?" Clare had talked about that plan at first and then let it slide into the background. There had been so much else to do, and Jamie was keeping the local craftsmen so busy. She had, however, ordered the large tin tub she'd visualized and drain piping on the expedition to Penzance, along with her new sofas and chairs. These materials were currently sitting in a dark corner of the stables.

"He's a skilled carpenter and all-round builder, and a pleasant young man. Also, he's quite intrigued with the innovations you suggest. A forward-looking lad."

"Why isn't he too busy then?" Clare wondered.

"He was working up in Penzance when he was taken ill and returned to his parents' house here to recover." Carew smiled. "Apparently, he's now smitten with a neighbor girl who helped with the nursing, and not eager to leave the village just yet."

"If you think he's up to it." What a pleasure it would be to have the bath in place, Clare thought, to be able to indulge in a thorough soak with so much less trouble.

"He can deal with drains?" Selina asked.

Reverend Carew nodded at her, his face softening in a way that confirmed all of Clare's surmises about his frequent calls. "So he says."

"Have him come and see me," Clare decided. "I'll show him what I have in mind and see what he thinks." And so it was arranged.

The vicar rose to go. Clare and Selina walked with him as far as the front door, where Clare said her farewells and continued on to the kitchen. Lingering in the entryway, Carew said, "I wondered if you would care to join me on a mission tomorrow?"

"A mission?" The term made Selina smile.

"I'm assigned to 'encounter' the twins during their expedition to the Merry Maidens and make sure all's well."

"Merry Maidens, is that a pub?" Selina couldn't imagine why Tamsyn and Tegan would be anywhere near a taproom.

Carew burst out laughing. "There's a vision of havoc. No, the Maidens are a circle of ancient stones, a matter of two miles from here. Perhaps a bit less. It's a pleasant walk." He awaited her answer with some trepidation, conscious that the invitation was a significant step. As vicar, he was subject to close scrutiny by his parishioners, or at least by a small prying group of them, and held to a very high standard of behavior. He couldn't be seen out with a woman unless he was sure. But in the last few weeks, as his acquaintance with Selina Newton grew through their talks, he had become so. "We would have a worthwhile purpose, you see."

"To make sure the twins don't get up to any mischief," said Selina slowly.

"Or in any trouble," he replied, with a diffidence that was new to him. It had been decades since he last went... courting. There was no other word for it. Her response would tell him how much of their cordial conversations had been simple politeness and how much something more.

Selina hesitated. It wasn't entirely proper to go walking alone with a gentleman, even a man of the cloth. She was of an age where it didn't matter so much, of course. But Selina could almost hear the sly whispers of some of her former employers—delightfully shocked, mockingly disappointed, deploring... oh, all sorts of things. Edward Carew certainly had parishioners who would raise their eyebrows at such an invitation, if not worse. And he certainly knew it. So he was asking... Selina's heart beat faster. She'd wondered whether he was really singling her out on his calls. He'd seemed quite attentive, but it was hard to be sure. Now she had her answer. If she chose to take a step beyond the bounds of the strictest propriety and routine, it might also be a step into a previously unimagined future. Was that so very difficult? Old habits and newly awakened desires fought a brief, fierce battle within her. A zest for adventure that she barely remembered rose up and wrestled the disapproving voices into silence. "Yes," she said. It came out loud, and Selina flushed. "That is, a walk sounds quite pleasant."

The warmth of her companion's smile burned away any lingering doubts. He took his leave with a promise to return for her early the following day.

Selina watched him walk toward the stables, his tall, thin figure limned by the afternoon light. When he was out of sight, she made her way to the sewing room. It was empty; her helpers had gone home to prepare their families' evening meal. Selina sat down to work on something simple, a long seam that allowed her fingers to be busy while her mind ranged far and wide.

When Clare came in half an hour later, she had to speak twice before Selina turned to her. "My father was a clergyman, you know," Selina said.

Clare blinked, startled. "I didn't know. You never mentioned it."

"Yes. My mother was a great help in his parish work. She enjoyed that very much."

"I'm sure she did." Clare examined her friend, noting the distance in her hazel eyes, the slight curve of her full lips.

"Life is a continual history of the unexpected," Selina said. "We may pretend it can be tamed through routine, but it can't. We don't have that power."

"Very true. I often marvel at the surprising changes in my own life these past months."

"Yet as unsettling as that can be, it is sometimes also wonderful."

Clare's puzzlement gave way to delighted surmise. "Do you have some news, Selina?" she asked.

The older woman started as if she'd been pinched. "What? News? No."

Despite her denials, Clare thought smugly that she soon would have.

❧

Reverend Carew returned soon after breakfast the next morning, and he and Selina set out together on a path that meandered across the countryside. It was a lovely day—sunny with just a few drifting clouds, a soft breeze that cooled without chilling. They were both fond of walking and moved at a compatible pace. The vicar carried a small knapsack and a serious hiker's stick. Selina wore a broad straw hat to shade her face and sturdy shoes below her muslin gown.

For the first few minutes they walked in silence, finding their strides, savoring the fresh air. Then Carew said, "Do you like Cornwall?" It sounded a bit abrupt to his own ears. Being alone with Selina Newton had turned out to be a mixed blessing. It was a relief to know that they could talk without reservation, but an uncharacteristic self-consciousness had descended upon him.

"I do," Selina replied. "It is wilder than the landscape where I grew up, but very beautiful."

"I find it so. I expect I shall spend the rest of my career in the church here." Which meant the rest of his life, most likely.

Was this a place where she could live permanently? Selina wondered. She'd never planned to remain. But that was before she met Edward Carew. "I can see why you would be glad to do so," she answered. "Have you no family to draw you elsewhere?" They'd had little opportunity to exchange intimate histories, with others always present during their conversations.

"I have one son and one daughter," the vicar said. "Both of them married well, before my wife died six years ago. Sarah lives in Hampshire. Robert helps his father-in-law manage his wife's inheritance in Kent. He complains of being under the man's thumb, but I think he's all right. They're both happy to visit here with their families in the summer, so I have the opportunity to see them. I have three grandchildren, all infants yet."

"I envy you that," Selina admitted. "Children were never granted me." There had been little opportunity, with her husband at sea for most of their marriage.

They walked awhile in silence. Birdsong and a sough of soft wind filled the air.

"It was another thing for my husband's mother to complain of," Selina found herself saying then. "She had a positive genius for complaint. I suppose that experience made my later posts more bearable. None of my other ladies was as bad."

"Still, it must have been difficult, catering to their whims and crochets," Carew said sympathetically.

"Sometimes... not generally. Of course there were moments of exasperation and... loneliness. But I liked feeling useful. And two of my... charges became good friends."

It was another way that they were kindred spirits, the vicar thought. Like him, Selina enjoyed helping people.

"But I admit it was a relief to gain some independence with the annuity Clare provided," she added, "and not to have to search for a new post."

This remark lay between them as they walked on. Edward Carew wondered if she meant she valued her independence too much to give it up. Selina was happy to have him know that she wasn't a penniless dependent, on the lookout for a more permanent source of support.

At midmorning they reached their goal, a circle of ancient gray stones in a grassy field. One or two had fallen, but most were upright, and they looked to have been carefully chosen for their shape and size. The inner faces and tops of the stones were flat and level, and they rose in size so that the tallest stones stood in the southwest quadrant of the circle. Selina walked among them. "Why is it called the Merry Maidens?" she wondered.

"Some talk of dancing maidens turned to stone for merrymaking on the Sabbath," replied Carew lightly. "The place is also called 'Dans Maen,' which is Cornish for, roughly, 'dancing stones.' Far too old to have anything to do with our Christian Sabbaths, of course."

"So what do you think it was?"

"A ritual spot, where people expressed their spiritual beliefs in their own way."

"You aren't bothered that it is a… pagan place?" Selina asked.

"Do you think I should be?"

Selina met his bright blue gaze. He always looked so engaged with whatever she said. Now, she knew he was sincerely interested in her opinion. Such attention had been rare in her life. She looked around the bright landscape. The place felt peaceful. "No. It was all so long ago."

"I think we can respect those who have a sincere faith that is not ours," he said. "Even if we don't agree with them."

Nodding, Selina realized that this was one of the things she most admired about him. He always treated others with respect, without ever compromising his own beliefs.

Carew's head came up. "Here come our charges," he said. "Be sure to act surprised."

Selina heard it then, the sound of hooves on the path. In another moment, Tamsyn and Tegan came into view, in their breeches again, riding easily on their ponies. She tried to assume a startled expression.

"Hello there," called Reverend Carew. "Well met. I was just showing Mrs. Newton the Merry Maidens."

The twins pulled up just outside the circle of stones. They looked at each other, then back at the vicar. Their faces indicated that they weren't fooled, and also that they were so happy to be out riding that they didn't much care about the supervision. "Look," said Tegan. She tapped her heels, and her pony trotted around the circle. "Isn't he wonderful? I call him Angwen." She pulled up beside her sister again. "That means 'handsome,'" she informed Selina.

Tamsyn leaned forward and patted her pony's neck. "Mine's Purdy, 'beautiful.' Because she is."

Feeling remarkably in charity with the world, Selina said, "You ride very well."

"We're 'naturals,'" said Tegan smugly. "Albert said so."

"Born to the saddle," added Tamsyn.

The phrase seemed to inspire them, and they set the ponies racing up one side of the field and down the other. Their sheer delight was a pleasure to watch.

Later, the group pooled their food and picnicked beside the stone circle. The vicar and girls talked about history, and Selina enjoyed listening. Though the twins were only children, he treated them respectfully, too, she thought. She found herself a bit surprised to be enjoying the girls' company in these circumstances.

All too soon, the sun had moved past the zenith, and it was time to go. The twins waved as they rode away. The older pair turned back to the path that had brought them. For a while, they walked in silence. Birds sang all about them; the breeze whispered in the long grass. At last Edward Carew cleared his throat. "Mrs. Newton. Selina. There is something I wish to say to you."

His serious tone slowed her steps.

"I don't know if you may… if you have observed…" He paused to gather himself. "Over these last weeks, as we have become better acquainted, I have developed a deep regard for you. I hoped you might… return that sentiment and… and consider becoming my wife." Before Selina could think of answering, he made an exasperated sound and said, "Could I sound more pompous? As if I didn't know how to express myself better…"

"It's all right." Her heart was pounding.

"It is not. You are an exceptional woman, with so many engaging qualities, I... Oh, blast."

"Perhaps you should let me speak?" Selina said.

He looked rueful. "I'm afraid to, for fear you'll tell me I'm an impertinent old fool."

"I had not thought to marry again," Selina began.

"Ah." The distressed look on his thin face and the disappointment in his voice made her hurry on. "Until I met you." Edward Carew stepped closer, hope in his eyes. "And came to care for you, as we talked together these weeks."

He took her hand, his blue eyes on hers. "Is... I beg your pardon... is that a yes?"

Selina looked up at him. He was just the slightest bit stooped, determinedly scholarly, so very earnest—and the most admirable man she'd ever met. She laughed. "I believe it is."

He moved closer still, near enough to slip his arms around her. "I love you."

"And I, you," she answered breathlessly.

The kiss was everything such embraces had never been in that long-ago marriage when Selina was a green girl.

"Oh!" she said sometime later. "You make my head spin."

Edward Carew drew back a little and gave her a delighted smile. "My dear, you could not have offered me a sweeter compliment."

"Goose." Selina reached up to straighten her hat, which had tilted over one ear. "This has all happened so fast. I hardly know where I am."

Carew tucked her hand into the crook of his arm and started walking again. "Well, we needn't hurry now that things are settled between us," he assured her. "Not that I wish to wait to be married. Not at all! But I would like to write my children before we announce it generally."

"Of course." Selina was conscious of a twinge of relief. She would have some time to adjust to this revolution in her circumstances. "Will they be... glad, do you think?"

"They will be cautiously pleased, I believe, until they meet you."

Selina tried, unsuccessfully, to pull her hand free. "Until...?"

"And then they will be awed by my incredible good luck."

"Oh, Edward." Selina pretended to hit him with her free hand.

"Say it again," he replied.

"What?"

"My name."

"Edward?"

"Ah, I look forward to hearing you say it, in every imaginable tone, for the rest of my life."

This sentiment naturally caused a short delay in their progress. Later, as they walked on arm in arm, they formed the very picture of amity and contentment.

Fourteen

THE YOUNG BUILDER CAME UP TO TREHEARTH HOUSE
the following day, and his comments on Clare's plans
were so intelligent and helpful that she engaged him
on the spot. He promised to begin work the very
next morning, bringing along two boys who were
interested in learning the building trade.

The trio arrived as promised, rucksacks of tools over
their shoulders. They cleared the small bedchamber
Clare had chosen for the bath and set to work.

Jamie discovered them there when he passed by
the room after breakfast, on his way out for the day.
He was startled, and then humiliated, by his ignorance
of their project. The young builder didn't appear to
notice, full of ideas on how best to add a drainpipe that
would take the water carried up from the kitchen out
and away from the house. He naturally assumed that
milady's husband had added his ideas to the plan and
approved it. Jamie went to look for Clare and found
her in the solar going over the household accounts.
"You hired builders without telling me," he said.

Clare held up a hand to show that she was totting

up a long column of numbers. When she was finished, she said, "It all happened so quickly, I forgot to mention it. Reverend Carew recommended—"

"Repairs and alteration to the estate are my responsibility," interrupted Jamie tightly.

At his tone, Clare abandoned her account book. "We had discussed adding a bath to the house."

"And I told you it had to wait."

"Yes, because your builder had more important work to do on the tenants' cottages. I understand that and agree it must come first. But I found a way to manage the project without taking any workers away from…"

"By engaging a complete stranger to work here in our home."

Clare could see that Jamie was angry, but she didn't understand why. "I told you, the vicar recommended him. And I spoke to him myself. He seems a…"

"Seems! And that is beside the point. You hired him behind my back, against my express wishes."

This seemed to Clare utterly unfair. "You said I could change whatever I wished in the house."

This perfectly true remark only added to Jamie's rage. The unexpected sight of the young workmen in his house had touched off all his objections to their financial situation. It also reminded him that he hadn't yet told Clare that the repair work on the estate was costing more than he'd estimated, and what he'd done about that. His resentment at having to beg for permission to cover his far-more-vital projects flared. "We had set aside a certain sum for renovation and repair. This was not included."

Was he simply worried about the cost? Clare wondered. "No. But it doesn't matter. His fee is quite reasonable, and I will cover it from…"

"When will you give up this ridiculous idea of controlling our money?" burst from Jamie. "You have a home now and more proper things to occupy your mind."

"What?" Clare couldn't believe she'd heard him correctly.

"You are a wife; you stand in the position of mother to my sisters. Surely it is time you acknowledged that the oversight of our accounts should be left to me."

"But… we made an agreement. You promised that the fortune I brought—"

Jamie's temper had overwhelmed his reason. The cause was trivial, but the pent-up ambivalence was not. "I did what I had to do in order to save my land," he snapped.

Under his scowl, Clare felt she didn't know him. He seemed a different man from the one she'd been learning to love over these last weeks. Had she been alone in that? She'd thought he felt the same, but now he was glaring like a stranger and claiming that their connection was all about her money. "You never meant it?" she whispered.

Warning bells went off in Jamie's mind. She looked stricken. He tried to backtrack. "I thought you would soon see that I am better qualified to manage business matters. As time passed and you… we—"

"You've just been waiting for me to hand the reins over to you?" Clare interrupted. "You thought I would do that?" She couldn't believe it.

Jamie tried to gentle his voice. "It's the way of things, Clare. Men are formed by nature for such tasks." The annoyance was still there; he couldn't quell it.

"So all this time you've been deceiving me? You had no intention of keeping your word?" Rising anger helped Clare cope with her crushing sense of betrayal.

"I assumed you would come to your senses, and it would not be necessary," he snapped back, stung.

In the dining room, Selina and the twins could hear them shouting, if not exactly what they were saying. Tamsyn and Tegan exchanged anxious glances. Selina was torn between her own uneasiness and doubt as to what she should do. Was it her place to interfere between husband and wife? She could not think so.

"My senses are perfectly clear," Clare responded, "and were when we made our agreement. The one you signed your name to."

"It is an idiotic agreement. The whole world expects that the head of the household—I—will have control of—"

"Well, you don't!" The years of being powerless, pushed this way and that by others' demands, treated as a servant, welled up in Clare, stronger even than the hurt and betrayal. "And you shan't. I will not change my mind, Jamie."

"If you could just be rational for one moment—"

"Rational is precisely what I am being!" Clare's voice had gone icy. "That is why I had documents prepared—which you had every opportunity to read and examine. If anyone here is irrational, it is you, expecting that I would make such careful preparations and then simply discard them."

Jamie felt he scarcely recognized this adamant woman who pinned him with her fierce tiger eyes. "You can't expect me to tolerate being overridden by my wife, letting all the world see me living under the cat's foot."

"When have I done that? When have I shown the least sign—?"

"You hired this fellow without consulting me, as if my wishes didn't matter." He was conscious that this wasn't a particularly strong point of argument. The discussion had somehow spiraled right out of his control.

"That isn't true."

"You did *not* hire him without consulting me?" It came out as a taunt.

"I had spoken to you about my wish for a bath. You agreed that it might be done."

In truth, he'd hardly paid attention when she mentioned it. He'd had so many more important things to think of. "I believe I said we had no time for fripperies," Jamie replied. "That is not quite the same thing."

Clare made an impatient gesture. This wasn't the heart of the matter. She hardly cared about the bath just now. The real issue went so much deeper. He'd given his word without meaning it. He'd promised things he never meant to deliver. *How could she trust him now?* she wondered. What else might he be hiding from her? She'd thought he was the companion and partner she'd longed for, dreamed of, but… he wasn't. The sound of hammering from upstairs accentuated the cause of the dispute. Should she tell the workmen to go? But that was not what she wanted. Why should she give up this simple pleasure? Clare couldn't think.

She was very much afraid she might give way to tears, which would be too humiliating to bear. She turned toward the door.

"Clare."

"Yes." She turned back. Perhaps he would say that he'd spoken too hastily, that he didn't mean it.

"Everything would be so much easier if you would just let me take care of you," Jamie said earnestly. He wanted to do that. He'd never wanted anything more. Couldn't she understand?

Clare stood rigid in the doorway. It sounded lovely—to be taken care of, to have no worries, to shift every burden onto someone else. But she knew from bitter experience that it was an illusion. The reasons to worry didn't go away. They were simply hidden from you until circumstances grew so dire that they had to come out, and life collapsed around you like a house of cards. She would never let that happen to her again. She'd thought that Jamie understood the feeling, the fear. She'd thought... imagined that he accepted her as intelligent and capable. But he hadn't accepted anything except her money. It hurt too much to talk any more.

Hurrying from the room, Clare encountered Selina hovering in the great hall. "Are you all right?" the older woman asked uncomfortably. "Is there anything I can do for you?"

"No." Selina had had doubts about the marriage scheme from the beginning. Now, Clare was ashamed to admit that her friend had been right, that Jamie had never really accepted her conditions. She rushed off, and then stood in the upstairs hallway wondering what to do. If she shut herself in her bedchamber, Selina might follow with more questions. Worse, the tears that threatened would overwhelm her there; she could feel it. Clare turned to the back stairs and descended to the kitchen to consult Mrs. Telmore, the cook, about the day's meals. After that, she moved on to other tasks, keeping her hands and her mind busy, shoving the conversation with Jamie out of her thoughts.

Jamie had to leave for an important appointment on the other side of the estate and had no opportunity to speak to Clare for the rest of that day. As he rode from place to place, he pondered his mistake. He'd let his resentment govern him and raised the topic of finances too soon. He would have to make amends, and then wait until she saw the truth of his arguments for herself. Eventually, she would. It was inevitable.

That night, when he put his hand on the knob to her bedroom door, he found it locked. So she was sulking, he concluded. Which just proved his point about her childishness. He definitely needed some scheme to placate her.

Clare, alone in her bed, choked on tears. This was far worse than the loneliness she'd felt as a governess. That had been impersonal, a matter of misfortune and position. It didn't strike to the heart like a hunter's bullet. She'd opened all of herself to Jamie. She'd trusted him and… and she'd fallen in love with him. Or… with the man she'd thought he was, the man who respected her wishes and valued her abilities, who understood and entered into her plans. Now the foundation of that love was crumbling beneath her. She couldn't bear it.

At breakfast the next morning the twins looked at Jamie and Clare with apprehensive eyes, and Selina sat stiffly, as if braced for a new storm. The couple pretended all was well, but Clare didn't think anyone was convinced. Dejected, weary from a nearly sleepless night, she left the dining room. Jamie followed her at once. "I was thinking you might make another visit to Penzance," he said. "I'm sure there are things you still want for the house." Realizing this might be dangerous territory, he quickly added, "You enjoyed yourself last time."

"Like a child's treat?" she responded.

"Well, you're acting like a child, which just proves my point." As soon as the words were out, Jamie wanted to bite his tongue. But her intransigent attitude, and the distance in her eyes, clawed at him. She was blowing up this minor incident out of all proportion. It was time to let it go.

"And what point is that?" asked Clare through gritted teeth.

He would not let this discussion go the way of yesterday, Jamie told himself. Yet he couldn't help resenting her obduracy. The whole world acknowledged that the male sex was better suited to understand business and finance. Women had other talents. Many admirable talents. Look at what Clare had accomplished in her brief time at Trehearth. Perhaps he hadn't made his respect and gratitude for that clear. He ought to compliment her more. "You've made a home here," he said. "The transformation is amazing. Trehearth is a different, and much pleasanter, place. Coming back to it every day is a wonder to me."

"With the new draperies and furniture, and the staff to cook and clean for you," Clare replied in a toneless voice.

"Exactly. And I know you've enjoyed doing it. Anyone could see that." Perhaps this was the key. If he took her step by step through his reasoning, she would agree with him. He'd already acknowledged that he'd been going too fast.

Clare looked around the spotless hallway, noted the colorful carpet runner. She had enjoyed it, and she knew she'd done a good job. Didn't this prove that she was a canny, skillful manager?

"This is your realm." Jamie gestured at their surroundings.

"Queen of the household," Clare replied. Jamie nodded and smiled, clearly missing the irony in her tone. She'd thought they were growing so close; actually, she hadn't had any idea what was going on in his mind. She'd been deluded, and now he was humoring her as if she were the twins' age. Younger! Tamsyn and Tegan would never have been taken in by this drivel. Abruptly, Clare felt invisible once again—not by her own choice this time, but because her husband saw only what he wished to see when he looked at her.

"Absolute monarch." Jamie smiled at her, confident that she was beginning to understand. They were not quite there; he could see that. But they were moving toward harmony.

Clare just gazed at him, realizing the full enormity of their misunderstanding. He actually believed that their detailed, written agreement was a whim she would get over. And she couldn't make him see that this view was insulting and misguided. It was pointless to try. "Perhaps I will go to Penzance," Clare said.

"Splendid." Relieved that she'd finally seen the futility of going round and round on a matter that would eventually resolve itself, Jamie took her hand. "You deserve some amusement after all your hard work," he said, dropping a kiss on her fingers. The journey would settle her down, he thought. And then all would be well between them again.

Clare and Selina traveled up to Penzance the following day, in the same hired carriage as before. Selina found her young friend's silence on the journey worrisome. Clare hadn't even noticed the twins' hopeful expression when the expedition was mentioned at dinner. That was not like her at all. But when she tried to probe, Clare brushed her inquiries aside. Selina was not one to force a confidence, but the younger woman's dire mood threw a pall over their expedition.

They took a room at the same inn and walked about the town looking into the shops. As the afternoon waned, Clare decided to visit the offices of her banker, and they parted ways. Selina dropped in at the draper's to see if he had any new stock on hand. There was a length of drapery material that drew her, and for a while she indulged in a pleasant daydream about how she would make the vicarage an even more inviting home.

When Selina returned to the inn, she found Clare pacing their room like a caged leopard. "Jamie has been corresponding with *my* banker," she declared, the skirts of her gown swishing like a big cat's tail. "He authorized a draft for a sum much larger than the one we agreed upon for repairs to the estate."

Her pale green eyes flashed. Selina had never seen her so angry.

"He also informed them that he would be taking over administration of the account as soon as 'some details were settled.' And of course the banker accepted this, because everyone knows that husbands control their wives' money. When I told him that was not the case with us, he… he acted as if I were a simpleton!" The pompous little man had been sickeningly patronizing. She'd nearly throttled him. "He practically patted me on the head and told me to run along."

Selina didn't know what to say.

"If Jamie had shown me what was needed, I would have agreed to the larger expenditure," Clare almost wailed. "It was no great matter. Except it *is*. He went behind my back. He broke his promise to me!"

The emotion vibrating in her voice shook Selina. She didn't know how to deal with such intensity. "Perhaps he was aware that you would agree and simply didn't want to bother…"

Clare was too furious to listen and too frightened to think. "Any man I speak to will see it just the same way," she said, half to herself. "I can claim whatever I wish about my special situation; they will simply not hear me. Because they will think Jamie must be right. That is the way things are." She had to do something. She remembered this desperate feeling all too well; it was the same that had swept her when her brother died and her family disintegrated. "I need to speak to Mr. Billingsley. We will go up to London."

"But, Clare…" It was a long, hard journey, for which they were completely unprepared, and this was not a time when Selina wished to undertake it.

"I must see what else can be done. I can't go about waving documents in people's faces and insisting on my rights. They'll think me mad."

Selina thought her worrisomely overwrought right now. "Clare, what has happened between you and your husband? Please tell me. You didn't know about this correspondence until we came here?"

"Of course I didn't!" She would have… Clare didn't know what she would have done. Broken something?

"So it wasn't the cause of your dispute the other night?"

"No." She bit off the word.

Selina waited. One thing she'd learned very well in her years as a lady's companion was not to put herself in the middle of family disputes. It helped no one and brought all parties down upon your head when the conflicts were resolved. It got you dismissed, if bad enough. Not that she had to worry about that any longer.

"He never meant it," Clare said finally. "When he signed the documents before our marriage. All along, he expected… he expects that I will change my mind and hand over all financial decisions to him."

"Oh." It was the way of society. Actually, Selina could see how he might make that assumption.

The single-word response didn't satisfy Clare. "He promised me! He gave his word without meaning it. How can I ever trust him again?"

Though Selina had had some doubts about the

marriage at first, she'd thought it was going well. She'd even come to like young Lord Trehearth. "Clare, do you really think your husband would oppress you, do things with your money that you don't like?"

"Are you siding with him?" Clare felt beleaguered. "I can't believe you would do that!"

"I'm not. Definitely not. I simply mean that you don't have to fear him as a... a domestic tyrant."

"I don't! Because I'm not giving up control of my fortune. I shall see Mr. Billingsley in London and put further guarantees in place."

"It's such a long journey. Perhaps a letter would do?"

Clare's jaw hardened. "I'm going. Will you come with me, or shall I go alone?"

Selina subsided. She did not wish to go. But it was not the act of a friend to send Clare off alone in her current state. Or to use her own good news to cry off. "I'll come with you." Once she said it, Selina realized how impossible it would have been to return to Trehearth on her own and face the swarm of questions that would ensue.

"Good. That's settled then." Clare stifled doubts. "You never planned to live in Cornwall forever. I'm sure you'll enjoy being back in London. The season is beginning. I never had a season. We could go out to... the theater."

With Clare so distraught, almost babbling, Selina merely nodded.

"We can see all the latest fashions," Clare went on. "You'll like that." She tried to find some enthusiasm in herself for the trip, and discovered only desolation.

Selina was a little tempted. She could dazzle Edward in a new gown at her wedding. "Very true. A short visit then."

"I'll ask about hiring a post chaise." Clare started toward the door.

"But… do you mean to just leave right now? With no warning?" Despite all that had transpired in the last few months, she was not yet inured to sudden changes, Selina acknowledged.

"I shall send a note." She didn't want to face Jamie. It was cowardice, Clare admitted, and told herself she didn't care.

"But we have no luggage…"

"We will buy new gowns in London, and whatever else we need. I have the authority to do that! I only wish we didn't have to stay at a hotel." But hiring a house was a step further than Clare wished to go.

Clare was immune to argument just now, Selina saw. She would make this ill-advised trip no matter what anyone said. Selina frowned and tried to gather her own scattered thoughts. She had said she would go; she should try to help. "Ah, my last employer's niece offered me a place to stay in town whenever I liked. We became good friends as I cared for her aunt."

"Would she have me as well, do you think?" Clare was feeling ruthless. She would impose on a stranger. She would do whatever she had to do.

"She'll be happy to have the company," Selina replied, certain it was true, though still full of conflicting feelings. "She's a widow with no children, and I think a bit lonely." Martha Howland might have sensible advice for Clare, Selina thought. No one was better attuned to the ins and outs of society. She might even know of other cases like Clare's and what was best to be done. The idea of another woman's support in these circumstances was appealing. "She goes about in society a good deal. She often urged me to join her at an evening party."

Aching to do something, to take control, Clare opened the door. "We'll leave tomorrow morning," she said, and strode out.

Selina sat on, wondering if she'd made the right decision. Clare appeared absolutely determined to make this journey. And however Selina framed matters, she could not see sending the younger woman off alone in her current emotional state. They would set off, and Clare would calm down, and surely the visit would not be long. With a sigh, Selina rose and went to find paper and pen to write a letter to Edward Carew.

⊷

When Jamie received his wife's brief note the following afternoon, he sat staring at the scribbled lines for several stunned moments. She had set off to London without even consulting him? This was not a year when they could go up to town for the season. There was far too much work to do. Another time, it might be possible, but... She was taking her revenge for his perfectly rational rebukes, he realized. Just as he'd said, she was behaving like a child—running away from home, showing him she could use their money however she liked. It was like one of the twins sticking out her tongue at him, daring him to react.

Well, he wouldn't. No doubt she expected him to

come pelting after her and beg her to return. In short, to grovel. He might just be able to catch a post chaise if he rode hard, but he didn't intend to enact such a scene on a public road. He had important things to do here, work that couldn't wait. If his wife chose to abandon her responsibilities—let her! He would not. And when she found that she got no reaction whatsoever from him, she would change her tune. Jamie crushed the sheet of notepaper in his fist and threw it into the fire.

"Where is Clare?" asked Tamsyn at breakfast the next morning.

"Why has she not come back?" wondered Tegan.

"What is she buying in Penzance to take so long?"

"Do you think it's a carriage?" Tegan suggested. "The wheel fell off the old one."

"Or something for the new bath?"

"It must be a surprise."

"Do you think it's for *us*?" Tamsyn said.

They both turned to Jamie, speaking in unison. "When will she be back?"

"Can you be quiet!" Silence fell at once. His feelings too lacerated to be careful, Jamie told them the bare truth. "She's gone to London. I don't know how long she intends to stay there." This statement, or perhaps the clenched teeth through which he made it, stopped his sisters' flow of conversation dead. They gazed at him with wide dark eyes, and it seemed to Jamie that he saw blame there.

"Oh," said Tamsyn finally.

"She won't come back," said Tegan.

"Or only to visit."

"Everyone likes London better."

Their glum assessment infuriated him further. "If you are referring to the governesses you chased away with your pranks, this is an entirely different case." Two woeful little faces stared back at him. "And I cannot conceive why you did chase them away, if you wanted them to stay."

"We don't mean *governesses*," said Tegan. They gave him the "you don't understand" look that he'd been familiar with for several years now.

"If you're referring to me, I always came back, didn't I? And, I might point out, I'm here now."

They surveyed him with the large solemn eyes of martyrs. "Now," said Tamsyn.

"For what that's worth," muttered her sister.

"I beg your pardon? Where did you even learn that expression?" Jamie held on to his self-control by a thread. "It's quite impertinent, you know."

The twins nodded in unison, which was always a bit unsettling.

Jamie rose to leave the table. "We will be perfectly fine until Clare returns."

"She won't—" began Tegan.

"As she most certainly will, quite soon." Of course she would, he assured himself. "I know Clare and Mrs. Newton set a course of study for you. Go on to your books."

"But who will correct our work?" Tamsyn wondered.

"I shall," answered Jamie, and realized that his jaw was clenched again.

"You?"

Their surprise was insulting, and then, blessedly,

amusing. "I went to school, you know. Quite a good school. I can even parse Latin, and a bit of Greek. Or I could, once upon a time."

"You're not going to make us learn Greek?"

He had to smile at their obvious horror. "Not if you behave yourselves."

His sisters headed for the dining room door. Then Tegan turned back. "Do we get to keep our ponies?"

"Of course, why wouldn't you?"

"*She* got them for us."

Oddly hurt that they seemed to think more of Clare than their own brother, Jamie said, "As a matter of fact, I found them and purchased them."

"But they're ours now?" Tamsyn asked.

"Forever?" Tegan added.

"Yes." It came out curt. And then the twins were gone, and Jamie was left alone with his cooling cup of tea. The room felt curiously forlorn. He shoved back his chair and headed out to the stables. He had important projects to oversee, workmen to advise. He couldn't waste any more time on domestic upheavals. Jamie was mounted and ready to go when he hesitated, then went back inside to fill his silver flask with brandy from the bottle in the estate office.

Fifteen

THE TRIP BETWEEN CORNWALL AND LONDON WAS NOT much easier in April than it had been in January. The air was warmer, and they had less need of hot bricks and layers of blankets, but the road was deeper in mud. Several times the coach bogged down and had to be heaved out by the driver, postilions, and helpers they fetched from a nearby farmstead. Tiring days in the carriage were followed by restless nights in posting houses, and Clare's dark mood made conversation sporadic and stilted. Both women reached the metropolis very ready to be still and sleep. They took rooms in Mivart's Hotel, where Clare had stayed before, then Selina went to call on her former employer's niece, Martha Howland. Weary as she was, Clare sat down at once to write a letter to the twins. She'd promised herself, when she made the decision to leave, that she would send them frequent reassurances. Then she made her way to Everett Billingsley's offices.

He looked just the same and greeted her very cordially. "This is a pleasant surprise," he said. "I didn't realize you were coming up to town." She looked vastly better, he thought. Her figure had filled out and rounded; her cheeks had bloomed. Despite some tension in her expression, she seemed quite a different person from the wan, self-effacing governess he'd encountered a few months ago.

"Yes, Selina and I have come."

"Lord Trehearth is not with you?" That was a bit odd.

"No. It was a… a spur-of-the-moment journey. There are some things I wished to take care of."

"Yes?" He looked alertly ready to help.

Now that she was here, Clare wasn't sure just how to put her case. What if Billingsley agreed with Jamie? The man of business had known him far longer than he'd been acquainted with Clare. They might have plotted the whole thing between them. Billingsley's earnest gaze and expression said otherwise, but… she remembered that he had urged her to hire her own representative during their negotiations. Surely he would not have suggested that if he was plotting against her? "Most people expect that my husband has control of my fortune," she began slowly, "because that is the usual way of it." Billingsley nodded, and Clare suppressed a tremor of unease. "So, if they are told that is the case, they see no reason to doubt the assertion. Why would they?"

"Ah?" He said it more cautiously. Clearly, something was wrong.

"I can tell them the true situation, but some… many may find me unconvincing."

"Has some problem arisen, Lady Trehearth?"

"I wondered… what is my recourse in that event?"

Billingsley frowned, uncertain what she meant. "If someone refuses to believe you, you mean?" He shrugged. "Well, you cannot compel belief."

"But if they refuse to act as I wish? About some financial matter."

He frowned. "I know the truth, and your bankers. So you could apply to us, and anything you want done should be easily accomp—"

Clare's heart was in her throat. "What if Jamie, Lord Trehearth, came to you and said that I'd changed my mind? That I had settled down to be a proper wife and wished to leave all the financial decisions to him? What would you do?"

Billingsley heard the tension in her voice; she was vibrating with it. "I would verify the change with you, and then alter the papers, before asking you both to sign new marriage settlements."

"You wouldn't just take his word, because that is the way things ought to be? And you have always thought so."

"No, I would not," said Billingsley firmly. "And even if I did, it would not alter the legal arrangement set forth in the documents. That cannot be changed without your signature. Please tell me what's wrong. Have you encountered a problem that I can help you with?"

It was what she'd come for. Clare found herself reluctant to reveal the cracks in her marriage, but she needed an ally. "Jamie told the banker's representative in Penzance that control would pass to him as soon as some 'details' were settled. Which is quite untrue, as you know. The man accepted this assertion without question and gave him a sizable draft on the account, without my knowledge."

"Ah." Billingsley's heart sank. He'd thought the match he'd promoted was such a splendid solution for both parties.

"When I expressed surprise that he had done so, and pointed out that he was required to consult me, this banker treated me like a willful child, or a simpleton, as if monetary questions were quite above my head." Clare grew furious all over again when she remembered the man's patronizing manner.

"Perhaps it was a misunderstanding? Lord Trehearth—"

"Has told me that he expects I will soon turn into a proper wife and hand the reins over to him. He always expected that, even when he was signing the documents you prepared. He said so." Clare gazed at the older man. She didn't precisely blame him. On the other hand, Jamie had been his suggestion. Clare had trusted his judgment, along with her own. She'd been wrong, but Billingsley had known Jamie far longer.

Billingsley felt the full weight of her regard. "I'm surprised at that."

"Are you?"

"I am indeed." His young client had seemed satisfied with the arrangement. And Billingsley knew him as a man of his word.

"What if it was your wife and her money?" Clare was moved to ask.

"I beg your pardon?" His wife had no money to speak of. He supported his family.

"If she had a fortune and asked of you what I

required of Jamie?" She had to test him, had to know if he was really on her side.

Billingsley simply couldn't imagine such a circumstance. His placid Emily speaking with bankers and choosing investments? It was inconceivable. Why, she wouldn't have the first idea how to conduct such a conversation. But this was beside the point. "If I sign a document, I keep to the letter and the spirit of the agreement. I do not sign papers that I mean to circumvent or ignore." It distressed him that young Lord Trehearth might have done so. Perhaps Lady Trehearth had misunderstood?

This was the crux of it, Clare thought. Jamie had broken his word. Worse, he'd never meant to keep it. He'd signed the documents deceptively, like a child crossing his fingers behind his back. Clare couldn't change the law or the opinions of the majority of men, but she'd thought she found someone who could be trusted. She hadn't. The fact went through her like a knife.

"Perhaps you are mistaken," the man of business tried. "Might you have misinterpreted some casual remark...?"

"Jamie was quite clear. He assumed I would change, and that made our... arrangement all right for him."

Billingsley looked at the papers on his desk. He'd seen families wreck themselves over money, and it was always dreadful. "I can write this bank representative a letter correcting his misapprehension," he said heavily. He hated the thought of getting between husband and wife. It had been a mistake, representing them both. His first impulse had been right. He ought to have refused to act until Clare found her own advocate.

Clare nodded. "But if Jamie speaks to others in the same way, what can I do? What actions can I take to prevent him?"

"I… I suppose I can give you a general letter, setting out the circumstances…"

"So I am reduced to proving my case over and over? Pulling out documents like a demented petitioner? Waving them under people's noses as they back away from me?"

"That is an exaggeration…"

It wasn't much of one, Clare thought. The world saw what it wanted to see, and a married woman in charge of her own fortune was not among the accepted versions of reality. "And if it doesn't work? If I am still treated like a child? Is there no way to make him stop?" Some part of Clare was aware that one small incident had been blown all out of proportion in her mind. But she couldn't seem to let it go.

"You could take Lord Trehearth to law," Billingsley said with great reluctance.

"Go to court?"

He nodded. "But it would take a long time and be very expensive. Fortunes have been exhausted in the toils of the chancery court. And…"

"I might lose," Clare finished, reading his expression.

"Court cases are chancy things. And, I must say, you have as yet no real cause for complaint. You have not been materially harmed. One reported conversation…"

She waved this aside. She had no intention of exposing her personal life to strangers in a courtroom.

As she'd expected, she would have to find a way to solve this herself. She had gotten what she came for, confirmation that Billingsley remained reliable. "You will verify the arrangement to anyone I send to you?" she asked.

"Of course."

"Splendid." Clare rose to go. "That is all I need at present."

The desolate look on her face made Billingsley wonder if he should write to Lord Trehearth. But what would he say?

⁓

Selina was having a more pleasant visit at Martha Howland's London mansion. Martha had always been cordial while Selina was living with her aged aunt, treating Selina more like a friend than an employee. She was even more so at this social call. Stout, rouged, and dressed in the height of fashion, Martha had a round face creased more by smiles than any other expression. Her gray hair was crimped *à la mode* and covered with a wisp of lace. She made up for a lack of family with a keen interest in the doings of her friends. "You are in town with a new employer?" she asked Selina.

"No, with a young friend. I have... come into a competence and have no need for employment any longer." At Trehearth, this change in her circumstances hadn't really sunk in. Now that she was in London again, Selina felt the full force of her financial freedom. She could order that gown to dazzle Edward. She could procure tickets to a play without an agony of careful calculation and the guilty sense that she should add the amount to her savings rather than squandering it on a night's entertainment.

"Congratulations, my dear. That's wonderful."

"My friend, Lady Trehearth, is… ah… making a short stay in town. She had some business here, and she's… umm… interested in experiencing a bit of the season. Without taking the trouble of renting a place and setting up a household, you know."

Martha's expression showed that she got the unspoken implication immediately. Selina was dangling for an invitation to stay. "Trehearth? I don't know the name. A respectable family, of course?"

"A fine estate in Cornwall." It would be, Selina told herself, with all the repairs made. "Quite an ancient barony, I believe. And a comfortable fortune."

"The husband?" Martha's arched brows rose.

"Occupied with improving his land."

"One of those new agriculturists, I suppose." Martha Howland grimaced. "What they can find to interest them in mud and turnips, I cannot conceive. Poor dear. Bring her to stay with me."

"I admit I was hoping…"

"I know." Martha gave her a sly smile. "It's a capital idea. I have nothing but empty bedchambers in this old pile."

Her "old pile" was a large house near Grosvenor Square. Since she'd inherited her aunt's fortune, Martha Howland must be richer than ever. Selina suspected she was one of the richest women in the *haut ton*. "Thank you. You're very kind."

Her hostess waved this aside. "It will be a favor to me. The season is always much more interesting with a newcomer to introduce. I've had too many seasons myself. Gotten old and jaded." She loosed one of her rolling laughs. "Where is your friend now? You should have brought her to call."

"She had an appointment."

"Well, bring her by tomorrow. In fact, go ahead and have your things sent over. Where are you staying?"

"Mivart's Hotel. Surely you wish to meet her first?"

"I trust your judgment completely, my dear Selina. Consider the matter settled." Martha Howland leaned back in her comfortable armchair and settled in for a good gossip. "Tell me all about her."

This was a game that Selina knew well. She'd observed it a thousand times, as she attended a series of old women and watched them chat with their callers. A vast, and vastly efficient, network of gossip underlay society, and much of it was informative rather than malicious. It allowed shortcuts, and wordless alignments of rivals and coalitions. It offered opportunities, like the one she now had to describe Clare and establish her friend's history as she wanted it to be known. Much as she liked Martha, Selina never forgot that she was speaking for public consumption, to position Clare in an intricate hierarchy of alliances. "Clare, Lady Trehearth, was married in January and has been down in Cornwall since then."

"Oh my, no wonder she wants a bit of gaiety."

Selina let this idea stand. "As I said, Lord Trehearth has a great deal to do on the estate. It had fallen somewhat into disrepair, you see…"

"And the gel had money," finished Martha shrewdly. Selina nodded.

"I wonder I haven't heard of her. Heiresses always create a stir. What was her name before she married?"

"Clare Greenough. She received an unexpected legacy from a great-uncle. She'd been working as a governess for several years before that." There was no sense trying to hide this. Clare had been working in London, and someone would winkle it out. Better to tell the story herself and remove any whiff of secrecy or hint of shame.

"Greenough," Martha mused. "Lincolnshire family?"

"I believe so."

"Hah. I've heard the name. And this Trehearth fellow snatched her up before anyone else got a chance at her fortune? How'd he manage that?"

"Ah… they were introduced by a mutual friend." Selina had heard Clare put it that way.

"A friend indeed. Unhappy match?" Martha was looking at her with uncomfortably canny blue eyes.

"No, it seems to be going well." And so it had, right up to the last day or so. "But he is deeply involved in setting his estate to rights."

"With her money."

"Umm."

"And your young friend wants a bit more out of life than crops and acres? As what gel wouldn't?"

This was the conclusion Selina had been aiming for, a story anyone in the *ton* would easily accept. No undercurrents, no complications. She nodded again, added a conspiratorial smile. When Martha matched it, Selina felt she'd slotted Clare into a safe social haven. There shouldn't be many uncomfortable questions after Martha had spread these facts about.

"Well, I'm just the person to show her that there *is* more—a vast deal more." Martha practically rubbed her hands together. "I don't suppose she's pretty?"

"Quite pretty."

"Oh, splendid. This will be great fun!"

Belatedly, Selina recalled Martha's weakness for... social manipulation, she supposed you would call it. Mainly it was matchmaking, which couldn't apply here. But her little... schemes extended into other areas as well. They'd always been so amusing to hear about—when Selina hadn't been acquainted with anyone she mentioned. "There must be no nefarious plots," she said, adopting a teasing tone.

"La, what a word. I have no idea what you mean."

"Clare hasn't gone about much in society. She will need guidance, not... a push. She doesn't mean to make a big splash. I thought just an evening party or two..." Enough to divert her young friend's mind from her troubles, cheer her up.

"My dear! You know you can trust me."

She could trust Martha to enjoy herself, to be generous with her hospitality, and to know the intricacies of London society down to the least detail. But could she trust her to give Clare good advice? Selina knew she couldn't draw back now without causing serious offense. She would simply have to supply the advice herself, she thought uneasily.

Returning to their hotel, Selina was assailed by regrets. She'd spent most of her life working to make certain other people were comfortable and content. Now, just when she'd begun to slough off that responsibility, here she was, thrown back into the role of caretaker. No one else knew how much she'd left behind in Cornwall. Clare would be mortified if she found out, and insist she return. But Selina didn't see how she could go back to Trehearth House as things stood. Besides, only a heartless creature would leave Clare alone among strangers in her despondent state. With a sigh, Selina concluded that she had one last term of duty before she broke free.

⚜

Clare, meeting her new hostess the following day, was surprised to find herself being carefully surveyed through a jeweled lorgnette. "Oh my goodness," Martha Howland said. "You'll be all the rage. A young married lady as lovely as you."

"You're very kind, Mrs. Howland."

"Call me Martha, dear. And I shall call you Clare, for I know we are going to be such great friends."

"Thank you… Martha." It felt awkward addressing a new acquaintance in this familiar way, particularly a much older woman. But how could she object?

Her hostess's eyes sparkled with plans. "We'll take my barouche to the park this very afternoon. Whet the *ton*'s curiosity, you see. Get them talking."

Clare felt as if she'd stepped into a rushing stream and was about to be carried off by the current. "I haven't brought many clothes," she said. In fact, her meager luggage contained only one other gown, packed in case of mishaps on her day trip to Penzance. And both dresses had endured a long coach drive. "I'm sure I have no proper things to wear."

Martha brushed this aside. "Easily remedied. My

dear Selina, how can I repay you for bringing me this diversion? I declare, I haven't looked forward to a season this much in ten years."

Martha Howland was like a force of nature, Clare thought over the next few days, as she was pulled into a whirl of shopping and morning calls and outings. The older woman never seemed to have the least hesitation about what should be done or how. She appeared determined to offer Clare up to society like a newly wrapped gift, and Clare was at once anxious and relieved to put herself into someone else's hands and think about matters other than the state of her marriage.

&

At Trehearth, the April days passed. The staff continued to put good meals on the table and keep the house neat and clean. The new furniture and hangings were just as colorful and comfortable. But Jamie felt that a vital spark had gone out of the place. Despite all the changes for the better, it seemed hollow and empty. Perhaps it was Clare's abandoned bedchamber, he thought, as he stood there one night and looked around. Her most personal items were gone—the hairbrush that always roused such vivid memories in him, the small litter of bottles, and her reticule. But she'd left clothes in the wardrobe. Her scent lingered there and in the linens, like a promise. She would be back soon; he had to believe that.

Her absence was a continual irritant that ran beneath everything he did. He wasn't sleeping well. His body ached for her. The twins missed her; the servants were furtively puzzled by her absence. Things were going wrong, and it was all her fault.

When ten days had passed with no word, the twins marched into the estate office after dinner and confronted Jamie where he sat with the brandy bottle at his elbow. Their appearance startled him. His sisters had never before approached him at this time and place. And he wasn't used to seeing them in their dresses, even yet. He'd been surprised when they continued to wear them and to abide by all the other conditions Clare had set.

"Clare has not come back," Tamsyn stated when they stood before him.

"Obviously." Like last night, and the one before, and the one before that, he'd had a bit too much brandy. His mind was mildly befuddled.

"She hasn't sent any letters," Tegan said. It was half a question.

"No." Immediately he realized that he should have lied and said he'd heard from her. If he'd had his wits about him, he could have made up some story to satisfy the whole household. Perhaps he still could. "That is to say…" He tried to come up with a plausible tale of a letter delivered in the village, and found his thoughts too fuzzy. "She's busy. She had some things to take care of in town."

"What things?" wondered Tamsyn.

"Matters that… came up unexpectedly." Jamie's tongue tripped a bit on the final word.

"Matters?" echoed Tegan, as if the word were foreign.

"Nothing that need worry you."

"What if she doesn't ever come back?" said Tamsyn.

A tremor went through Jamie, as if the hollowness of the house had somehow gotten inside him and scooped out his heart. It felt perilous, like walking too close to the cliff edge beyond the terrace. "She will, of course, come back. There's no question about that."

"But what if she…?"

"You should go and get her," said Tegan.

"You should tell her you're sorry," added Tamsyn.

"Sorry for…?" What the devil could his little sisters know of their quarrel?

"For whatever you did to make her go away," said Tegan.

"I didn't do any—"

"You shouted at each other," Tamsyn pointed out.

"You told her to go to Penzance," Tegan went on. Their alternating voices were like buzzing flies around his head.

"And she did."

"And she didn't come back."

He tried to break in. "I know th—"

"So you should go and talk to her and bring her back."

Jamie started to tell them that it wasn't so simple. But then he realized that this was what he really wanted to do. By God, he would fetch Clare home, where she belonged. "Dashed if I won't."

"You'll say you're sorry?" urged Tamsyn.

"You'll make her come?" asked Tegan at the same time. Her voice was eager and doubtful at once.

Jamie thumped his empty glass on the desktop. "I will!"

"But what if she doesn't want to live here anymore?" asked Tamsyn sadly.

"Don't be ridiculous!" He shoved the thought

savagely aside. Clare was his wife; she would live where he dictated.

He hadn't meant to shout. As he watched Tamsyn tug her twin away toward the door, he tried to think how to remove the anxious expressions from their identical faces. But before he could imagine a way, they were gone.

Sixteen

"IT IS HER, ISN'T IT?" ASKED HARRY SIMPSON, LOOKING across the crowded reception room at a stunning blond. The big, bluff guardsman was the target of numerous glances himself. He looked as handsome in evening dress as in his uniform, his close-cropped red hair shining in the candlelight.

Small, wiry Andrew Tate nodded, his eyes on the same lovely young woman.

"You are sure? She looks rather different."

"That's Jamie's wife. Lady Trehearth. I have it on unimpeachable authority."

Harry nodded. Andrew always knew all the latest *on dits*. He'd never known him to be wrong. Still, he could scarcely believe this was the subdued girl who had stood beside his friend at the wedding a few months ago. "Jamie's still down in Cornwall though?"

"As far as I am aware. Have you heard from him?"

"Not a peep." Harry continued to survey his good friend's wife, still comparing the vision before him to the figure he'd briefly met at the ceremony. She had the same pale golden hair and delicate features, but now they topped an entrancing frame draped in sea green silk. He didn't see how he could have forgotten those curves. Well, he couldn't have. Her head turned at some remark from the older woman beside her. She also had a ravishing smile. That hadn't been much in evidence in January. "Shall we go and speak to her?" Harry's deceptively innocent blue eyes met Andrew's ironic gray ones.

"Oh, I think so," was the response. "I think so indeed. If Jamie don't keep us up to date, we'll just have to find out for ourselves. But first…" Andrew swept his gaze across the crowded room and carefully calibrated the crowd. "There she is." Martha Howland stood amid a formidable congregation of dowagers, but it took more than a flock of old biddies to intimidate Andrew Tate. His source had named Mrs. Howland as young Lady Trehearth's entree to this party, and Andrew wanted to discover how that connection had been made. It bothered him a bit. Martha Howland adored intrigue. She wasn't malicious—not a dangerous gossip like others Andrew could see in the room—but she definitely… savored romantic complications. He'd heard her say as much, if not in exactly those words. And she wasn't above giving them a little push, if chance sent the opportunity her way. Just to see what might happen. "Come on," he said to Harry.

Andrew's bow to Mrs. Howland was impeccable, and his face showed none of his apprehensions. Harry offered a similar salutation and his patented smile, guaranteed to flutter any feminine heart, of whatever age.

"Aha," said Mrs. Howland. "I think I can predict what you two are after."

"Have you taken up prognosticating?" Andrew responded lightly.

She laughed. "Hardly. I've taken up squiring a lovely young lady about town. You wouldn't credit how many fellows have suddenly developed an urge to speak to me, as they haven't done in twenty years. And all to wangle an introduction. Well, she don't want to meet a lot of people just yet, so you'll have to wait…"

"We're already acquainted with Lady Trehearth," Andrew inserted smoothly. "We're old friends of her husband."

"Really?" Mrs. Howland's gaze sharpened. "You know the family then?"

"Very well. Quite a respected old line. Jamie is the seventh Baron Trehearth." There was no harm in pumping his friend up a bit. No need to mention the decline in fortune. "And you? Are you a friend of Lady Trehearth's family?"

"No. We have a mutual acquaintance. You familiar with her side as well?" Mrs. Howland's curiosity was obvious and boundless.

"We only met her at the wedding," responded Harry, earning a monitory glance from his friend. He took the hint and kept quiet.

"Ah yes. Was that a grand affair? Before the season started, I gather."

For the next ten minutes, Andrew and Mrs. Howland engaged in an oral sparring match, each trying to get information without giving any. Harry admired the cut and thrust and judged that the contest ended in a draw, with neither much the wiser.

Andrew finally gave up, acknowledging Mrs.

Howland's social prowess with another enviable bow, and led Harry over toward their friend's wife.

Clare smoothed a hand over the sumptuous fabric of her new evening gown. It was quite the most beautiful dress she'd ever had. Martha Howland had taken them to her own modiste, and even Selina admitted that the woman was a genius. Her skills had tempted Selina into a new gown as well, and the deep red brocade gave her friend a fetching glow. They both looked very fine, Clare thought. She was aware of curious glances from the crowd.

Perhaps she'd made a mistake in asking Martha not to make too many introductions on her first night among the *ton*. Now that she was accustomed to the room and the chattering crowd, she was finding it hard to stand here with Selina and watch the party go on without her. It was also making her something of a mystery, she realized, and attracting more attention than she would have garnered otherwise. When the two young men came up and spoke to her, she was relieved as well as startled.

"Lady Trehearth," they said with courteous bows.

One was tall and redheaded, the other wiry and blond, each handsome in his own way. There was something familiar about them, as if she should recognize them. But she couldn't quite recall why.

"We met at the wedding," Selina said, saving her.

"Indeed, ma'am. Andrew Tate, at your service."

"Harry Simpson," said the taller one.

"Of course. You're Jamie's friends." Clare decided to reciprocate on the reminders. "You remember Mrs. Newton."

This elicited another elegant bow. "Nice to see you again, ma'am."

"You're up to town for a visit?" Harry inquired.

"Yes." Clare was realizing that their connection with Jamie was an unanticipated complication.

"We haven't heard much from Jamie lately," said Andrew, confirming her fears.

"Not that he was ever a great correspondent," added Harry, earning another admonitory glance.

"He's very busy on the estate," Clare replied. "There's so much to do."

"Indeed." Andrew surveyed her, noting uneasiness. "So, he decided not to come up to town with you?"

"Yes." What else could she say? She could hardly tell them that he hadn't been given the opportunity to decide.

Andrew could see that his question made her even more anxious. Jamie's few short letters since January had sounded buoyant, as if he was smugly pleased with his decision to wed. But his wife's manner told a somewhat different story.

"Enjoying yourself in the metropolis?" Harry asked.

"We've only been here a few days."

"Be happy to show you around," the large guardsman added. Clare had roused his ready sympathies.

"Oh… thank you."

"Jamie would want us to make you feel at home," put in Andrew smoothly. "May we call?"

"Well… I'm not sure…" She was behaving like a newly hatched deb, Clare thought. But Andrew Tate's gaze was unnervingly shrewd. She didn't want to answer any more inquiries about Jamie.

"We're guests of a friend," Selina interjected, seeing Clare's unease. "We can't speak for her."

"Oh, I'm well acquainted with Mrs. Howland." Andrew was stretching the truth a bit, since he seldom called on elderly matrons. But it wasn't a lie. "We were just talking. I'm sure she'll be glad to receive us."

"Ah, you…" *How had he known the name of their hostess?* Clare wondered. Suddenly the curious glances around them seemed intrusive.

"We're happy to meet any friend of Martha's." Selina was politely dismissive, and the two young men took the hint and moved on.

"What was all that about?" Harry asked when they were well away.

"We have to keep an eye on her," Andrew replied. "Before other fellows get ideas."

Harry stood still, the implications washing over him. "Pretty young wife on the town without her husband might be looking for some… alternative company?"

"Exactly. Sometimes you surprise me, Harry." His bluff friend could be quicker than expected.

"I like being underestimated. It gives me a tactical advantage."

Andrew nodded.

"Are you going to write Jamie?"

Andrew frowned. "I suppose so. Yes. But perhaps not immediately."

Harry raised his ruddy brows.

"I want to be sure about what to say first. I'd like some idea about what's going on."

"Doesn't seem much mystery to it."

"Indeed? What would you say to him, Harry?" Andrew wondered.

"Your wife's on the loose amidst a bunch of jackals. Come and get her."

Andrew's bark of laughter attracted a few glances. "That would certainly get a reaction."

"So it should. Look, there's Fitzhugh eyeing her like a sweetmeat. Did you see?"

"No, I seem to have missed that." Andrew looked up at his friend with rapidly increasing respect. "I'm surprised that you did not."

The tall guardsman glowered around the room. "Thing is, you don't have a sister. Lily being out gives me a whole new perspective on the season. It's like setting a kitten down amongst a rabble of tom cats."

Andrew laughed again. "Surely not quite so bad as that, Harry."

"I've got it." Harry brightened. "I'll take Lily to see Jamie's wife, have her make friends."

"That's kind of you."

"Not being kind," Harry sniffed. "If they go about together, I can watch them both at once."

"My dear fellow, I had no idea you could be devious."

"As I said, you haven't got a sister."

❧

Lily was only too glad to oblige her adored older brother, and so the next morning the two Simpsons joined Andrew in a call at Martha Howland's. They found all the ladies at home. What might have been a rather awkward occasion was lightened by red-haired, seventeen-year-old Lily, who was delighted to be out of the schoolroom and ready to savor everything she encountered. Her enthusiasm won Clare over in the first few minutes, and soon had Selina and Martha smiling benevolently.

"Would you credit it? I attended a balloon ascension only three days ago," Lily informed them. "It was the most astonishing thing. The gas bag was quite huge." She opened her blue eyes wide to emphasize the point. "It knocked off three chimney pots as they went shooting up in the air."

The girl made Clare feel far more than six years her senior, and yet at the same time some of her excitement about the thrills of society rubbed off.

"Mama has gotten us vouchers for Almack's," Lily went on, "though Harry claims it's a dead bore."

"Not for you," her tall brother replied.

"No dicing or rum punch," Lily said archly. "I've heard you complaining about it."

He ignored the teasing. "You'll like the dancing."

"I love to dance," she agreed, a smile lighting her pretty face. "Shall you be at the Condons' ball, Lady Trehearth? It is my very first one!"

Clare did not reveal that it would be hers as well. She merely nodded and let the girl's chatter flow on. There seemed to be several parties every night of the London season, and Martha Howland had invitations to them all. No hostess appeared to mind including a safely married young lady and her older companion. They were no competition in the marriage stakes. And so Clare had attended more social gatherings in the last week than in all of her life before.

"I have had dancing lessons, of course," Lily was

saying. "But I have only danced with Harry and Cousin Daniel." She gave the group in the drawing room a flashing glance. "What if no one asks me to stand up with them?"

"They will," Harry assured her, with an expression that suggested he found this a mixed blessing.

"Will you make them, Harry?" Lily laughed. "Will you wear your uniform and fetch me dancing partners at sword point?"

"More likely beat them off with the flat of the blade," her brother muttered.

Clare envied Lily's peal of laughter at this mock threat. The girl looked so carefree, no thought in her head but of the fun she would have in her first season. Lily had a mother to consult and manage her debut, and a brother obviously watching out for her welfare. From Clare's perspective, her life looked gloriously uncomplicated. Perhaps she shouldn't have allowed Martha Howland to talk her into ordering a ball gown, Clare thought. It had been years since her own dancing lessons, and as for partners—she seemed to have forgotten how to flirt, if she ever knew. The years as a governess had changed her. Entering crowded rooms under a battery of eyes, talking to the people Martha introduced, Clare was plagued by sudden qualms, urges to step out of the limelight and protect herself.

"So you will be at the ball?" asked a baritone voice at her elbow.

Clare suppressed a start. She hadn't noticed Andrew Tate slipping into the chair beside her. The man moved about a drawing room like a slinking cat, and his shrewd gaze posed questions she didn't wish to answer. "Martha insists I go." When evading inquiries, blame others, Clare thought, mocking herself.

"I hope you will honor me with a dance," Andrew said.

It wasn't what she'd expected him to say. When he and Harry arrived this morning, she'd seen them as Jamie's emissaries, here to spy, to interrogate, and maybe even reproach her. But Mr. Tate's expression was bland and courteous. Today, they'd made no mention of Jamie at all, which was odd. Not sure whether she was relieved or disappointed, Clare nodded.

When the callers had gone and Clare went up to her bedchamber, Selina remained in the drawing room with Martha. She was worried. She'd thought this trip to London would be brief, no more than an interlude while Clare cleared her mind. But there'd been no mention of returning, and Martha was planning more and more outings, stretching well into the season. Selina wanted their hostess to stop encouraging Clare to stay, for a number of reasons, some admittedly selfish. But she wasn't sure how to broach the matter. Living in someone's home, seeing them for hours every day, revealed unsuspected facets of personality. If Selina had understood the extent of Martha's mischievous streak, she thought, she never would have asked for her hospitality. At times, Selina felt that the other woman viewed Clare as a kind of experiment. She tried this or that event, one or another set of people, and sat back waiting to see what interesting results might transpire. Yet "interesting" could apparently include actions that Selina saw as disastrous. Finally, nothing better having occurred to her, Selina spoke directly. "I think it's time Clare went back to Cornwall."

"Has she heard from her husband?" Martha asked, her eyes bright with curiosity.

Their hostess knew everything that occurred in her household. She would be aware that no letters had been delivered. "No. That's one reason why I—"

"If they're quarreling, she shouldn't give in. She must show him that she will not be tyrannized!"

The remark, and the militant glance that went with it, made Selina wonder about Martha's marriage. She'd never met the late Mr. Howland. Martha had been a widow for years.

"Take it from me, the lines of demarcation must be established early on. Before bad habits take root. What are they quarreling about, precisely?"

"I don't… they aren't, Martha." It was a lie. She hated to lie. Selina wished she'd never begun this conversation.

"They don't care a fig for each other, you mean?" Martha had a habit of lobbing outrageous statements into a conversation, like wild throws at a cricket match, to see what sort of response she could provoke.

"No. That is not what I mean," Selina said firmly. "Don't you think newly married couples should take ample time to get to know each other?"

"Well, if they're complete strangers…" Martha waited to see if the phrase elicited any further details. When they weren't forthcoming, she surged on. "I think the habits of a lifetime together are established in the first year of marriage. And Clare is doing just the thing to get the upper hand." Her eyes narrowed, then she smiled like a gourmand at a lavish buffet table.

"You should write Lord Trehearth and tell him how much his wife is admired here in town. Light a fire under that young man."

To her own chagrin, Selina was tempted. It would be a gross interference, yet there could be no resolution if Clare and her husband didn't communicate. The longer the silence, the more portentous it became. Clare clearly was not happy with the current situation. If she could help resolve it... At this point, Selina was forced to acknowledge that Clare's happiness was not her sole consideration. She wanted to go back to Cornwall for her own reasons. A letter had come from Edward, declaring how much he missed her. He had not precisely complained about her absence, but he had wondered a trifle plaintively when she would return. She wanted it as much as he did.

"*I* would write Lord Trehearth," Martha went on, "but we are not acquainted."

"No!" Thoughts of what their hostess might say galvanized Selina. "That would not be a good idea. Please do not."

"Of course, my dear." Martha's smile made it clear that she understood Selina's reaction perfectly. "Only tell me if there is anything I can do. I'm quite clever about these matters, you know."

Blessedly, more callers were announced, ending the exchange. Under the cover of light conversation, Selina's mind raced. But nothing like a plan emerged.

Upstairs, Clare adjusted her shawl in the mirror and once again appreciated the transformation Martha Howland's recommendations had made in her appearance. She could see why they called it "town polish."

She felt almost like a piece of silver that had been buffed to a marvelous sheen. The idea made her smile. Then she watched the smile fade from her reflected face.

She deserved a bit of frivolity after the years of scrimping and self-effacement, she thought. And when they were gadding about town or receiving callers, she was sometimes almost content. But as soon as she was alone, her thoughts turned to Jamie. What was he doing? Why had he sent no response to her note? She hadn't written either, of course. But she had nothing to apologize for! She hadn't promised him things she never intended to perform. Did he not even care that she was gone? She imagined walking back into the house she'd come to love as her own. What would he say? How would he look at her? Would he apologize or accuse?

It was worst at night, when she lay in bed and remembered the feel of his arms, his lips on hers. When they'd been together in the bedchamber at Trehearth, he'd spoken to her as if she meant everything to him. They'd been completely open to each other, with no possibility of deceit. Or, at least, so she'd believed. Apparently, she was a fool.

Seventeen

Jamie sat in his estate office late into the night, the brandy bottle at his elbow. His satisfaction in seeing new tenant cottages rising and repairs made on other buildings seemed to have lost its savor. Still, how could he simply abandon the work? He'd waited years—nearly all his life—to see it begin. So despite what he'd said to the twins, he lingered in Cornwall. His mood swung between sadness and anger, and only a good dose of brandy managed to drown both.

It was all Clare's fault. Her ridiculous flight was an insult and an embarrassment. She didn't care, apparently, that the twins missed her, that neighbors were asking where she was, that the vicar seemed positively pugnacious about the situation. What people thought when told she was in London he didn't know, because he always made sure the conversation ended there. Her responsibilities clearly meant nothing to her. He—her husband!—didn't even know where she was staying. It was an outrage. Savagely, Jamie refilled his glass. And if she thought such behavior would bring him back under her thumb, she was sadly mistaken.

On the contrary, it was clear evidence that she needed his guidance. She must be taught how to behave!

On top of it all, his sisters were driving him mad. They went about with long faces, now and then intoning, like a dashed Greek chorus, that Clare would never come home. He regretted shouting at them. But what was a man to do, beset on all sides by infuriating females? He drank, and he welcomed the fog that thickened about his endlessly circling thoughts. One thing at least he could count on—the oblivion of the bottle.

It was after a night such as this, and the wretched morning that followed, that the letter from Andrew Tate arrived. Jamie squinted at the lines through a pounding headache and tried to decipher his friend's meaning. Andrew seemed to imagine that he was being tactful, but his hints and careful wording struck just the wrong note with Jamie. How dare his friend stick his nose into his affairs, he thought with furious humiliation, and why the devil had he taken so long to send word? Clare was rousing "a good deal of interest" among the *ton*? What the devil was he to make of that phrase? Who was interested? In what? His mind supplied several unwelcome answers, and the paper crackled as his fist closed around it. Did she think he would stand for this? Would she taunt him with the kind of behavior that fueled the gossip mill? This was it. He'd had enough.

Calling for a mug of ale to ease his pounding head, Jamie gave the order for his valise to be packed and his horse readied. The servants scurried to do his bidding. They'd learned in recent days that their master had a temper. For Jamie's part, now that he'd made his decision to leave, nothing could be done quickly enough, and every question about arrangements seemed idiotic.

The twins observed this flurry from the sidelines, careful to keep out of their brother's way. With Randolph seated between them, his head level with their shoulders, they watched Gwen rush by with a pile of freshly pressed shirts, and John carry up a pair of boots polished to a high sheen. "Do you think he'll get her back?" Tamsyn said quietly.

"He'll shout at her," Tegan replied. "You know how he shouts."

"She won't like that."

"How could anybody?"

"Perhaps he won't. Perhaps they'll make it up. They're *married*."

Tegan considered this. "Married people are supposed to be together," she agreed finally.

"But they don't have to be here."

Tamsyn's expression showed that she too was remembering all the times they'd been left at Trehearth while their brother stayed in London. "Reverend Carew said he was sure the ladies would be back very soon."

"But he didn't really sound sure."

"He sounded annoyed," admitted Tamsyn.

"Which was odd."

"He likes Mrs. Newton," her sister informed her.

"I know but—"

"He *likes* her."

"Oh. Does she...?"

"Yes, Tegan."

"Oh." She pondered this information. "That's good, isn't it? Mrs. Newton must want to come back."

"She'll do what Clare says." Tamsyn sounded distracted. Jamie was tossing terse orders over his shoulder as he went down to his waiting mount. None of his remarks were addressed to them. The sisters looked at each other, then away.

Jamie didn't notice two forlorn little figures standing in an upper window, watching him ride away. Or he didn't allow himself to notice. They'd done it before, so many times. He had no remedy for their mood, and what couldn't be remedied was better off blotted from consciousness.

Unlike his past journeys, Jamie could have afforded a post chaise, but he hated being driven, bouncing around in the close confines of a carriage like a dried pea in its pod. On horseback, there was no getting a wheel stuck in the spring mud and spending an hour hauling it out. They'd take a chaise on the way back. Next week.

He'd ridden this road so many times. As the familiar landscape passed by, it reminded him of the days when it seemed his only problem was money. He'd been desperate then, true, but that desperation appeared pure and simple compared to his current predicament. He spent hours in the saddle silently arguing with Clare, rehearsing what he would say to her. In his mind, she was first amazed and then quickly overborne by his telling points. Tearful and apologetic, she threw herself into his arms and begged for his forgiveness, which led to quite another kind of fantasy, and left him aching for the nights they'd spent together. How could she have welcomed him so sweetly then and be so obdurate now? It made no sense.

Jamie arrived at Andrew Tate's rooms tired from days on the road and liberally spattered with mud. He was cordially offered his old bed there, even though he'd come without warning. When Harry stopped by later that evening, and they cracked a convivial bottle, it was almost as if his marriage had never happened. The thought irritated Jamie no end. "You might have sent her home, I think."

It was not the first time Andrew had heard this complaint, and he was losing patience with his old friend's morose intransigence. "Precisely how would we have done that, Jamie? When it was none of our affair?"

"We only met her at your wedding," Harry chimed in. "Not as if we were well acquainted."

"Well enough to be calling on her at this old biddy's where she's staying," Jamie growled. He saw the exasperated look his friends exchanged and caught himself up. None of this was Harry's or Andrew's fault. They had at least known Clare's current address. And he'd been relieved to hear she was putting up at the house of a respectable older woman. "Never mind, I'll go and see her and end this farce." He shoved his chair back from the table, now littered with selections from Andrew's excellent wine cellar.

"You're not going out like that?" his host said.

"Why not?" Jamie frowned at him.

"Want to put on evening dress," said Harry, who wore an elegant ensemble himself.

"No I don't."

"It's London, my dear fellow," Andrew pointed

out. "You can't go visiting in filthy riding breeches." He didn't add that it was no proper time for a call, and still less that he knew Clare would already be at the Condons' ball. He'd had his head bitten off quite enough for one evening. Nor was he about to say that Martha Howland was far from an old biddy, and that Jamie was most likely diving headlong into trouble. Let him go to her house, and find no one home, and come back and cool off. Far better for him to see his wife when he was calmer. And soberer.

Jamie stalked out. Andrew and Harry listened for a moment, and realized with relief that he'd headed upstairs to change. "You still going to the Condons'?" Harry asked quietly.

"I don't know." Andrew was conscious of a craven desire to stay home this evening and avoid all possibility of a scene.

"I have to." Harry looked grumpy at the prospect. "Promised Lily a dance. She's still afraid no one will ask her to stand up." The big guardsman shook his head. It was endearing, of course, that his little sister didn't notice the admiration she was attracting. But that didn't make it any easier to watch men whose habits he'd never before thought to deplore flocking around her.

"Of course you must go."

"Shall I tell her Jamie's here?"

Andrew knew he wasn't referring to his sister. He looked up at his old friend and sighed. "I simply don't know, Harry. Can't say I like being in the middle this way."

"I flat out hate it myself."

Andrew nodded. "You must use your own judgment. I believe I'll stay home tonight."

"Coward."

"Nothing like it. I'll be here to hear how he feels and what he means to do when he can't find her."

"Ah." Harry gave him a mock salute.

In a crowded, overheated ballroom not too far away, Clare had just come face to face with her cousin Simon. It had never occurred to her that she might encounter the man who had shattered her family, who had callously let her mother die, in the midst of the London season. She'd not only had many other things on her mind, but she never thought of Simon if she could help it. Now she was paying for her own lapse.

As always when she saw her cousin, she was struck to the heart by his resemblance to her dead brother. Tall, with blond hair more golden than Clare's and the male Greenoughs' hawkish cast of countenance, Simon looked down at her with raised brows, his lips curved in a sneer. Her brother's features had been softened by a ready smile and a constant twinkle in his light blue eyes. Simon's gaze was invariably sardonic. His manner always hovered on the edge of mockery. Now, he looked her up and down as if she were a piece of defective merchandise that would need to go back to the shop. "Cousin." He gave her a very small bow. "I heard you were in town. Without your new husband, too. So very… fashionable of you."

Clare nearly choked on her dislike of the man and

of the disdainful way he spoke to her. "Hello, Simon," she managed.

One corner of his mouth quirked up. "Still holding a grudge, are we? But you won the last round so handily, my dear cousin, raking in Uncle Sebastian's money. Surely we're all even now?" His tone implied that she was petty and unreasonable. His gaze taunted.

He hoped to provoke her into an outburst, Clare realized. He wanted her to lose her temper in public and make a spectacle of herself. How her despicable cousin would love it if people began whispering about her. He would revel in spreading old stories even as he proclaimed his bewilderment at her enmity.

And who was he to talk of grudges? Clare had asked him once why he hated them so much. It had been a cry from the heart when her mother was dying. Her cousin had replied that he did no such thing, and when she pointed out that he was acting as if he hated them, he replied that she gave herself far too much credit. He didn't think about them enough to hate. She hadn't believed him. She remained convinced that some twist in their family history, some bitterness his parents had instilled in him, made him relish their suffering. But he would never tell her what it was. She wondered if he even knew the details.

Clare suspected that even if he could explain, it might seem like no great thing to her. Once, a school friend had confided the story of a childhood wound, from which she swore she would never recover. To Clare, the incident had sounded more like a mistake than an attack, but when she tried to explain this alternate perspective, she'd nearly lost the friendship.

Simon's eternal grievance was probably made up of a whole sequence of such occurrences. It would never be assuaged. Quite the contrary, she was certain her rage and grief fed the vendetta and his malicious soul.

"Something wrong, cuz?" He smirked at her.

He was, rightly, taking her silence for upset. Not giving Simon what he wanted was far more important than venting her feelings. *Refuse to go along, don't give him the satisfaction*, Clare thought. The idea of thwarting him helped cool her tone to iciness. "No, why should there be?" She thought, hoped, that he looked a bit disappointed.

"Are you enjoying being a baroness? Uncle Sebastian's money did buy you a title, if a rather moth-eaten one. Lovely gown by the way."

It was like being hit by random shots, each trying a new angle and hoping to hit a vulnerable spot. Clare gritted her teeth. "Are you up in town for the season?" she responded. She prayed he would say it was just a flying visit.

"Oh yes. A bit later than I meant to arrive. I had a few things to take care of at the house." He emphasized the final word, a wholly unnecessary reminder that her former home was now his. "Finally got around to demolishing that old wreck of a pavilion."

The pavilion! It had been a favorite refuge of her childhood. Clare had loved curling up on the frayed cushions and reading through long, hot afternoons, shaded by the oaks and willows that leaned over the airy structure. From the spiteful glint in his eyes, she was sure Simon knew that. For a moment, she wanted to ask him again why he had to be so unpleasant, after all this time. But she knew he would simply raise those pale brows and wonder what she could possibly mean. She hadn't seen a crack in his smooth facade since he was eleven years old and had thrown a tantrum at being denied a ride on a spirited new horse in their stables. His father, her uncle, had responded with cold indifference to his upset, she remembered. No doubt that was part of what had made Simon such an odious person. But after what had happened with her mother, she didn't really care.

He was waiting for a response. The longer she was silent, the more certain he'd be that he had hurt her. "Pavilion?" said Clare. "I don't quite recall… Oh, you mean the place down by the stream?"

"The very one." His sly smile said he wasn't fooled by her show of indifference.

"I'm surprised it took you so long to attend to it," Clare added. She thought that hit might have gotten through, but she was vastly relieved when Selina came to join them. She couldn't keep up this pretense much longer.

Something in Clare's stance, evident from across the room, had caused Selina to ask about the identity of her companion. When she was told the man was Simon Greenough, she moved at once to join them. Clare had told her a bit of the history with her cousin, certainly enough to know that his appearance would not be at all welcome.

Clare introduced them and was relieved when Selina said, "I hope you will excuse us, sir. Our hostess, Mrs. Howland, wishes to present Clare to an old friend."

Simon Greenough could do nothing but bow at this. "Of course."

Everything Clare might have wished to say was impossible. She silently vowed to avoid her cousin in future.

As if he could read her expression, he added, "I shall look forward to seeing you again soon, Clare."

Clare made herself smile. Head held high, she walked away with Selina. But she murmured, "I don't really feel like meeting anyone new just now."

"It was a lie, I fear. An excuse to get you away. But we'd best join Martha for a bit."

"Thank you, Selina." They headed toward the group that included Mrs. Howland. "If I'd known Simon would be in London, I don't think I would have come."

"Perhaps it's time to go back to Cornwall." Maybe this was a goad to send them back? Selina felt a rush of hope.

"Perhaps." *Which was worse?* Clare wondered. To encounter her wretched cousin in crowded rooms and endure his gibes, or to return to her new home and face Jamie? Clare wished it wasn't so complicated. Was Jamie angry? Hurt? Despite his silence, she couldn't believe he was simply indifferent.

❧

At that particular moment, her husband was wildly frustrated. All his faculties concentrated on a meeting with Clare, Jamie had knocked on the door of Martha Howland's fashionable town house and been told no one was at home. The doorkeeper had looked down his nose at a visitor who knew no better than to call at a quite inappropriate hour, and informed him that the "ladies" had gone out for the evening. When Jamie had asked where they'd gone, the fellow had told him he really couldn't say and tried to shut the door in his face. It had been the last straw. Jamie put his shoulder to the door and shoved inside, demanding, "Do you know who I am?" Giving the young footman no time to answer, he said, "I am Lord Trehearth, the husband of one of your houseguests. Tell me where she is right now."

The footman, perhaps not so long at his job, was not up to thwarting an enraged nobleman. He edged away from Jamie until his back hit the wall. Trapped, he stammered out the ladies' destination and then sagged with relief when the gentleman turned and stalked out.

In the street, Jamie searched for a cab. Here was what Clare had reduced him to: he'd bullied a servant. And this after carping at his best friends in the world and abandoning a host of responsibilities at home. He had to get hold of himself, and this idiocy had to end, tonight.

No one questioned him when he presented himself at the mansion where the Condons' ball was taking place. In his evening dress, he looked as if he belonged, and the hostess had long since left her post at the top of the stair. He moved swiftly into the ballroom and began to scan the chattering, dancing crowd.

It seemed an interminable time before he spotted Clare. She was dancing—dancing!—with some chinless town blade, and she looked—astonishing. Jamie stood quite still and stared. He'd always thought his wife beautiful. Hadn't he told her so? Of course he had. But here, amongst the *ton*, in a silken gown he'd never seen before, she looked... radiant, polished, sophisticated. He didn't understand how she could have changed so much in so short a time. It made her seem even more distant from him, and lowered his mood even further, if that was possible. The music ended; he made his way through the crowd to her side.

"Jamie!" Clare felt a surge of joy to find him suddenly standing beside her.

"What do you think you're doing?" he muttered. He wanted to sweep her into his arms. But there were people all around them, beady-eyed scandalmongers, most of them.

Clare's euphoria collapsed. "Attending a ball," she replied. "I didn't know you had come up to..."

This was unbearable. The musicians struck up again. Jamie pulled his wife into the dance. The feel of her body was intoxicating and tantalizingly forbidden, here with all these eyes upon them.

"Jamie, it's a waltz." Martha had said something about waltzing. One was supposed to be approved before... or was that just for debs? Had she been speaking to Lily? Clare's thoughts spun, and then she could think of nothing but Jamie's nearness. His arm encircled her waist. His hand held hers as if he would never let go.

Clare's magnificent eyes were inches from his. It was all he could do not to crush her to him. He turned her in the dance, trying to edge closer to the door with each step. "This... tantrum of yours is over," he said. "You're coming home with me tomorrow."

Clare stiffened in his embrace. She'd wanted him to ask her to come home. She'd hoped that he missed her, longed for her, as she did him. She'd dared to imagine that he regretted the things he'd said and done. But he spoke to her now in that same hateful tone, as if she were an errant child who required discipline. "I'm enjoying the season," she replied.

Jamie was afraid she was enjoying it all too much. "You belong at Trehearth."

"Were your meals not being served on time?" Clare taunted. Hurt and disappointment lent her voice a bitter edge.

"You are my wife, and I command you to come home." His voice had risen. Heads turned nearby.

"Command? I'm not your horse or… or Randolph, that you can order me about."

Jamie jerked her closer. Her lips were so close now that it killed him not to kiss her. The ballroom doorway was just a few steps away.

People were definitely noticing their exchange. Clare was aware of an increasing number of avid stares. "We cannot talk about this here…"

Jamie whirled Clare in a dizzying turn and whisked her through an archway and out into the corridor. It was blessedly, momentarily, empty. There was a line of recessed windows across the hall. He swept her into one of the niches, yanked its draperies closed, and captured her lips with his. This was what he needed. This would show her the way things were meant to be.

Clare stiffened only briefly, then she couldn't help it: she melted at his touch. The kiss ran through her like a raging fever. She'd missed him so much.

Her arms curled around his neck, and she yearned toward him.

Jamie drew her closer still. Her tantalizing curves fit his body as if they'd been molded for it. She had to see that they were designed for each other. He pulled back slightly; he needed to get her out of here, to somewhere private, and then home.

The curtains twitched, then parted slightly. Martha Howland stood in the narrow opening. "Lord Trehearth, I presume?" They jumped apart. "Indeed, I sincerely hope so." The older woman's tone was prim, but curiosity danced in her eyes. "Whatever do you think you're doing?"

Jamie took a further step back, clenching his fists at his sides to control a flood of thwarted desire.

"Yes," stammered Clare, crimson with embarrassment. "That is, this is my husband. Jamie, this is Mrs. Howland, my kind hostess in London."

Somehow, he managed a bow, though he longed to throttle her for the interruption. "Mrs. Howland."

"Come out of there at once. Before someone else sees you." Martha's sharp eyes had followed the young man's maneuver, as had Selina's. She'd left her other guest dithering in the ballroom, assigned the task of making excuses, should they prove necessary. Martha eyed the couple like a stern schoolmistress. They responded to the look, and her tone, by stepping briskly out of their hiding place.

His automatic obedience annoyed Jamie further. "Thank you for your hospitality to my wife. We are returning to Cornwall immediately."

"Really? I had no notion."

"I am not!" cried Clare. How dared he speak for her as if she had no say in the matter?

Oh, la, Martha thought. Under other circumstances, she might have nudged this pair toward each other, but it was clear to her that Lord Trehearth needed a small lesson. And she was just the person to administer it. "You're most welcome to stay as long as you like, Clare. So many handsome men have come calling at my house because of you. I haven't seen the like in twenty years." The wild spark in *this* handsome young man's eyes told her that she'd hit her mark.

Jamie eyed the stout, rouged older woman—a busybody and a slave to fashion from her crimped gray hair to her ridiculous evening slippers. Her meddling in his affairs was unconscionable, and he longed to say so. But he restrained himself. "Perhaps we might have some privacy, so that I can discuss this matter with my *wife*?" he said tightly.

"Well, I don't think we dare risk that." He really was amusing. Martha couldn't resist goading him a bit further. "It doesn't seem as if I can leave you two alone, even in the midst of a crowded ball, without provoking a scandal."

Clare put her hands to her flaming cheeks. "It's not necessary." She slipped past Martha and rushed back to the ballroom, searching the crowd for Selina.

Her friend had been watching for her. She came up at once and stood so as to shield Clare from the battery of prying eyes. There was no need to ask if all was well; obviously, it wasn't.

Back in the corridor, Martha Howland savored Lord Trehearth's thunderous expression. Clearly this was a young man who needed curbing. What she must determine was: did he really care for Clare, or was he simply a possessive young idiot? "You're making a hash of things, you know," Martha said to him. "If you want my advice—"

Jamie ground his teeth. "I do not!" He stalked down the hallway toward the stair. He had just enough control left to realize that he couldn't go back into the ballroom. If he did, he would seize Clare in full view of the dancers, and damn the consequences. Society would never forget it.

"Very well then," Martha murmured to his departing back. "I shan't offer again." She put a placid smile on her face and made her stately way back to the ballroom. Clare most likely required some... encouragement in order to act as if nothing had happened.

Jamie walked back to Andrew's rooms. It was a goodly distance, and the streets were dark, but he relished the physical activity. Let a footpad accost him, he thought; he would be only too glad to hit something. No obliging target appeared, however. His boots pounded the cobbles; his arms swung like scythes; he muttered and fumed and reached his destination safely. Upstairs, he headed straight for the array of bottles on the sideboard.

"What luck?" asked Andrew, lounging in the armchair before the fire.

Jamie poured a large brandy.

"Bad, apparently." Andrew sipped his own drink and wondered what to say.

"Clare has fallen into the clutches of an insufferable...

this Howland woman. She intends to keep her here in town against my express wishes." Jamie silently acknowledged that this wasn't quite the whole story, but he couldn't admit to his friend that Clare had refused to listen to him. "We will see about that!"

"Ah, you… met Mrs. Howland?"

"Clare was at a ball! Dancing with some damn fool." Jamie glowered. "I didn't get his name. When I tried to speak to her, this Howland creature sent me packing."

Andrew suspected it wasn't quite as simple as that, but this was clearly not the time to ask. Nor did he inquire how Jamie had gotten himself to the Condons' ball, or whether he had seen Harry there.

"She cannot keep me from her forever," Jamie growled. "The next time I get my hands on Clare, we're off to Cornwall, and the rest of them can go straight to perdition!"

Andrew observed the scowl on his face. He liked what he'd seen of the new Lady Trehearth. And he had a great affection for his boyhood friend Jamie. He would have liked to see amity between them. This plan did not seem likely to promote it. Andrew watched Jamie raise the glass. Though he didn't take Jamie's mutterings as gospel, he was concerned about what he might do. Especially if he continued drinking as he had since he arrived. "You know, you might try wooing her a bit. Get her to understand…"

"What?" Jamie gave him a confused glare. "She's already my wife, for God's sake!"

"Yes. But you never wooed her properly."

The brandy was hitting. "Don't know what you're talking about. Didn't have to."

Andrew nodded. "Because the marriage was arranged. I know that. But you see, she might feel she's missed out. Alice always said…"

"Oh, God, no!" Jamie dropped into the second armchair, spilling a drop of brandy on his shirtfront. "Don't begin on your dalliance with that milksop. I don't need to 'woo' Clare. We…" Jamie realized he'd been about to say that they could scarcely keep their hands off each other. He snapped his mouth shut.

Andrew had stiffened. "Of course, what you're doing is working so very well." He rose to head for bed. "But as you say, I'm no expert."

Left alone, Jamie glared at the dying fire and brooded. His life had been going so well—splendidly, even—and then, seemingly in an instant, it had crashed like a felled ox. And he could not for the life of him figure out why. Was one ridiculous argument enough to topple a marriage? Could Clare be that shallow and silly? He knew she wasn't. And yet, she'd run away and was refusing to return.

Tonight, when he'd held her again, she'd responded to his touch just as she had in their blissful nights together. She wanted him, as he so urgently wanted her. He was certain of it. So why didn't she simply come home? The brandy dulled but didn't dissipate his bewilderment and pain. It took another glass, and then another, before he finally fell asleep in the chair.

Eighteen

"GOOD MORNING," SAID ANDREW TATE TO HIS ERRANT houseguest. Then he said it again, louder. He wasn't particularly penitent when his old friend woke with a start. Perhaps it was the deep, gurgling snort that influenced him.

"Ow!" Jamie had a savage crick in his neck from the night spent in the armchair. He couldn't turn his head without a slash of pain. He also had a brainpan that felt like it was stuffed with hot coals and a queasy stomach. He was grumpy as a bear. "Coffee?" he growled.

"Coming, *my lord*," Andrew replied. "Perhaps you'd like to change first? And even wash?"

Jamie looked down at his crumpled evening dress. His shirtfront showed dried spatters of brandy. His mouth tasted like stable sweepings. "After coffee," he croaked. "Please?" He winced as the door banged and Harry Simpson swept in, resplendent in his Guards uniform and disgustingly chipper.

"There you are," Harry said to him. "Missed you last night."

Behind Jamie's slumped form, Andrew shook

his head and waved his hands, but he failed to snag Harry's attention.

"Saw you at the ball, but you left before I caught up with you."

Jamie jerked upright. "Ow! You were there?"

By this time, Harry had noticed Andrew's gestures and grimaces. "Right. Ah, watching out for Lily, you know."

"Lily?"

"My sister?" Harry looked at Andrew, who shrugged.

"Right. Of course. Sorry." Jamie's mind was moving at the speed of cold molasses. "How is Lily?"

"Blooming like a dashed rose," grumbled Harry.

This was a bit beyond Jamie's current mental capacity. "Did you see Clare? She was there."

In fact, he'd danced with her. But Harry didn't think this was the moment to say so. "Believe I may have, as a matter of fact."

Jamie turned his head too fast. Lancing pain ran down into his shoulder. "Ow!"

"Something wrong, old man?" asked Harry.

"Jamie slept in my armchair," replied Andrew dryly.

"Ah, dipped a bit deep last night?" Harry nodded sympathetically. "Got just the remedy. Drop a raw egg into—"

"Don't!" Jamie held up a hand. "Don't speak to me of raw eggs."

Andrew's man arrived with a tray and poured coffee. Andrew took his own cup before offering one to Jamie.

Jamie gulped the hot liquid, burning his throat. In the harsh light of day, he felt more depressed than belligerent. He had to see Clare again, but he couldn't face her in this condition. "Tell me what's happened to my wife," he requested, chastened.

"Happened?" Harry looked to Andrew again; once more, he shrugged. "Well, she's staying with Mrs. Howland."

Jamie groaned. "That much I know. How did she end up there?"

"I believe her hostess is an old friend of Mrs. Newton's," Andrew said.

"Ah." Jamie got a second cup of coffee and drank. His wits were slowly emerging from the remains of his alcoholic haze. "Look, you wrote me and said I should come up to town. You must have meant something by it."

The thing was, they hadn't expected this erratic version of their friend, Andrew thought. He wondered now if it had been a mistake to interfere.

Harry felt compelled to fill the silence. "It's like Lily," he said. "Lady Trehearth's just been going about a bit, enjoying herself. But I thought she should have someone to look after her."

Jamie slowly sorted through the pronouns. "You think Clare needs looking after?"

"Well, she's new to town, surrounded by all sorts of fellows. Some of them aren't quite the—"

In an instant, Jamie was on his feet. He ignored the lancing pain in his head. "Has some blackguard been making up to her?" Oddly, Andrew found his friend's murderous look quite gratifying.

"No, no," said Harry. "Nothing like that. It's just… You can't be too careful, eh?" He looked to Andrew for help.

"What aren't you telling me?' Jamie demanded. He very nearly grabbed the front of Harry's fine uniform and shook him.

"Nothing, Jamie," Andrew answered. It was time to step in. "My word on that. It's just… your wife might like you by her side."

"And isn't that where I want her? At home, in Cornwall! But how am I supposed to get her there if she won't listen to me?" Jamie sank back into the chair and cradled his throbbing head.

Uncomfortable at the near wail in his friend's voice, Andrew turned to pour a bit more coffee.

"Andrew thinks I should 'woo' her," Jamie informed Harry.

"That's not a bad notion," replied Harry.

Jamie rubbed his hands through his hair. Even the dark strands seemed to hurt. He ordered his mind to clear. "So, you think a bit of flattery and attention—a few flowery compliments—and she'll come to her senses?" He hadn't seen Clare as so vain, but she was a woman, after all. They were susceptible to all kinds of flummery.

It was not what Andrew thought, but he chose to say no more. It didn't seem the moment.

As Jamie began to plot his siege on his own wife, a windfall fell in his lap. An old school friend was being sent on an extended mission to India and needed someone to take over his rooms, furnishings and all. Jamie jumped at the chance to feel more his own man and less like the impoverished hanger-on he used to be. The digs weren't as elegant as Andrew's, but there was a decent parlor and bedchamber and a pleasant landlady who provided breakfasts and the odd cup of tea. Andrew seemed pleased at the change as well— perhaps a bit too pleased. Jamie wondered if the years of offering him a bed in town had worn thin. It was a lowering thought to add to his surfeit of such ideas.

He called at Mrs. Howland's formidable house and saw Clare again. But somehow, he could never get her alone. Her hostess seemed to delight in interrupting private conversations. Selina Newton was equally omnipresent. And Harry's little sister, often there as well, exhibited an innocent delight in talking to him, one of her few prior acquaintances in London. All in all, it was soon apparent that he would have to catch Clare elsewhere in order to say anything important.

The fact that Jamie had no invitations to *ton* parties was a problem that Harry and Andrew easily solved. As attractive, eligible males they were much in demand, and a request to bring along a presentable friend, even though married, was never denied.

Jamie attended several such events—dead bores— before he hit upon one where Clare was present. Finally, at a musical evening, with threats of an operatic performance later on, he saw her walk in with her two dragons. She looked so lovely his breath caught. This was the night. He felt it in his bones. Of course he knew how to make up to a female. He'd had his share of successes in the past. He'd bowl her over, and then sweep her off home.

Jamie started across the room, threading his way through the chattering crowd, resisting the impulse to shove a few of the more insipid out of his way, only to see Clare snatched up by some coxcomb in a striped waistcoat. He had no idea who the fellow was, but he did know that he hated the way he bent over Clare and offered his arm. Jamie covered the rest of the distance between them in five long steps. "Clare!" It came out too strong. He knew the tone was a mistake as soon as she turned and blinked at him.

"Oh, Jamie. Hello." Her heart lifted and beat faster every time she saw him. But the expression on his face told her nothing had changed.

"I need to speak to you." Less heat and more flattery, he told himself. But he had to get Clare's hand off this idiot's coat sleeve.

"This is Mr. Travers. Mr. Travers, my husband, Lord Trehearth."

"How d'you do?" The man made an elegant bow.

"We're just going for some lemonade," Clare began.

"I fear you will have to excuse us, sir." Jamie moved forward to detach him.

Travers seemed to take it as a joke. "Can't keep your wife in your pocket, old man. Not at all the thing."

"I don't care a whit about the 'thing.'" He reached out to pull her away.

Did loving someone make you more susceptible to annoyance? Clare wondered. She was an even-tempered person, but Jamie continually made her want to shake him these days. Or give him a blistering setdown. She settled for stepping out of range. "We'll speak later," she said coolly.

She actually walked off with this Travers. As they went, Jamie heard him say, "Have you heard Orsini yet? Divine voice." How could she prefer such drivel to being with him? He stood there, oblivious to the crush of people, staring after her and struggling with a desire to throttle the man whose arm she held instead of his. He had to get control of himself. She was driving him mad.

Becoming aware of sidelong glances, Jamie retreated from the center of the large reception room to lean on one of the walls. He'd recover, lie in wait, and try again. Like a cat crouched over a mouse hole, he watched the archway through which Clare had disappeared. Snagging a glass of champagne from a passing servitor, he didn't notice a gentleman stroll over to join him until the newcomer cleared his throat.

"I beg your pardon," the man said when Jamie turned. "Forgive my forwardness in introducing myself, but as we are family now..."

"Family?" The man was tall and blond, with a hawk nose and a lanky frame.

"I'm Clare's cousin, Simon Greenough."

He seemed to watch Jamie rather closely as he said this. Jamie met shrewd blue eyes and reluctantly shifted his attention from the arch. "Indeed. I didn't realize Clare had family in town." On the contrary, he'd had the impression that she hadn't any family to speak of. Certainly none had been invited to their wedding.

"I only arrived recently."

Had she mentioned cousins? Maybe there'd been something, back at the beginning of their acquaintance... he'd forgotten. She wouldn't like that. He'd be expected to know the fellow existed, to make an effort. "Ah, enjoying the season?" Jamie asked.

Greenough seemed to relax. "Very much. You?"

"Oh, yes," Jamie lied.

"I hope we'll have the opportunity to get better acquainted."

Clare appeared in the archway, without Travers, thankfully. All other thoughts went out of Jamie's mind. He abandoned his champagne glass on the chair rail. "We must certainly do so. I fear you must excuse me now, however." He bowed, and Greenough had hardly responded when he was away.

Simon watched him move across the room and examined the couple's expressions when he accosted Clare. Something odd going on there. They didn't look like blissful newlyweds; yet they certainly weren't indifferent partners in a marital arrangement either. One glance at their faces showed that. Perhaps the situation offered possibilities. Simon hadn't gotten over the fact that his cousin had snatched their great-uncle's money from under his nose. It ate at him, soured his triumph at winning the entail game. He couldn't get his hands on the money; she'd finessed him there. But there might be other ways to make her sorry. This marriage that no one seemed to know anything about, for example. He sensed a lever.

"I was rather short with your friend," Jamie said when he reached Clare. "Forgive me." Now that Travers wasn't in evidence, he could wish he'd been more polite to him. And he was determined to keep his temper in check. Clare mustn't walk away from him again—as it was all too easy for her to do in this blasted mob.

Clare actually found Mr. Travers extremely tedious.

She'd slipped away from him as soon as possible. But Jamie didn't deserve to know that. "I was going back to Selina," she replied.

"Allow me to escort you." He offered an arm. "Perhaps we could take a turn about the room first?"

He was being suspiciously punctilious. Still, Clare couldn't resist tucking her hand through his elbow, and she couldn't suppress a slight shiver at his nearness. How could it be so different—one man's touch over another's? Mr. Travers, and all the other fashionable men she'd met in London so far, left her unmoved. Their compliments and attentions were pleasant, flattering of course, but they meant nothing to her. Then, a mere brush of Jamie's coat sleeve raised her pulse and jumbled her thoughts.

"You look lovely," he said. Indeed, now that she was close to him, it was impossible to notice any other woman in the room.

"Thank you."

He ransacked his brain for something more to say. But he seemed to have forgotten the pretty nothings that he'd used on females in the past. She wasn't a random female; she was Clare. "I've missed you," came out of his mouth. "Trehearth isn't the same with you gone." When her pale green eyes met his, and her expression softened, something stuttered deep in Jamie's chest.

"I've missed you, too," Clare admitted. The conversational roar of the party receded, as if they walked in a bubble separate from the din. "How are the twins?"

"Constantly asking when you're coming home," he

answered, and saw at once that it was a misstep. Her nearness was driving him mad—the scent she used, the delicate line of her jaw, the light pressure of her fingers on his arm. He couldn't watch every word when his senses were starting to swim. "Clare, can't we go somewhere and talk? I've hardly been able to get near you since I arrived in town."

Martha had advised her to keep him at arm's length, to wait until he cracked and came crawling. But Clare had no wish to humiliate Jamie. She simply wanted him to understand and to keep the promises he'd made to her. "Where would we...?"

"I have rooms in Duke Street. A friend lent them to me." As he spoke he was steering her toward the doorway. "Just for a bit, Clare. So we can hear ourselves speak."

Clare couldn't resist those warm dark eyes or the memory of how happy they'd been together. "I must tell Selina."

Jamie turned his head and found, as he'd expected, Mrs. Newton's gaze fixed on them. He forced himself to smile at her. "She sees us." He nodded as if she must understand what he meant to convey and whisked Clare out of the room.

It seemed to Clare as if they were wafted out of the house, into a cab, and then out again into a dark street. In a very few minutes, Jamie was offering her a chair in a comfortable sitting room, putting a match to kindling in the fireplace, going to the sideboard and pouring wine. She looked around as she took the glass from his hand. The furnishings were masculine, the colors muted. It felt suddenly as if they had separate residences. "You're living here?"

Jamie sat in the other armchair flanking the hearth. "An old school friend was sent on a mission abroad. He let me borrow this place."

She sipped her wine and wondered what to say. Once, they'd spoken so easily to each other; then they had disagreed. And now it seemed that any phrase she chose might provoke another quarrel. Sadness washed through her. The small room seemed full of tension.

Sitting opposite Clare in the strange room, washed by candlelight and firelight, Jamie was filled with memories of other nights—of soft murmurs in the dark, of skin touching skin. In one fluid motion, he set aside his wine and surged from his chair to kneel before her. "I can't bear this." He took her hand. "We were so in harmony with each other. I can't believe that is gone. It isn't! It can't be." He bent closer, intoxicated by her scent.

Clare put down her glass and gazed into his eyes—a smoldering darkness. His fingers clutching hers felt like a lifeline. Her heart yearned for him. Her blood heated. She swayed closer.

Jamie slipped his arms around her in the chair and leaned in to take her lips with his. All the sweetness and fire he remembered were there. He drew her closer; her arms encircled his neck. As the kiss grew deeper, he pulled her out of the chair to kneel with him. She arched against him. Their bodies pressed together in the warm firelight.

How she'd missed him, Clare thought. It seemed

an age had passed since he held her, since she felt this lightning running along her nerves. His hands moved over her body; his lips strayed down her neck to the curve of her shoulder. Her breath caught, and she let her head fall back. Jamie's dark hair tangled in her fingers as he eased her down onto the thick hearth rug. His face above her was warmed by the orange flames. The next kiss made her forget everything but his touch.

Jamie exulted in the arch of her hip, the tumble of her pale hair as pins scattered. He pushed down the sleeve of her evening dress and revealed the luscious curve of her breast. When he set his mouth there, he heard the answering gasp he so loved to rouse. All was well. She wanted him as much as he did her. The only trouble was all these damned clothes. Slipping his hand up the smoothness of her silk stocking, Jamie loosed ties and laces. There was the sound of something ripping, and at last he found his goal. Clare cried out when he reached that liquid warmth, and his own body jerked in reaction.

Sensation drowned Clare. Nothing existed but the two of them as she rose and shattered under his touch. They met in a kiss that said everything words could not. Her own hands grew busy with the fastenings that kept Jamie from her. They resisted, frustrated her, then finally gave way. She cried out again when they came together.

Mad for her, Jamie plunged into ecstasy. The glory of physical sensation, relief at having her in his arms again, fierce tenderness, all joined to overwhelm him. Reality blurred, and he let it go. This was so much better. Together, they found their way to rapturous oblivion.

Afterward, they lay entwined in a tumble of clothing, firelight dancing on glimpses of skin. As their breath slowed and their pulses moderated, Clare became aware of the disarray. Her lovely new gown was twisted and crumpled. Her hair was falling about her face. Jamie's breeches were falling off him. Her cheeks reddened at the spectacle they made, sprawled on the floor. She pushed her skirt down and sat up.

Jamie stretched, smug with satisfaction, the fire warm on his side. "You can go back and pack your things. We'll leave tomorrow."

"Leave?" Clare pulled the short sleeves of her gown back into place.

"For home." He watched her adjust her clothing with tolerant amusement.

Clare pushed to her feet and shook out her skirts. The wrinkles stayed. A torn ruffle on her petticoat sagged toward the floor. "So, you've changed your mind? You will honor our marriage agreements after all?" Clare gazed down at him, hope dawning.

Jamie sat up and began to adjust his own attire. "Clare. Do we have to start that ridiculous wrangle up again? Surely we don't need to talk about that now? What just passed between us shows that we—"

"Yes or no?"

Jamie thought of lying to her. He very nearly did. The words were on the tip of his tongue. But before he could speak, he realized that she'd seen the truth in his face. Well, why should he have changed his mind? He was in the right.

The uncomprehending stubbornness in the set of his jaw ripped through her heart. "I see. Your answer is no. In that case, so is mine. I'm staying in London."

"A few moments ago you were in my arms. Do you expect me to believe that you didn't enjoy it?"

"Of course not. I enjoyed it very much. As you did. But it doesn't change anything."

"But you… we… you're my wife, damn it!"

"I am. On the terms we set out together, which you now wish to ignore. It's just like breaking a wedding vow, Jamie."

"It's no such thing!"

"It is to me!" Clare snatched up her cloak and flung it around her. She fought tears as she marched from the room.

Jamie went after her, but luck had gone against him. By the time he reached the bottom of the stairs, Clare had found a cab and was climbing into it. She paid no attention to his shout. He ran a few futile steps behind the moving carriage, then stopped. There was no way to catch her on foot, and no other cab in sight. Jamie turned back, only to find his landlady on the doorstep.

"My lord! I declare I didn't believe my Sam when he said you'd brought some… young person to your rooms. And now I see with my own eyes. This is not the sort of behavior I'm used to. I can't permit it." She looked him up and down, making Jamie aware of his disheveled appearance.

"You don't understand. It was my wife."

"Your wife, my lord?" She stood in the door, blocking his way inside.

"Yes. Lady Trehearth. We… we have no house

in London as yet, and she is staying with friends near Grosvenor Square."

The address clearly impressed her. "You wouldn't be trying to cozen me, my lord?"

"I swear I am not. I will introduce her to you the next time she visits." *Would there be a next time?* Jamie wondered.

"Well…"

"I promise you it is the truth."

"It's quite irregular, my lord."

He could see she was weakening. "A temporary situation, I assure you." Which it had to be. This couldn't go on.

"All right then." She stepped aside and let him through. "I'm trusting you, my lord."

As he started up the stairs, Jamie wondered why the blazes his wife could not do the same.

Nineteen

ONE MORNING SOON AFTER THIS, A MAID CAME TO Selina's bedchamber to say that a caller was asking for her particularly. For a moment Selina feared it might be Lord Trehearth, come to reproach or argue with her, but when she inquired, she was told it was a young lady. Puzzled, since morning callers always asked for Clare or Martha, she made her way down to the drawing room. A tall, thin, sandy-haired woman of perhaps twenty-five rose from the sofa. She wore a well-cut but not terribly fashionable dress in a rose shade that flattered her skin and fixed on Selina with sharply curious blue eyes. "Good morning," Selina said, trying not to sound perplexed at facing a total stranger.

"Hello," the caller replied. "I am Mary Finch, Edward Carew's daughter."

"Oh." Now that she knew the relationship, Selina could see a resemblance. Surprise, and a mild nervousness, replaced her bewilderment. "I didn't realize… how kind of you to call."

"We're passing through London on the way to

Bath, so that my husband's mother can drink the waters. I took the opportunity to meet you."

"I am so happy you did. Please sit down." As they settled themselves, Selina endured the younger woman's close scrutiny. Of course she would want to evaluate the woman her father meant to marry.

There was a short silence.

"I hope your journey so far has been pleasant," Selina said.

"Yes, thank you." The younger woman's mouth curved in a half smile, the expression very reminiscent of Edward Carew. "This is rather odd. My father and I had several conversations over the years concerning gentlemen who might, or might not, want to marry me. But I have never been... on the other side of the fence, so to speak."

Her wry tone, her gestures, all reminded Selina of her father and made her feel rather wistful.

"You haven't known my father long," Mary Finch continued.

Or he me, Selina supplied silently. "It's true. I was surprised myself at how quickly we established a... close connection. He is such an admirable, amiable man." She couldn't keep her tender feelings out of her voice, and Mary Finch's face softened at her tone.

"And you think you will like living in a country parsonage far from the, er, gaieties of London?" She eyed Selina's very modish gown as she said it.

Selina smiled at her. "I grew up in a country parsonage, just as far from town. And I was very happy there. My father was a clergyman."

"Indeed?" Mary's blue eyes met her hazel ones.

Something in the gaze seemed to satisfy the young woman, and she sat back more comfortably. "My father's letters sound so happy," she admitted. "I'm glad for him, for you both."

"Thank you." Selina's heart felt full.

"But when are you going back to Cornwall? Papa is all eagerness to go forward and set a wedding date."

This sounded like one of Edward's letters, and Selina almost sighed. It was hard to be continually urged to do something you very much wanted to do, and remain unable to comply. "I'm here in town with a young friend," she explained.

"Lady Trehearth? Papa mentioned her."

"Yes. She is having a somewhat... difficult time, and I have been lending her support."

"You've known her a long time, I suppose?" Mary probed.

"Ah, well, no. Only a few months."

"But you are obligated to her in some way?"

Selina wondered if Edward had primed her for this interview. "As a friend."

"Of course." Mary smiled at her. "Your dedication to friendship is admirable. But if Lady Trehearth knew of your plans, would she not urge you to go? As a friend to you?"

"Did Edw... your father provide you with a list of arguments?" Selina asked.

Mary Finch laughed. "I may have echoed some of the sentiments in his letters."

Selina contemplated the figured carpet. Her visitor obviously put her father's concerns first, as any good daughter would. But when it came down to it, how did Selina explain lingering in London when she longed to go to Cornwall? Had she become so accustomed to catering to others' needs that she didn't know how to meet her own? "At some point, I will simply go," she said, realizing the truth of the statement as it came out of her mouth.

Mary Finch heard it. "When?" she asked softly.

Was she actually helping Clare? Selina wondered. She'd seen no change in the rift between the Trehearths, and she didn't know how to promote one. If she was doing no good, could she not address her own happiness instead? When, indeed?

Before she could find an answer, Clare came into the drawing room. "Selina, I was thinking we could... Oh, I beg your pardon. I didn't realize we had a visitor."

Selina sprang to her feet like a schoolgirl caught in some infraction. Her introductions were clumsy, and at any other time in her life Clare would have noticed and wondered at it. But today, her mind was wholly occupied with her own concerns. She was aware of mild surprise that the vicar's daughter had called, and she managed to play her part in the commonplace conversation that followed. Most of her attention remained elsewhere.

Mary Finch departed soon after, and Clare was able to offer her suggestion that they take a walk in the park. She longed to be outdoors, to breathe deep and move quickly. The park was a poor substitute for a brisk tramp in the countryside, but it was the only choice.

The outing did little to calm her, however. The London season was not so entertaining when you were always on edge, waiting to see whether one person would appear. One darkly handsome person whom you longed to see, and yet also wanted to avoid. It roused such turmoil in Clare's breast that she didn't even notice Selina Newton's pensive silence.

Over the next week, Clare and Jamie had a series of unsatisfactory encounters at parties and balls. Clare engaged in empty conversations, offending a few high sticklers when she lost the thread as Jamie approached her. When they talked, they got nowhere, repeating the same litany that had brought them to this pass. When they were silent, tension vibrated between them, even across a crowded reception room. Jamie took to leaning on walls and brooding over the chattering crowds like Lord Byron.

Clare grew more and more afraid that he would make a scene in public. He was like a tempest brewing on the horizon of various fashionable reception rooms. Cataclysm loomed, with no way to predict when it would break over her. On top of all this, she had at last noticed that Selina grew quieter and more preoccupied every day. Clare wondered if her friend was thinking of leaving to set up on her own. She would not have blamed her if she was, yet she feared to hear it. This new tension between them curtailed their private conversations and made Clare feel even more lost. Even an encounter with her former employer, Edwina Benson, and daughter Bella, in which they fawned over her in a blatant attempt to benefit from her change in fortune, did not amuse her. Her current position felt like a trap. She missed Trehearth and the twins and all the plans she'd been making there, but she couldn't go back as things stood with Jamie.

In the end, Clare simply turned away from all these
buzzing questions and pretended she was enjoying the
entertainments Martha Howland was kind enough to
arrange. She was charming to Selina to convince her
to stay. She spoke to Jamie when he called and evaded
every important topic. And soon, she felt that everything she did was to placate other people and sustain
an unhappy situation for fear of worse.

Harry and Andrew observed the stalemate between
Jamie and his lovely wife, and finally threw up their
hands, at their wits' end. Their old friend had always
been convivial, but now he'd ventured far beyond the
line. A gentleman didn't stumble home through the
streets, barely able to walk for drink. They got tired
of helping Jamie back to his rooms and having their
heads snapped off when they tried to curb his excesses.
"What do you do," Andrew asked Harry, "with a
friend who refuses to hear a word you say?" Harry had
no satisfactory answer.

ꙮ

As he stood in yet another overheated ballroom, on
yet another vastly frustrating night, Jamie scowled
at the rotating dancers and consigned them all to
perdition—his wife and her interfering friends, his
own equally nosy comrades, and the whole of London
society for that matter. He simply didn't know what
to do. It felt like earlier times, when he'd been about
to lose Trehearth, and there was no way to avert
calamity. Or even before that, when his parents had
been ripped from his life, and he'd been left alone to
pick up the pieces. The fears and desperations of his

younger self threatened to drown him. It felt as if his only option was to stifle them first. He snagged his fifth glass of champagne from a tray and held it like a lifeline. So far, it wasn't helping.

"Good evening, Lord Trehearth."

Jamie turned his head and discovered Clare's cousin standing next to him. The fellow kept popping up in odd corners at parties, always ready to chat or to keep silent, always with a sympathetic look. Lately, he was one of the few people who was pleasant to him. Jamie nodded a greeting and drank.

Covertly watching him, Simon Greenough decided that "drunk as a lord" was an apt phrase in this case. Perhaps tonight he would finally winkle some information out of Trehearth. Simon kept trying to get at the nub of what was troubling this marriage, and finding his only informant obscure or resistant. He couldn't leave it alone, though. The childhood years, when he'd been the despised poor relation, would not leave him. He couldn't shake the conviction that Clare, the only one remaining of those privileged relatives, should pay. Her rise in the world chafed at him like a wound that refused to heal. "Clare is looking particularly lovely tonight," he said, knowing it would goad his companion.

"Huh." Jamie exchanged his empty glass for a full one as a footman passed by.

"It appears you're staying for the full season, then?" Jamie had told Simon they were not, but he'd shown no sign of departing.

Jamie's fingers tightened on the goblet. "We ought to have been back home weeks ago!"

"Well, why don't you just order her home? If you cut off the funds, she'll have to—"

"Can't," Jamie growled. "She arranged it so she holds the purse strings. Billingsh... lee... man of business won't listen to me, damn his effrontery." Jamie had called on his old adviser and received a prosy lecture for his pains. That's what he recalled, anyway; he'd been about half sprung. A pang of shame went through him. Billingsley had been a mainstay when he needed one, and he had not behaved well.

Simon's blue eyes lit. Here was an opening at last. "How can that be? When you married, you naturally assumed control..."

"Made me sh... sign a document." Jamie scarcely noticed that his voice was slurred. His attention was riveted on Clare a few yards away, and miles from his arms. "Had to. Trehearth going to be taken away."

"Ah." Simon could certainly understand Clare's impulse. The thought of someone else getting his hands on one's fortune was intolerable.

Jamie took the single syllable as criticism. "Well, I ash... ashum... I thought she'd change her mind once she was married and settled. Why wouldn't she? Ish unnatural for a woman to manage the money. Don't you think?"

"Indeed." Simon didn't mention that he was the son of a woman who'd done precisely that, who'd had to scrimp and make do for years because his father was hopeless with money. The point was irrelevant. "You know, I'm certain you could break that agreement if you contested it." He had no idea if this was true. Truth wasn't the issue here.

"Really?" Jamie gazed at him owlishly.

"Of course. The law is on your side."

"True." Jamie nodded, noticed his half-empty glass, and drained it.

"And I know just the man who could arrange it for you. He's done a good deal of that kind of work for me. He's very sharp."

Jamie tried to force his reeling brain to focus. If he had control of the money, Clare would have to go home. And once she was there... He'd take care of her, treat her like a queen. Anything she wanted. She'd soon see how much better it was, when she was far away from people like Mrs. Howland. Selina Newton, too. Time she was out of his house. They were all against him.

"Why don't I take you to meet him tomorrow?" said Simon Greenough. "You can hear what he has to say and then decide."

"Well..." Some distant inner voice told Jamie this wasn't a good idea. He should wait until his mind was clearer to decide. But another piped up urging him to be a man and take the reins; that one sounded a bit like his old headmaster at school.

"I'll come for you at ten," Clare's cousin added smoothly.

"I don't know..."

"Please, it's no trouble at all. I'm happy to help."

Her own cousin thought he was in the right, Jamie told himself. Still... He turned to tell the man that he must think it over first. But Simon was gone. The footmen weren't, however. One glided by, and Jamie took a fresh glass.

❧

Jamie woke the next morning feeling fouler than he ever had before, with no memory of how he'd gotten from last night's ballroom to the tumbled bed in his rooms. His evening clothes were twisted and crumpled around his body, his neckcloth nearly choking off the air. His mouth tasted like putrid ashes. But all of this was as nothing to the fiery pounding in his head.

Jamie sat up, and the room spun. His stomach twisted and threatened to spew its meager contents. He had to struggle to get it under control. He lurched from the bed and into the sitting room, heading for the only quick remedy for his condition—the brandy bottle.

The first sip burned the sour taste from his mouth. After a little while, his body responded to this tonic, and he felt slightly better. He stripped off his wrinkled clothes and splashed his face with cold water from the basin. If he was home at Trehearth, it would be hot, and there would be tea… He clenched the towel and threw it across the room. He searched through the piles of raiment dotting the chamber floor and dressed in an ensemble that might best have gone to the laundress instead of onto his back. He made no request to his landlady for breakfast because he didn't think his stomach would stand it. Dropping into an armchair, he wondered how to face the day. A bottomless sadness threatened, almost palpable. Jamie stood. He had to go somewhere, do something, even though his brain had not yet recovered from the previous night's overindulgence. When the knock came on the outer door, he welcomed the diversion. Though when he opened it to reveal Simon Greenough, perfectly

groomed and disgustingly cheery, he very nearly shut
it again.

"Ready for our appointment? All's set on the other
end." Simon could smell brandy on his host's breath.
He was starting early in the day.

"Appointment?" Jamie had no memory of an
appointment but was ashamed to say so. If only his
head would stop pounding. "I'm not really feeling up
to it. Perhaps another day…"

"Oh, they're all ready for us. And I have a cab waiting. Best just get it done."

Get what done? Jamie wondered. *Who were "they"?*
Without quite knowing how, he allowed himself to
be hustled down the stairs and into a cab. As they
rode through the morning streets, he searched his
memory for the reason behind this expedition. Finally,
he pulled up some talk about money, and his unusual
situation. He shouldn't have spoken of that. He
couldn't remember what he'd said. At least the man
was Clare's cousin, not some random stranger.

They left the cab in front of a narrow building
that wasn't too far from Everett Billingsley's offices.
Greenough herded him up two sets of stairs and into
a solicitor's chambers. Jamie didn't catch the name
properly, but the balding man inside had an insinuat-
ing, confidential manner and seemed to know all
about why they were there. Which was more than
he did, Jamie thought. The other two kept talking
and talking, and gradually he understood that they
proposed overturning the agreement he'd signed with
Clare. They spoke of it as a simple matter, a sure thing
really, easily accomplished without much fuss. All he

need do was sign an authorization for this solicitor fellow to act on his behalf.

At some point during this explanation, a large glass of brandy appeared at his elbow, and he sipped from it automatically as he listened. It seemed that the action they proposed—he didn't quite comprehend what it was— could be accomplished quickly and discreetly. It was a mere nothing, beneath notice really, a simple solution to his dilemma. Badgered, cajoled, taunted—and increasingly befuddled—Jamie finally gave way and signed.

After that, everything was bustle once again. Papers were whisked away. Simon Greenough escorted him to the street and put him in a cab on his own. Jolting over the cobbles on the way back to his rooms, Jamie nodded off. The driver had to wake him when they arrived. Inside, slumped into the armchair before the hearth, Jamie let his head fall back, eyes closed. He'd be better after more rest. He hadn't been sleeping well, and he was so tired. Maybe his headache would be gone when he woke.

The next thing he knew, Andrew Tate was shaking him and practically shouting in his ear. "Wake up!"

Jerked from unconsciousness, Jamie put up his hands to fend him off. "What are you doing? Let me be."

"There's news from Cornwall." Andrew waved a letter under his nose. "Must be important, because it came by special courier. Wake up, damn you, Jamie!"

❧

Not too far away, Clare and Selina were reading letters that had arrived with the same special courier. They came from Anna Pendennis and Edward Carew and brought the same worrisome information. "The twins have gone missing?" Clare exclaimed. "But how… where…?" She'd written the girls faithfully, but they hadn't responded, possibly because her letters had been superficial, she thought guiltily, never addressing the issue of when she would return.

Selina nodded. "Edw… Reverend Carew says that he has searched all the places he can think of where they usually go."

Clare sprang to her feet. "We must go home at once and help find them."

Selina nodded again and couldn't repress a wave of gladness. Immediately, she reproached herself. It was complicated to be granted your dearest wish through such dire news.

Clare turned one way, then the other. "We must pack. Will you tell Martha? And Jamie…" She turned back to Selina. "We must tell—"

"The vicar has written to him as well. I'm sure Anna has, too."

Fleetingly, Clare cringed at the thought that everyone knew they had separate addresses. Then she thrust the thought aside and rushed to make preparations.

In the end, they could not get off until the following morning. There was a post chaise to hire and belongings to pack up. Notes flew back and forth from Mrs. Howland's mansion to Jamie's rooms, and it was agreed that he would ride alongside the carriage that transported Clare and Selina.

Their meeting beside the chaise in the cool dawn light was stiff and unsatisfying. Worry about Tamsyn and Tegan had superseded all other concerns. But beneath that anxiety lay the fact that nothing had been resolved between them. Jamie was grim-faced and laconic, Clare nervous and sad.

They traveled as fast as they could, and there was little conversation when they stopped in the evenings at some post house or inn. Dinners were merely an occasion for refueling weary bodies, and Jamie barely took advantage of these opportunities. Clare began to wonder if he was ill; he looked so pale and drawn. He was thinner, too. And he drank more than she would have liked. She noticed that he kept a flask with him on horseback, and his first call when they stopped at the end of the day was for brandy.

Jamie fought an uncertain stomach for much of the journey, eating little and assuaging his pains with sips of brandy, and more after the women had gone to bed. He'd so often imagined their trip home, but not like this. Clare spoke very little to him. When she gazed at him with her intoxicating eyes, he imagined that she was blaming him for leaving the twins with only servants to watch over them—again. More than once guilt had so agitated him that he nearly burst out that it was all her fault for running away. If she'd stayed home like a proper wife, none of this would have happened.

They reached Trehearth late in the afternoon and were quickly surrounded by a clamoring staff, all eager to explain how Tamsyn and Tegan had slipped away, and everything they had done to try to find them. The Pendennises were stricken. The newer servants defensive. Jamie felt as if he'd fallen into the middle of a street mob. The noise and confusion were maddening. And then the vicar showed up to add his contributions to the melee, enumerating all the places he'd searched and everyone he'd recruited to be on watch.

"Please, please." Clare held up her hands, and gradually the group fell silent. "I'm sure that you have done everything you could, and we will hear it all. But one by one. Let us go in and sit down, and then we will speak to each of you."

Jamie admired her calm, the more because he'd seen on the journey how worried she was. They did as she suggested, and gathered more detail, but the upshot was—his sisters had gone out on an expedition, as they often did. On foot, not on their ponies. No one remembered if they'd taken anything unusual with them, because their behavior had been so ordinary. And then they had simply not come back. It was hours before anyone noticed; it was none of the staff's particular responsibility to monitor their movements, as individuals were quick to remind him. Now, they'd not been seen for days, and nobody had the least idea where they were.

The day declined into darkness and grew late. Jamie met with the various search parties and suggested a few spots that hadn't been scoured. Clare talked for quite a time with Anna Pendennis, trying to discover what the twins might have been thinking. Edward Carew caught Selina as she hurried down a corridor and pulled her into the empty solar. They stood there a moment, holding a long gaze, then fell into each other's arms. "I've so longed to see you," he murmured into her dark hair. "I cannot help but be glad you're here, even though the reason for it is terrible."

Holding onto him like a lifeline, she nodded into his shoulder. "I know."

He drew back a little so that he could see her face. "When the twins are found, there can be no more delays. I could not bear it."

"No. We will tell everyone as soon as…" Selina's throat grew tight. She hadn't always gotten along with Tamsyn and Tegan, but the thought of the little girls perhaps lost in the sea or… "As soon as they are back home," she finished resolutely.

"Tell everyone… and marry," he answered.

"Yes. Oh, yes."

He pulled her close once again.

After hours of circular discussions and increasingly wild suggestions, at last exhaustion triumphed, and the household retired to bed. Clare and Jamie tried unsuccessfully to sleep, separated by a few feet, the panels of a door, and an obdurate wall of misunderstanding.

Twenty

"THEY KNOW THIS COUNTRY SO WELL," CLARE repeated to Selina. "And they left on their own. They took food from the kitchen." The girls often packed a picnic for their ramblings. "Even if one of them were hurt," Clare continued, reassuring herself, "the other could go for help. Randolph is gone as well, and can only be with them. So they must be all right."

Selina said the same to the vicar, who agreed it must be true when talking with Jamie. Jamie assured the Pendennises. And the words went round and round the house, while searchers combed the area and turned up no sign of the girls. Selina had her own theories, which she shared only with Edward Carew. Tamsyn and Tegan had left no note, but she strongly suspected they had run away with the express purpose of bringing everyone home to search for them. The vicar agreed, and deplored, and refrained from pointing out that the travelers were all now returned. Yet the twins remained missing.

Jamie swung between acute anxiety and anger. Under the influence of the first, he grew certain that something terrible had happened to his sisters. A portion of the sea cliff had collapsed under them, or they had been robbed and killed, or fallen victim to some illness brought on by exposure. They were lying out there somewhere, off all the known tracks, feverish and starving. When his mood shifted, he railed at them for playing this trick, so much more than a simple prank. He imagined them hiding in some remote den and giggling as they spied the parties looking for them. He spent long days riding the land with the searchers, and longer nights soothing his lacerated emotions with bottles from the wine cellar.

Clare walked the nearby fields with other groups. She and Selina searched the twins' bedchamber from top to bottom, even though this had already been done. She canvassed the village for any word. The twins had to be getting food from somewhere, but no one admitted supplying them. Clare didn't think anyone was lying to her, and she refused to consider the possibility that the girls had no more need of food because of some disaster.

Edward Carew continually fought an agony of self-blame. He began to imagine that his encouragement of the girls' interest in the history of the area had given them the idea of running away. Selina did her best to soothe him, pointing out that Tamsyn and Tegan had been fascinated by the ancient stones before he started teaching them. But her reassurance had little effect. He would not be consoled for his supposed dereliction.

Trehearth became a house brimming with tension. Emotions hovered at a fever pitch, and the least thing could cause a wild reaction, in the servants' quarters as well as the family's. Shouting had grown commonplace, and all and sundry vented their anxiety in excessive blame for small infractions.

The storm broke over dinner on the third evening, as Jamie poured the last of a bottle of wine, which only he had touched, into his glass and sagged back in his chair. He watched the ruby liquid glint in the candlelight and fuzzily hoped it would bring sleep. He hadn't had a good night's rest since the news reached them in London. No, that wasn't true. He hadn't slept well in weeks.

"Drinking yourself into a stupor again isn't going to help," Clare commented tartly. Jamie had always liked his wine a bit too much. But she was appalled by the amount he was drinking now.

"Oh? What exactly will help?" He drank off half the glass defiantly. "You have some bright idea?"

"At least I'm keeping my wits about me trying to think of one," she answered.

"You! This is all your fault for running off and leaving them."

His voice felt like a blow. "Mine? How many times have you left them here alone? If you had ever taken care of them properly…"

"What do you know about it?" Jamie shouted. Her accusation was like a lash on his raw sensibilities. "You think because you were *employed* to care for children that you have some special insight? I didn't require payment to watch over my sisters."

Clare felt as if he'd really struck her. It wasn't the words as much as the fury in his eyes. Though she told herself that worry had driven him half mad, and that he was drunk, it didn't stop the pain cutting through her. "Neither did I," she said.

She should intervene, Selina thought. But she simply couldn't bear the strident voices and the anguished looks on their faces. Rising from her chair, she slipped out of the dining room.

"You deserted them without a thought," Jamie accused.

"That isn't true!" She had thought about the twins while she was away, Clare told herself. She had. She'd written to them. She'd sent them gifts from London. But it was a fact that her own concerns had overwhelmed her care for them. "And what of you? Did you write them even once?"

Jamie flinched from the question and flailed for words that would divert her from his failings. "You're a uh… unnatural woman," he spat. "Want all the reins in your hands. Money. Tell everybody what to do." He waved his glass, splashing wine on the linen cloth. The stain spread, red as blood.

"You are their brother, and you deserted them!" Clare cried. Every feeling lacerated, she pushed back from the table and stumbled to her feet. "Just as you always did. How many times? When you were all they had? Can you even remember?"

Jamie surged upright, rage roaring through him like a tempest. Enflamed by the wine, it pounded in his temples, raced along his veins. His arm drew back, and he flung his wineglass with all his strength. It shattered on the wall opposite Clare, bright splinters flying. Crimson dripped down the plaster in screaming runnels.

Clare ran—out into the corridor, up the stairs to her room. She locked the doors and went to rest her hands on the back of the armchair by the hearth. She was shaking all over. Her dinner felt like a ball of lead in her stomach, and her eyes burned. But she was too upset even to cry. How had her life come to this?

Trying to follow, Jamie grew entangled, somehow, with his chair. It tripped him, and he fell, bringing it down on top of him. He writhed and fought like a trapped animal, finally casting it aside in a flurry of hands and limbs. Then he crouched there on the floor, panting, terrified. What had he done? How had he so lost control of his emotions? At least he hadn't thrown the glass *at* her. He'd never meant to hurt her. Of course he hadn't. Just to make her stop flinging accusations at him, making him feel even worse about the fate of his sisters. It wasn't his fault.

Images of the twins' forlorn faces rose in his mind. He'd seen them, and refused to notice them, time after time. Now they spun about him like mocking ghosts. The shards of glass on the floor and the red splatter on the wall mocked his excuses. As the maid peeked nervously around the door frame, Jamie let his head fall into his hands. What was happening to him?

The next morning dawned in due course, after an anxious, sleepless night for most of the denizens of Trehearth. There was no news. Nothing had changed. Noting the overcast day through the windows, and thinking of the mud it would bring as she tramped with the searchers, Clare pulled her oldest gown from the wardrobe. She didn't care a fig what happened to this drab, gray garment.

As she pulled the dress over her head, she heard an odd crackle in the fabric. Running her hands over the cloth, she discovered the source, a piece of paper in one of the pockets. She pulled it out, expecting a forgotten laundry list or receipt, but when she unfolded the page, she found a note signed by the twins.

Grasping it with both hands, so hard the paper wrinkled, she ran her eyes over the words. She was at the bedroom door when she finished reading. She stopped and read it again.

> Dear Clare,
>
> The vicar is very sad with all of you gone. He's lonely and tired of people leaving and not knowing when they'll ever come back. We decided to help him. That's why we're going away.
>
> Everyone will have to come and look for us. You won't find us though. Or Randolph either.
>
> We're writing to you because you listen, and Jamie doesn't. Come to Moore's Rock alone, at ten o'clock in the morning. We'll see you and meet you there.
>
> If you bring other people, we'll hide, and you'll never find us!

Clare's first surge of relief was tinged with a fleeting amusement at the way the girls used the vicar as a proxy for their own feelings. Then worry clamped down again. This note must have been in her gown the whole time. Why had they left it in such an obscure place? She examined the page again in a futile attempt to elicit more information about where the twins were or how they were surviving. It gave no clue. The note was written in alternating handwriting—very similar, but she could see the difference. They both had written it, and she felt she could almost tell which sentiments were whose.

Poised to move, Clare wondered what to do. She knew Moore's Rock. Tamsyn and Tegan had pointed it out to her on one of their walks. The huge boulder crowned a small hill and could be seen from a great distance. It was a walk of around two miles from Trehearth along a secluded path. Should she do as they instructed, or take this note to the others?

If she gave it to Jamie, he would insist on going in her place. It was true that he didn't listen. And after last night... Clare shivered. She believed the twins' threat. If anyone else showed up, they would stay hidden, and they'd proved how skillful they were at that. Still, it didn't feel wise to just set off on her own across the countryside, not after all that had transpired. She had to tell someone what she was doing.

There was one person she could trust to do as she asked. She sat down at her desk to pen a note of her own to Selina. She folded the twins' missive into it, asking her friend to keep these matters confidential until late in the day. If Clare was not back by then, she should send John Pendennis after her.

It was still quite early. Clare got out her old cloak and a thick scarf, added sturdy boots, and slipped from her room. Creeping down the corridor, she slid the sealed note under Selina's bedchamber door and hurried on. She didn't want to explain where she was going to anyone else. That meant the kitchen was out of bounds, but she could endure a little hunger if it got the twins back home again.

The sun was barely up, but it wasn't visible. Clouds scudded across the sky, and a cool sea wind bent branches and long grass. Clare clutched her cloak to keep it from billowing and walked down the drive to a twisting path that led away inland. She'd wrapped the scarf around her neck. Although it would be June in a few days, the air was chilly and smelled of rain. Hoping it would hold off, she trudged along. At least there was no possibility of getting lost. She could see the hill she was aiming at through each opening in the vegetation.

She reached the great rock less than an hour later. It loomed gray and craggy above her head. Clare positioned herself on the lee side, out of the wind, and set herself to wait.

Time passed at a crawl. Although she knew it was well before ten, she still found her anxiety rushing back. It warred with the fatigue that had become a fact of her life lately, and made the wait even harder. Clare stood by the rock. She walked a few steps in one direction, then in another, to keep warm. She rubbed her gloved hands together inside her cloak. She pulled the scarf tighter about her neck. After a seemingly endless time, she sat on a mossy stone and leaned back against the much larger rock behind her. Tented in her cloak, the hood up, hands tucked into folded arms, she actually found her eyelids growing heavy. It had been so very long since she slept well. She relaxed against the stone and drowsed.

The sound of her name woke her. Clare blinked, momentarily disoriented, and focused on the two small forms standing before her. Tamsyn and Tegan wore their boy's breeches and shirts under thick, rough jackets. The clothes were smudged with dirt, and their dark hair was bundled up into cloth caps, only a few wild tangles escaping. Their faces looked clean, however. Nearby, Randolph was tethered to a sapling.

Clare was overwhelmed by a flood of gratitude when she saw that they were unhurt and seemingly healthy. The terrible burden of anxiety that she'd been carrying lifted like clouds burned away by the sun. She jumped up and enveloped them in a breathless embrace, one to an arm, holding as tight as she could. Their small arms gripped her just as hard. Tears of joy spilled from Clare's eyes as for an endless moment they swayed together in loving relief.

At long last, Clare drew back. She was so happy, and… so angry. "What do you think you've been doing?" she said. "Have you any notion how worried everyone has been?"

Two pairs of dark eyes gazed back at her. Tamsyn's lower lip trembled.

"Where have you been? How could you do this?"

"We left a note," Tamsyn said.

"It took you forever to find it," Tegan added.

"I should not have had to do so. Because you should not have run away. Come along. Let's go home."

The twins backed away from her. "We're not going unless you promise that no one will leave again," declared Tamsyn.

"And you won't take away our ponies," her sister

added. Tamsyn turned to glare at her, then shifted her gaze back to Clare.

Two pairs of dark eyes pleaded with her. This had gone on far longer than they meant it to, Clare realized. The twins were on the edge of desperation. "I can't guarantee..." she began. Then she stopped herself. This was not a negotiation. They had bargained over lesser matters, but the girls could not be allowed to do so over this. "You are in no position to set conditions. Your behavior has been outrageous."

The girls backed up another step. If they ran, Clare knew she could never catch them. They would disappear into whatever hiding place had concealed them for so long. Though she was sure they wanted to go back to Trehearth, she also knew they could be fantastically stubborn. Thinking quickly, Clare strode over and untied Randolph's leash. The huge dog welcomed her with a juicy swipe of his tongue. She held the leather strap firmly. "Randolph and I are going home." *Could the dog track his mistresses if they fled?* she wondered.

"He won't go with you," cried Tegan. "Randolph! Come here."

The great dog leaned in her direction, pulling at Clare's arm. "Home, Randolph," Clare said firmly. "I'll find you a good meaty bone."

The dog recognized this last word. The twins had used it often in his training, as Clare was well aware. He gazed up at her, brown eyes bright, his tongue happily lolling. When Clare took a step toward the path, he came with her. A spatter of rain darkened the rock.

"Randolph!" repeated Tegan.

He stopped and looked back over his massive shoulder.

"Come," ordered Tegan. Tamsyn seemed on the verge of tears.

Randolph pulled at the leash. Clare resisted and wondered how to break this impasse. And then, like an answer to a prayer, Selina and the vicar walked around the far side of the rock and positioned themselves behind the twins. The girls were now surrounded.

"You told!" cried Tegan, her eyes hot with betrayal.

Clare refused to be moved. "I could not go out all alone, leaving no idea where I was headed. I would never worry people that way. I consider it wrong."

Tamsyn hung her head.

"Very wise," said the vicar. "I'm extremely disappointed in you, Tegan, Tamsyn, for running away as you did. We have all been quite frantic. It was a thoughtless and irresponsible thing to do."

Under the reproving gaze of their mentor, the girls wilted. They offered no further resistance on the walk home, particularly when the rain began in earnest about halfway there. It soon soaked the whole party and made the walk a miserable slog. Even so, the twins' steps lagged as they neared the house. "I suppose Jamie will be very angry with us," Tegan murmured. It wasn't a question, and no one replied.

Inside the house, amidst the exclamations of Anna and other members of the staff, Clare inquired as to Jamie's whereabouts. She expected to hear that he was out searching, but Gwen said he had come back just ahead of the rain and gone into the estate office. This was not good news. Clare now knew that he

kept a brandy bottle there. But they couldn't delay.
The three adults herded the girls along the corridor
to find him.

When the bedraggled party came into the estate
office, Jamie was dumbfounded. For a fleeting instant,
he thought they were an illusion brought on by drink.
But he hadn't downed that much today, yet. He took
in his sisters' unharmed, if wet and grimy, condition.
They were back; they were all right. The crisis was
over. Relief ran through him in a heart-shaking tremor.

Two pairs of dark eyes gazed at him with their
customary challenge. The strength of his worry for
them flipped into a burning anger. "Where the devil
have you been? Do you have any notion of the worry
you've caused? You set the whole household on its
ear. We've been searching... if any tenant of mine has
been hiding you, I swear I will turn them out..."

"They haven't," interrupted Tegan. "We... we
hid ourselves."

Jamie recollected that he had visited every tenant on
his land, and a good few on others' estates. "Where?"
Seeing his sisters' obdurate expressions, he turned to
the others. "How did you find them?"

"They left a note in the pocket of this old gown,"
said Clare. "In my wardrobe. I only found it this
morning when I put the dress on."

Selina, ever prepared, held out the note. Jamie
snatched the page and read it. The words "you listen
and Jamie doesn't" seared his sensibilities. He grappled
with the fact that his sisters had trusted Clare rather
than him, and that she hadn't told him before going
after them.

"We wouldn't have come out if she hadn't been alone," Tamsyn said.

"Looked like she was alone," muttered Tegan.

Clare turned to look at Tamsyn, surprised by the little girl's immediate grasp of her brother's thought process.

"We thought she'd listen to us," Tamsyn ventured.

"And promise," said Tegan.

"But she didn't," murmured her sister.

"Promise what?" Jamie snapped.

"That everyone wouldn't leave us again," Tamsyn said. And she burst into tears.

"Tam." Though she looked disgusted, Tegan went and put an arm around her sister. She glared at the adults as if daring them to comment or offer sympathy. Jamie blinked at the scene. He hadn't seen either of his sisters cry in years.

"We need to get out of these wet clothes," said Clare. Further discussion could wait until everyone was warm and dry.

The admirable Anna Pendennis had already begun filling the bath with hot water. Clare left the twins in her hands and went to change her own clothes. How insignificant her bathroom plan had become compared with all that followed, she thought as she pulled off her soaked boots. She'd returned to find the project completed and hardly had the attention to care.

When she returned to the estate office some minutes later, Jamie was drinking coffee and staring out the window at the rain. Relief at his sisters' return, and the anger, had given way to a host of other emotions. They flitted in and out of his mind in no particular order, and he couldn't seem to organize them into a coherent plan of what to do next. When Clare walked in, he felt a surprising gratitude, as if all would now become clear. "Thank you for bringing them back," he said.

The simple openness of his tone touched her. "I only wish I had taken out that old gown earlier."

He waved this aside. "Last night... I... That was outrageous, inexcusable. I apologize. It will never happen again." He saw Clare looking at the coffee cup. He raised it in a small salute. He couldn't quite bring himself to say it aloud, but he hoped she would understand that he meant to limit his drinking from this day forward.

After a moment, she nodded and sat in the chair opposite his desk. "We must decide what to do. I feel that there must be severe consequences for the girls' behavior."

"I couldn't agree more. Shall we lock them in the cellars?" He tried a smile to show he was joking. He seemed to have forgotten how to talk to Clare, a skill that had once been so easy. "Pack them off to school?" he added more seriously.

"I don't think so." Clare shook her head. "No. They love this place so much. I think that is too harsh. There must be punishment, of course. Running away is absolutely unacceptable. But what Tamsyn said... Obviously, they've also been hurt by being left alone."

Jamie winced. Clearly leaving them here at Trehearth with only the Pendennises—this time and before—had been a mistake. He'd made so many mistakes with his sisters.

"To send them away from the home they adore... from all of us..." Clare cringed internally. Was there an "all of us" any longer? She'd thought they were building a family; she'd given the twins the impression that they had one and then fled without a word. In her anguish, she'd hurt them cruelly. But resolving the crisis that had brought her back to Trehearth didn't solve the problems that had precipitated it.

"They would hate that," Jamie acknowledged.

Throat tight, Clare nodded.

"Clare." His voice broke on the syllable. "I've acted like… an ass. I'm sorry. Can you forgive me?"

Was he apologizing for going back on his word? She should ask him, Clare thought. But the idea of rehashing that sore subject was too painful. And perhaps she was afraid of the answer.

"I'll do better." He would forego the brandy entirely, Jamie vowed. "Can we not go back to the way things were… before? Try again?"

"Just as they were before?" Clare said. She gazed at him steadily, the whole history of his betrayal in her eyes. If he would honor their agreement… She swallowed. How she yearned for their days here together when all had seemed well.

Jamie didn't pretend to misunderstand her. He knew he'd made a host of mistakes. The drinking. And he'd been hasty and short-tempered. He'd pushed for his own way when there was really no necessity. They'd easily reached agreement on what was to be spent, after all. Why had he not let any change that was to come in their understanding develop at its own speed? Strangers—which was what they'd been at first—did not trust each other in an instant. "Yes," he said firmly.

Clare was shaken by the strength of her reaction. A tightness around her heart, an ache she'd been carrying for weeks, eased. She blinked back a film of tears and nodded.

Jamie wanted to leap up and sweep her into his arms, but he didn't quite dare. He was afraid of making any missteps in this fragile dance. He cleared his throat. "So, the twins, what shall we do about them?"

With a deep breath, Clare pulled her mind back to the present problem. "I think… what about… no ponies for… a month? And even then, they are not allowed to wander around the countryside on their own. If they go riding or walking, they must be escorted."

Jamie nodded. This would be a real hardship for his sisters. "We should find out where they were, so they can't pull that trick again."

"If we can." Clare doubted that the girls would part with this information. "Also, they must concentrate on *all* of their studies without any complaint and…" She smiled slightly. "Learn to cook."

"Cook?" Jamie raised his brows in surprise.

"Just some simple dishes. Tamsyn and Tegan are rather contemptuous of domestic tasks."

"Ah." There was a gratifying symmetry to the scheme.

"What do you think?" They were his sisters, Clare reminded herself, even though she had developed a deep affection for them.

"I agree absolutely, on every point. And I believe it would be best if we tell them together, to make it clear there is no room for… jockeying or playing one of us off against the other."

"A good idea." Clare smiled at him, wondering if he understood that this would also reassure the twins.

She smiled at him, and for the first time since he was sixteen, Jamie nearly wept. It seemed an endless time since she'd looked at him so affectionately, and he'd missed her so much.

Judgment passed, they went to find the twins and deliver the sentence. Tucked into their own great bed, washed, in clean nightclothes and supplied with mugs of hot milk, the girls were sliding toward sleep. Their relief at being home again was obviously taking hold, and they received the news of their punishments with little protest. That would come later, Clare thought as she shut the door upon them. This weary docility would soon wear off. But she found she didn't mind. Tamsyn and Tegan wouldn't be themselves without a good dollop of mischief.

Jamie returned to the estate office to take up the myriad projects that had fallen behind as they searched for his sisters. Clare went to the kitchen to share the terms of the twins' punishment with Anna and Mrs. Telmore, the cook. The latter looked a bit apprehensive until Anna promised to join in the culinary lessons. She also promised to tell her husband about the ban on the ponies. Feeling that she'd done her duty, Clare headed for the solar, anticipating the first moments of true relaxation she'd experienced since returning from London.

She was a bit surprised to find the vicar there, hovering over the fire to dry his damp garments. Selina sat on the sofa, and Clare had the sense that they'd been talking of serious matters until she arrived. "I asked…

Reverend Carew to dinner," Selina said, her voice a little constrained. "It's so wet and dreary outside."

And would be all that, as well as dark, later on, thought Clare. She said nothing, however. She was content to have his company. Perhaps he needed to be here, to assure himself that all was really well. He'd been as worried about twins as any of them.

The rainy afternoon darkened toward dusk, and the four adults gathered in the dining room for a quietly celebratory meal. Jamie ordered up a single bottle of wine and partook of only one glass. With each hour that passed, the restoration of the twins sank in more deeply. They were able to truly enjoy the cook's efforts, as they had not in days.

When the last dish had been cleared, leaving them alone, Selina sat up straighter in her chair and said. "We have something to tell you."

"We?"

"Selina and I," said the vicar.

Before Clare could react to his use of her friend's first name, Selina added, "Edward has asked me to marry him."

"And she has done me the great honor of accepting." Carew reached across the table and took Selina's hand.

So that was why the vicar had been hanging about Trehearth so much since they brought Mrs. Newton here, Jamie thought. He hadn't suspected an attachment. "Congratulations," he said.

Clare was stunned. Had she become so self-absorbed that she didn't notice such a great change in the life of a friend? Her cheeks warmed a bit with shame. But Selina was looking at her, gaze slightly anxious.

"That's wonderful news!" As soon as she spoke, Clare realized the truth of her statement. Selina would be her neighbor. She would stay right here rather than going off on her own. And still she was thinking of herself! "I'm so happy for you," she added.

"We should break out a bottle of champagne from the cellars," Jamie said. He saw Clare looking at him and flushed. Did she think drink was always his first thought? At the same time, he was aware that a part of him longed for a sparkling glass. Or two.

"Not for me," said the vicar. "One glass of wine is my limit, and in any case, I must head home. My housekeeper will be wondering what's become of me. I simply wanted to share our happy news before... any new disruptions occurred. Or Selina could change her mind." The couple smiled at each other so tenderly that Clare finally discovered the joy she should feel at a friend's happiness.

Reverend Carew rose. Selina did too. "I'll see you out," she said.

Clare and Jamie sat on in the dining room. There was no thought tonight of her retreating to the solar and leaving him to his bottle. "So, a romance right under our noses," Jamie said.

"Yes."

"Aren't you pleased? I would have thought you'd be delighted."

"I am. I'm just... startled that I didn't notice it happening."

"I didn't either. They were very discreet."

Clare didn't say that men rarely noticed such things. "I thought Selina and I were so close. She listened very patiently to all my… worries. I feel I haven't paid enough attention to her concerns."

As the undoubted object of many of these worries, Jamie didn't know how to respond to this.

Clare shook herself. "I'm just being foolish. Selina looked very happy, didn't she?"

"She did." He smiled with raised brows. "Carew, too."

Clare laughed. "As he should be! Selina will be a perfect vicar's wife."

"A happy ending."

She looked up and met his dark gaze as it turned serious.

"Clare." He lost himself in her tiger eyes, thinking back to the first time he'd seen her, on the dim stairs of Billingsley's offices. It wasn't so very long ago in the greater scheme of things, but so much had happened since then it seemed an age.

The happiness on the faces of Selina and the vicar came back to Clare. She and Jamie had been moving toward that kind of harmony before all this began. She knew they had. And now they'd weathered this emotional storm. If he was willing—as he seemed to be—surely they could find their way? As someone had said to her long ago— her mother?—marriage was about compromise.

As Carew had done, Jamie extended his hand across the tablecloth. "I've missed you so."

Tears pricking, Clare took it. Their fingers curled together, and they rose. Jamie stepped around the table. Clare moved into his arms and rested her head on his shoulder. They stood there, intertwined, in a silence broken only by the ticking of the mantel clock.

Then Jamie pulled back a little and looked down. The tentative hope he saw in her face shook him to the core. "Come upstairs," he murmured.

She could not have done anything else. His arm still around her, they went quietly up to her bedchamber. Though it was still early, they saw no one in the corridors. They slipped into Clare's room, and Jamie locked the door. When he turned to her, her pale hair gleamed in the light of the low fire, her slender form outlined by orange light. He'd thought she was beautiful as soon as he saw her; now that he knew her, she seemed so much lovelier, as if the kindness and intelligence inside lent more beauty to her physical lineaments.

Clare's skin warmed under his appreciative gaze. Memories of their nights in this room made her heart beat faster. She smiled at him.

In three steps, he was with her, pulling her close and capturing her lips in a kiss that held equal parts tenderness and desire. Clare melted under his hands. Doubts and hesitations couldn't withstand the depth of this kiss. It paused and resumed until it shut out the world, leaving only the two of them, together.

Jamie's body and spirit had caught fire. Yet he didn't want to hurry. He wanted these exquisite sensations to go on forever. When Clare arched against him and tangled her fingers in his hair, he whispered in her ear, "Slowly, my darling, let us tantalize each other."

Clare drew back and looked at him. His eyes were pools dark enough to drown in, but a slight smile curved his lips. She caught his mood and responded with a shy smile of her own.

As his fingers played with the row of buttons down

the back of her dress, she loosened his neckcloth and teased it away, letting the length of starched cotton slither down from the strong column of his neck. She pushed his coat from his shoulders. Jamie straightened his arms, and it fell to the floor with a sigh of fabric.

Her gown went more softly, with a mere whisper. Clare's breath escaped in a long sigh as Jamie dropped kisses down her neck and onto her bare shoulder. She undid the buttons of his shirt and slipped her hands inside it, running them over the muscles of his chest, making his breath catch as she let them stray across his hard belly. Then she eased the shirt back and over his broad shoulders. It fell, then caught briefly, until he once again straightened his arms and freed the cuffs from his hands.

Bare-chested in the firelight, Jamie untied strings and loosed her petticoat. It whispered down to join the pool of cloth at their feet, and Clare stood inches away in her half transparent shift. Firelight danced through, outlining her body. Boots, he had to get rid of his boots. He stepped back long enough to yank them off, and then pulled her into his arms again.

This kiss was more urgent. He couldn't sustain this game much longer, not when her fingers were on the fastenings of his breeches. Jamie ran his hands up her sides, lifting her shift until he found the hem. He drew it over her thighs and hips, lingered at the curve of her waist, and then, in one swift movement, yanked it up and over her head. Distracted by the glorious sight of her naked body, he almost threw it in the fire.

Under his burning eyes, Clare put her shoulders back and stretched a little. She'd never felt this way before. She wanted to rouse him even further, wanted the fire she saw in his eyes to flame higher. Holding his gaze, she undid his breeches and let a hand stray behind the laces.

"Ah," Jamie groaned. This was the end of the game; he could bear no more. In one swoop, he picked her up and carried her to the bed. She smiled seductively as he set her down, a vision of pale gold and cream and rose on the blue counterpane. He pushed off the rest of his clothes and joined her.

At last there was nothing between them. The heat of skin to skin built toward conflagration. Jamie's hands, browned by the sun, roamed over her, leaving trails of sweet fire. The ache of desire rose in both of them.

Clare panted his name, and Jamie gave in to her unspoken plea. His fingers caressed the soft arch of her ribs, the arc of her hip, the silk of her inner thigh. They drifted inward and slipped to the center of that ache, teasing and appeasing.

Clare's whole body responded to his touch. She yearned toward him, entwined a leg with his, and tightened her arms around him. She danced into a blaze of light that built to a magnificent intensity before it broke in a million sparkling pieces.

When her head fell back, and she cried out, Jamie's control shattered. He could wait no longer. He rose over her and let himself go. It was like discovering new realms of pleasure and coming home, all at once. As they moved so sweetly in unison, it seemed as if they could never be out of harmony again. They rose to the peak together, lingered there for a timeless moment, then dropped into paradise side by side, hanging onto each other as if they would never let go. He wouldn't, he vowed to himself; he would never let go. He took her lips again with that silent promise.

Sated, entangled, gradually their pulses slowed, their breathing eased. Jamie turned on his back, keeping Clare close. She rested her head on his shoulder as if it belonged nowhere else. One hand gently stroked his chest. In its own way, the tender aftermath was as moving as the passion, and Jamie realized then that he'd fallen in love with his wife. It was like an old joke, but this was dead serious. Over these last tumultuous weeks, as he'd come to know her many facets, as he'd won her and then very nearly lost her and finally won her again, he'd given his heart to this woman in his arms. She'd become vital to his existence. He had to do whatever it took to keep her in his house, in his arms. If he had to change, it was worth it, more than anything before in his life. As he pushed a strand of pale hair off her brow, following his fingers with a kiss, he silently determined to bend all his efforts to keep her close to him for the rest of their days.

Twenty-one

"WHAT DO YOU THINK OF THIS RIBBON TRIM FOR THE bonnet?" Selina asked anxiously.

"It's perfect," Clare answered. "You're going to be a beautiful bride."

"I don't want to look beautiful," was the fretful reply. "I want to look suitable and reverent and…" Selina's voice trailed off, hearing the tone and absurdity of the sentiment. "I do beg your pardon, Clare. It's just…"

"I know."

The marriage of the local vicar had turned out to be a momentous event in the eyes of at least some parishioners. Many, of course, were simply glad for Reverend Carew. But others seemed to have an almost proprietary interest in him and had eyed Selina with doubt and touches of envy. Questions flew about the parish like a swarm of bees. While Edward took it all in stride, used to his doings being more or less public, Selina had some difficulty enduring the beady gazes at church and in the village streets. They roused in her a desire to ensure that every element of her conduct, and the upcoming ceremony, was above reproach. Uncharacteristically, she consulted Clare about the smallest details of her planned costume and arrangements.

Clare was glad to offer her support, and well able to do so now that her own life had shifted back into happiness. The two women spent many pleasant hours in the solar or the sewing room talking over busy hands.

Jamie had thrown himself into the building projects that had slowed without his supervision, his enthusiasm for restoring his estate renewed. On one afternoon, he showed Clare all the figures for the new and repaired tenant cottages. Tentatively, nervously, they worked their way through this fraught experience. At one or two points, Jamie had to fight the impulse to tell her he simply knew best. Though his dark eyes snapped, he did fight it, and Clare noticed and appreciated his efforts. Once all was explained, he found her quite understanding about the higher costs.

What Jamie did not tell his wife was how difficult he was finding it to keep his promise to reduce his drinking. Though he freely admitted that he'd been overindulging, changing his habits was far from easy. Each evening he vowed he would drink less. But it shook him to find just how much he wanted one more glass, which he knew would lead to another, and another. The change in the amount he imbibed affected his physical state, too. He sometimes felt rather ill and had to struggle to hide this from the household.

Clare returned to her work of refurbishing the house, continuing to add brightness and color to their surroundings. She also involved herself more closely in the twins' lessons and activities. They seemed genuinely contrite about their escapade, eager to earn back riding privileges and the right to roam. Though she sometimes wondered how long their repentance would last, Clare enjoyed the increased closeness and the buoyancy of their company. Occasional remarks revealed that their anxiety about people leaving without warning had been assuaged but not erased.

All in all, however, it seemed that their household had found its way through the tempests to contentment. Clare didn't imagine that all tumult was past, but she thought they would be able to navigate new bumps in the road as they appeared with much more aplomb.

She was thinking something like this on a bright morning in late June as she and Gwen hung new draperies in one of the guest bedchambers. Jamie was out at some distant building site. Selina had gone down to the vicarage to consult Edward's housekeeper about a list of details. The twins actually seemed content over their books in the library.

Clare had no thought of trouble when Anna Pendennis came in and held out a letter, saying that a messenger from the village had brought up a packet that had arrived with the mail coach. The envelope was addressed to Clare, and when she unfolded the fat document, she found it came from a hated source, her cousin's solicitor. She'd long ago learned to dread communications from this man. His missives—Simon's communications—were always unpleasant or insulting. This time, though, she held the pages with less trepidation. There was nothing Simon could do to hurt her now. She was beyond his control. She was even tempted just to put the thing aside. It was too fine a day to be ruined by her cousin. But she couldn't quite manage; better to know the bad news than to worry about what it might be.

Clare folded the document up again and took it to the solar. She sat down and started to read. After the first few sentences, her sight blurred, and she swayed in the chair. This couldn't be right. She'd misunderstood. She started again from the beginning. But there it was on the page, in careful, clerkly handwriting. This hateful solicitor claimed that he'd been given the authority to act on Jamie's behalf, and that her husband was suing to set aside the document they'd signed upon their marriage. He would ask a judge in chancery to turn over all control of her inheritance to him.

Clare refused to believe it. It couldn't be true. She read faster, the legal language twisting in her mind. Under the larger document, she found a note from her cousin, explaining that he had been present when Jamie signed the authorization. Clare could almost hear Simon's snide voice in the written words. She could see his sneering smile. A paragraph at the end, in a different hand, stated that a clerk named Cyrus Gorrige had also witnessed Lord Trehearth's request for legal assistance and would so swear.

The stiff pages dropped to the floor of the solar. Simon's part in this was no surprise. He would do anything to hurt her. He never seemed to tire of it. She was accustomed to her cousin's malice. She'd learned to expect nothing else. But Jamie! Her husband had joined her cousin to betray her. Far worse than that, he had smiled at her, held her in his arms, talked of their future together as if all was now well between them. And all the time he'd known that this suit was being prepared. It was like the time she'd visited the banker in Penzance and found that he'd secretly undermined her position with the firm. Only far, far worse!

Clare crossed her arms over her chest and bent over them, as if to hold herself together. Before, he had at least stated his position openly. There'd been no sneaking subterfuge, no sly intermediaries. This time, betrayal came with smiling hypocrisy. He'd kissed her and caressed her as he waited for this blow to fall. Clare had to stifle a sound that was humiliatingly like a whimper.

Every time she thought she knew him, she found she was wrong. When it came to Jamie, it seemed her judgment was fatally flawed. He clouded her perceptions, made her trust without reason. Places inside Clare that had opened and expanded in what she saw as the warmth of his affections now felt like slashing wounds. When she was poor and a governess, she'd put up inner barriers to protect herself. She needed them back! She couldn't stand this; she couldn't function while she was dizzy with anguish.

Minutes ticked past on the mantel clock. Fortunately, no one entered the solar while Clare grappled with her pain. The household was occupied; the staff was busy elsewhere. She sat there, alone, and panted like a wounded animal. At last, after an endless time, she was able to straighten in the chair. After a bit more, she could wonder what to do.

Part of her longed to run—the part that had sent her fleeing before. Hire a coach, race to London, confront Everett Billingsley, hire some other representative to help her. Of course she would not have Selina's companionship this time. She couldn't separate her friend from the vicar, spoil her wedding plans. And she had promised the twins not to abandon them again. Why had she made such a rash promise? Why had she trusted in the future? Thoughts raced around her brain in chittering chaos. Go, stay, go. She felt very much alone.

Clare knew that running away wouldn't solve her problems. She'd proved as much. But the thought of facing Jamie in this devastated state made her shudder. To see him walk in, perhaps smile at her, hold out his hand... The image cut through her like a knife. It was all she could do not to run down the hallway and out the front door into the fields.

Clare swallowed, took a tremulous breath. She bent and picked up the stiff pages from the floor. They shook in her hands. She must write to Billingsley, find some other solicitor, have him prepare a response to this suit and... other things. She couldn't put two thoughts together. The vision of Jamie changed to a sight of him in a courtroom. What would she say, how would she endure it, as she fought her husband in court? She had to grit her teeth to keep from weeping. If she started, she didn't think she'd ever stop.

There was a slight sound at the doorway, and the twins came in. "We were looking for you because it's time for our..." Tegan trailed off.

"What's the matter?" said Tamsyn.

"Nothing." Clare's voice sounded completely false in her own ears.

"Something's made you sad," Tamsyn went on.

"And mad," added Tegan.

These girls were far too canny for their age. Clare searched for an excuse they would accept.

"We didn't do anything," said Tegan.

Clare swallowed. "No, you didn't."

"Did Jamie do it?" Tegan wondered.

She couldn't help it, her eyes flashed to theirs, then dropped again. She had to regain her composure. It wasn't fair to involve the twins in her turmoil. She didn't want to lie to them, but neither could she share the truth. "There's nothing for you to worry about," she tried.

Immediately, the girls looked worried. "Are you going away again?" asked Tegan.

"I promised I wouldn't do that," Clare replied. Could she keep that promise? She'd made promises to Jamie, too. Vows that she never meant to break. Clare couldn't help it; she rested her forehead on her hand. She wanted to keep up appearances for Jamie's sisters, but she felt so broken, so tired. "If I could just get away for a bit, not long, have some time to think," she murmured, too quietly to be heard, she thought.

But the twins had ears like foxes. "You want to hide for a while?" asked Tegan.

Clare looked up into two pairs of dark eyes, so like Jamie's she wanted to cry. "Hide?" That was exactly it; she wanted to go to ground, like an injured animal crawling off to lick its wounds in solitude.

"We know a place you can hide," said Tamsyn.

Clare gazed at the girls. They'd never discovered where the twins went when they ran away. They had some secret lair. She shouldn't pull them into this. It wasn't right. But she was dazed with hurt and confusion. Clare struggled with her doubts.

"It's not a hole in the ground or anything," added Tegan. "You'd be all right there." Tamsyn nodded.

It was so tempting. Too tempting. "Perhaps... just for a few days. I... I need to think."

Tamsyn and Tegan looked at each other, then back at Clare. "A few days," said Tegan.

"Then you'll come back?" Tamsyn asked.

"Yes." She had to, Clare thought. Her whole life was in question here. She had to find a solution.

"We can take you," Tegan said.

"It's a longish walk," said her sister.

"But no one will find you. They didn't find us!" Tegan grinned.

"And we won't tell. We never tell." Tamsyn looked quite proud of herself.

She shouldn't allow them to take on this responsibility, Clare thought. But if she didn't get away, very soon, she would break down completely. "All right. Just for a little while." She would organize her thoughts and come back to face Jamie. They would have it out, once and for all.

The girls nodded solemnly.

Once she'd made up her mind, Clare was goaded by the thought that Jamie could come home at any moment. She quickly packed a few things in a small valise and scribbled a note to Selina, telling her that she was all right, just going away for a few days. The final matter was what to do with the hateful document the mail had brought. In the end she decided to leave it on Jamie's desk in the estate office. Despite everything, she felt he deserved some idea of why she had left the house.

It was after noon when they set out, Clare with her valise and the twins each carrying a parcel of food purloined from the kitchen. Randolph bounded along beside them as they followed a path heading southeast. It ran near the ocean for a while, then veered inland. Clare scarcely noticed its twists and turns. All her faculties were occupied by her inner turmoil. After an hour, though, she grew tired. "How much farther is it?" she asked the twins.

"We're more than halfway," Tamsyn replied.

"It's beyond the bounds of Trehearth," Tegan explained.

That was why none of the tenants had known where they were, Clare concluded. She wasn't sure why she was so tired; she'd often walked farther than this in the past. It must be the shock of receiving the document and trying to figure out what to do. She set her valise on the ground and stretched her back. The twins paused as she did. "Are you tired?" Tamsyn asked.

"Randolph could carry your bag for you," Tegan said.

"What?"

"He can carry it. We do it all the time." The girl pulled a length of rope from her bundle and went to pick up the valise. "Randolph." The huge dog obediently stepped over to her, and he stood still as she set the small bag on his back and began to wrap the rope around it and his chest and belly. Clare watched in amazement.

"We trained him to do it," said Tamsyn.

"It's lots better when we have his pan-ears."

Clare blinked at a momentary fantastical image.

"Panniers," corrected Tamsyn. "They use them on donkeys. I saw a picture in a book."

"And we made them out of feed sacks from the stables." Tegan knotted the rope, pulling on the valise to make sure it was secure. "Randolph likes to help."

The dog's red tongue lolled, and he turned from one of his mistresses to the other. Clare thought he looked more indulgent than pleased, but she was once again impressed by the twins' ingenuity.

The walk became easier without her burden. They went on past some cultivated fields and a long stretch of waste ground, then into a forested dip with a small stream at the bottom. Randolph slurped water in sloppy gulps. They'd been on the move for nearly two hours when they rounded a hill and came upon one of the oddest dwellings Clare had ever seen. It was built on one of the round stone foundations of the ancient peoples, raised higher by a motley collection of timbers, and with a crude fireplace added at one side. Grass and wildflowers grew so thickly on the thatched roof that the place seemed like an extension of the nearby hill, or perhaps a fairy mound.

Tamsyn and Tegan led her around to a low doorway on the south side. An old woman emerged as they arrived, small enough to walk through the low opening without stooping. She wore an ancient stuff gown, and her white hair was twisted into a bun at the nape of her neck. Despite her age, attested by a face as brown and wrinkled as old parchment, her back was straight. Eyes so dark they seemed black danced from one to another of her visitors. She held Randolph's gaze the longest.

"Tess, we've brought Clare," said Tegan.

"Lady Trehearth," corrected Tamsyn, then frowned as if wondering if she'd made a mistake.

"She needs to hide," continued her sister.

"I need a day or two to think," amended Clare. She peered into the dark doorway uncertainly. Could she really stay in such a place, with a total stranger?

The old woman made no bow or curtsy. She came close and examined Clare with those fathomless eyes. Indeed, she held Clare's gaze for so long that it began to be uncomfortable. At last she said, "All right. Ye're welcome to think here." A smile shifted her wrinkles into a surprisingly warm expression. With a gesture, she indicated her home. The twins skipped through the entry, Randolph on their heels. Clare followed more slowly. "Careful now," said Tess. "It's a step down, inside."

Clare ducked through the opening and negotiated the step. The earthen floor had been dug down almost a foot, so that the ceiling was higher than she'd expected. The dirt was rock hard and swept clean. The circular interior space was also more expansive that it had seemed from without. It held two low beds, one on either side, and a rough table and chairs before the hearth directly opposite the door. A small fire burned there, with an iron teapot hanging over the coals. A covered, three-legged pot nestled among them. Planks had been fixed against the thatch above, so its tiny residents couldn't drop on unwary heads. Little horizontal windows, not visible under the overhanging eaves outside, admitted fresh air but not much light. A candle burned on the table.

The twins seemed very much at home. They'd set their bundles beside the candlestick. "You can sleep there." Tamsyn pointed at the bed on the right.

"That's where we stayed," Tegan agreed. She was untying the rope that girdled Randolph.

"Tess takes care of sick people sometimes. That's why she has two beds."

Clare surveyed the rustic mattress.

"The straw gets changed right regular. And there's pennyroyal and lavender in it, to keep off fleas and such," said the old woman, as if she could read Clare's reservations in her face. Tess sounded amused.

"We have to get back," said Tamsyn.

Tegan nodded, setting the valise on the earthen floor. "Before anybody notices."

"We'll go much faster alone."

"We can run. No one will know we were gone."

"Wait," said Clare. Should she just go with them? Was this a mistake? But she'd spoken too softly. They were out and gone, Randolph on their heels, moving fast. Could she even find the way back on her own?

Tess went over to the fire. If she'd heard Clare's protest, she was ignoring it. "Got a bit of chamomile here. I'll brew up some tea." She used a rag to remove the iron teapot from its hook and poured steaming water into a china one sitting on the hearth stones. "Be good for you. You should sit down. That's a right long walk for a woman with child to be taking."

"What? I'm not…" With the words buzzing in her head, Clare swayed on her feet. Calculations raced through her mind, until she was dizzy with them. Her body's timing told its own story. "How… how could you know that? I didn't realize it myself until you said…"

Tess took two chipped cups from a shelf by the fireplace. "It's a sort of knowing that comes to me. My granny had it, too."

Clare went over and sank into one of the rough wooden chairs. Was this why she'd been so tired lately? But she hadn't been sick or… "Oh, my God." She was glad and uncertain and excited and despairing.

"Is that why you've really come?" The old woman gazed at her from those deep black eyes. "There's ways to deal with it."

At first Clare didn't understand what she meant, then she crossed her hands over her midsection and leaned away from her. "No! How dare you even suggest—?"

"There can be reasons." Tess hung the iron teapot back on its hook. "I have to hear some powerful good uns 'afore I give anybody anything, you understand."

"I didn't come for that. I didn't even realize… I don't know why I came, really." That sounded foolish.

"Had a lot on yer mind, eh?" The old woman poured tea and set one of the cups before Clare on the table.

"This won't hurt…?"

"Not a bit of it. Told yer, I have to hear powerful reasons. And I ain't heard any." She smiled at Clare and took up her own cup, drank a little, then sat down opposite her guest.

Clare was thirsty. She sniffed at the liquid. She'd had chamomile tea before, and this smelled like it.

"Child, I wouldn't hurt you for all the world. My granny taught me healing, and healing's what I do. Naught else."

Reassured, Clare sipped the warm beverage. "You live here all alone?"

"Aye. Though I get a good bit of company from those wanting this and that. Some just come to the spring 'round t'other side of the hill, to tie up bits o' cloth or ribbon for luck. You'll want to stay inside when I tell you to, else you'll be seen."

"But how do you live? Do you farm?" She hadn't seen any sign of it. Wondering how Tess survived so far from any village took her mind off her own worries.

"I've a vegetable patch, along with my herbs, but no, I'm no sort of farmer. I trade for what I need in the village. And people bring me bread and such when they come looking for a salve or a tincture. And even when they don't, betimes." Tess smiled, showing surprisingly white teeth. "Staying on my good side for when they might need one, y'see." Her enjoyment of this fact seemed quite good-humored.

Clare finished her tea. When Tess started to rise, she held up a restraining hand and bent to refill her own cup.

"And now and then I have a visitor who needs to be safe away for a while. Betimes they need dosing and betimes they need rest. Or they want a quiet place to ponder, like you maybe. They bring along some provisions." She gestured at the bundles Tamsyn and Tegan had carried.

"You kept the twins here." Clare didn't quite approve of that.

"Well, they kept themselves. Showed up with that lummox of a dog and flat refused to leave. Mayhap you think I should have sent word up to Trehearth."

"They're children," Clare pointed out.

Tess nodded. "It was a near thing. But they kept after me, day and night. They're not ones for listening to 'no.'"

That was certainly true.

"Point is, I was afeard they'd run off someplace less safe if I told or turned them out. And then…"

"What?" asked Clare, wondering at the bemused expression on the old woman's face.

"Somethin' told me it were best that you and his lordship come home. And that were their reason for running, after all."

"Best? What 'something'?"

Tess shrugged. She rose and busied herself putting away the food the twins had brought. Clare drank her cooling tea and hoped it would calm the whirling chaos of her mind.

Twenty-two

As the sun sank toward the western horizon, Jamie rode home whistling. The day had gone very well. Each project he visited had shown progress. He felt as if the massive work of restoring Trehearth was actually happening. It had seemed overwhelming at first, and so slow. There was still much to accomplish. But step by step, it was moving along.

Leaving his horse with Albert in the stable, he went into the house. The entryway was quiet, servants busy elsewhere at this time of day. Slanting light fell across polished paneling and a rug in deep notes of cobalt and ruby. Furniture gleamed with beeswax polish, and lavender scented the air. Jamie felt a great contentment hum in him. Somewhere in his home his wife went about her tasks, making it ever more welcoming. His sisters were in their room or out in the gardens with Randolph demonstrating their… not docility. That would be unnerving, and he didn't even wish for it. Call it a new willingness to compromise, or an appreciation of the value of cooperation. Jamie smiled. Selina Newton might be here, or down at the vicarage, as she increasingly was. Jamie was very happy for the older woman, and Carew as well. She'd make a fine vicar's wife. He was pleased that she'd be nearby as a friend for Clare, and even more that she would be out of their house. Despite Mrs. Newton's amiability, he never felt absolutely at ease with her. It was always so clear that if it were a question of sides, she took Clare's.

Jamie walked down the corridor that led to the estate office. He needed to note down some tasks for tomorrow and a list of materials to order from Penzance. Then he would go and find Clare and tell her about the nearly completed cottage at the northern boundary of the Trehearth land, and the fine new roof on another nearer the manor. He'd discovered that a great part of the pleasure of the work came in recounting it to her, and explaining how the investment would improve both the tenants' lives and the profitability of their acres. Moving by old habit, he started to pour himself a small celebratory brandy from the decanter on the side table, then remembered his resolutions and replaced the stopper. He didn't need to numb his senses, he reminded himself. He was a happy man. He sat at the desk to make his lists.

A fat document lay there, one he didn't remember seeing this morning. Puzzled, he pulled it closer and scanned the first page. Jamie frowned, reread, and scowled with bewilderment. This was incorrect and outrageous. He'd authorized no suit against Clare. He never would have done such a thing, not even in his angriest moments. Chancery court was a mire of time and expense that had swallowed more than one fortune.

He flipped quickly through the rest of the maze of legal language and came upon Simon Greenough's note beneath the legal copperplate. What was the man talking about? Claiming to be "present" in the solicitor's offices when Jamie signed the authorization. He'd signed no such… Thinking of Clare's cousin, a vague memory stirred. Greenough had dragged him out one ghastly morning, when his head was splitting, to some sort of business premises. It was all very fuzzy. Chiefly, Jamie remembered his gratitude when Greenough had urged a restorative glass upon him. There'd been another at the place they ended up, and he'd attended to little else. Jamie groped for a clearer recollection. Perhaps… there had been some sort of paper. Had he…? Perhaps a pen had been thrust at him. Jamie's pulse accelerated. He supposed he might have… had… signed something, just to make them leave him alone. And when they'd let him go, the whole incident had swiftly fallen out of his consciousness. There'd been so much else to worry over. But he'd never meant anything like this! These pages were an outrage; he'd write immediately to put a stop to the suit.

Jamie threw the packet back onto the desk in disgust. And then it felt as if his heart stopped beating for a long moment. How had this document gotten here—opened? He rustled through the pile and found the direction written on the outside. It was addressed to Clare. She'd seen it, read the contents. But she couldn't have believed that he plotted this treachery. On the other hand, why wouldn't she, with the evidence laid out before her? She'd put it here for him to find. Good God, how must she feel? Jamie's pulse resumed, pounding like a frantic drum. He stood so quickly that his chair toppled backward and ran to find his wife.

She wasn't in the solar, where she often sat at this time of day. She wasn't in her bedchamber changing for dinner, nor in the kitchens consulting the staff about the meal. She wasn't with the twins, who were romping with Randolph in the courtyard. Jamie rushed to the stables, only to be told that she hadn't taken out a horse or sent for a carriage. Receiving increasingly odd looks, he questioned every servant. None of them knew where she was. He stood with his fists clenched, at a stand, then cursed aloud. One person would know. He should have gone first to her. His brain wasn't working properly.

Jamie had glimpsed Selina Newton returning to the house as he raced from stables to kitchen. He went to knock at her bedchamber door. Receiving no answer, he dared to open it. The room was empty. He found her in the solar, sitting on the sofa, hands idle in her lap. This was so unlike Mrs. Newton that Jamie knew his suspicions were correct. "Where is she?"

"I don't know. What has happ—?"

"Don't lie to me!"

Perplexed and deeply disheartened, Selina didn't bother to object to his tone. "I would do so if I thought it necessary. But in this case, I'm telling the truth. Clare left me a note…"

Seeing a folded sheet of paper in her lap, Jamie snatched it, propriety be damned, and opened it so hastily that it tore a little. He devoured the words and found a maddening lack of information. "She can't just say she's going away for a few days and not tell me where!"

Resisting the impulse to say that she had, Selina eyed him. "What has happened, Lord Trehearth?"

Jamie crushed the notepaper in his fingers.

"Do you know *why* she's gone? I think perhaps you do."

Jamie turned away, throwing the note into the fireplace.

"Lord Trehearth."

Her tone made him turn despite himself. He couldn't control his expression.

"Clearly you do," Selina said. "If you have done something to hurt Clare, I swear I…"

"Let me be!" He fled to the estate office, closing the door and locking it behind him. Automatically, he headed for the decanter on the sideboard. Before he'd even thought, his hand had poured a large brandy and was bringing it to his lips. He stopped the glass inches away, then held it out, gazing at the amber liquid in the last of the sunlight. Its allure was palpable. Part of him longed for it with a frightening intensity.

Jamie's hand trembled. Drinking had gotten him into this coil. It wasn't going to solve anything now. He had to stop, he realized. Completely. No half measures, fewer glasses, rationed excess. His taste for brandy threatened to bring his whole world crashing down about his ears. He had to excise it from his life.

But he wanted the familiar taste on his tongue, the warmth traveling down his throat and into his chest, the glow that took the hard edges from the world. He wanted them all so much that it terrified him.

Carefully, Jamie set the glass down beside the decanter. He watched his hand hover there, still shaking slightly, reluctant to retreat, and clenched it. He stepped back, away from the sideboard—once, again. Flooded with a longing to destroy something, he started to throw the hateful document into the fire. Only just in time did he realize that he needed the name and direction of the thrice-damned solicitor in order to cancel the suit. He sat down at his desk, yanked out a sheet of paper, and composed a blistering letter withdrawing his previous authorization and ordering the man to cease all activities on his behalf. He signed it with a slash that nearly went through the page, then wrote it all again as a copy for Everett Billingsley, and again as proof to show Clare. He scribbled another missive to Billingsley himself, informing him that the suit was false, and ordering him to make very certain it was stopped immediately.

Folding and sealing the letters, Jamie felt slightly better. At least he was doing something. He ached to move, to act, to mend the balance he'd broken. He would take these down to the village himself and find a trustworthy courier to ferry the packets up to London. He couldn't remember just now when the next mail coach was due, and he didn't intend to wait a moment longer than necessary to send these on their way.

He made the short ride at a gallop. Ignoring speculative looks at the inn, he found his courier and negotiated the arrangements. Back at the house, Anna caught him coming in and told him that dinner was being served. Jamie merely shook his head and returned to his desk.

Elbows on its polished wood, head in his hands, he tried to think what else he could do. How could he find her? There must be some way. But instead of solutions, his mind filled with images of Clare— laughing, thoughtful, her green tiger eyes drowning in passion. He'd just barely recognized how desperately he loved her, and now perhaps he'd lost her forever. His stomach twisted. If it hadn't been for her odious cousin…

No. It was no good trying to shift the blame onto others. Drunk or not, he… *he* had done the thing that appeared to be an attack on her. Heedless, irresponsible, he'd allowed this tangle to happen. When she opened that document and read… The recurring pain of that picture, and a terrible fear of loss, made him turn to the decanter again. The glass still sat beside it, ready to numb the despair, to help him forget. He wanted it. His hands were shaking again, and his empty stomach was sour. He needed something to get him through the coming night. Jamie went over to the sideboard. He reached out. His fingertips brushed the glass. He picked it up. The familiar bouquet of fine brandy rose to fill his nostrils. Frighteningly, he could feel his whole body react to its lure. What could one drink matter, here, tonight? He felt so desperate. Tomorrow, he would begin… His gaze brushed the note from Simon Greenough, open on the desk. Gritting his teeth, he forced himself to set the glass aside.

In the dining room, Selina and the twins ate a mostly silent dinner. Selina was preoccupied, her mind going over the events of the last few days, trying to see what might have made Clare leave without warning.

Thus, it took her much longer than usual to notice that Tamsyn and Tegan looked far too innocent. Oh, they'd made a few remarks about Clare's absence. They'd asked questions, but not with their customary relentlessness. And they'd given up far too easily. Selina examined the girls on the other side of the table. Belatedly, again, it occurred to her that they had hidden themselves somewhere nearby for quite a long time. "You know where Clare is, don't you?" she said.

Two pair of dark eyes looked back at her. They didn't appear guilty or worried. Indeed, their direct gaze was surprisingly adult and resolute. It communicated that the twins were ready to resist any pressure she might exert. But Selina didn't feel inclined to badger them. If she knew where Clare was, she'd have to lie—to Jamie, and perhaps to Edward as well. And she hated that idea. She would never betray Clare's confidence. But if she possessed that information, she would be torn by conflicting loyalties and duties. Clare had known that, and she hadn't wanted it. That was why she hadn't revealed more in the note. Selina stifled her doubts and said only, "It's a safe place?"

A flicker of surprise danced in the girls' eyes. They didn't reply, however. They wouldn't be caught so easily. Yet it seemed to Selina that they didn't wish to lie outright either, which was comforting. She decided to be content with this and see how matters developed. If she had to, she could get it out of them. And if she judged it necessary, she would not hesitate.

There followed one of the worst nights of Jamie's entire life. Perhaps the night after he'd heard of his father's death had been worse. It had marked the end of everything then. Clare wasn't dead; she was safe and well, he trusted. But if she didn't come back to him... That would be an end of another kind, and he didn't know how he could bear it.

He sat at his desk in the estate office as the hours ground slowly by. Each minute was a millstone added to the weight oppressing him. He paced the floor in front of the fireplace. He couldn't face his bedchamber, next to the room where he and Clare had been so happy together. And since there was no question of sleep, it was better to be here, surrounded by evidence that he could affect his life, could make changes.

The brandy decanter continually tempted him, whispering of oblivion right there at hand, mocking his resolution. It beckoned like a false friend. In the depths of the night, when all the others in the house slept, he carried the tray of bottles from the sideboard to the kitchen and left it there. It didn't stop him longing for a drink, but at least the temptation was out of sight.

The sky was turning gray when he laid his head on his crossed arms and fell into a fitful doze at the desk. Not much more than an hour later, he was wakened by a sharp exclamation when the maid Gwen came in to rake the ashes and re-lay the fire, and was startled to find him in the room. Jamie finally retreated then, going upstairs to splash water on his face and change his crumpled shirt. The man who stared back at him from the mirror was pale and strained.

When he went back downstairs, he discovered that Selina Newton had repeated the message in Clare's note to the servants. Her absence had apparently been accepted without question. His behavior was drawing sidelong looks, however. No doubt Gwen had already spread the tale of finding him asleep in the estate office.

Jamie tried to eat some breakfast. To preserve the fiction that all was well, he should ride out and visit the projects on today's schedule. But he couldn't. He had to be here in case she came back. What if she only returned to pack all her things? He had to be on hand to explain and make amends. If Clare had just waited until he came home yesterday… No, this wasn't her fault. The document, which must have been crushing for her to read, had come of his own weakness and stupidity. He wanted to put that right. He had to be given the chance.

Jamie shut himself in the office once again. And the day began its endless reel toward another empty night. There were tasks waiting on his desk—orders to be sent, proposals to approve. But his drive to restore Trehearth suddenly seemed hollow and meaningless. Why was he doing it, except as a home for his family? Clare was his family. If she wasn't here to share the place… He'd have to carry on, of course. He owed it to his sisters, to his name. All his life, he'd tried to carry on, even when he made a hash of it. But it would be mere plodding without the… the glow, the joy, she'd brought to his efforts.

As darkness approached, Jamie's wish for a drink came back even stronger. The longing for oblivion made him sweat and tremble, almost distracting him from other pains. He forced himself to appear at dinner, though he couldn't manage much conversation. Back in the estate office, he paced again. It was terrible to realize how his body urged him toward the liquid solace he'd used for so long. He had reason to be glad he'd moved the bottles. If they'd been in their old spot, he feared he would have succumbed.

Sometime after midnight, he dragged himself up to bed, and exhaustion at last let him sleep for a few hours. When he woke more rested, it was with an idea fully formed in his mind. His sisters had a hiding place that no one had ever found. He couldn't believe that he hadn't remembered this before. He was an idiot, a fool. If he hadn't been so agitated and tired, he would have recalled it sooner. Jamie threw on his clothes and went to find Tamsyn and Tegan. But they weren't in their room, or the dining room waiting for breakfast. They weren't in the stables cosseting their ponies. They weren't throwing a ball for Randolph on the grounds. In fact, they were nowhere to be found. Again.

Furious, no longer caring what anybody thought, Jamie went to rap on the door of Selina Newton's bedchamber. When she opened it—fully dressed, thank God—he said, "My sisters know where Clare has gone." It wasn't a question.

"I think they do," Selina replied with little sign of surprise. "But they didn't confide in me."

"You expect me to believe that?"

Selina hadn't slept well, and she was becoming rather weary of the Trehearth family drama. "I don't really care. You will believe what you like, Lord Trehearth. I do not lie."

Even through his anger and disappointment, Jamie knew she prided herself on this quality. He glared into her hazel eyes and saw no deception there. She didn't know. He'd hit another dead end. And now his sisters were gone as well as his wife. Jamie had no idea what to do next.

Twenty-three

TESS'S COTTAGE WAS A PEACEFUL PLACE, IF MORE rustic than any other dwelling Clare had inhabited. She enjoyed the serene atmosphere, the clean herbal scents, and the quick sensitivity of the old woman who lived here. Tess always seemed to know when she wished to be silent and when a few words of conversation would be welcome. She didn't offer specific advice, as Clare never asked for any. But she had an ever-ready store of cheerful and sympathetic words. At the same time, Clare acknowledged that she found the interior of the little house dim and missed hot water in the morning, and real tea, which was too expensive for Tess's simple larder. She knew that she caused more work for her hostess as well, though she tried to be helpful. She would have to go soon. And so she would have to decide what that meant, exactly.

Fortunately, the weather remained warm and sunny, and Clare was able to sit outside for hours, tucked into a hidden dell near the little spring on the other side of the hill. The unfamiliarity of each detail of her day and the distance from home gave her the respite she needed to grapple with her thoughts, and also to consider what was happening in her body. Now that she was consciously aware of it, she could feel internal changes. A child coming altered so many things. She was a wife, and soon to be a mother. What could be more important?

Yet Jamie's betrayal couldn't be simply set aside. If he could treat her so… smile and caress and still plot to undermine their promises, what sort of man was he? What other moral lapses lurked behind his handsome face? The question felt so wrong-headed. She'd lived with him and seen him act nobly. She knew him! She couldn't believe her judgment was so flawed. Yet the proof had been there on the page. All this time he'd just been lulling her, waiting for his trap to snap shut. Could she let her child learn from such a blackguard? But he wasn't!

At this point in the debate, which came round again and again, Clare usually had to resist tearing her hair. Exhausted, miserable, she found no way out of the maze that her life had become. The only certainty was: she had to go home and confront Jamie. Let him explain what he thought he was doing! She'd weathered the initial shock. She no longer had that excuse. It was time to leave.

She told herself this on the third morning, as she sat on a bit of old blanket under the spreading oak beside the spring. Bits of cloth and ribbon fluttered from the branches, tied there by supplicants from around the countryside. Clare was wondering if they'd gotten their wishes when Tamsyn walked slowly around the hill and stood before her. Her posture and expression told Clare that something serious was amiss. "What is it?" she said, ready to rise. "What's wrong?"

Tamsyn lifted one shoulder, ambivalence in every line of her body. "I know we promised. And we never break our promises. But Jamie's very sad. And tired. He hardly ever talks. Except when he shouted once. He just stays shut in the estate office. Tegan thinks we have to bring him here." She hung her head.

The strain of holding Clare's secret showed on the girl's face. It wasn't fair to leave this weighing on the twins. She'd indulged herself too long already.

"Also, he's going to figure out that we hid you," Tamsyn added. "Mrs. Newton already did. She asked us right away. But we didn't tell!" She looked at Clare anxiously.

"You did very well. Thank you. I'm grateful to you both. But you've done enough. Tegan's right. You should bring your brother here." It would be better to talk to him far from the house, Clare realized. They could say what they liked without being overheard. They could settle things and present the result with a united front. A tremor went along Clare's nerves. What would he say? How could he justify what he'd done? As much as she yearned for the way things had been, she didn't see how it was possible.

Tamsyn let out a sigh of relief. "Tegan's hiding near the house. She's going to bring him if I don't come back in two hours."

Even in her turmoil, Clare had to smile.

༄

It was midmorning. Jamie was back at his desk. The twins were still missing. Selina Newton had fled to the vicarage. So he'd been abandoned by every vestige of family. The servants knew enough not to enter this room. Here he could brood in solitary state, he thought savagely. It was a splendid opportunity to review every tragedy that had befallen him, every mistake he'd ever made in his life. And imagine, oh yes, with the infuriating clarity of hindsight, what he should have done instead. Jamie purposely stoked the energy of anger, using it to stave off his growing despair.

He didn't hear Tegan slip into the room; she was simply there, suddenly, standing before him, solemn as a judge. Jamie shot to his feet. "Where is Clare?" he demanded, coming around the desk. "Don't bother to tell me that you don't know, because I won't bel…"

"I came to take you to her."

"…lieve you." Her words penetrated, and he stopped short, arms outstretched to grab her in case she tried to flee. "What? Where?"

Taking this literally, Tegan said, "It's about an hour's walk. More, maybe."

"We'll ride," said Jamie curtly. He started for the door, paused, went back for the copy of his letter to the solicitor. With the page in his pocket, he headed for the stables, only belatedly noticing that Tegan had to run to keep up.

"We're not allowed on our ponies," his sister pointed out, trotting beside him.

"You are if I say so." Jamie called for Albert and ordered his horse and Tegan's pony to be saddled. Impatience tore at him. He went to help the stableman adjust and buckle.

"Tamsyn's pony too," put in Tegan.

Jamie didn't object. He did gibe when Randolph rose

from a nest of straw in an empty stall and attempted to join the party, remembering the dog's first rough greeting of Clare in the courtyard. It would not do to repeat that now. At least he could ensure this one small thing.

It seemed an endless time before they set off, Tegan leading Tamsyn's pony behind her. All his faculties were concentrated on getting to Clare. Restraining his urge to kick his mount into a gallop, Jamie followed his sister along a twisting, overgrown trail.

The ride seemed to last forever, but it wasn't actually very long. Jamie noticed when they left the bounds of Trehearth. He wasn't as familiar with the holdings in this direction, though he would have sworn they'd come this way during the search for the twins.

Tegan led him through a patch of forest and into a dell. He didn't realize until they were quite close that it contained a dwelling. The place looked like part of the adjoining hill. He started to pull up, but an ancient woman standing in the low doorway waved them on. His sister rode around the mound of thatch and the hill. Beyond the rise stood a great oak tree, fluttering with bits of colored cloth.

Peripherally, Jamie noticed this, as well as Tamsyn jumping up and running to greet her pony. But really his attention was focused on Clare, sitting under the branches like a fairy in her bower. He threw himself off his horse and ran to kneel beside her. "It was a mistake," he cried. He pulled the letter from his pocket and thrust it at her. "I never meant it."

As Clare smoothed out the page and began to read, Tamsyn jumped onto her pony. She tugged at Tegan's pony's reins as well, urging her away. Tegan resisted briefly, her dark eyes fixed on the pair under the tree. Then she gave in, and the twins rode off toward Tess's cottage.

When Clare's pale green eyes came up to look at him again, Jamie added, "I was drunk. I barely remember anything about that morning. I never would have signed such a document if I'd had my wits about me." He wasn't going to spare himself. "It's no proper excuse, and I am so sorry."

"Drunk," repeated Clare. She looked bewildered and deeply pained.

Wincing at her expression, Jamie started at the beginning. "I was… you know I was behaving like a damn fool in London. I'd had far too much champagne, and I was talking with your cousin. I suppose I must have… complained about how matters stood between us. Your cousin took it upon himself to ferry me over to this solicitor." That was odd, come to think of it. Jamie started to add that he hadn't asked the man to do anything of the kind, that it had been a surprise. But that didn't justify his actions. "I was befuddled by drink, and they gave me more. Not that it wasn't my fault. It was. They shoved some document in front of me and kept at me to sign it. And I did." Clare was scowling. He couldn't bear it. "I didn't even know what it was about. But I know that doesn't excuse it. I've vowed never to touch a drop again. Clare. Please say you'll forgive me."

"Simon," Clare said. Slowly her frown eased. "It was Simon." At last, she met Jamie's gaze. "He saw a chance and took advantage of it. He's very good at that. He would do anything to hurt me."

"Your cousin would?"

"My cousin, yes, but no friend." Slowly, Clare told the story of the family estrangement—of Simon's taking her home, of his refusal to help her mother when she was ill. "I don't know all the history of it," she finished. "Or why Simon can never let it go. But he hasn't, not for a moment."

"If I'd known that you and he were at odds…" Would that have prevented him from sharing his sodden ramblings? Jamie truly believed that it would. "You never spoke of your family."

"It seemed like old bad news. I saw no reason to bring it up." Clare smiled sadly. "But then, the things we didn't know about each other have proved treacherous. I should have confided in you."

Jamie nodded. "Old wounds trip us up." He swallowed and pushed on. "Everyone suspects my father took his own life, you know. I've always believed it, that he chose the coward's way out. Everything in my life went out of control on the day I got the news of his death."

Clare nodded. "It feels like the end of the world."

Jamie looked at her and saw real understanding in her eyes. It wasn't anything like pity or even simple compassion. It was the comradeship of shared anguish. "I've hated him for it." Jamie had never said this aloud before. "Whether he was heedless because of his grief over my mother's death, or he jumped from that cliff… The thing is, he knew how badly the estate stood. He had two infant daughters. He knew very well the responsibility would fall to me."

"And you were only a boy."

"Shouldn't he have taken more care?" It came out like the plea of a much younger Jamie.

Clare reached over and took his hand. They gazed into each other's eyes, recognizing similar struggles, acknowledging the daring of honesty, the risk of trust.

But one more admission weighed on Jamie. "When it happened, I told myself I'd never be a father like that. I'd never abandon any child of mine. But then, when I would come home to Trehearth, the memories and the... the doom hanging over the place made it unbearable. I broke that vow. I stuck my head in a bottle, and I left my sisters alone."

He tried to pull his hand away, but Clare kept hold of it. "I think the strain was just too much for a boy still in school."

"I can't excuse myself so easily. I've made so many mistakes." His free hand struck the blanket.

"Who among us has not?" Clare pointed out.

Jamie turned to her. "I'm going to do my utmost to be someone my sisters can rely on from now on. And you. If you'll forgive me?" Unconsciously, his hand tightened almost painfully on hers.

There wasn't so very much to forgive. He hadn't been the sneaking hypocrite she'd feared when she opened that dreadful envelope. She'd known he couldn't be! They'd been getting on so well before that thunderbolt ripped through the household. He'd been trying so hard. "Yes. Of course. If you will forgive me as well."

"For what?" Jamie wondered.

"I should have waited to speak to you instead of running away. I should have trusted that there was an explanation."

"I hadn't given you much reason to trust. But I shall, every day, for the rest of our lives. I swear it."

"That's fortunate." Clare felt as if light was running throughout her body. "Because you're going to have a new opportunity to demonstrate your reliability quite soon."

"What?"

Clare laid her free hand on her midsection. "There'll be a child in the winter. We'll both have many chances to get it right… and wrong, I imagine." She gave him a tremulous smile.

Jamie stared at her—delight and fear and hope and surprise muddling his mind. A torrent of love swept all of them away. With a cry of triumph, he pulled her into his arms.

ॐ

Tamsyn and Tegan eased back from the thicket near the oak from which they'd been observing this interesting meeting. It wasn't hard to slip away. Jamie and Clare were unaware of anything outside themselves. The twins made their way back to the spot where they'd tied their ponies and stood for a moment sharing a solemn gaze. Some of what they'd heard had stirred up sadness. They didn't need to speak to see it in each other or to offer comfort. Gradually their expressions eased.

"They'll stay here now," said Tamsyn.

More silent communication passed between the twins. Their faces lightened further.

"And we'll have a new brother," Tegan said.

"Nephew," corrected her sister. "Or niece."

A slow smile spread over Tegan's elfin features. "He'll have to call us auntie."

Tamsyn smiled back. "And treat us with proper respect."

Tegan nodded appreciatively. "We'll teach him—"

"Or her."

"Or her. The way out the cellar window."

"And how to get round Anna when she's cross."

"And the best berry patch."

"The trunk full of old sabers in the attic."

"And... and everything!"

The twins' dark eyes sparkled. Minds bursting with plans, they waited with what patience they could summon for their family to be ready to head home.

Read on for an excerpt from Jane Ashford's
Once Again a Bride and see why *Publishers Weekly*
calls it "a near-perfect example of everything that
makes this genre an escapist joy to read"

CHARLOTTE RUTHERFORD WYLDE CLOSED HER EYES
and enjoyed the sensation of the brush moving rhyth-
mically through her long hair. Lucy had been her maid
since she was eleven years old and was well aware that
her mistress's lacerated feelings needed soothing. The
whole household was aware, no doubt, but only Lucy
cared. The rest of the servants had a hundred subtle,
unprovable ways of intensifying the laceration. It had
become a kind of sport for them, Charlotte believed,
growing more daring as the months passed without
reprimand, denied with a practiced blankness that
made her doubly a fool.

Lucy stopped brushing and began to braid Charlotte's
hair for the night. Charlotte opened her eyes and faced
up to the dressing table mirror. Candlelight gleamed
on the creamy lace of her nightdress, just visible under
the heavy dressing gown that protected her from drafts.
Her bedchamber was cold despite the fire on this bitter
March night. Every room in this tall, narrow London
house was cold. Cold in so many different ways.

She ought to be changed utterly by these months,

Charlotte thought. But the mirror showed her hair of the same coppery gold, eyes the same hazel—though without any hint of the sparkle that had once been called alluring. Her familiar oval face, straight nose, and full lips had been judged pretty a scant year, and a lifetime, ago. She was perhaps too thin, now that each meal was an ordeal. There were dark smudges under her eyes, and they looked hopelessly back at her like those of a trapped animal. She remembered suddenly a squirrel she had found one long-ago winter—frozen during a terrible cold snap that had turned the countryside hard and bitter. It had lain on its side in the snow, its legs poised as if running from icy death.

"There you are, Miss Charlotte." Lucy put a comforting hand on her shoulder. When they were alone, she always used the old familiar form of address. It was a futile but comforting pretense. "Can I get you anything…?"

"No, thank you, Lucy." Charlotte tried to put a world of gratitude into her tone as she repeated, "Thank you."

"You should get into bed. I warmed the sheets."

"I will. In a moment. You go on to bed yourself."

"Are you sure I can't…?"

"I'm all right."

Neither of them believed it. Lucy pressed her lips together on some reply, then sketched a curtsy and turned to go. Slender, yet solid as a rock, her familiar figure was such a comfort that Charlotte almost called her back. But Lucy deserved her sleep. She shouldn't be deprived just because Charlotte expected none.

The door opened and closed. The candles guttered

and steadied. Charlotte sat on, rehearsing thoughts and plans she had already gone over a hundred times. There must be something she could do, some approach she could discover to make things—if not right, at least better. Not hopeless, not unendurable.

Her father—her dear, scattered, and now departed father—had done his best. She had to believe that. Tears came as she thought of him; when he died six months ago, he'd no longer remembered who she was. The brutal erosion of his mind, his most prized possession, had been complete.

It had happened so quickly. Yes, he'd always been distracted, so deep in his scholarly work that practicalities escaped him. But in his library, reading and writing, corresponding with other historians, he'd never lost or mistaken the smallest detail. Until two years ago, when the insidious slide began—unnoticed, dismissed, denied until undeniable. Then he had set all his fading faculties on getting her "safely" married. That one idea had obsessed and sustained him as all else slipped away. Perforce, he'd looked among his own few friends and acquaintances for a groom. Why, why had he chosen Henry Wylde?

In her grief and fear, Charlotte had put up no protest. She'd even been excited by the thought of moving from her isolated country home to the city, with all its diversions and amusements. And so, at age eighteen, she'd been married to a man almost thirty years older. Had she imagined it would be some sort of eccentric fairy tale? How silly and ignorant had she been? She couldn't remember now.

It wasn't all stupidity; unequal matches need not

be disastrous. She had observed a few older husbands who treated their young wives with every appearance of delight and appreciation. Not quite so much older, perhaps. But… from the day after the wedding, Henry had treated her like a troublesome pupil foisted upon his household for the express purpose of irritating him. He criticized everything she did. Just this morning, at breakfast, he had accused her of forgetting his precise instructions on how to brew his tea. She had *not* forgotten, not one single fussy step; she had carefully counted out the minutes in her head—easily done because Henry allowed no conversation at breakfast. He always brought a book. She was sure she had timed it exactly right, and still he railed at her for ten minutes, in front of the housemaid. She had ended up with the knot in her stomach and lump in her throat that were her constant companions now. The food lost all appeal.

If her husband did talk to her, it was most often about Tiberius or Hadrian or some other ancient. He spent his money—quite a lot of money, she suspected, and most of it hers—and all his affection on his collections. The lower floor of the house was like a museum, filled with cases of Roman coins and artifacts, shelves of books about Rome. For Henry, these things were important, and she, emphatically, was not.

After nearly a year of marriage, Charlotte still felt like a schoolgirl. It might have been different if there were a chance of children, but her husband seemed wholly uninterested in the process of getting them. And by this time, the thought of any physical contact with him repelled Charlotte so completely that she didn't know what she would do if he suddenly changed his mind.

She stared into the mirror, watching the golden candle flames dance, feeling the drafts caress the back of her neck, seeing her life stretch out for decades in this intolerable way. It had become quite clear that it would drive her mad. And so, she had made her plan. Henry avoided her during the day, and she could not speak to him at meals, with the prying eyes of servants all around them. After dinner, he went to his club and stayed until she had gone to bed. So she would not go to bed. She would stay up and confront him, no matter how late. She would insist on changes.

She had tried waiting warm under the bedclothes but had failed to stay awake for two nights. Last night, she'd fallen asleep in the armchair and missed her opportunity. Tonight, she would sit up straight on the dressing table stool with no possibility of slumber. She rose and set the door ajar, ignoring the increased draft this created. She could see the head of the stairs from here; he could not get by her. She would thrash it out tonight, no matter what insults he flung at her. The memory of that cold, dispassionate voice reciting her seemingly endless list of faults made her shiver, but she would not give up.

The candles fluttered and burned down faster. Charlotte waited, jerking upright whenever she started to nod off. Once, she nearly fell off the backless stool. But she endured, hour after hour, into the deeps of the night. She replaced the stubs of the candles. She added coals to the fire, piled on another heavy shawl against the chill. She rubbed her hands together to warm them, gritted her teeth, and held on until light showed in the crevices of the draperies and birds began to twitter outside. Another day had dawned, and Henry Wylde had not come home. Her husband had spent the night elsewhere.

Pulling her shawls closer, Charlotte contemplated this stupefying fact. The man she saw as made of ice had a secret life? He kept a mistress? He drank himself into insensibility and collapsed at his club? He haunted the gaming hells with feverish wagers? Impossible to picture any of these things. But she had never waited up so long before. She had no idea what he did with his nights.

Chilled to the bone, she rose, shut the bedroom door, and crawled into her cold bed. She needed to get warm; she needed to decide if she could use this new information to change the bitter circumstances of her life. Perhaps Henry was not completely without feelings, as she had thought. Her eyelids drooped. Perhaps there was hope.

Lucy Bowman tested the temperature of a flatiron she'd set heating on the hearth. It hissed obligingly. Satisfied, she carried it to a small cloth-draped table in the corner of the kitchen and applied it to the frill of a cambric gown. She was good at fine ironing, and she liked being good at things. She also liked—these days—doing her work in the hours when most of the staff was elsewhere. This early, the cook and scullery maid had just begun to prepare breakfast. Barely out of bed, and sullen with it, they didn't speak. Not that there ever was much conversation in this house—and none of it the easy back-and-forth of the servants' hall in Hampshire.

The Rutherford manor had been a very heaven compared to this place. Everyone below stairs got along; they'd gone together to church fetes and dances and formed up a kind of family. For certain, the old housekeeper had been a second mother to her. When Lucy'd arrived, sent into service at twelve to save her parents a mouth to feed, Mrs. Beckham had welcomed her and looked after her. She'd been the first person ever to tell Lucy that she was smart and capable and had a chance to make something of herself. Thinking of her, and of that household, comforted and hurt at the same time.

Lucy eased the iron around an embroidered placket, enjoying the crisp scent of starched cloth rising in the steam. She'd made a place for herself in Hampshire, starting in the laundry and working her way up, learning all she could as fast as she could, with kindly training. She'd been so proud to be chosen as Miss Charlotte's lady's maid eight years ago. Mrs. Beckham had told her straight out, in front of the others, how well she'd done, called her an example for the younger staff. It had warmed her right down to her toes to see them smiling at her, glad for her advancement.

And now it was all gone. The house sold, the people she'd known retired or scattered to other positions, and none of them much for letters. Well, she wasn't either, as far as that went. But she couldn't even pretend she'd be back in that house, in the country, one day.

Not that she'd ever leave Miss Charlotte alone

in this terrible place. Lucy put her head down and maneuvered the iron around a double frill.

Mr. Hines tromped in, heavy-eyed and growling for tea. A head on him, no doubt, from swilling his way through another evening. Cook's husband, who called himself the butler, was really just a man of all work. Lucy had seen a proper butler, and that he was not. What he was was a raw-boned, tight-mouthed package of sheer meanness. Lucy stayed well out of his way. It was no wonder Cook was short-tempered, shackled to a bear like him. As for the young women on the staff who might have been her friends, both the scullery maid and the housemaid were slow-witted and spiritless. If you tried to talk to them which she didn't, not anymore—they mostly stared like they didn't understand plain English. And if that wasn't enough, the valet Holcombe took every chance to put a sneaky hand where it didn't belong. Him, she outright despised. Every word he said to her was obviously supposed to mean something different. The ones she understood were disgusting. She'd spent some of her own wages on a bolt for her bedroom door because of him. Couldn't ask Miss Charlotte for the money because she didn't need another worry, did she?

The iron had cooled. She exchanged it for another that had been heating near the coals and deftly pressed the scalloped sleeve of a morning dress. The rising warmth on her face was welcome, though the kitchen was the most tolerable room in this cold house. She had to pile on blankets until she felt like a clothes press to sleep warm.

The scullery maid brushed past her on the way to

the pantry. "Mort o' trouble for a gown no one'll see," she said.

Lucy ignored her. Any remark the staff made to her was carping, about her work or her mistress, though they'd eased up on that when they saw they weren't going to cause any trouble. But they baited and humiliated Miss Charlotte something terrible. It still shocked Lucy after all this time. She couldn't quite give up expecting *him*—she refused to name the master of this house—to step in and stop them. But he was a pure devil; he seemed to enjoy it. Lucy liked to understand a problem and find a solution for it if she any way could, but there was nothing to be done about this pure disaster of a marriage.

Holcombe surged into the kitchen. He'd be after early morning tea for *him,* and nothing in the world more important, in his book. Lucy turned her back and concentrated on her ironing. "Have you seen Mr. Henry?" he asked. "Hines?"

"Why would I?" was the sullen reply from the man sitting at the kitchen table.

Holcombe stood frowning for a moment, then hurried out—without any tea. Which was strange, and interesting. Lucy eyed the others. They showed no signs of curiosity. As far as she'd been able to tell over the months, they didn't have any.

The scent of porridge wafted from the hearth, and Lucy's stomach growled. Mrs. Hines could make a decent porridge, at least. She wasn't good at much else. On the other hand, *he* ordered such bland dishes that it was hardly worth any bother.

Holcombe popped back in. "Hines, come with

me," he said. The cook's husband grumbled but pushed up from his chair and obeyed. This was one of the things that showed Hines wasn't a real butler. He snapped to when the valet spoke in that particular tone and did as he was told. The two men left the kitchen, and they didn't come back.

Something was up, Lucy thought. *He* next to worshipped his routines, threw a fit if any little detail was altered. Despite months of grinding frustration, she felt a shred of hope. Any difference had to be for the better, didn't it? She took her finished ironing and headed upstairs to see what she could see before waking her mistress.

❧

When Lucy pulled back the curtains, Charlotte swam slowly up from her belated sleep. Her memory sputtered and cleared. She sat up. "You should have told me, Lucy."

"Told you what, Miss Charlotte?"

"That Henry spends nights away from home. The knowledge could hardly hurt my feelings at this point."

"Away…?"

"Come, Lucy, the household knows these things."

"They don't talk to me." Was this it then? *He* hadn't come home last night?

"I know they haven't befriended you, but there must be gossip…"

"Never, miss. I don't know what you're talking about." Lucy opened the wardrobe and surveyed the row of gowns. "Except… Mr. Holcombe's in a right taking this morning."

Charlotte threw back the covers. "I'll dress at once and see him."

"You know he don't like to be…"

"I don't care." And she didn't. Not a whit. Holcombe might be the most insolent of all the servants, but Charlotte was finished with being cowed.

She hurried Lucy through their morning routine. She would demand that Holcombe appear, and if he refused, she would hunt him down wherever he lurked and force him to tell her the truth. Chin up, eyes steely, Charlotte marched out of her bedchamber and down the hall. In what passed for a drawing room in this house, she jerked the bellpull. Minutes ticked by; no one answered the summons. Charlotte rang again, then gave it up and started for the stairs.

A heavy knock fell on the front door; it sounded as if someone were striking it with a stick. Charlotte looked over the banister. The knock came again, echoing through the house. Who could be calling at this hour?

The housemaid hurried out and began to undo the bolts. Charlotte heard the swinging door at the back of the hall and knew that other servants were behind her. The front door swung open.

"Miss," said a deep voice from the stoop. "Is there a gen'lmun at home pr'haps?"

Charlotte hurried down the stairs.

"Who wants to know?" demanded Holcombe, surging out of the back hall.

"It's the watch," replied the deep voice. "Are you…?"

Charlotte moved faster. "I am the mistress of this house," she said, more for Holcombe's benefit than

the visitor's. "My husband is apparently not at home."
A glance at Holcombe showed him pale and anxious,
completely unlike the snake who delighted in taunting her. Charlotte turned her attention to the burly
individual on her doorstep. Bearded, in a long stuff
coat and fingerless gloves, he looked like any of the
men who patrolled the streets of London. His staff was
tall beside him.

"Ma'am," he said, shifting uneasily from foot to
foot. "Er…"

"Is there a problem?"

The man held out a visiting card, which seemed so
incongruous that Charlotte just stared at it. "I wonder
if you might recognize that, ma'am?"

She took the small pasteboard square and read it.
"This is my husband's card."

"Ah." The watchman didn't seem surprised. "Might
you want to sit down, ma'am?"

"Just tell us what has happened!" exclaimed Holcombe,
typically ignoring her authority, her very existence.

"Yes, please tell us," Charlotte agreed.

The man on the step stood straighter. "Regret to
inform you, ma'am, that there has been an… incident.
A gent'lmun was found earlier this morning. His purse
was missing, but he had a card case in his waistcoat
pocket. That there card was inside it."

"But… what happened? Is he hurt? Where have
you taken…?"

"Sorry, ma'am." The visitor grimaced, looking as
if he wished very much to be elsewhere. "Regret to
tell you, the gent'lmun is dead. Footpads, looks like.
Caught him as he was…"

"Dead?" Somehow, Lucy was at Charlotte's elbow, supporting her. "But how… are you sure? I cannot believe…"

The man shuffled his feet. "Somebody must come and identify him for sartain, ma'am. Mebbe a…?"

"I shall go!" interrupted Holcombe. He glared at Charlotte, at the watchman, at the other servants. No one argued with him. The watchman looked relieved.

They all stood in stunned silence as Holcombe ran for his coat and departed with the watch. Charlotte never remembered afterward how she got back up to the drawing room, only that she was sitting there when Lucy entered some indeterminate time later and said, "It's him. He's dead."

Charlotte half rose. "Holcombe is…?"

"He's back with the news. Right cut up, he is." Lucy's lip curled.

"Henry is dead?" She couldn't help repeating it.

"Seems he is, Miss Charlotte. Happens more often than we had any notion, Holcombe says. Streets aren't half safe, after dark. London!" Lucy knew that many people saw the city as thrilling, with every sort of goods and amusement on offer. She hated the filth and the noise—wheels clattering, people shouting at you to buy this or that from the moment you stepped into the street. Strangers shoving past if you walked too slow. She had discounted Holcombe's horror stories, however. He enjoyed scaring the scullery maid out of the few wits she possessed with tales of hapless servants who wandered into the wrong part of town and never came out. Lucy had refused to show any fear just to irk him. Now it seemed he was right, after all.

Charlotte sank back onto the sofa. She hadn't wanted this, not anything like this. She'd longed for change, but she'd never wished...

"Can I get you something? Tea? You haven't eaten a crumb."

"I couldn't."

"You have to eat."

"Not now."

Lucy bowed her head at the tension in her voice. "Shall I sit with you?"

"No. No, I'd like to be alone for a while."

Lucy hesitated, then bobbed a curtsy and went out. Charlotte folded her hands tightly together, pressed her elbows to her sides. This wasn't change, this was life violently turned upside down. This was the fabric of daily existence ripped right in two.

She hadn't ever loved Henry. She had tried to like him, almost thought she did, before he made that impossible. In these last months, she hadn't hated him, had she? No, she hadn't gone that far. She had wished, over and over, that he had never entered her life. But she hadn't wished him dead. Yesterday, at about this time, he had been haranguing her about his tea, and now he was removed from the face of the earth. How could this be?

David

by Grace Burrowes

New York Times Bestselling Author

David, Viscount Fairly, has imperiled his honor…

Letty Banks is a reluctant courtesan, keeping a terrible secret that brought her, a vicar's daughter, to a life of vice. While becoming madam of Viscount Fairly's high-class brothel is an absolute financial necessity, Letty refuses to become David's mistress—though their attraction becomes harder to resist the more she learns about the man…

Perhaps a fallen woman can redeem it.

David is smitten not only with Letty's beauty, but also with her calm, her kindness, her quiet. David is determined to put respectability back in her grasp, even if that means uncovering the secrets Letty works so hard to keep hidden—secrets that could take her away from him forever…

Praise for Grace Burrowes:

"Ms. Burrowes continually presses the bar and goes above and beyond the normal to give her readers phenomenal love stories that keep us manic for more."—*Romantic Crush Junkies*

"[Grace Burrowes's] stories are not only intriguing, fast-paced, and filled with passion, but also have the human side that only a talented author could provide."—*My Book Addiction Reviews*

For more Grace Burrowes, visit:

www.sourcebooks.com

Sapphires Are an Earl's Best Friend
by Shana Galen

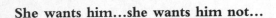

She wants him…she wants him not…

Lily Dawson, dubbed the Countess of Charm by the Prince Regent himself, plays the role of the courtesan flawlessly while her real purpose is spying in the service of the Crown. Her mission now is to seduce a duke to test his true loyalties. She'll do it, even though the man she really wants is Andrew Booth-Payne, Earl of Darlington—the duke's son.

Andrew is furious when he finds himself rivaling his father for Lily's attention. When he uncovers Lily's mission, Andrew is faced with impossible choices. It seems he is destined to betray either his family, his country, or the longings of his own heart…

Praise for Shana Galen:

"Shana Galen is one of my favorite, go-to authors for books filled with adventure, humor, and passion…"—*Rogue Under the Covers*

"Galen can do no wrong when it comes to historical romance! Her writing draws you in and lets you fall in love with her exciting and passionate characters."—*The Romance Reviews*

For more Shana Galen, visit:

www.sourcebooks.com

Much Ado About Jack
by Christy English

How to become London's most notorious widow:

1. Vow to NEVER remarry

2. Own a ship and become fabulously wealthy

3. Wear the latest risqué fashions in your signature color

4. Do NOT have a liaison at the Prince Regent's palace with a naval captain whose broad shoulders and green eyes make you forget Rule #1

Angelique Beauchamp, the widowed Countess of Devonshire, has been twice burned by love, and she is certain that no man will ever touch her heart again. But that doesn't mean she can't indulge a little—and it would be hard to find a more perfect dalliance than one with the dashing Captain James Montgomery.

After a brief but torrid affair, James tries to forget Angelique and his undeniable thirst for more. The luscious lady was quite clear that their liaison was temporary. But for the first time, the lure of the sea isn't powerful enough to keep him away…

Praise for *Love on a Midsummer Night*:

"With its quick and engaging characters, here's a pleasurable evening's escape."—*RT Book Reviews*

For more Christy English, visit:

www.sourcebooks.com

What the Groom Wants

by Jade Lee

USA Today Bestselling Author

— ❧ —

An honest love…

Radley Lyncott has been in love with Wendy Drew as long as he can remember. When he went to sea, she was too young to court. Now that he's returned to take up his Welsh title, he is appalled to find that debt has ruined the Drew family, and—even worse—Wendy is being courted by another man.

Or a dangerous attraction?

Family comes first for seamstress Wendy Drew, who is forced to settle her brother's debt by working nights at a notorious gambling den. But her double life hasn't gone unnoticed—she has captivated none other than Demon Damon, a nefarious rake who understands Wendy's darkest desires and is hell-bent on luring her into his arms.

— ❧ —

Praise for Jade Lee:

For more Jade Lee, visit:

www.sourcebooks.com

Miss Molly Robbins Designs a Seduction

by Jayne Fresina

She designs dresses for London's leading ladies

Molly Robbins is finally stepping into the spotlight. Her unique dress designs have caught the eye of London's elite. And if it means her own dress shop, proper Molly will make a deal with the devil himself—the notoriously naughty Earl of Everscham. But becoming his mistress is not a part of their arrangement. It's right there in the contract's fine print: No Tomfoolery.

He's an expert at taking them off

Carver Danforthe has a reputation for beautiful mistresses, cutting remarks, and shirking his responsibilities—not for indulging the ambitions of his sister's maid. He must have been drunk when he signed that blasted contract. The stubborn female may think she's gotten the best of him, but what this situation calls for is a little hands-on negotiating…

All's fair in love and fashion

Praise for Jayne Fresina:

"Jayne Fresina writes with great skill, creating characters that you won't soon forget."—*Bookworm 2 Bookworm*

For more Jayne Fresina, visit:

www.sourcebooks.com

Must Love Dukes
by Elizabeth Michels

She can't resist a dare

Lillian Phillips could not imagine how her quiet, simple life had come to this. Blackmailed by the Mad Duke of Thornwood into accepting one wild dare after another…all because of a pocket watch. Desperate to recover her beloved father's pawned timepiece, Lily did something reckless and dangerous and delicious—something that led to a night she'd never forget.

He has a reputation for scandal

When Devon Grey, Duke of Thornwood, runs into the mesmerizing, intoxicating, thieving woman who literally stole from his bedchamber—with his new pocket watch—Devon plots his revenge. If the daring wench likes to play games, he's happy to oblige. After all, what's the use of being the Mad Duke if you can't have some fun? But the last laugh just might be on him…

Look for more titles by Elizabeth Michels:

Desperately Seeking Suzanna

How to Lose a Lord in 10 Days or Less

For more Elizabeth Michels, visit:

www.sourcebooks.com

A Hint of Seduction

by Amelia Grey

New York Times Bestselling Author

———— ✆ ————

Seeking: a cad of a father

The *ton* believes Miss Catherine Reynolds has come to London to find a husband. They would be surprised to know her real purpose, or that it was Catherine herself who stole the horse of the dashing Earl of Chatwin practically out from under him (it was an emergency, of course). Catherine has learned that her real father—the scoundrel who broke her mother's heart—is still out there somewhere, and she intends to find him.

Found: an enchanting earl

Irritated, intrigued, and highly eligible, John Fines, Earl of Chatwin, finds his name on the tongues of half the ton as they speculate about his mysterious lady horsethief. Catherine needs his help to uncover the secrets of her birth, but if he becomes embroiled in her quest, he may be in danger of losing not only his horse and his reputation as a charmer, but also his heart.

———— ✆ ————

Praise for Amelia Grey:

"I love an Amelia Grey book because of the lightness, the wonderful characters and their interaction with each other, and just an overall warm and easy read."—*A Bluestocking's Place*

For more Amelia Grey, visit:

www.sourcebooks.com

Between a Rake and a Hard Place

by Connie Mason and Mia Marlowe

❧

Lady Serena's list of forbidden pleasures

Attend an exclusively male club.

Smoke a cigar.

Have a fortune told by gypsies.

Dance the scandalous waltz.

Sir Jonah Sharp thinks Lady Serena Osbourne will be just like any other debutante, and seducing her will be one of the easiest services he's ever done for the Crown. Then he catches her wearing trousers and a mustache in his gentleman's club and she demands he teach her to smoke a cigar. But what will truly be Jonah's undoing is finding out he's an item on her list too, which makes him determined to bring her all the forbidden pleasure she can handle.

❧

"Shimmers with romance... Well-rounded characters and effortless plotting make this installment the best in the series."—*Publishers Weekly*

For more Connie Mason and Mia Marlowe, visit:

www.sourcebooks.com

One Rogue Too Many

by Samantha Grace

From the betting book at Brooks's gentlemen's club: £2,000 that Lord Ellis will throw the first punch when he discovers Lord Thorne is wooing a certain duke's sister.

All bets are off when the game is love

Lady Gabrielle is thrilled when Anthony Keaton, Earl of Ellis, asks for her hand in marriage. She's not so pleased when he then leaves the country and four months pass without a word. Clearly, the scoundrel has changed his mind and is too cowardly to tell her. There's nothing to do but go back on the marriage mart…

When Anthony returns to town and finds his ultimate rival has set sights on Gabby, his continual battle of one-upmanship with Sebastian Thorne ceases to be a game. Anthony is determined to win back the woman who holds his heart—but he's not expecting Gabby herself to up the stakes…

Praise for Samantha Grace:

"Anything written by Samantha Grace deserves a coveted spot on my 'keeper shelf.'"—*The Romance Reviews*

"There is a charm in Grace's prose that will delight readers."—*RT Book Reviews*

For more Samantha Grace, visit:

www.sourcebooks.com

About the Author

The Bride Insists is a brand-new Regency romance from bestselling author Jane Ashford. Jane discovered Georgette Heyer in junior high school and was captivated by the glittering world and witty language of Regency England. That delight was part of what led her to study English literature and travel widely in Britain and Europe. She has written historical and contemporary romances, and her books have been published in Sweden, Italy, England, Denmark, France, Russia, Latvia, and Spain, as well as the United States. Jane has been nominated for a Career Achievement Award by *RT Book Reviews*. Born in Ohio, Jane now divides her time between Boston and Los Angeles.

And look for these classic Regency romances
from Jane Ashford, reissued by
Sourcebooks Casablanca and available
in print and digital format!

Read on for excerpts from:

Man of Honour

The Three Graces

The Marriage Wager

Man of Honour

"WHAT DO YOU MEAN YOU HAVE NOTHING AVAILABLE?" demanded Mr. Eliot Crenshaw. The cold anger in his eyes made the small innkeeper quail.

"I swear it's true, sir. My missus has took the gig, being as my youngest daughter is about to be brought to bed in Hemsley, the next village but one, you know. She won't be home for a sennight. There's the old cob left in the stables, but he won't draw a carriage, and with this snow now…" He looked out the window of the taproom at the driving blizzard. "Well I can't see as how any animal could." He paused apologetically, conscious of the gentleman's impatience.

"Damn the snow," said Mr. Crenshaw, but he too looked out the window. It was obvious that the weather was worsening rapidly, and having already endured one accident on the road, he had no wish to risk another. But his situation was awkward. "Your wife is away, you say? Who else is here?"

Mr. Jenkins showed signs of wringing his hands. "There's just me tonight, sir, begging your pardon. Betty, the girl as comes from the village to help out, went home early on account of the storm. And my stable boy broke his fool leg last week, climbing trees he was, the witless chawbacon, at his age! I don't see how I'll serve a proper supper. And the lady!" This last remark ended with something like a groan, and the man shook his head. "This ain't a great establishment, you see, sir, off the main road like we are and keeping no post horses. We ain't used to housing quality, and that's the truth. I don't know what I'm to do."

Mr. Crenshaw eyed the distraught host with some contempt. His mood had been decidedly soured by recent events. In the course of a relatively short daylight drive, his fine traveling carriage had been severely damaged by a reckless youngster in a ridiculous high-perch phaeton. His horses had been brought up lame and their high-spirited tempers roused, and though he knew he was fortunate to have escaped without serious injury, the problems which now faced him as a result of the accident did not make him thankful.

He had been escorting a young visitor of his mother's to the home of her aunts. Only his parent's most earnest entreaties had persuaded him to do so, and he was now cursing himself roundly for giving in, for Miss Lindley's maid had been badly hurt in the accident, forcing them to leave her at a cottage on the scene and walk alone to this inn. Here he found there were no females to chaperone the girl; the blizzard was steadily increasing in intensity, and there was no conveyance of any kind available, even had it been possible to go on. Eliot Crenshaw was not accustomed to finding himself at a stand, but now he passed a hand wearily across his forehead, sat down at a taproom table, and stared fiercely at the swirling snow outside. He clenched a fist on the table top. "Bring me a pint," he said resignedly.

In the little inn's one private parlor, the Right Honorable Miss Laura Lindley, oldest daughter of the late Earl of Stoke-Mannering, sat miserably holding her hands out to the crackling fire. She was chilled to the bone, her bonnet was wrecked, her cloak torn and muddy, and her green cambric traveling dress was as disheveled as her black curls. There was a nasty scratch on her left cheek and a bruise above her eye. But these minor discomforts worried her less than the rising storm and the smashed chaise they had left leaning drunkenly by the roadside. What was she to do? Her aunts had expected her a full three hours ago, and these two elderly ladies, by whom she had been brought up, were notoriously high sticklers. The smallest deviation from the rules of propriety was enough to overset them completely. What then could they feel when they knew that their cherished niece was stranded alone at a country inn with a man she scarcely knew?

Laura caught her breath on a sob. She had only just persuaded her aunts to allow her to spend a season in London. Though her twentieth birthday was past, she had never been to the metropolis, and it had required all of her argumentative skills and the help of some of her aunts' old friends, Mrs. Crenshaw among them, to get the necessary permission. She was to have gone to town next month, but now... Laura sighed tremulously. Now, it appeared that she would never have a London season. She had waited two years after her friends' debuts and argued her case with the utmost care, only to see it all come to naught because of this stupid accident. She grimaced. That was always the way of it—the things one wanted most were snatched away just when they seemed certain at last. She took several deep breaths, telling herself sternly to stop this maundering. Perhaps Mr. Crenshaw would find some way out of this dilemma. He seemed a most capable man.

But in the taproom, at that moment finishing his pint of ale, Mr. Crenshaw did not feel particularly capable. He had badly wrenched his shoulder falling from the carriage; his exquisitely cut coat, from the hands of Weston himself, was torn in several places and indisputably ruined, as was much of the rest of his extremely fashionable attire. In fact any member of the *ton* would have been appalled to see this absolute nonesuch in his present state. This was not the top-of-the-trees Corinthian they knew, and though he would not have admitted it, the elegant Mr. Crenshaw was just now at his wit's end.

With a sigh he rose and walked stiffly to a small mirror which hung over the bar. He made some effort to straighten his twisted cravat and brush back his hair. The face in the mirror was rather too austere to be called handsome. Mr. Crenshaw's high cheekbones and aquiline nose gave his dark face a hawk-like look, and this was intensified by black hair and piercing gray eyes. The overall effect was of strength but little warmth; very few men would wish to cross this tall, slender gentleman, and fewer still would succeed in beating him. Pulling at his now disreputable coat and brushing the drying mud from his once immaculate pantaloons and tall Hessian boots, Mr. Crenshaw turned from the mirror with a grimace and walked across the corridor to the private parlor.

Miss Lindley rose at his entrance. "Did you find...?" she began, but the realities of the situation made it seem foolish to ask if he had gotten another carriage, and she fell silent.

Mr. Crenshaw bowed his head courteously. "Please sit down, Miss Lindley. I fear I have bad news." And he explained what the innkeeper had told him.

Laura put a hand to the side of her neck. "Oh dear, how unfortunate that his wife should be away just at this time." She tried to speak lightly, but a sinking feeling grew in her stomach. Her aunts would never forgive her, even though this predicament was certainly not of her own making.

"An understatement," replied Mr. Crenshaw drily, "because I fear we must spend the night at this inn. It will be impossible to go on in the snow, whatever vehicle we may be able to discover." A particularly loud gust of wind howled outside as if to emphasize his point. "I would willingly ride the cob back to the village and try to persuade some woman to return and stay with you," he went on. "But I do not think any would consent to come, and frankly I am not certain I could find the village in this infernal storm."

Laura nodded disconsolately. "Of course you must not go out in such weather." She clenched her hands together and fought back tears once more.

Mr. Crenshaw looked at her. "I say again how sorry I am, Miss Lindley."

"Oh, it is not your fault. I know that. You saved us all from being killed! If only Ruth had not been hurt or if I had stayed with her at the cottage. But when that young man was taken in there as well and the woman was so eager that I should *not* stay… and I was certain we would find another carriage. I did not realize that the snow…" Her disjointed speech trailed off as she watched the storm uneasily.

"Nor did I," replied Mr. Crenshaw. "Weather like this should not come at this time of year. However, it remains that it has. We must make the best of it."

"Yes. I suppose there is no way to send a message to my aunts? No, of course there is not."

He shook his head. "I fear not. But surely they will realize that you have been delayed by the weather. I wager they will be glad you are not traveling today."

Laura smiled weakly. "I see you are not acquainted with my aunts," she said. She looked down at her clasped hands and swallowed nervously. She had suddenly become conscious that she was completely alone with a man and a stranger, a thing her aunts had never permitted in the whole course of her life.

Mr. Crenshaw frowned. "I am not. They are very strict with you, I take it."

She nodded. "They are… older, you see, and…" she faltered.

"I am beginning to," he responded grimly. "What an infernal coil! Why did I allow Mother to bully me into escorting you?"

Laura's eyes widened. "I am sorry," she said miserably. She had a somewhat clearer idea of Mrs. Crenshaw's motives than her son had. That lady had told her that the carriage ride would be a perfect opportunity for Laura to try out her social skills. No one knew better than Mrs. Crenshaw the restrictions her aunts had put on Laura, and no one felt for her more keenly. She had added jokingly that Laura must do her best to captivate her son, for she had been trying to get him safely married these past five years. The girl stole a glance at the tall figure standing beside the sofa. There could be little question of that, she thought to herself. Mr. Crenshaw appeared to take no interest in her whatsoever; indeed she found him very stiff and cold.

But the thoughts running through her companion's mind would have surprised her. He was observing that the Lindley girl was very well to pass, even in her current state of disarray. In other circumstances, at Almack's for example, he might have asked her to dance without any fear that she would disgrace him. A tall, willowy girl, Laura Lindley was a striking brunette, with a thick mass of black curls and eyes so dark as to be almost black as well. Her skin was ivory pale, particularly now after this strenuous adventure. The customary deep rose of her cheeks and lips, an enchanting color Mr. Crenshaw had noted earlier, had drained away and she looked very tired and disheartened.

Resolutely Mr. Crenshaw redirected his thoughts. This was an utterly improper time to be thinking of the girl's looks. He and the lady were in a damnable situation. The lines around his mouth deepened as he reconsidered the problem.

Watching him, Laura shivered a little. He looked so grim and angry.

"Are you cold?" he asked quickly. "Draw nearer to the fire. I have not even asked if you would care for something. Some tea, perhaps?"

Laura allowed that some tea would be most welcome, and Mr. Crenshaw went out to find the landlord.

Two hours later they sat down to dinner in somewhat better frame. Though they had not changed their attire—Laura's luggage remained with the wrecked chaise and Mr. Crenshaw had none—Laura had tidied her hair and dress and washed, as had her companion. The scratch on her face was shown to be minor when the dirt and dried blood were sponged away, and though the bruise had turned a sullen purple, it too was clearly not serious. Both felt much better as they started on the oddly assorted dishes the innkeeper had assembled. There was bread and butter and cheese, a roast chicken, some boiled potatoes, and a large pot of jam. Mr. Crenshaw eyed the repast ruefully and made Laura laugh as he, with a cocked eyebrow, helped her to chicken.

As they ate, he began to talk lightly of London. He had heard from his mother that Laura would be making her come-out, and he told her of the places she would see and the things she might do.

"There is Almack's, of course," he said. "I have no doubt that you will spend many evenings dancing there. And there will be routs, Venetian breakfasts, musical evenings, and the like. You can have no idea how busy your life will become."

At this catalog of delights, Laura could not keep a tremor from her voice when she agreed, and her expression was so woebegone that her companion said, "What is wrong? Have I said something?"

She shook her head. "No, no, it is just that… well I shall not go to London now, I daresay, and I was feeling sorry for myself." She looked wistfully down at her plate.

He was frowning. "What do you mean you will not go?"

"Oh my aunts will never let me leave after this, this… that is…" She stammered to a halt, not wishing to burden him with the certain consequences of their misadventure. There was nothing he could do, after all, and the incident was no more his fault than hers.

"Nonsense," he replied. "Why should they not? You have simply an unfortunate accident on the road."

"Yes I know, but you do not reason as my aunts do, of course. They worry so, and they do not understand modern manners. At least that is what they say. When the curate wished to visit my sister… to pay attentions, you know, they forbade him to enter the house ever again." She smiled slightly at the memory. "It was very awkward, because they are the heads of the relief committee, and the curate was in charge of that. The vicar was nearly driven distracted." Raising her eyes, Laura saw that Mr. Crenshaw had returned her smile, and hers broadened, showing two dimples.

"Was your sister heartbroken?"

"Clarissa?" Laura gave an involuntary gurgle of laughter. "Oh she did not care. She wishes to marry a duke."

He was taken aback. "A duke? Which duke?"

Laura looked mischievous. "It doesn't matter; she is determined to make a grand marriage." Her smile faded. "That will be impossible now, of course. I mean, she will never be married after this. My aunts will keep us so close, I suppose we shall not be allowed even to go to the country assemblies." Her momentary high spirits dissolved in melancholy reflection.

Mr. Crenshaw frowned once more. "You must be mistaken. They cannot be so gothic."

Laura remained unconvinced, but she did not argue further, not wishing to tease him with her problems. Silently the two finished their repast.

After a time Laura rose. "I shall go to bed, I think. I am tired out."

Mr. Crenshaw also stood. "Of course. The landlord has left your candle." He fetched it and lit it at the fire. "There is no one to take you up. Yours is the room at the head of the stairs."

"Thank you." She took the candle and started out of the room. As she was about to enter the hall, he spoke again.

"I shall spend the night in the innkeeper's chamber. It is the best I can do."

Laura's mouth jerked. "Haven't you a sword?"

"I beg your pardon?"

"Like Tristan."

Mr. Crenshaw looked blank. The girl must be on the edge of exhaustion, he thought to himself. He fervently hoped he would not be called upon to deal with an attack of the vapors.

Laura shrugged. "Never mind. I didn't mean anything. My aunts call levity my besetting sin."

The man looked at her.

"Good night," she said.

"Good night," said Eliot, much relieved.

The Three Graces

THE THREE MISSES HARTINGTON SAT BEFORE THE schoolroom fire, sewing sheets. Though their surroundings were decidedly shabby, the dull brown carpet worn and the furniture discarded from more elegant apartments and earlier times, they presented a charming picture. Their close relationship was evident in their appearance; all had hair of the shade commonly called auburn, a deep russet red, and the pale clear ivory skin that sometimes goes with such a color. The eldest sister, who was but nineteen, had eyes of celestial blue, while those of the two younger girls, aged eighteen and seventeen, were dazzling green. An observer would have been hard put to pick the prettiest of them. All were slender, with neat ankles, elegant wrists, and an air of unconscious distinction that did much to outweigh their dowdy gowns and unfashionable braids. He might perhaps venture that Miss Hartington's nose was a trifle straighter than her sisters' and her mouth a more perfect bow. But the second girl's eyebrows formed a finer arch, and the youngest one's expression held the greater promise of liveliness. Altogether, there was little to choose among this delightful trio.

Silence had reigned for some time in the room as they plied their needles with varying degrees of diligence. Having lived together for all of their lives and served during that short period as each other's only companions and confidantes, they knew one another's moods too well to chatter. And nothing of note had occurred this day to cause discussion. Miss Hartington had had occasion to recall her youngest sister to her work once or twice, but otherwise the circle had been silent. The afternoon was passing; soon it would be teatime, and the girls would put up their sewing and join their aunt in the drawing room.

A sound at the door across the room attracted their attention. It was followed by the entrance of first a very large yellow tomcat, then a smaller gray tabby, and finally three kittens of varying hues, bounding forward awkwardly and falling over one another in their eagerness to keep up with their elders. Miss Hartington smiled. "Hannibal's family has found us already," she said, "I told you it would not be long."

The youngest girl wrinkled her nose. "I cannot understand his behavior in the least. They are not even his kittens."

Her middle sister smiled. "But he has adopted them, you see, so they are all the more precious to him."

"I don't see why you say that," sniffed the other. "Our aunt adopted us, but we are certainly not dear to her."

"Euphie!" Miss Hartington looked shocked. "Mind your tongue. How can you say such a thing?"

"Well, it is true. If she cared a button for us, she would let us go about more and visit and... and do all the things other young girls are allowed to do. Indeed, she would bring you out this season, Aggie, as she should have done last year."

"Hush," replied her sister repressively. "Aunt has done everything for us, and you must not speak so of her. If she had not given us a home when Father died, we should be in desperate straits, and you know it."

The youngest girl sighed, shaking her head. "Yes, I know it. Not but what Father showed a decided lack of sympathy, too. Only think of our ridiculous names. He can't have considered what it would be like to go through life being called Euphrosyne."

Miss Hartington frowned at her, but the third sister laughed. "It was not he, Euphie. It was our mother. Aunt Elvira has told me that she was inspired by a passage the vicar read aloud to her just before Aggie was born. From Homer. How did it go? Something about the three Graces." She concentrated a moment, then quoted in Greek, translating for the others: "Most beauteous goddesses and to mortals most kind."

Euphrosyne Hartington wrinkled her nose once more. "Well, I never knew her, since she died when I was born, but though I do not wish to be disrespectful, I think she showed a shocking lack of sensibility. It is very well for you two to tease me. Your names are not nearly so queer."

Her middle sister smiled again. "I suppose you would prefer Thalia? I must say it seems just as burdensome to me."

Miss Hartington rallied at this. "Well, neither of you

was persecuted by Johnny Dudley as I was. He could never pronounce 'Aglaia' properly, and he used to dance around me singing 'Uglea, Uglea,' until I thought I should scream. He thought it excessively witty."

"Johnny Dudley," echoed Thalia meditatively. "I have not thought of him in years. What became of him, I wonder?"

Aglaia shrugged. "I daresay he is still in Hampshire. We were both eight when Father died and we left the county."

Exasperated, Euphrosyne jumped up and faced her sisters. "How can you sit there calmly chattering about nothing?" she exclaimed. "What are we to do?"

Thalia only looked amused, but Miss Hartington said, "Do about what, Euphie? Please try to control yourself; you mustn't fly into a pelter every second minute, you know."

Euphrosyne put her hands on her hips. "Someone must," she retorted. "I am tired of hearing about propriety and what I must do and must not. Sitting meekly in our rooms sewing will do us no good at all. We must make a plan, Aggie. We must *do* something!"

Thalia smiled at her ironically. "What do you suggest?"

"Oh, if I only knew what to suggest," Euphie cried. "You are the scholar. Surely you can tell how we are to escape this dreadful situation."

Aglaia looked bewildered. "What situation? I declare, Euphie, you get no conduct as you grow older. What are you talking about?"

"Can you ask? We are trapped in this house. We never go out; we meet no young people, only Aunt's crusty old friends and the cats!" She directed a venomous look at Hannibal where he reclined luxuriously in the window seat. Ignoring her, he yawned hugely and began to lick one of the kittens. "What is to become of us? How are we ever to marry, for example?"

Thalia laughed. "Take care that Aunt Elvira does not hear you, Euphie. She would give you a thundering scold for presuming to think of marriage."

Euphrosyne whirled to face her. "Oh, sometimes I think I hate Aunt Elvira." This drew a shocked gasp from her eldest sister, and she hastened to add, "I do not, of course. She has been wonderfully kind to us. But I get so angry. She never cared to marry. I understand that. But she cannot expect that we will feel as she did at every point in life. It is selfish of her to keep us hemmed up here."

Thalia sputtered, "Never cared to marry? You are a master of understatement, Euphie."

But Miss Hartington looked disapproving. "You are exaggerating all out of reason. And you should not encourage her, Thalia. We often go out; we are certainly not prisoners in our aunt's house. And she does what she believes is best for us and gives us all we ask. Did she not engage special teachers for you, Euphie, when you wished to continue your music beyond what Miss Lewes could teach? And did she not allow Thalia to study Greek and Latin and anything else she wished, again with special, and very expensive, teachers? I think she has been a very generous guardian."

Euphrosyne pushed out a rebellious lip, but before she could speak again they were all frozen by a bloodcurdling shriek coming from the direction of the drawing room. Hannibal leaped up, his fur prickling, and spat. The shriek came again. Thalia stood, and Euphrosyne started toward the door. There was a patter of footsteps in the hall outside; then the door was thrown open by an hysterical maid. "Oh, miss, miss," she gasped, "it's your aunt!"

As one, the sisters hurried down the stairs to the drawing room. In the doorway they paused, for there was clearly something very wrong. They could see the top of their aunt's head, as usual, above her tall chair before the fireplace, but most unusually, they did not see any other creature.

"Where are the cats?" asked Euphie, voicing their puzzlement. They had never seen their aunt's drawing room without at least five, and more commonly ten or twelve, cats. And now there were none at all.

Aggie hurried around the chair, stopped, and put a hand to her mouth. At this moment, the maid caught up with them, and seeing Miss Hartington's expression, she screeched again. "That's just how I found her, miss, when I come in to ask about the tea. Gave me the nastiest turn of my life, it did. She's gone, ain't she?"

Aggie, rather pale, nodded. "I think she is. But you had best send for the doctor."

The maid ran from the room.

Aglaia's sisters had joined her by this time, and the three girls looked down wide-eyed at the spare figure in the armchair. It would have been hard to imagine a greater contrast. Elvira Hartington was, or had been, a harsh-featured woman, with deep lines beside her mouth and a hawk nose. In death, her face had not relaxed, but held its customary expression of doubting disapproval. Her hand was clutched to her chest, and her pale gray eyes stared sightlessly at her nieces.

Aggie shuddered and turned away. "Poor Aunt Elvira," she murmured.

Thalia took the old woman's wrist. "Cold," she said. "She is indeed dead, and has been for some time, I think."

Aggie shuddered again, but Euphie merely stared at the corpse curiously. "She does not look peaceful," said the youngest girl. "I thought dead people were supposed to be peaceful. Aunt looks just as she did before giving me a scold."

"Euphie, please!" said Miss Hartington.

The other looked abashed. "I didn't mean anything. I wonder what happened? She seemed fine this morning. Remember, she was going to write a letter to the *Times* about Wellington?"

"We are at least spared that," murmured Thalia.

"I don't know," replied Aggie. "She seems to have been taken suddenly. The doctor will tell us."

"Well, I am only sorry for St. Peter," added Euphie, looking sidelong at her middle sister. "She will probably tell him he is not at all what she expected and is used to."

Thalia choked back a laugh and turned away as the maid came hurrying back into the room. "Dr. Perkins will be here directly," she said. "Should I send for anyone else, Miss Hartington?" She spoke to Aggie with a new respect, as her new mistress.

Aggie put a hand to her forehead. "No, I don't think quite yet... Oh, you might send word to Miss Hitchins. She will want to know immediately."

"Yes, miss." And the girl was gone again.

The next few hours passed in a kind of muddle. The realities of death soon depressed even Euphie's spirits, and by the time the doctor had come and gone and all the details were settled, the three sisters were weary and silent. They went up to bed much subdued, for all of them had been attached to their aunt, whatever they might sometimes say.

The next morning, two early visitors arrived almost together—Miss Hitchins and their aunt's solicitor. The former, a forbidding woman of fifty-odd, had been Elvira Hartington's closest friend for many years, ever since they had met at a meeting of the Feline Protectionist Society and discovered like feelings on this important subject. Miss Hitchins often gave her friend's nieces the impression that she disapproved of them, though she remained unfailingly polite, and they greeted her with some nervousness on this solemn occasion. She pressed each of their hands in turn. "So sudden," she murmured. "Poor dear Elvira. None can count himself secure in this world."

Miss Hitchins looked even more somber than usual this morning. She habitually wore black, but today, she had added a black bonnet and veil to her customary dark gown. Her gray hair was washed out by this attire, and her pale skin looked whiter than ever. All of the girls were relieved when the solicitor, Mr. Gaines, came in behind her.

But even the usually jovial Gaines seemed oppressed today. "Tch, tch," he said as he returned the sisters' greeting. "This is an uncomfortable situation. More than uncomfortable. Outrageous, I call it. But she never would listen."

Euphie exchanged a puzzled glance with Thalia.

"Each of us must face death," replied Miss Hitchins reprovingly. "And we must all endeavor to do so with Christian resignation, as I am certain Elvira did."

"Oh, death," said Mr. Gaines, dismissing the question with an impatient wave of his hand. "I daresay, I was speaking of the will, you know."

Miss Hitchins's eyes sharpened. "The will?"

The solicitor scanned four pairs of unblinking eyes. "None of you knows? No, of course you don't. She left that to me. Just like her, too. I've been urging her for years to change the blasted thing, and she always said she meant to. But she didn't. And so, here we are, aren't we? Outrageous."

"I don't understand, Mr. Gaines," said Aggie. "Is there some problem with my aunt's will?"

"There is, and there isn't. And I shan't say another word until the reading this afternoon. If you'll excuse me, I'll go to the library now. I want to go over Miss Hartington's papers as soon as may be."

"Of course. I'll…"

"That's all right. I know my way." Mr. Gaines started out of the drawing room, but in the doorway he paused. "You'll want to come for the reading, Miss Hitchins," he added gruffly. Then he was gone.

Miss Hitchins looked highly gratified.

"Whatever can be wrong with Mr. Gaines?" wondered Euphie. "He is not at all like himself. I have never seen him so abrupt."

Aggie shook her head. Thalia stared at the doorway where he had gone out, a worried frown on her face.

"Oh, I daresay he ate something that disagreed with him at breakfast," said Miss Hitchins brightly. "Men are sensitive to such things, I believe. Women are really much the stronger sex, in spite of what they say."

One of the cats, who had returned to the drawing room when their former mistress left it, stood up on the mantelshelf, stretched mightily, and leaped to the floor, evidently intending to go out. Miss Hitchins bent as it passed her and held out an eager hand. "Cato," she said, "there's a good puss. Come here, Cato."

The cat, a large gray, turned his head fractionally, eyed Miss Hitchins's fingers with a distinct lack of enthusiasm, and passed by and out the door. A black cat draped over the back of the sofa yawned.

Euphie made a slight choking sound, and Aggie said quickly, "Would you care for a cup of tea, Miss Hitchins?"

The older woman straightened and indicated that tea would be welcome. Euphie made a face at Thalia, who shook her head slightly, though she too smiled.

The following half hour was very uncomfortable, and the girls were painfully wondering if Miss Hitchins meant to stay to luncheon when she got up at last and took her leave. "I shall return in the afternoon," she told them, "as Mr. Gaines has asked me to. I shouldn't have dreamed of doing so otherwise, of course." She pressed each girl's hand once again. "If there is anything I can do, you need only call on me," she finished, and the maid showed her out.

"Whew!" said Euphie when she was gone. "I

thought she was settled for the day. What a dreary woman!" The girl fell back on the sofa dramatically.

"Euphie!" Miss Hartington glared at her.

"Well, it is the truth, and I do not see why I should not tell the truth, even if it is impolite."

Her sister opened her mouth to reply, then shut it again. The question seemed too large to grapple with at this moment.

"I wonder what is wrong with the will?" said Thalia, who had been sitting in a corner, very quiet, for some time.

"What do you mean?" asked her younger sister.

"There is something wrong with it. Mr. Gaines said as much. But what?"

"He said, 'There is, and there isn't,'" responded Aggie.

Thalia nodded. "Yes, but that means there is. Why bring it up otherwise? Oh, I wish he had told us. I shall worry about it all day."

"But what could be wrong?" Aggie frowned. "Our aunt was always very careful in business matters. I am sure all is in order."

"In order, yes. But for whom?" Thalia was also frowning.

"What do you mean?"

"Never mind, Aggie. Perhaps Mr. Gaines was right. We should wait until the will is read. Come, let us see if Cook has managed to make us lunch today, or if she still has the vapors." And with this, Thalia strode out of the room. Her sisters followed more slowly, looking concerned.

The Marriage Wager

COLIN WAREHAM, FIFTH BARON ST. MAWR, STOOD AT the ship's rail watching the foam and heave of the English Channel. Even though it was late June, the day was damp and cool, with a sky of streaming black clouds and a sharp wind from the north. Yet Wareham made no effort to restrain the flapping of his long cloak or to avoid the slap of spray as the ship beat through the waves. He was bone-tired. He could no longer remember, in fact, when he hadn't been tired.

"Nearly home, my lord," said his valet, Reddings, who stood solicitously beside him. He pointed to the smudge of gray at the horizon that was England.

"Home." Colin examined the word as if he couldn't quite remember its meaning. For eight years, his home had been a military encampment. In the duke of Wellington's army, he had fought his way up the Iberian Peninsula—Coruña, Talavera, Salamanca—he had fought his way through France, and then done it again after Napoleon escaped Saint Helena and rallied the country behind him once more. He had lived with blood and death and filth until all the joy had gone out of him. And now he was going home, back to a family that lived for the amusements of fashionable London, to the responsibilities of an eldest son. His many relatives, at least, were pleased. According to them, as baron, he should never have risked himself as a soldier in the first place. Their satisfaction at his return matched the intensity of the outcry when he had joined up at twenty.

Reddings watched his master with surreptitious anxiety. The baron was a big man, broad-shouldered and rangy. But just now, he was thin from the privations of war and silent with its memories. Reddings didn't like the brooding quiet that had come to dominate St. Mawr, which the recent victory at Waterloo had done nothing to lift. He would even have preferred flares of temper, complaints, bitter railing against the fate that had decreed that his lordship's youth be spent at war. Most of all, he would have rejoiced to see some sign of the laughing, gallant young lad who had first taken him into his service.

That had been a day, Reddings thought, glad to retreat into memories of happier times. His lordship had returned from his last year at Eton six inches taller than when he left in the fall, with a wardrobe that had by no means kept up with his growth. The old baron, his father, had taken one look at Master Colin and let off one of his great barks of laughter, declaring that the boy must have a valet before he went up to Cambridge or the family reputation would fall into tatters along with his coat. Colin had grinned and replied that he would never live up to his father's sartorial splendor. They had a bond, those two, Reddings thought.

He'd been a footman, then, and had actually been on duty in the front hall of the house when this exchange took place in the study. He had heard it all, including the heart-stopping words that concluded the conversation. The old baron had said, "Fetch young Sam Reddings. He follows my man about like a starving hound and is always full of questions. I daresay he'll make you a tolerable valet." And so Reddings had been granted his dearest wish and never had a moment's regret, despite going off to war and all the rest of it. It was a terrible pity the old baron had died so soon after that day, he thought. He'd be the man to make a difference in his lordship now.

The ship's prow crashed into a mountainous gray wave, throwing cold spray in great gleaming arcs to either side. The wind sang in the rigging and cut through layers of clothing like the slash of a cavalry-man's saber. It had been a rough crossing. Most of the passengers were ill below, fervently wishing for an end to the journey or, if that were not possible, to their miserable lives.

The pitch and heave of the deck left Colin Wareham unscathed. What an adventure he had imagined war would be, he was thinking. What a young idiot he had been, dreaming of exotic places and wild escapades, fancying himself a hero. Colin's lip curled with contempt for his youthful self. That naïveté had been wrung out of him by years of hard campaigning. The realities of war made all his medals and commendations seem a dark joke. And what was left to him now? The numbing boredom of the London Season; hunting parties and the changeless tasks of a noble landholder; his widowed mother's nagging to marry and produce an heir; the tiresome attentions of insipid debutantes and their rapacious parents. In short, nothing but duty. Wareham's mouth tightened. He knew about duty, and he would do it.

A movement on the opposite side of the deck caught Colin's eye. Two other passengers had left the refuge of their cabins and dared the elements to watch the landing. The first was most unusual—a giant of a man with swarthy skin, dark flashing eyes, and huge hands. Though he wore European dress, he was obviously from some eastern country, an Arab or a Turk, Colin thought, and wondered what he could be doing so far from home. He didn't look very happy with his first view of the English coastline.

The fellow moved, and Colin got a clear look at the woman who stood next to him. A gust of wind molded her clothing against her slender form and caught the hood of her gray cloak and threw it back, revealing hair of the very palest gold; even on this dim day, it glowed like burnished metal. She had a delicately etched profile like an antique cameo, a small straight nose, and high unyielding cheekbones, but Colin also noticed the promise of passion in her full lips and soft curve of jaw. She was exquisite—a woman like a blade of moonlight—tall and square-shouldered, perhaps five and twenty, her pale skin flushed from the bitter wind. His interest caught, Colin noticed that her gaze at the shore was steady and serious. She looked as if she were facing a potential enemy instead of a friendly harbor.

As he watched, she turned, letting her eyes run

along the coast to the south, her gaze glancing across his. Her expression was so full of longing and loss that he felt a spark of curiosity. Who was she? What had taken her across the Channel, and what brought her back? She turned to speak to the dark giant—undoubtedly her servant, he thought—and he wondered if she had been in the East, a most unlikely destination for a lady. She smiled slightly, sadly, and he felt a sudden tug of attraction. For a moment, he was tempted to cross the deck and speak to her, taking advantage of the freedom among ship passengers to scrape an introduction. Surely that pensive face held fascinating secrets. He took one step before rationality intervened, reminding him that most of the truly tedious women he had known in his life had been quite pretty. It would be unbearable to discover that only silly chatter and wearisome affectation lay behind that beautiful facade. Colin turned and saw that they were approaching the docks. "We'd best gather our things," he said to Reddings, and led the way below.

The other pair remained at the rail as the ship passed into the shelter of the headland and the wind lessened. The dark giant huddled his cloak closer, while the woman faced the waves head-on. She seemed to relish the cut of the spray and the salty damp of the air. "There it is, Ferik," she said after a while. "Home." Her tone was quietly sarcastic.

"When I left here seven years ago," said the woman, "I had a husband, a fortune, six servants, and trunks of fashionable gowns. I return with little but my wits."

"And me, mistress," answered the giant in a deep sonorous voice with a heavy accent to his English.

"And you," she replied warmly. "I still don't think you will like England, Ferik." He looked so odd in narrow trousers and a tailcoat, she thought, utterly out of place.

"It must be better than where I came from, mistress," was the reply.

Remembering the horrors she had rescued him from, Emma Tarrant had to agree.

"Except for maybe the rain," he added, a bit plaintively.

Emma laughed. "I warned you about that, and the cold, too."

"Yes, mistress," agreed her huge servitor, sounding aggrieved nonetheless.

Emma surveyed the shore, drinking in the peaked roofs of English houses, the greenery, the very English carriage and pair with a crest on the door, waiting for some passenger. Seven years, she thought, seven years she'd been gone, and it felt like a lifetime. Probably it was a mistake to come back. She would find no welcome, no feast spread for the prodigal daughter. Indeed, she had no intention of seeing anyone from that old, lost life. She only wanted to live among familiar surroundings again, to speak her own language, to feel other than an alien on foreign soil. She was asking so little. Surely, it would not be denied her.

The sailors were throwing lines to be secured and readying the gangplank. Men bustled on the docks. "Come, Ferik," said Emma. "We'd best see to our boxes."

On the steep, ladderlike stair leading below deck, they had to squeeze past a tall gentleman and his valet who were coming up. Even their few pieces of worn, battered luggage jammed the opening, so that for a moment, Emma was caught and held against the ship's timbers on one side and the departing passenger on the other. Looking up to protest, she encountered eyes of a startling, unusual blue, almost violet, and undeniable magnetism. From a distance of less than five inches they examined her, seeming to look beneath the surface and search for something important. Emma couldn't look away. She felt a deep internal pulse answer that search, as if it was a quest she too had been pursuing for a long time. Her lips parted in surprise; her heartbeat accelerated.

Colin Wareham found himself seized by an overwhelming desire to kiss this stranger to whom he had never spoken a word. Her nearness roused him; the startled intelligence of her expression intrigued him. It would be so very easy to bend his head and take her lips for his own. The mere thought of their yielding softness made him rigid with longing.

Then the giant moved, backing out of the passage and hauling one of the offending pieces of luggage with him. The woman was freed. "Are you all right, mistress?" the huge servant asked when she did not move at once.

She started, and slipped quickly down the stair to the lower deck. "Yes," she said. "Thank you, Ferik."

"Beg pardon," murmured Reddings, and hurried up.

Colin hesitated, about to speak. One part of him declared that he would always regret it if he let this woman slip away, while another insisted that this was madness. Reddings leaned over the open hatch above him. "Can I help, my lord?" he asked. The outsized man started down the stair again, effectively filling the opening. It *was* madness, Colin concluded, and pushed past the giant into the open air.

❦

A week later, Emma sat at a card table in Barbara Rampling's drawing room and pondered which suit to discard. It was a matter of some importance, because for the past year her only means of support had been her skill with games of chance. She considered a minor club, then a diamond. Her opponent was a wretched player, but overconfidence was always a mistake. It had been the downfall of her late husband, Edward, who never stopped believing that the next hand of cards, or the next turn of the wheel, would favor him. He had run through all of Emma's substantial fortune on the basis of that belief, and had managed to maintain it up to the very moment he was killed in a tavern brawl over a wager.

Emma laid down her card. While her opponent considered it, she glanced up and caught Barbara Rampling's eye. Though she had only just met the woman, she felt she knew her. Barbara, too, had had a husband whose grand passion was gaming rather than his wife. When his insurmountable pile of debts had caused him to put a bullet through his head, Barbara had opened this genteel gaming hell in her own house in order to keep from starving. Emma was quite familiar with such places; she had spent the last year in them. She was even grateful. She could not enter the clubs where gentlemen played deep. It was only thanks to people like Barbara that she could survive at all.

Edward's only legacy, besides debts and disappointments, had been the lessons he gave Emma in gambling. Under his tutelage, she had learned to play all sorts of card games and, surprisingly, had proved to have real talent. It had driven Edward nearly mad—that she could be so skillful and yet have no desire whatsoever to play. In the last days she had kept them afloat for a while by winning. But no one could have kept pace with his continual losses. His death had ended an accelerating spiral of ruin that had very nearly pulled Emma under with it.

Her opponent frowned. She was a careless player who did not seem to grasp the principles of the game. She was also, Emma had been reliably informed, easily able to afford substantial losses. Emma need not feel guilty if she came out of this evening set up for a month.

Hiding her impatience while her partner decided on her play, Emma gazed around the room once again, automatically cataloguing the crowd at the tables. Most of them were tiresomely familiar types; she had encountered them in grand salons and mean inns all across the Continent and as far away as Constantinople. They made up a floating international population of sharps and gulls, the cunning and the lost, who shared just one overriding characteristic— they cared for nothing but the game. The usual mixture of contempt, pity, and dislike that assailed her in such places gathered in Emma's throat. Sir Edward and Lady Emma Tarrant, she thought with bitter humor. She had certainly never imagined it would end like this.

Her gaze paused and then froze on a young man at a corner table, playing faro with a single opponent. He could not be more than seventeen, she thought, and he exhibited all the terrible signs she knew so well—the obsessed glitter in his eyes, the trembling hands, the intent angle of his body bent over the cards. He was losing money he did not have. The sight made Emma sick. She would have stopped him if she could, but the last seven years had made her only too familiar with the gamester's mania. He would not hear anything she said.

She started to turn her back on that corner of the room, refusing to watch the debacle, but just then, the young man made a quick gesture and turned his head so that she could see his full face. Emma frowned. The gesture, his hair, the set of his shoulders—his features were at once hauntingly familiar and completely new to her. There was only one person he could be.

Emma's heart began to pound, and she grew hot. She had not expected to find any of them in a place like this. As the fat woman on the other side of the table at last laid down her card, Emma said, "Do you know that young man in the corner?" Though she fought to keep her voice steady, it wavered a little.

The woman was too engrossed in the game to notice. She glanced idly at the boy and said, "Name's Bellingham, I believe. Your play."

The name rang in her ears, confirming her suspicions. It could not be, but it was. The past, which she had thought to evade, had surfaced despite all her plans.